OFF SEASON

A DETECTIVE RYAN MYSTERY

CLIVE FLEURY

coffeetownpress

KENMORE, WA

coffeetownpress

A Coffeetown Press book published by Epicenter Press

Epicenter Press
6524 NE 181st St.
Suite 2
Kenmore, WA 98028

For more information go to:
www.Camelpress.com
www.Coffeetownpress.com
www.Epicenterpress.com
www.clivefleurywriter.com

This is a work of fiction. Names, characters, places, brands, media, and incidents are either the product of the author's imagination or are used fictitiously.

Cover design by Scott Book
Design by Melissa Vail Coffman

Library of Congress Control Number: 2023945732

ISBN: 978-1-68492-147-8 (Trade Paper)
ISBN: 978-1-68492-148-5 (eBook)

Thanks to my wife Rose for providing a springboard for my ideas, and for keeping me sane while writing.

ACKNOWLEDGMENTS

THANKS TO JENNIFER MCCORD FROM COFFEETOWN Press for all the help and assistance she gave in the editing of *Off Season* and to everyone else at Epicenter Press for their help in marketing the novel.

ONE

A S THE NIGHT DREW ON, THE rain poured down ever heavier, and the waves grew bigger and stronger. They tossed the twenty-foot boat from side to side and up and down. The skipper had never been out in weather like this before. Nor had his friend, who was now clutching tight to the underside of his seat, his face green, his breathing labored.

"Almost there," the skipper yelled, though, in truth, neither he nor his friend had decided where *there* was. They just needed to be a reasonable distance from the shore.

"This is fine," his friend shouted back. "Let's do it."

The skipper cut the engine. "You take the helm."

His friend tried to stand but fell back as the boat rocked violently. He shook his head. "I can't."

Standing and releasing the wheel, the skipper leaned over, yanking the man to his feet. "Hold on," he said, placing his friend's hands on his shoulders and guiding him onto the captain's seat. "Now, take it."

His friend lurched forward, catching the spinning wheel and clutching it tightly.

"Don't let go," the skipper ordered.

Leaning into the buffeting wind, the skipper set off for the stern. He reached the waterproof covering, stooped, and pulled the wrapping away. He tasted vomit rising in his mouth as he peered at the lifeless body. Swallowing hard, he composed himself. *"What was that song?"* the man thought. "*Always look on the bright side of life.*" He grabbed the dead man's arms and yanked the corpse forward, sliding it along the sodden wooden deck. Then, wrapping his arms around the dead man's ribs, he heaved it up, balancing it on the side of the boat. One more push, and it would be over. He stood, winded, and peered back through the rain up to the bow. Good, his friend was still holding tight to the wheel.

The skipper wrapped his arms around the corpse. Its head, which had been leaning back, lurched forward, knocking into his stomach. He tried to think of something else besides the cold dead eyes that were staring up at him. What about how lucky they had been? No one had seen them when they had set out. He smiled. So there it was. The bright side!

"Time to do this," he thought. Grabbing the cadaver's legs tight, he tipped them forward, at the same time pushing hard. In one fluid movement, the corpse cleared the side of the boat, dropping into the churning ocean. It disappeared almost immediately, leaving no trace.

TWO

15 YEARS LATER

Dᴇᴛᴇᴄᴛɪᴠᴇ Iɴsᴘᴇᴄᴛᴏʀ Rᴀᴍᴇsʜ Rʏᴀɴ ɴᴇʀᴠᴏᴜsʟʏ ғʟɪᴄᴋᴇᴅ open his jacket button and brushed the collar before tugging at his trousers to stop them from bagging at the knees. Ryan was facetious about his appearance. For him, being well dressed wasn't just an option; it was a necessity. He had always taken the saying 'clothes maketh the man' seriously.

Today the detective was wearing his blue suit. He put it on when a verdict was about to be delivered. But after ten years of wear, the clothing was showing its age. The cuffs were fraying, and the butt shiny after hours of sitting and sliding on uncomfortable court seats. It didn't fit Ryan as well as it used to, either. Now it was a little snug around the waist, the suit pants clinging too tight to the detective's long legs.

For Ryan, the blue suit was more than just a piece of clothing. It was a talisman. True, it didn't always work—the occasional not guilty verdict was part and parcel of any cop's life. But without it, Ryan was confident that the odds would be stacked even more in the defendant's favor. The detective couldn't prove this, of course. But then, it was not a matter of proof, more of faith, which was odd since the detective wasn't religious. However, he was superstitious. He believed in things like misfortune coming in threes and that a black cat crossing your path brought you bad luck.

His mother, Mumta, had attributed these beliefs to him 'being Indian.' "We Indians are spiritual creatures," she had said when he had mentioned one of his superstitions. But Ryan knew that wasn't true. He had spent most of his thirty-eight years on earth in Australia. So, that's what he was, an Australian; not an Indian.

"All rise," the clerk announced, interrupting the detective's thoughts while instantly silencing the court chatter. Everyone stood, and awaited the arrival of the judge. Seventy-year-old Sir Patrick Blackburn, KBE, QC, came out of his chamber and shuffled to his seat. Once a tall, imposing figure, Sir Patrick had started to show signs of age. Arthritis had almost crippled his legs, hence the shuffle, and his back was now severely bent. But whatever his physical ailments, the judge remained sharp as a tack.

As Sir Patrick gingerly lowered himself into his chair, a stocky, robed and wigged middle-aged man glanced back at Ryan and offered him a quick, nervous smile. Police Prosecutor Fred Park knew a lot rested on what happened in the next few minutes. Park was pleasant enough, but no lawyer. This wasn't a criticism. It was a fact. And as a police prosecutor, he didn't need to be either, though most prosecutors did have a law degree. However, Park had one much more impressive credential, his father—the late Cedric Park. Park Senior had until recently been the Superintendent of the NSW Police. This was more than enough to ensure his son's rapid rise through the ranks and eventual promotion to his current role. But although Park's lawyering had improved over the years, he remained a middling prosecutor, and one the detective would not have chosen to go to trial with if he had his way—which, of course, he didn't.

Fred Park wasn't Detective Ryan's only concern. The other was the wigged defense barrister sitting down from the police prosecutor. Benjamin 'Benjie' Gould of the renowned law firm Gould, Brook, and Cohen was recognized by many as Sydney's best criminal lawyer. His approach to a defendant was never to ask the question, "Did you do it?" In Benjie's eyes, this didn't matter. What was important wasn't the evidence against them but neutralizing it. In Benjie's mind, a defense barrister's job was to bury the proof, or if that wasn't possible, to turn it gray—since gray was the color of reasonable doubt.

Even though he was the opposition, the detective had a sneaking admiration for Benjie. He liked the way the man dressed, always in beautifully tailored suits. And he admired the barrister's ability to hypnotize juries with his extravagant gestures and deep baritone voice. But most of all, Ryan approved of Benjie's skill at 'selling' a story, however outlandish. And that was what he had tried to do in this trial.

At first, the detective hadn't been concerned. He believed he had a watertight case. Ryan had found the seven kilos of coke in the kitchen freezer of the defendant's Pizzeria. No one could dispute that. So the case was closed! But the defense lawyer hadn't bothered to argue about the facts. Instead, Benjie had chosen to sell the story that his client had no idea the drugs were there. As outlandish and ridiculous as this argument appeared—the Pizzeria was owned and run by the defendant, and he even had an office there—there was still a possibility that this tale could gain traction with the jury. And if it did this, it was down not just to Benjie's lawyering skills but to the ability of his client—sixty-year-old Oscar Bruno.

Oscar Bruno had sat in a wheelchair throughout the three-week trial. Swathed in a fluffy red dressing gown, with a yellow blanket spread across his knees, the defendant cut a pathetic figure. His jowly mouth was constantly open, saliva dripping down, while his head slumped down as he slept, which he did, most of the time. If he awoke, his eyes would roll around confused while he swiveled his head from side to side, apparently unsure of exactly where he was.

When Detective Ryan had first seen Bruno's court antics, he had almost laughed out loud. Hadn't he seen a documentary on TV about a New York mafioso who had pulled the same stunt? And surely no one would buy that Sydney's 'alleged' number one drug dealer had run an empire in this condition? But then Benjie had introduced a series of experts, all with impressive academic credentials. Each had certified that Bruno's mind had succumbed to dementia. They all agreed he was now scarcely capable of making himself a cup of coffee.

The more the detective had studied Bruno, the more impressed he had become. There was no doubt that the drug dealer could have pursued a career as an actor if he had so wished. His performance was beyond impressive. It was masterly. Even so, Ryan was still unwilling to believe that the twelve down-to-earth Australian men and women on the jury could be taken in by Bruno's ridiculous antics.

The door in the far corner of the wood-paneled courtroom swung open. All watched the jury file in and take their seats. Everyone remained quiet, waiting for what was to come—everyone that was except for Oscar Bruno. Sleeping, his head down, he suddenly let out a series of searing snores.

The detective ignored Bruno's performance and tried to read the juror's faces. Most had their eyes down. What did that mean? Experts choose the right people for the jury, and then, during the trial, they try to predict what individual jurors are thinking and feeling. Detective Ryan didn't have time for what he considered a voodoo science. He chose to make his mind up about the jurors' emotions, and he was concerned about their refusal to make eye contact. The jury had been deliberating for a mere four hours before signaling they had reached a verdict. To Detective Ryan, this could mean one of two things. Either they were so confident of Bruno's guilt that they needed little time to examine the facts or . . .

The detective took a deep breath. He didn't want to think about that alternative. He had worked on this case for over a year, obsessively watching the antics of Bruno and his men while praying for the canny drug dealer to make a mistake . . . and finally, he had; seven keys worth of mistakes. But was it enough? If Bruno was found guilty, Ryan would be the hero of the hour. If not, then most would question why he was in charge of a case that would have been won but for the 'Indian' cop leading it.

Detective Ryan turned his attention back to Sir Patrick. The judge nodded to a woman in her late-fifties who sat just in front of him. The court clerk stood up and waited, milking the moment, before signaling for the jury foreperson, a skinny man in his forties, to rise.

"Oscar Roberto Bruno is charged with one count of trafficking seven kilograms of a prohibited drug. How do you find the Accused, guilty or not guilty?"

The foreman hesitated before speaking. "Not guilty," he announced finally.

Detective Ryan felt a wave of nausea sweep over him as he tried to block out the cheers that erupted in the court.

"Silence, silence," the judge said, slamming down his gavel. "Mr. Bruno, you are free to go."

Oscar Bruno looked up for a moment and then let his head slump. His nurse, a constant presence in the court, grasped the man's wheelchair and started to push it out.

The detective rose to his feet too. He wanted to leave as quickly as possible. But whether by design or coincidence, the nurse and his charge reached the central aisle first. If the detective stepped out, he would block Oscar Bruno's path! He could either barge ahead or wait until the drug dealer had passed.

He had no choice. He signaled to the nurse to move ahead of him. As he did, Bruno lifted his head and, making eye contact Detective Ryan, moved his right hand from under the throw. He formed his fingers into the shape of a gun and pointed it at the detective. The action was only visible for a split second before the drug dealer pushed his hand back under the blanket, and the wheelchair trundled on past Ryan and headed for the exit.

THREE

OUTSIDE, OSCAR BRUNO'S GRAY BULLETPROOF V8 Rover Autography pulled up at the court steps. Taking his hand off the wheel, the driver, The Owl, adjusted his red and white striped tie, tightening and centering it around his thick neck. Satisfied, he peered out of his round pebble glasses at the chaos unfolding all around. His boss's consigliere, Big Jay, had paid for a rent-a-crowd to wave placards and shout for justice. A gaggle of reporters standing nearby watched them, filling time while they awaited the arrival of the main event—Oscar Bruno. And suddenly, there he was, sitting in the wheelchair in his dirty red dressing gown.

Seeing this, The Owl leaped out of the car and raced up the stairs. Reaching his boss, he helped the lawyer and the nurse lift the drug dealer down the steps to the Range Rover. All ignored the shouted reporters' questions, the flashing cameras, and the TV hacks thrusting microphones.

Usually, attorney Benjie Gould would have relished this moment, lecturing to the assembled media about the 'injustice' of the trial and how his client had been railroaded and demeaned. But Benjie's cameo would have to wait until Bruno had been helped into the car and the Rover had driven away.

Reaching the vehicle, The Owl yanked the back door open, and the nurse lifted Bruno into the plush black leather seats. Then he helped the nurse stow the wheelchair in the trunk before climbing back into the driver's seat, clipping on his seat belt, and switching on the motor.

"Okay, boss?" The Owl asked, moving his right foot over the accelerator pedal.

There was a grunt from the back. The Owl waited for more. Nothing came. It was the first hint that perhaps things weren't entirely right. But he accepted the sound as the only affirmative needed and accelerated away.

"Big Jay organize that?" Bruno asked suddenly.

The Owl glanced into the driver's mirror. His boss had his head turned. He was watching the media scrum receding behind him.

"Yes, boss."

Bruno nodded, unclipped his belt, and, helped by the nurse, started to peel off his bath robe. The Owl saw the movement in the mirror. He hesitated. Should he say something?

"It might be best to leave the gown on, boss. There's a load of paparazzi outside the mansion gates."

Bruno thought about that, then he pulled the robe back on. The Owl breathed out and again glanced into the driver's mirror. For a man that had just dodged a huge bullet, his boss didn't appear to be thrilled. He should warn the others. The Owl took his right hand off the steering wheel and reached down to the center console to pick up his cell.

"Leave it," Bruno ordered.

The Owl pulled his hand back quickly, returning it to the wheel.

"I was just going tell them that you're on your way?"

"They'll fucking know that when they see me, won't they?"

The Owl quaked. "Yes. Right, boss."

IT TOOK ANOTHER FIFTEEN MINUTES BEFORE the Range Rover arrived at the grandly named Villa Bruno, a sprawling eleven-bedroom house in Point Piper's most prestigious street. The mansion, built last century, was designed to allow expansive views over Sydney's breathtakingly beautiful harbor and to impress the bejeezus out of anyone who saw it. And it certainly did that. But, although Bruno appreciated the building's fuck-you qualities, he had bought the home because it afforded him the kind of security that was necessary for his line of work. Surrounded by high concrete walls, topped by barbed wire, monitored by surveillance cameras and motion detectors, it was at the end of a cul-de-sac and backed onto cliffs. To breach its defenses from the cliffside would require the skills of a platoon of soldiers. The city's underworld was practiced at organizing beatings, presiding over tortures, and carrying out gruesome murders; but SAS soldiering expertise was not in their skill set.

And any would-be invaders who attempted to ram through the building's ornate front gates would be in for a nasty surprise too. Built from titanium with a tensile strength of 63,000 psi, the closed barriers could withstand virtually any impact.

Even getting in legally was difficult. Vehicles waited for five or more minutes while a drone flew low, and wall-mounted surveillance cameras examined the occupants. If the gate was opened, armed guards interrogated the passengers, holding back large snarling German Shepherds and Rottweilers. The gray V-8 Rover didn't have to endure any of this. As the vehicle approached, the gates immediately slid open. The SUV sped past the crowd of paparazzi and rubberneckers and entered the mansion grounds.

BIG JAY AND THE LION HAD already come out to greet their boss. They were the highest-ranking employees in Bruno's organization. Big Jay, Jay Russo, was the consigliere. A tall, muscular man in his mid-thirties, he had a rotund face, squinty blue eyes, and a shiny bald head. Today, he'd dressed up to greet the boss and wore a tight-fitting black suit and open-necked red shirt. The Lion was a shade shorter than his compatriot and boasted a mane of black hair that reached down over his shoulders. The hair and his name Leo Moretti provided the reason for his nickname. Like Big Jay, The Lion looked a lot like a brick wall. He had the same substantial build as Big Jay but a more triangular visage and, his dead eyes were brown and not blue. He, too, wore a black suit but a more restrained blue-colored open-necked shirt.

The others in the gang—the twenty or so men who were the beating heart of Oscar Bruno's organization—surrounded Big Jay and The Lion. They watched as the Rover wound its way up the long concrete driveway and let out a cheer as the vehicle halted in front of the building's impressive white-columned entrance.

The Owl quickly got out and opened the car's back door. As he did,

Bruno flicked his hand, indicating the nurse should leave. But he didn't move. He remained inside the Rover, silently staring ahead.

"Boss?" said Big Jay stepping forward.

Bruno turned. Vicious, mean eyes stared out at his employee. He lifted his head to take in the banner tacked across the first floor of the stone building. It read: **"Welcome back."**

"What the fuck's that?" Bruno asked, pointing up as he climbed out of the car. "I've been coming back every night of the trial, you idiot."

"Sorry, boss. We'll take it down."

Big Jay twisted around and nodded. Immediately, two men peeled off and retreated into the house. The banner would be removed in moments.

Bruno walked through the now-silent crowd heading for the open front door.

"Great win. You showed those fuckers!" Big Jay said as he hurried to catch up to his boss. Ignoring him, Bruno entered the home's stately hallway. Inside, a jazz group started to play.

In the world of Oscar Bruno, Big Jay was considered a deep thinker—a man who could read a person and a room at a glance. It had taken him mere seconds to work out that his boss was in no mood to party. So, as he entered the hallway, Big Jay was already waving his hand frantically, signaling for the band to stop. But it was too late.

"Oh, for Christ's sake, get those people out of here. NOW!" Bruno yelled. Then, tossing aside the tatty bathrobe, the drug dealer headed up the sweeping marble staircase.

FOUR

DETECTIVE RAMESH RYAN WAS RECEIVING A similar reception to Big Jay on his arrival at his office. Cops are gregarious animals—bombastic and talkative. Ryan had always taken the nosey camaraderie for granted. So when he walked in, the silence was unnerving. The detective crossed to his desk while the other cops kept their heads down, apparently engrossed in their work.

Ryan stopped before sitting and turning to address the room.

"Okay, for those that haven't heard, and I'm betting that's no one here, Bruno was found not guilty. The bastard got away scot-free." He paused. "That means that next time, we've got to try even harder to nail the asshole. Got that?"

An overweight bald man in his mid-thirties broke the silence.

"Come on, you lot. We were robbed." Detective Inspector Rob Headley waited. "I said we were robbed. You all know Ryan did his best. Right?"

It was like a dam had been breached.

"The bastard escaped by the skin of his teeth."

"Lucky dickhead."

"What a sick verdict!"

This could have gone on if Chief Inspector Dan Dudley hadn't stuck his head out of his office at the far end of the room.

"Ryan, in here now," the big cop yelled. "And you lot get back to work."

"SIT DOWN, RYAN," DUDLEY SAID AS the detective entered. He indicated a wooden chair in front of an expansive glass table.

At a smidge over six feet with a well-built, muscular body, Detective Ryan could never be described as a small man. Even so, the Chief Inspector's bulk made the detective look and feel diminutive. Standing six feet four and weighing in at around two hundred pounds with cauliflower ears, a pug nose, squinty eyes, and a large head, Dan Dudley looked more like a prizefighter than a man chosen to run one of the most powerful police units in Australia. And he used his bulk to intimidate, which was why he remained standing while instructing Detective Ryan to sit down.

The detective had a theory that Dan Dudley spent much of his free time scouring the latest books on the psychology of undermining your enemy. Of course, those tomes weren't in his office. That would have been too obvious. Instead, space on the Chief Inspector's bookshelves and the desk had numerous photographs of the beaming Inspector surrounded by family, friends, and high-ranking officials, like the Mayor and the Premier.

"So you lost, Ryan," the Chief Inspector thundered, uttering the sentence as a statement rather than a question.

The detective hesitated, twisting his head around and indicating the door. "Sir, could you close the door, please?"

"I want it left open Ryan, that way, they can all hear what I'm about to say," Dudley said. "The fact is I don't like losing, and that's what just happened."

"Yes, unfortunately, we did," the detective concurred.

"We?" The Chief Inspector paused. "There's no we about this. As my lead detective, you persuaded me to take this case to court because of what turned out to be flimsy evidence."

So that was the tack that Dudley was taking, Ryan thought. Chief Inspector Dudley wasn't known as Teflon Dan for nothing! Dudley had risen through the ranks with the agility of a large goat scrambling up a mountain, his open smile and backslapping bonhomie on show for all he considered valuable. His charm offensive had worked. For five years now, he had headed the all-important Organized Crime Squad. He had survived and prospered because of his ability to read the political winds better than most.

The detective opened his mouth to say something, but Dudley raised his hand.

"I haven't finished yet. If I recall, you couldn't lose the case. Bruno would be, to use the vernacular, 'banged to rights.'"

"Sir, with due respect, I said that I thought we . . . I . . . should win the case."

"Let's not argue semantics Ryan. Maybe it's part of your culture to nit-pick over words, but . . ."

"Culture, Sir? You mean the Australian culture?"

"No, I mean your culture. Your Indian culture."

"Sir, I'm not Indian; I'm Australian."

"You've got brown skin and your mother's Indian. In my book, that makes you Indian."

The detective went to speak and then changed his mind.

"Did you hear what the defense counsel had to say about the verdict, Ryan?"

The detective shook his head. He hadn't stuck around while Benjie Gould gloated.

"You should have," Dudley said. He grabbed a copy of the Evening News from his desk and held it up. A photo of the defense lawyer and his bemused client Oscar Bruno filled the front page. The headline was just two words long: "Not Guilty."

"Gould specifically mentions you, Ryan," the Chief Inspector said, waving the paper in the air.

"He does?"

"Yes, he says," the Chief Inspector peered at the newspaper, ". . . blah, blah, blah, and Detective Ramesh Ryan, who headed the investigation, should resign from the Force after his despicable attempt to imprison an innocent, sick old man."

The Chief Inspector slammed the paper back down on the desk.

"So, what do you say to that, Ryan?"

"You're quoting the defense barrister, Sir. Of course, he's going to claim that," Ryan said in a voice that revealed just a sliver of anger.

"He mentions you, Ryan. Just you. Not We. Not police in general. Do you get my drift?"

And like a blinding flash of light, the detective suddenly understood the true Machiavellian nature of the Chief Inspector's words.

"I do, Sir. You're saying that by mentioning me, I have become a tar-get?" he said slowly and loudly.

"Exactly."

Then the Chief Inspector abruptly changed tack. "Have you ever heard of a little place called Barton, Ryan?"

"No, Sir."

"Well, it's a small beach town north of Sydney on the Central Coast."

The Chief Inspector stepped over to a large map of Australia pinned to the wall. "It's here," he said, pointing a finger at a small dot. "Population six thousand, with a few pubs, a couple of cafes, and shops selling trinkets for the tourists. The usual."

Now the detective saw where the Chief Inspector was heading.

"You want me to go to Barton, Sir?"

"For your safety."

"Of course, Sir."

"I met the Sergeant up there at one of those tiresome conferences I have to go to from time to time. He was a nice enough guy but complained that there was just him and another few cops to look after everything. And he mentioned he was short a detective."

For the next few minutes, Ryan let the Chief Inspector's words wash over him. Dudley painted a picture of a dull beach town with nothing to do. The Chief Inspector finally stopped talking. He waited for a response from the detective.

"Well?"

"When am I to leave, Sir?"

"The Sergeant is expecting you tomorrow. You'll find all the details in the file on your desk."

"How long will I be there, Sir?"

"It's open-ended."

"And if I were to refuse?" the detective asked.

The Chief Inspector glared at him.

"I don't think you would want to do that, Ryan."

FIVE

O F COURSE, EVERYONE HAD HEARD. THE Chief Inspector's booming voice had easily carried through the open door into the main office. Detective Ramesh Ryan, the high-flying detective who had 'inexplicably' lost the Oscar Bruno case, was on the out—exiled to a tiny town on the Central Coast for an unspecified amount of time.

As the detective left the Chief Inspector's office, the cops avoided eye contact with the doomed man. Ryan wasn't surprised. It was all about self-preservation.

To put his colleagues out of their misery, Ryan immediately announced that much as he'd like to go for a drink to say a 'temporary' goodbye to everyone, he had to go home and sort a few things out before leaving. Then the detective scooped up the manila file from his desk, quickly packed up his laptop, and left. Only Detective Headley said goodbye, slapping him on his back as he walked out, promising to give him a call soon "to catch up."

PARKING OPPOSITE HIS POTTS POINT APARTMENT block, Ryan flicked through the file of notes the Chief Inspector had left him. The detective preferred the reassurance of paper to that of a flickering computer screen. And Chief Inspector Dan Dudley had known that. It was why he had given Ryan the hard copy notes and not emailed them to his laptop.

Opening the file, the detective scanned the first page and stared at the photo at the top. A fat, rosey-faced man smiled back at him. Sergeant Gary

Acton—the head of Barton's police station. The Sergeant had been living and working in Barton for all of his thirty-seven years. Not much ambition there then, Ryan thought.

The detective flicked the page over to reveal a photo of a pretty Asian woman in a police uniform. Unlike Sergeant Acton, she wasn't smiling. She stared aggressively at the camera, her lips pursed, her eyes wide and piercing, and her arms crossed. This was Senior Constable Zoe Yang—twenty-six years old, and the number two in Barton's cop station—a woman who clearly wanted to be taken seriously.

According to the notes, Zoe Yang had a Chinese father and an Australian mother, so, she and the detective had something in common. Zoe had probably encountered the same kinds of prejudices as Ryan had. What's more, Constable Yang was a woman—an extra cross to bear.

Ryan scanned more of the file. There was the background on the town, much of which the Chief Inspector had already outlined: Barton was a beachside location with a mix of tourist attractions—surfing, swimming, and cliff walks. The town had several pubs, a few restaurants, a post office, and a cafe. It also had a pier, with a boat shed and a mooring dock. Years ago, it was known as a fishing town, but trawling had gone the way of the dodo. Getting up at four o'clock in the morning for three hundred plus days a year to go to sea was hard work. The alternative—capturing the tourist dollar—had proved much more attractive to most.

The annual crime figures were listed. Serious felonies were rarer than rocking horse droppings. But if you were a cop leaving 'the big smoke' for a quiet life by the coast while counting down the days before retirement, the statistics would be like manna from heaven. Ryan wasn't that cop.

As he stared at the pages, the detective's mind turned back to the trial. Usually, when he lost in court, he tried to forget it. These things happen. But losing to a man like Oscar Bruno was just too personal. He despised Bruno, hating him for his callous use of violence, disregard for the law, and willingness to do anything to make money, whatever the human cost.

Sitting back, the detective breathed in and out slowly. He had taken up meditation some years back, and now everything he had learned came into play. The trial had been a disaster. Ryan had underestimated the wiles of his opponent. The police prosecutor was incompetent; the expensive defense lawyer was masterly; and Oscar Bruno's acting was worthy of his namesake's trophy.

Ryan rubbed his hand over his face and returned to reading the papers. There was a breakdown of tomorrow's itinerary on the final page. It included an already-arranged time to meet Sergeant Acton. Ryan was booked into a room in a local pub, incongruously named the "Singing Pelican." As far as he knew, pelicans didn't sing, and there had been no mention in his notes of mass sightings of the bird in the town, so the pub's owner either had a wacky sense of humor or was drunk when he decided on the name—or both. The detective closed the file and grabbed his laptop case. He hated the beach town already.

Getting out of the car, he crossed the one-way street to the metal barred front gates of his art-deco block. He jammed his security key into the lock and pushed the door open. It creaked and scraped over the concrete. The gate was old and stubborn, but for Ryan, there was something reassuring about its refusal to do what it was meant to do.

Ryan lived in what was, in estate agent jargon, the Paris-end of Potts Point. Perched on a hill overlooking the naval base, the bay, and the city, the district had finally succumbed to gentrification back in the mid-eighties. Before this, Potts Point, with its myriad of one and two-bed apartments, had housed a mix of poor older people and even more impoverished youngsters. But with the developers' arrival, derelict land was brought up, and ancient terraces were bulldozed to make way for gleaming high-rise blocks. Today the area was a 'happening place' filled with hip restaurants and expensive boutiques . . . well, most of it was. A little of the 'old' Potts Point remained, and that's where Ryan chose to live.

The detective closed the gate, strode up the redbrick steps, and entered the lobby. His apartment was on the third floor. To reach it, he had to climb worn stone stairs that curved around the building's innards. When he had rented the unit two years ago, Ryan was told that most occupants had lived in the block for at least thirty years. Many had bought their flats when prices were still just four figures. But, despite the numerous agents who came calling, many remained, refusing to leave. Ryan knew why.

Despite the district's noise, buzz, and cosmopolitan feel, his apartment, with its view over the city, remained quiet and serene—a perfect place to hide away from the world.

Ryan paused outside his unit. He could hear the sound of a TV inside. The detective lowered the file and laptop onto the floor. Reaching into his blue suit jacket, he unholstered his Glock semi-automatic gun. Holding the weapon in one hand, he unlocked the door, twisted the handle, pushed hard, and entered.

SIX

"R AMESH?" THE PORTLY MIDDLE-AGED WOMAN SAID as the detective burst into the living room, his arm out, the Glock gripped tight.

"Mom?"

She peered up at the detective from the couch. "Why have you got that gun out?"

Ryan looked at the weapon before hastily holstering it. "What are you doing here?"

"Watching the TV, of course. What does it look like?"

Ryan squinted his eyes. "How did you get in?"

"With a key."

Ryan strode across to his mother, lifted the remote, and turned the TV off. "A key?"

"That is the way you usually enter an apartment. And thank you, Ramesh. Now I won't know if anyone won the million dollars today."

Ryan sniffed the air. "What's that smell?"

The detective's mother stood up and brushed down her green sari over her substantial stomach. "Curry."

"You've cooked curry?"

"Yes, for you. It's your favorite. Now come over here and kiss your mother." Mumta opened up her arms to embrace her son.

"That's better," she said. Releasing him, she walked out of the living room into the kitchen.

Ryan, still confused, followed. "You have a key?"

"You gave me one last year, don't you remember?"

"That was for you to let the electrician in while I was at work."

"For which you never thanked me properly."

"I did, mom." He thought about that. "But you gave me that key back?"

Mumta dipped a wooden spoon into the pan of curry and offered the liquid to Ramesh. "Try it."

He sipped the curry. It was fantastic—deep and earthy from a blend of cumin, coriander, turmeric, mustard, and ginger. His mother was a brilliant cook, and as a result, he had never bothered to learn to do much in the kitchen himself. It was something the detective had always regretted. But the one time he had nagged her to teach him, Mumta had screwed up her nose. "That's my job. What do you want to do, put me out of work?" And that was that. He never brought it up again because he knew it was never going to happen. Mumta's stubbornness was legendary.

"You brought all the ingredients here?"

"Yes. Do you think I'd forgotten that you never cook?" Mumta said as she raised the spoon to her mouth and took a sip. "It just needs half an hour more."

"Mom, I've just left something outside. I'll be back in a moment."

The detective walked out of the kitchen and across the living room. He opened the front door, collected the laptop and file, and came back in.

"So, the key?" he said as his mom came out of the kitchen.

Mumta frowned as she brushed back her long dark black hair. "Didn't we go through that just now, Ramesh?"

"But if you returned it, how did you get in?"

"I said I returned that key, not all the keys?"

"You made a copy?"

"Of course." She smiled. "I knew it might be useful. And, when I saw that terrible news on the television, I was proved right."

"You heard about the trial?"

"You think your own mother doesn't follow your career?"

"Yes, but . . ."

"I never wanted you to be a policeman, but you're almost as obstinate as I am, so I knew I would get nowhere saying you had to do something else."

Ryan raised his eyebrows. He had never heard his mom ever admit to being stubborn. "But you're always saying that I should have been a doctor."

"Yes, it's a much better and more suitable career for an Indian."

"Australian."

Mumta stared at him.

"Mom, you are Australian too. You came here from Britain with my dad . . ."

"May God rest his soul," Mumta interrupted.

". . . thirty years ago, and when he died, you chose to stay."

"I chose to remain close to my son. That's what mothers do."

"But you wanted to go back to India permanently. You've only ever returned there for holidays."

"And when your grandfather died," Mumta corrected.

"Okay, but admit it, you like it here," Ryan said.

"I will do nothing of the sort."

They stared at each other—an impasse. Mumta blinked first. "Let's not argue. I just don't want you to forget that part of you is Indian."

"Well, we can agree on that." He reached across to hug her again. "You came over and made me curry because of the trial?"

"I saw the expression on your face outside of that court when you were behind that smarmy lawyer, the nurse, and that man. Boscar."

"Oscar."

"Yes. Him. The lawyer insulted you too when he was crowing about the case."

"That's what defense lawyers do when they win."

"Maybe, but he shouldn't have won. You should have."

"I can't always win," Ryan said.

"But that Boscar was acting." She paused." Your great grandfather Aakil used to do that when people were after him for money."

"He did?"

"Yes. And Aakil was much better at it than Boscar." She reached for her purse. "I'm off."

"Won't you stay to eat?" Ryan asked.

"Thank you, but no. I have an important bridge match tonight, and I can't let my partner down."

"A man ?" asked Ryan quizzically.

"He is."

"Hum."

"Don't you hum me, son. I know what you're thinking, but it's nothing like that" Mumta said, and headed for the door.

"Mom, I have something to tell you."

Mumta stopped and turned. "You've met a suitable girl?"

"No."

"I didn't think so. What is it then?"

"I'm going away for a few weeks," Ryan said.

"When?"

"Tomorrow." He saw the look on her face. "It was sudden. I was only officially told about it today."

"It's for work?"

"Yes."

"They're sending you away as punishment for losing the case?" Mumta asked.

Ryan had sometimes thought that at a different time in another place, his mother could have been a brilliant investigator herself.

"Not a punishment, no. My boss just needs me to go up to the Central Coast to a town called Barton to sort a few things out."

Mumta opened the door. She knew a lie when she heard one, but it had been a bad day for her son, so she wouldn't dwell on something neither of them could do anything about.

"Well, make sure you call me. At least once a week. And eat that curry. You're all skin and bones."

"Love you," said Ryan as his mother stepped into the corridor.

"You too," said Mumta, reaching across to kiss him.

"And next time, I'll make you something Australian—maybe a bacon and egg roll. I'm getting good at them," Mumta said and closed the door.

SEVEN

JACK BREEN HADN'T FELT THIS GOOD since he had won his silver medal, his head held high, the medallion around his neck, while the Australian national anthem boomed out over the speakers. That was a moment that, as the old cliche goes, you never forgot. Surely nothing would ever compare to that feeling? Yet now, four years later, Jack felt a similar sensation. And that didn't make sense.

How could being perched precariously on the bow of the fishing boat, his hands clutching tight to the rail, while rainwater streamed down his face, and the wind buffeted his body make him so happy? Well, in truth, Jack knew the answer. Finally, he had found a reason for living and was again experiencing the adrenaline high that he had searched for so long outside of his swimming career.

"Jack," a voice yelled.

Alfie Carlisle frantically gestured to his friend to return. Jack mouthed okay and headed over to the wheelhouse.

INSIDE, AT THE HELM, SKIPPER MARIO Hannan steered his boat, The Peggy Sue, towards the Korean cargo ship moored some four hundred yards away. The seven hundred feet long, fifty thousand-ton Chong San was small by today's standards, but it dwarfed the skipper's tiny vessel.

Mario was regretting his decision to sail. He should have called it off when he had read today's weather forecast. It warned of twenty to thirty-three-knot winds, heavy rain, and thunder and lightning—a vortex that was now threatening to engulf his boat. The skipper knew he should have listened to his gut. But he had ignored it. The thought of earning a cool half a million bucks had assuaged any doubts.

Running a deep-sea charter business earned Mario a good living—certainly more than in his previous job as a trawler fisherman. But running the company still hadn't meant that the skipper could live comfortably—not with his gambling problem and owing a loan shark called Lenny thousands. No! Then you did what you could to survive. And despite the weather, there was no way that either Alfie Carlisle, Jack Breen, or the Koreans would cancel the pickup. Mario knew that they had to collect the cocaine tonight.

"It'll be easy, Alfie," the rich kid had said. "I know a guy who knows people who know where to get the stuff. We go out, do the exchange, and Bob's your uncle."

Alfie and Jack had been out on Mario's boat, fishing for tuna and flat head when they had first made the pitch. The kids were regulars and always paid handsomely. Over time Mario had got to like the boys. Although twenty-four-year-old Alfie always carried himself with the kind of narcissism that only the wealthy have, his natural charm offset his arrogance. As for Jack, Mario knew of him already. The skipper had been watching TV the day that the lanky guy had won his medal. Like most of Australia, he had cheered as Jack had finished the swim just inches behind the Yank.

Mario had thought about the kids' proposal for all of sixty seconds and knew by then he would accept it—though, of course, he hadn't let on. "I'm not sure," he'd said. "What exactly do you want me to do?"

"Just ferry us to the ship and then back to shore," Alfie had said.

"That's it?"

"That's it."

"When will I get my money?"

"On the job's completion."

Mario had shaken his head. "I want at least twenty grand upfront."

Alfie had glanced across at Jack, who'd smiled. Mario had caught the look. He realized then that he should have asked for at least double.

"Okay, you'll get it before we leave," Alfie had said.

THE SKIPPER TAPPED HIS COAT POCKET, feeling the reassurance of the money the kid had given him earlier that night. So far, so good.

As the boat's lights cut through the spray and rain, Mario pressed the button for the horn. Two loud wails cut through the noise of the storm. The skipper slowed the engine and pulled the Peggy Sue closer into the Chong San as Alfie hoisted his backpack off the floor. The case contained the two million dollars payment, and he hadn't let it out of his sight since he'd got it.

Jack tapped Alfie on the shoulder and pointed up at the Korean ship that loomed over them. Moments ago, its deck had been empty. Now armed men swarmed across it, their AK-47s pointing down at their boat. What had taken months to plan had suddenly become very real.

"Alfie," Mario shouted, pointing to the satellite radio handset clipped to the shelf at the side of the wheel.

The rich kid pulled the transmitter from its holster, quickly tapping in numbers on its pad. "Hello," he said and waited.

"You have the money," an accented voice finally answered.

"Of course."

"Put it into the net."

"But . . ."

"First the money, and then the product."

Alfie hesitated. The rule was: Get the goods first and then pay the cash. "I need a sample," Alfie said.

Silence.

Alfie glanced over at Jack. Had he just blown it?

Then: "You have all the cash?" the voice finally asked.

"Yes."

More silence before: "Agreed."

Alfie released his breath. He raised his thumb to the others and clicked the radio off. The men watched as a blue net was flung over the side of the Chong San.

"Go," Alfie said to Jack.

LEAVING THE WHEELHOUSE, THE OLYMPIAD struggled to keep upright in the wind. Reaching over the side of the Peggy Sue, he undid the ropes that held a pike pole. Looking up, he saw the net descending from the Korean ship. Jack raised the rod, thrusting it forward, its curved tip hooking into the mesh. He pulled it on deck. Reaching in, Jack grasped a brick parcel. A gold tiger was embossed on its blue waterproof cover.

Jack returned to the wheelhouse with the package and handed it to Alfie. It took his friend seconds to run his Victorinox fish-gutting knife over the covering. It opened a small slit to reveal dense white powder.

"Jack?" Alfie asked.

The swimmer reached into his pocket and pulled out a small ampoule filled with clear liquid. Snapping off the top of the glass capsule, Jack offered it to Alfie. He scooped a sample of the white power up with his fingers and dropped the coke into the liquid. Alfie and Jack waited and watched as the fluid slowly changed color. Dark red!

"Jeez," said Alfie quietly.

"Almost 100 percent pure," echoed Jack, who turned and gave a thumbs up to Mario.

Then Alfie handed Jack the backpack, watching as the Olympiad returned to the deck and placed it into the mesh. After that the net was hoisted back onto the cargo ship.

Alfie and Jack waited. They had given the money up and had had only a sample of the promised coke. What if the ship just sailed away?

The satellite radio buzzed. "Yes?" Alfie asked anxiously.

"On its way," the accented voice said.

Relieved, Jack returned to the deck. He grasped the pike pole and watched as the full net was lowered. With his heart beating, he reached across and thrust the rod into the mesh. That's when things started to go wrong.

As Jack yanked on the pole, the net swung towards the Peggy Sue and began to tear. Seeing this, the man pulled harder. Two packages fell through the holed mesh into the churning water below. Cursing, Jack yanked the pole again, and the netting and rest of the packages fell onto the deck.

"Shit, Jack," Alfie yelled, appearing behind him. "Do something."

Pulling off his rainproof jacket Jack dived into the sea. It was a ridiculous thing to do. He may have been a great swimmer, but it was beyond

foolhardy to plunge clothed into the frothing, foaming sea. But Jack did it
without thinking. He knew it was his responsibility to solve the situation.
He was that kind of man.

Above, the netting was pulled back onto the Chong San, and the ship
started up its engines. The drug traffickers had completed the deal and
wanted to get away as quickly as possible. Mario heard the sound and panicked. He liked Jack, but he was not going to die for him. He knew he had
to leave now before the swell from the Korean ship engulfed his little boat.

Twisting the wheel around, the skipper motored away, leaving Jack to
his fate.

EIGHT

Last night's storm left as quickly as it had arrived—which was lucky for Detective Ramesh Ryan. He was no great shakes as a driver, and motoring through heavy rain made him nervous. The journey up had been trouble-free, and now, arriving in Barton, the detective felt strangely happy. Despite his reservations, the little town did seem to have a certain charm. Its flat, sandy beach lapped by the calm waters of the Pacific and framed by craggy majestic cliffs was easy on the eye. And being off season, there were none of the noisy distractions afforded by the flocks of marauding tourists.

Ryan rounded the bay, passing a picturesque pier, a boat shed, and a mooring dock where small boats bobbed up and down in the bright sunlight. The road began climbing up towards the center of town. The detective glanced to his right as he steered his blue Ford Focus around a bend on the narrow coastal road. He spied a small restaurant, wedged between an estate agency and a row of rundown shops. The name Sand Castle was printed on a board above its windows. Ryan made a mental note of it. Because he didn't cook, the detective was always on the lookout for places to eat. For him, good food was important.

The detective released one hand from the wheel and clenched his fist, trying to get the circulation back. He found driving boring, so to distract himself, he had let his mind wander. There were thousands of things the detective could have thought about, but he kept remembering the trial.

How had he lost what was considered an open and shut case? Bruno's wheelchair act and the charisma of the defense lawyer were obvious factors but were they enough? The detective had his doubts. He replayed the shocking moment that the foreman had read out the jury's verdict. He had addressed the judge confidently when he said the words "Not Guilty." And yet—Ryan concentrated, trying to remember what he'd seen in court. There was something he had missed, and if he put his mind to it, he would remember what it was. Though he never bragged about it, the detective had a phenomenal recall.

Ryan had discovered the talent as a child when he had played something called 'the memory game' at school. One day the teacher had spread out objects on a table for a minute or so. Then he had covered them with a cloth and asked the children to write down what they'd seen. When there were just a few items, everyone got it right. But, as the teacher repeated the game adding to the number of objects, it became increasingly difficult for most. But not for Ryan. He was just too good. Ryan never played the memory game again at school but had spent weeks at home honing his abilities.

The detective replayed the foreman's actions. He had dropped his head immediately after reading out the verdict. Then he had glanced to the right, making eye contact with Bruno. For just a split second, the foreman had blinked, and Bruno had nodded. Yes, that's what he'd seen. The man had signaled to the drug dealer, and Bruno had acknowledged it. So the foreman had been got at. Bruno had weighted the scales of justice!

Ryan came out of his revelry. He had forgotten he was driving. The car was heading off the road. He swung the wheel to the left, straightening the Ford's nose and narrowly avoiding catastrophe. It was a close call. Ryan drove on, relieved he was only minutes away from his destination.

WHEN THE SINGLE-LEVEL, BRICK-WALLED BUILDING came into view, the detective thought that he had made a mistake. The place looked more like a large cottage than a cop station. But then he saw the square blue-and-white checkered police sign attached to the top of the white tubing that advertised the building's true purpose. Yes, this was it.

Parking, Ryan glanced at his watch: three twenty-six. *Good.* His meeting with Sergeant Acton had been arranged for three-thirty, and the detective hated being late. He got out of his car and hurried down the concrete path to the front entrance. Pushing the heavy wooden door open, he entered the lobby. It was a small empty room. Four black plastic chairs linked together and bolted to a wall adorned with notices stood to his left. There was an L-shaped reception desk and office to his right.

The detective peered into the office. He pressed his hand hard down on the bell on the counter and waited—nothing. He tried again—silence. Ryan glanced at his watch: three twenty-eight. If he stayed here any longer, he was going to be late. Making a decision, he leaned over the desk and ran his hand along its underside. He knew there should be a button there that allowed entry into the main office.

Finding the switch, he pushed it. There was a buzz, a satisfying click, and the sound of the release of a lock. Turning, he stepped to the inner door and pushed it open. The detective entered a large room as behind the door closed and locked.

Ryan looked around. An old cloth-covered blue sofa was pushed hard against the far wall. A glass coffee table stood close by. A wooden corner desk took up the space between the couch and the back wall. A full-sized computer and untidy piles of papers spread out over the top of the desk while, jammed under it, was a battered leather swivel chair. Close-by sat another small table and chair. Over by the opposite wall was one more wood-topped desk, a rectangular white evidence board above it. Two words had been scrawled in black marker ink across it—Dry Cleaning. A full percolator of coffee bubbled on a metal bureau to the right of the board. White and blue striped mugs sat next to it. A small silver micro-wave cooker took up the remainder of the space. A compact fridge stood between the bureau and the door to the lobby.

Ryan scanned the room. There was no one there.

"Hello," the detective shouted and waited—nothing.

"Hello," he repeated—still nothing.

Ryan was unimpressed. Where was everyone? He was due to meet Sergeant Acton at three-thirty, which was in exactly one minute. Well, if the mountain wouldn't come to Mohammed, then he would find the mountain.

The detective walked over to the door on the opposite side. Most police stations were laid out in the same way. There was a lobby behind the main office, and then off the main office various other rooms. Ryan turned the door handle. He pulled the door open and entered a long narrow corridor lit by fluorescent lights. He walked down the hallway pushing open doors marked Interview Room One, Interview Room Two, and Evidence Room. There was no one in any of them—or in the unisex toilets, either.

The detective continued to the door at the far end of the corridor. Opening it, he saw stone stairs running down to the basement. He knew this was where the holding cells would be. Even in a police station as small as this one, criminals sometimes needed to be held overnight before they were either released or picked up for delivery to jail.

Gripping the metal banister rail, the detective walked down the stairs and into another corridor. Ahead Ryan saw a uniformed cop, his back to him, unlocking a jail cell.

"Can I help?" the detective shouted.

The policeman glanced back. "Detective Ryan, I presume?"

"Yes. Afternoon. Sergeant Acton?" Ryan said, arriving.

"That's me," the Sergeant said as he pulled open the barred door, and a suited young man stepped out.

"Finally!" the man said.

"Detective, meet Terry Sutherland, one of Barton's more ungrateful drunks. He's the reason I wasn't there to meet you upstairs. Terry was making such a row down here I had to deal with it."

"You know I've missed a day's work because of you?" Terry Sutherland said, glaring at the Sergeant. "You should have let me out hours ago. You'll be hearing from my lawyer."

"I look forward to it," the Sarge said. "Now, do you want me to lock you up again, or are you ready to leave?"

Terry hesitated. "Are my wallet and phone in the office?"

"Yes. And if you'll quit showboating, we can go up to collect your things."

"Okay."

"Good. Detective Ryan, please lead the way."

"HE'S A PAIN IN THE ASS," Sergeant Acton said, returning after seeing Terry Sutherland out of the station. "I don't know why we bother. Once a month like clockwork, he gets drunk and picks a fight with the biggest guy in the pub."

The Sergeant offered Ryan his hand. "By the way, it's good to have you here, detective."

"Good to meet you too, Sarge."

"This must be a bit of comedown from the Sydney Organized Crime Squad?"

"Well, it's different," the detective said diplomatically.

"I suppose that's one way of viewing it." The Sarge stopped. "Now you'll be over there," he said, indicating the desk on the right. "We'll get a chair and computer in for you tomorrow. I figured you'd need today to get the lay of the land."

He reached into his pocket and dropped a key into Detective Ryan's hand. "And this is for the back door, save you going through the lobby all the time."

As he spoke, the corridor door opened, and a young uniformed constable entered. She carried a clear plastic-covered coat over her shoulder with one hand and clutched a brown paper bag in the other. Ryan recognized Constable Zoe Yang from the file picture.

"Thanks," the Sarge said as he took the coat and the bag from the police officer. "Meet Detective Ryan," he said, slinging the overcoat over the back of his chair and sitting down. The Sarge pulled a burger out of the bag as the woman offered Ryan her hand. "Constable Yang. Nice to meet you, detective."

"Call me Ryan, everyone else does apart from my mother," he said, smiling. He waited for the constable to reply in kind. She didn't.

Silence.

"Hmm, that's good. It's got more ketchup in it this time," the Sarge said, breaking the embarrassing quiet.

"You know, Sarge, you really should think about eating more vegetables. Too many burgers aren't good for you," Constable Yang said, turning her attention away from the detective.

"But I've already cut back from having two at lunch." the Sarge glanced down at this stomach. It bulged over the top of his trousers. "At this rate, there won't be anything left of me." He lifted his hand to wipe his mouth.

"You know, Ryan, when I met your Chief Inspector, I mentioned that I had been trying to get a detective up here for eons. He said maybe he could help me with that. I never thought anything would come of it. Then I got this call about your assignment up here. You could have knocked me down with a feather."

"Me too, Sarge," said Constable Yang. "And yet here he is." The constable's tone was cold.

"I want you and Ryan to work together for a few days, Zoe. Show him around, fill him in on the town, that sort of thing," the Sarge said. He stopped. "If that's okay with you, detective?"

"No problem," Ryan said, though it was. Usually, he preferred to check things out alone.

"You've been booked in at the Singing Pelican pub. You'll love it there. A mate of mine owns it, and he's given us a great rate."

"Thanks, that's good," Ryan said and looked across at Constable Yang. "Shall we take a look around?"

Constable Yang hesitated. She didn't relish the idea of the tour.

"Off you go, constable . . . And I'll pay you back for the dry cleaning and the food tomorrow."

NINE

A s Detective Ryan and Constable Yang began their tour of Barton, back in Sydney, Sven Meyer thought that maybe he shouldn't have had so many whiskeys last night. He pulled away from the spyhole, blinked, and rolled his head. He pushed his eye onto the hole again. The sausage-shaped white furry animal with a pencil face, pointed ears, and short legs was still there. It stared at him from inside a small cage held by a thin-faced pretty girl with long blonde hair wearing a black t-shirt emblazoned with the slogan 'Be Kind.'

"Who the fuck is that?" a voice yelled from behind. Meyer turned. Alfie Carlisle stood by the open living room door.

"I don't know, boss, but I'm dealing with it."

"Well, deal with it quicker," Alfie said, retreating into the room and slamming the door.

Meyer sighed. Alfie, the shouty man, had hired him through a casual acquaintance he knew from the docks—a guy he'd nicknamed Captain Birdseye. Birdseye ran fishing trips for tourists, and one of his clients needed a favor. The 'favor' was for Meyer to provide a couple of days security at Alfie's multi-million-dollar terrace house in Surry Hills. The big man had asked who he was trying to be secure from. Alfie had given him a stare meant to intimidate. Now that was a joke! Working on the door at the Bada Boom Club in the Cross, Meyer met the Alfie-types all the time— little rich kids keen to impress their friends with how tough they were. But when guns, knives, bottles, whatever, threatened you, it took much more than a look from someone like this kid to frighten the big man. Anyway, it was usually Sven Meyer who scared the living daylights out of people. Standing six foot six tall and weighing in at three hundred pounds while boasting a tattooed face and scary dead black eyes, the man cut an intimidating figure.

Sven Meyer never did get an answer to his question about security but took the job anyway. He needed the money. And how difficult could it be? Arriving, he had been shunted into the kitchen and told to sit tight. From here, he had heard Alfie and Birdseye arguing in the living room. They were yelling about some guy called Jack. He had been left out in the ocean last night and from, what Meyer could glean, was now probably dead. Alfie and Birdseye each blamed the other for leaving Jack behind. Meyer didn't want to hear any of this. It was far too much information, and in his world, knowing too much could end up getting you killed. So, he'd tried to ignore the row, made a cup of coffee, and took a nap.

IN THE LIVING ROOM, ALFIE FINALLY STOPPED YELLING and listened to the skipper. Mario explained that Alfie's friend Jack was almost certainly a dead man.

"There's no way Jack could have avoided being sucked under the ship, however good a swimmer he was. And if we'd stayed, we would have probably gone the same way. So why don't we forget him and talk about us?" Mario had said, leaning back in the designer chair.

The skipper had a point. Alfie had only been making a scene to assuage his own guilt. His friend's disappearance actually benefitted him. Now Alfie could take Jack's cut too. But who was this 'us' the skipper was referring to?

"Mario, there is no us. You skippered the boat. Job done." Alfie pushed a large wad of hundred-dollar bills over the marble dining table. "There's the rest of the cash I owe you."

The skipper shook his head and grinned. "That doesn't work for me. Now that's Jack's gone, it's time to renegotiate the deal."

Alfie had seen Mario's ingratiating smile many times. It was the look of greed. The skipper didn't just want to be a hired hand. He wanted to be

Alfie's new partner. As a trust fund kid, Alfie had frequently been marked out as a soft touch. But nothing could be further from the truth. Growing up in a wealthy family had actually made him even more aware of the importance of money. He had viewed up-close how people acted around his late father. They were subservient and smarmy. They wanted just a taste of what Bernard Carlisle had, and they were willing to say and do almost anything to get it. But his father knew their game only too well. He would hire them and pay them as little as he could get away with while promising them more in the future. Then, when he had worked them almost to death, he would ditch them. "You have no loyalty to anyone except your family," was his father's mantra.

SVEN MEYER'S MANTRA WAS: "DO AS LITTLE for as much money as possible," so he wasn't too pleased when the persistent ringing of the doorbell had awoken him, and after he had had to check the visitors out. From what he could see, there was only the teenage girl and her pet outside. Both looked harmless enough. So Meyer unlocked the two security latches and eased open the heavy door.

"What do you want?" he asked.

"I have an appointment," the girl said with a big friendly grin.

"You do?"

"Yes, with Alfie Carlisle. This is his house, right?"

"Yes."

"So?" the girl said.

Meyer hesitated. What could Alfie want with this little girl and the animal? "Why?" he asked.

"Why what?" the girl said.

"Why would he want to see you?"

"That's between Alfie and me."

"Okay, then I'll go ask him," Meyer said and moved to close the door.

"If you must know, he wants to buy Bumpy," the girl said quickly, holding up the cage to Meyer's stomach.

"Oh. What is that thing?" the big man asked.

"A weasel."

"Weasel, huh? How come I've never seen one before?"

The girl waved Meyer down to her level and whispered. "Because weasels are illegal here, which is why Bumpy and I shouldn't be hanging around outside."

Meyer vaguely remembered a song called 'pop goes the weasel' but had had no idea what a weasel actually looked like until now. "Okay, you better come in then," he said.

Meyer opened the door wide, moved to let the girl and weasel through, and was about to close up when he heard two loud bangs and felt tremendous pain. Looking down, Meyer saw blood streaming from his stomach. Moments later, his eyes lost focus. Then he lurched backward onto the tiled hallway floor.

Micky Docker stepped through the door and pushed in front of Stacey "Stack" Lawrence. As she closed the door, Micky pointed his 9 mm Glock 19—a suppressor screwed to its barrel—and fired one more shot into Meyer's colossal head. It was known as a double-tap, but Micky didn't know that. He was just making sure the asshole was dead.

TEN

THE EVENTS UNLEASHED BY SVEN MEYER'S DEATH would soon impact Detective Ramesh Ryan's life, but at this precise moment, he was more concerned about matters closer to home. "Will the Sarge pay you back?" the detective asked as he climbed into Constable Yang's car.

"Why do you ask?" the constable said.

"Because I noticed the Sergeant's coat is at least ten years old, and he mentioned the low rate at the pub too. Those are both indicators that he's no big spender. And people who are careful with their cash are often not the best at returning money owed," he said, pulling on his seat belt.

The constable didn't answer immediately. She turned the ignition key on, pressed her foot down on the accelerator pedal, and pulled out onto the highway.

"It takes a time, but he will eventually. Not that he does much dry cleaning. The coat cleaning is a yearly ritual—always in winter," Constable Yang finally said.

"He's not married?"

"And you ask that because . . .?"

"Because you're the one who does his dry cleaning," Ryan said.

"You're assuming that if he was married, his wife would do that for him? That's very sexist."

"That's not it. When you suggested the Sarge ate more vegetables and fewer burgers, he didn't respond the way a man of his age who was married would normally answer."

"And how would that be?" the constable asked.

"By saying something about you sounding like his wife."

Constable Yang hesitated. Then: "Yes, well, he's divorced. Been that way for a couple of years now." She glanced over at the detective. "I can see I'm going to have to watch what I say around you."

Ryan didn't reply. He had initiated the conversation to find out more about Sergeant Gary Acton, but he would have liked to discover more background on Constable Yang too. However, she was still acting like he was something vile that had just landed on the sole of her shoe.

"You're taking me to the bus station?" Ryan said.

"Did you drive around town before you came to see us?"

The detective shook his head. "No. I came in along the coast road. But I did glance at the map last night."

'Glance' was an understatement. Ryan had studied the layout of the town for over an hour. He never liked to go anywhere or do anything unprepared. But the detective didn't want to tell Constable Yang that. She had been asked to show him around, and he wanted the constable to assume he knew next to nothing about Barton.

A TOWN TOUR FOR THE TOURIST IS VERY DIFFERENT from the one on which Constable Yang was taking Ryan. Police view a location tour through a unique filter. It's all about where the bad guys live and operate. And no town, however small, is totally crime-free. So, if you were looking for trouble in Barton, then it was a fair assumption that you would find it in and around the bus station. This was why Constable Yang was driving the detective there first.

As they parked, Ryan saw a group of scruffily dressed guys quickly move along. An old homeless guy with a black dog picked up his cap from the floor and shuffled away too. It was a scene played out day-in-day-out whenever a marked cop car pulled up.

"Are the homeless a problem?" Ryan asked.

"It's becoming a problem. There's more of them every year. But when the season ends and the tourists leave, most tend to go. There's just not the foot traffic for successful begging."

"Drugs?" the detective asked.

"Yes, but nothing large scale. So far, at least."

"Homicides?"

Constable Yang smiled. "There's been a couple of domestics over the last few years. But that's about it. Neither required much work to find the perps. The culprits were both arrested while standing over the bodies."

"What about suicides and the like?"

"We do have them from time to time. People come to settle, thinking they've found paradise. But there are the same difficulties here as anywhere else. The fact is if you're unhappy in a big city like Sydney, it's odds on you will be unhappy here too."

"And there's just you and the Sarge to deal with everything?" Ryan asked.

"And Jimmy . . . Constable Jimmy O'Hagan to give him his full title. He's a rookie that takes the lobster shift. He knows he can call me if something is up. And I can radio Gosford for reinforcements if necessary. The pathologist's there, and she comes out if needed." The constable stopped. "Course now there's you too."

Ryan studied her. "Constable, do you mind if I call you Zoe?"

She shrugged. "Fine, though you don't really need to ask. You outrank me."

Zoe turned the car ignition back on. "Let's go see where the rich live."

She drove up the hill and past a row of large detached houses on the cliff edge. Zoe explained that the wealthy families who had been in the town for years lived here. Following the road around, they passed rows of smaller single and two-story houses—middle management accommodation. Behind and further up was housing for the more recent new arrivals. Many of these had bought properties as second homes—investments and holiday homes. There was only one highrise.

"Locals call this the Tut Tut building," Zoe said, parking in front of a high wire fence surrounding a construction site.

Ryan stared out at the workers that swarmed over the half-built property. "Tut Tut?"

"It's going to be twenty levels tall when it's completed, and it'll be by far the highest building in Barton. For many, it's a monstrosity and should never have been put up. These people make the sound 'Tut Tut' when they walk past the site. It's a name that's struck."

Ryan pointed to the large board attached to the perimeter fence. "Plummer Construction. Who are they?"

"They are Charles Plummer and his family—the richest and the most powerful people around these parts."

"They live in Barton?"

"No. This place is far too small and dull for the likes of the Plummers. They have a huge mansion just outside Gosford." She paused. "Of course, that doesn't mean they can't mess up our town."

"Are you one of the Tut Tuts, Zoe?"

She shook her head emphatically. "We both know that the police must be strictly neutral in these matters, but . . ." She paused, weighing up what to say next.

"Go on, please," Ryan said.

"Charles Plummer made his four hundred-million-dollar fortune when he sold his used car distribution business and then invested in developing properties like this one along the Central Coast."

"Nothing wrong with that."

"Except, and don't take this as any kind of judgment, the business he sold was headquartered in Slovakia, and buying property is an excellent way to launder cash."

Zoe pulled out into the road again. "Well, I think you've seen enough of Barton for the time being. Let's get back."

They returned to the station in silence. Ryan didn't really mind. If Zoe didn't want to talk, that was her choice.

"You can find the Singing Pelican from here, can't you?" the constable said as she parked the car next to Ryan's Ford Focus.

"Sure. Strange name that Singing Pelican."

"Johnny Wilson is a bit of a joker. The pub was originally named The Kingdom Inn, but that was too boring for him. He wanted to give it a memorable name."

"Well, he certainly did that," Ryan said. "Thanks for the tour."

He reached for the door handle and then turned back. "Before I go, I have a question?"

"Which is?"

"Why do you stay here? Most people your age with any ambition would head to Sydney or Brisbane."

"I've only been a police officer for four years, so this is a good place to start. And my partner lives and works here, so it's okay, for now."

"And later?"

Zoe hesitated before taking the plunge. "The Sarge's been here all his life. He loves the town and seems happy to leave most of the policing to me. The way I see it, if I build a reputation up here as a reliable, honest cop, then maybe in a year or so, I can put in for a promotion to Gosford."

"As a detective?"

"Maybe." Zoe had confirmed what Ryan had already worked out. The detective's appearance could put the constable's ambitions on hold.

"Can I ask you a question now?" Zoe asked.

"Sure."

"How long are you here for?"

"I'm not sure," Ryan said, opening the door and climbing out.

"Yes, that's what the Sarge said too. See you tomorrow."

ELEVEN

ALFIE WASN'T SURE THAT HE WOULD SEE TOMORROW, which wasn't a good thought. It had all happened so fast. He'd heard the sound of the shots outside and opened the living room door to face a gun-toting man and a woman holding a cage with a ferret inside. They had quickly and efficiently bound Mario and him to the dining room chairs with cord and tape pulled from the man's backpack. Then the pretty woman had introduced herself as Stack, the animal in the cage as Bumpy the weasel, and the muscular tattooed man as Micky.

At first, Stack only appeared interested in checking out the room. "Wow, this place is something. Right, Micky? That sofa, snow-white and three-piece. Fabulous. White leather Eames chairs too. And that's an asymmetric Noguchi mid-century coffee table, right? This is the kind of room I want to live in one day."

Micky had just grunted. "Can we do this?"

She ignored him. "So, you are Alfie?" Stack said, looking across at him. "And you're Mario?" The skipper nodded. And for Alfie, that was the most frightening thing that had happened so far. They knew their names!"

"So, where's the coke?"

Alfie pulled a confused face, but Mario hadn't hesitated: "If I tell you, will you let me go?"

"Stupid fucking question," Alfie had just managed to say before the tape was slammed on his mouth. The skipper had the negotiating ability of a two-year-old. Did he honestly believe that this pair would just free them?

"Of course," Stack answered.

MARIO HAD TOLD THE GIRL EVERYTHING about the safe before she slapped tape over his mouth too. Now Micky was crouched next to the large fireplace, running his fingers up and down its marble frame.

"Well?" asked Stack.

"I can't find the catches."

"Why didn't you let Alfie or Mario open it for you."

"Cause I can do this. I'm good with my hands," Micky said, grinning at the woman.

Micky tightened his right hand. There was a single click. "Got it." He moved his left hand down the frame. There was a second clink. Micky curled his right hand around the fireplace's heavy surround and pulled. The entire structure, black grate, and iron fire-back swung to the left to reveal a large gun-metal gray safe.

"Dadar," he said, jumping to his feet and bowing to Stack. An irritating grunting sound came from behind. Micky spun around. Mario was shaking his head up and down and making strange mumbling noises through his gag.

"Go see what Mario wants, will you?" Stack said, still studying the safe.

Micky marched over to the skipper and yanked the tape off his mouth. "What's up?"

Mario gasped for breath. "I told you it was there. Without me, you'd never have found it."

"What do you want? A medal?"

"Micky!" Stack shouted.

He slammed the tape back over Mario's mouth. "On my way."

Stack was staring at the safe. "I don't know where you got the idea that I was a master safe breaker. I'm not. No one told me that the stuff would be locked away in something like this."

"You can't do anything with it?" Micky asked.

"If it was a simple little mother, sure I could, but this is a Guardall KCR with a pick lever pick-resistant key lock, a solid 32mm 4-way bolt work with 12 locking points on the door, large heavy grade steel block hinge, and two recessed bolting points in its base of for secure anchorage."

"Wow, that's impressive, Stack. How do you know all that?"

She held up her cell. "It's called the internet."

"And it doesn't tell you how to get into it?"

Stack sighed. "'Course we could open it if we had the code for the digital pad," she said, pointing at the board.

Micky smiled. He liked Stack—truth be told, he pretty much thought he loved her. They had so much in common. They had both knocked around foster care since they were little kids. Sometimes they'd been in the same foster homes. One time they'd even had the same foster parents. That was until they'd ripped off the family's money and credit cards and headed to the Cross for a good time.

"Problem solved then," Micky said and strode over to Mario. "Talk to me, skipper," he said and ripped the tape off Mario's mouth. "Give me the numbers."

"I don't know them. Only he knows." Mario pointed at Alfie.

"You don't?"

"Nope."

Micky smashed Mario in the face. Then he walked over to the couch and picked up his gun before returning to Mario.

"Micky, don't do it," Stack said urgently.

In the movies, shots fired from a suppressed gun usually make a slight pinging sound. In real life, this isn't the case. When Micky had killed Meyers, the sound of the gunshot had been deafening, so loud in fact that Stack had been shocked that someone hadn't come to investigate.

"Think of the neighbors, Micky."

"The neighbors?" the man repeated. "Yep, you're right." He reached for the small leather sheath attached to his belt. Unclipping it, he pulled out a knife. The Ka-Bar TDI Law Enforcement Knife sports a black blade a mere 3.6 inches long—half the size of the average hunting knife. Micky pushed his finger into the curved inset at the top of the weapon, yanked Mario's head up by his hair and dragged the knife across his exposed throat. Blood spurted out from the gash. Mario coughed, gulped, spluttered, and then went silent. Micky released the dead man's head, allowing it to slump forward. Red liquid cascaded down the front of Mario's shirt, forming a pool on the polished wooden floorboards.

Stack walked over. "You shouldn't have done that."

"Why? What use was he? He didn't know the digits?"

Stack liked Micky. She knew too that he loved her, which was flattering and kind of stupid to an equal degree. But if she spent too much time around him, he drove her crazy—doing things without any thought. Like now!

"You don't rip a guy's throat out just because he says he doesn't know the numbers," Stack said.

"Why not?" Micky asked.

"Cause he could have been lying. Now, all we've got is this guy," she said, pointing at Alfie.

ALFIE, WHO WAS TRYING TO HOLD himself together. Seeing someone murdered right before your eyes was shocking and horrifying, in equal measure. He started to sweat—not the odd bead of perspiration but like a tap had been turned on. He could feel the fluid dripping down his face and his clothes, now wet, clinging to his body. He had just seen the man called Micky cut someone's throat without a thought. And the girl had just scolded him like he'd just spilled something on the floor. She must be a sociopath too. Now Alfie knew for sure that they wouldn't hesitate to murder him, and he didn't want to die aged just twenty-four. Actually, he didn't want to die full stop. Alfie had always believed someone would have found a solution to the inconvenience of dying in the future. And being a rich guy, he would be able to afford the treatment. But that plan wouldn't work if these moron kids killed him now.

He took a deep breath and tried to pull himself together. Youth and too much money breed confidence. So Mario was dead. So what? He was Alfie Carlisle and could negotiate his way out of any situation. These idiots needed something from him. That was his ace in the hole.

Stack walked towards him, carefully stepping over Mario's blood and, reaching out, yanked the tape off his face.

"Speak," she said.

Silence.

Let them sweat, Alfie thought.

Micky moved forward, but Stack waved him away. "Leave it."

He shrugged and backed off.

"Just give me the numbers for the pad. Then we open the safe, take the coke and vamonos. We leave," Stack said, lifting her hand to stroke back his brown hair. "Sound good?"

Alfie smiled. Vamonos? Wasn't that Spanish for 'let's go'? That sounded fine. But it was complete and utter garbage. If they opened the safe and found the coke, he could kiss his life goodbye. He glanced down at the woman's wrist—at her cute pink, see-through Fossil watch. It was 5:40. Alfie suddenly felt better.

"You won't kill me?" he asked.

"No. Not if you give us the numbers," Stack said.

"But when you go, you'll take all the coke?"

"Yeah, shit for brains," Micky sneered.

"Micky!" Stack said, leaning in to smile sexily at Alfie. "Sure, we'll have the coke, but you'll still be alive. That's a promise."

Alfie furrowed his brow. "No. That still doesn't work for me."

"What about this then," Micky said, striding past Stack and smashing his clenched fist into Alfie. The pain was immediate and immense. The rich kid's eyes closed, his head dropped forward. The world was suddenly far, far away.

Darkness.

TWELVE

THE LIGHT WAS DROPPING BY THE time Ryan pulled into the pub car park. He peered out. The detective was no expert on bars, but he'd seen enough of them to know that the Singing Pelican was a bit of a gem. To start, it couldn't have been in a better location, sitting as it did on the cliff edge. And the old white and brown colored two-story building had a definite charm about it. A lovely historic pub overlooking the ocean had to be a winner.

Ryan pulled his blue Samsonite suitcase from the trunk and locked the vehicle. When traveling, most cops just throw a few clothes into a carryall. But that wouldn't do for the detective. He had never embraced the "travel light" concept. His two suits, shirts, trousers, underwear, and spare pair of shoes, were all folded neatly into the big case, leaving plenty of room for his laptop and toiletries.

Reaching the imposing yellow and beige entrance door, the detective pushed it open. Inside, a sprinkling of men and women sat at the wooden tables dotted around the room. A painted brown, yellow and white pelican, looked down from the ceiling above.

A man waved from the bar that ran along the far side. Ryan headed over.

"Johnny Wilson," the man said on the detective's arrival and held out his hand. "Owner, bartender, and general dogs-body. And I assume you are Detective Ramesh Ryan?"

In his early thirties, Johnny Wilson was central casting for a pub owner—extrovert and friendly with a broad smile splitting his chubby, bearded face.

"Yeah, that's me," Ryan confirmed.

"Good. It would be embarrassing if it wasn't. You've come for the room?"

Ryan nodded.

The bar owner stepped over to the cash register and picked up a pen and a large hardback registration book. Returning, he opened the book and offered the detective the pen. "Just sign in there." Johnny pointed to a clean page. "Name, address, cell number, all that jazz, then Katie over there will take you up." He indicated the young woman at the far end of the bar.

Johnny leaned across the counter and whispered: "You like movies, Ryan?" He stopped. "It is okay if I call you Ryan?" The detective nodded. "Well, Ryan, if you do like films, then keep an eye out for the name Kate Cassels. She may be this pub's longest-serving and best-looking barperson, but she's also about to head over to LA to make it big on the silver screen."

Johnny took a step back. "Hollywood, oh Hollywood," he sang loudly. "That's right, isn't Kate?" he shouted, signaling for her to join them.

"Kate meet our latest arrival, Detective Ryan," Johnny said on the young woman's arrival. "I want you to show him up to his room."

"Hi." Ryan held out his hand to the young woman. Kate Cassels was around twenty something and attractive, a thin woman with long brown hair framing a narrow face. She shook the detective's hand. "Nice to meet you."

Ryan pushed the register back to Johnny. "All done."

The detective would be glad to complete the formalities and get up to his room to unpack. There was only a certain amount of time he wanted to spend in the company of Johnny Wilson. The hail-fellow-well-met act didn't ring true. There was something not quite right about it.

"I'm sure you'll like it here," Johnny said, dropping a large metal key with a pelican engraved on it into the detective's hand. "Number four. It's our best room, with a fantastic view of the ocean. A couple of things, though. We don't offer meals to our guests. But there's a mini kitchen in your room, and of course, there are lots of places around here to get food.

Oh, and one other thing, you've arrived on our famous Karaoke night." He indicated the small stage set up on the far right of the room. "To be honest, without this regular Wednesday night treat, it would be tough to make a living in the off season. The kids love Karaoke, and in a couple of hours, this place will be packed to the rafters. That's good news for me. But, due warning, you might want to go out tonight. It does get a little noisy."

Johnny slapped Ryan on the back. "Look, I'm sure you'll enjoy your stay. Any idea how long you're here for?"

The detective shook his head. "No. Sorry."

"No problem. Just give me a day or so's notice."

"Okay." The detective bent down to grab his case.

"Tell Bluey thanks, by the way."

"The Sarge?" the detective asked.

"Yeah." Johnny paused. "One thing you'll discover here, Ryan, that's if you don't already know it. All of us, 'Barton lifers' of a certain age, know each other pretty well. Most of us, Bluey and I included, went to the same local school, Beach High. And, before you say it, not at the same time. He's a few years older. And unlike him, I have kept my youthful good looks . . . Okay, enough talk. Kate, show the man to his room."

Room four was one flight up a rickety set of stairs. Kate led the way, with Ryan following. "We take a left here," she said, reaching a small landing. Kate headed down a narrow wood-paneled corridor, stopping when she arrived at a door with the large letter four painted on it.

She held out her hand to the detective. "Key, please."

"It's fine. I can take it from here."

"No way. Johnny would go crazy if I just left you standing out in the corridor. Now please . . ."

"If you insist." The detective tossed the large key over to Kate. She caught it with one hand, pushed it into the lock, shoved the door open, and flicked on the overhead light. Ryan followed her into the room.

Painted in the traditional house beige color, the place had a low rent feel about it. A long, brown three-seater sofa was pushed against the nearest wall. A small TV on an old-fashioned wood sideboard sat opposite, next to a Formica-topped dining table with four plastic chairs jammed under it. Looking to his left, the detective glimpsed an open entrance to a small kitchen.

"Johnny's given you one of the best rooms at the rear of the building. Take a look." Kate pointed at the paneled glass window filling half of the back wall.

Ryan dropped his suitcase and strode over to gaze out. "The gloaming"—just after the sun sets but before it gets truly dark—was the detective's favorite time of the day. The stunning light could make most places attractive. Here was no exception. Peering down, Ryan saw the pier, the mooring shed, and a few small boats floating on the millpond-calm water. "Looks fantastic," Ryan said and meant it.

"Right now. But this part of the coast can get some pretty bad weather. There was a big storm just last night. And, be warned, there's a strong rip that runs across from the cliffs through the bay. The good news is that it's been known to dump some interesting articles onto the shore from time to time. The bad news is no one bothers to tell the tourists about it. We come close to losing a few of them every year. They get drunk, go for a swim, and—well, you know the rest," Kate said.

She opened a door on her left. "The bedroom."

Ryan peered in. A double bed, topped with a flowered quilt, sat in the center. A row of white closet doors ran along one wall. The opposite wall was broken by three small windows. Ryan walked over and looked out.

" I know what you're thinking—they should have put bigger windows in here too," Kate shouted from the doorway. "Johnny was too mean for that. He's never put any money into this place."

"Has he owned the pub long?" asked Ryan as he walked out of the bedroom to rejoin Kate.

"His parents bought it and gave it to him as a twenty-first present just before they went to live in Spain."

"Lucky man. And you've been working here since then too?"

"Over ten years?" Kate shook her head. "No way. Only two so far, and that's way too long." She smiled. "But soon, I'll be off to LA."

"So Johnny mentioned. You won't miss Barton?"

"I've been here all my life. But that doesn't mean I like it. It's a small boring town where nothing much happens."

"You could go to Sydney?"

Kate shrugged. "It's cheaper in Barton. I have a job, and I can save my money." She stopped. "Sorry, I'm a bit of a Debbie Downer. I'm sure you'll love the town. Anyway, there's one more thing to show you—the bathroom." She opened the door to the left of the bedroom. "No bath. Just a shower."

Kate placed the key down on a small side table by the front door and pulled it open. "That's it. Tour's over. I'll see you around." She took a step out into the corridor.

"Oh, Kate," said Ryan quickly. "Any suggestions for where to eat tonight?"

"There are a few cafes on the main drag that sell decent burgers and chips, but if you like good food and are prepared to pay for it, the Sea Castle is the place."

"The restaurant on the front?"

"That's the one."

"Thanks. One more question. We passed more rooms on the way, are they . . ."

"All empty. Yeah, that's Barton in the off season. Like a ghost town!" she said before closing the door behind her.

THIRTEEN

THE SINISTER WAILING AND HISSING NOISES woke Alfie. Opening his eyes, he saw that his view was blocked by a metal plate. Small rectangular holes had been cut into it. Alfie squinted. Through the gaps, he could see flashes of white fur.

Ignoring the throbbing pain, he tried to move his head. It was being pulled back hard against the chair. He flicked his eyes up, down, and sideways. Now he had worked it out. A metal open-ended mesh cage had been folded around his head and somehow attached to the chair.

"Help," Alfie screamed, his voice muffled by the metal contraption and the hissing and wailing. He waited. *Nothing.*

"Hey, help me," he shouted again.

There were another few moments of silence. Then, through the slats, Alfie saw the door open, and first Micky and then Stack came in. Both were chewing sandwiches. They headed over.

"What have you done to me?" Alfie said as they reached him, raising his voice over the hissing and wailing.

"What? You'll have to speak up. It's difficult to hear you," Stack said.

"I said, what have you done to me?"

"Nothing yet. But if Micky had had his way, you'd be dead by now."

"Stack was always the kind one," Micky said, taking another bite of his sandwich and leaning forward. "You hungry? Bet you are."

Alfie said nothing. Stack leaned in too and placed her hand on the plate, lifting it up to reveal a tiny gap. Alfie saw the white furry edges of a pencil face dissected by a row of chiseled, razor-sharp teeth.

"Bumpy's hungry as well," Stack said.

Now Alfie knew what was making the noise. The weasel.

Stack banged the plate back to its original position. The fur and teeth retreated from view.

"Have you ever read a book called 1984 by a guy named George Orwell?" Stack said.

"No."

"1984 is set in the future." She stopped. "I mean, I know the book was set in 1984, but when George Orwell wrote it, that was the future."

Finishing his sandwich, Micky yawned. "Get to the point, Stack."

"The guy in 1984, the hero, is in love. And he thinks he'd be willing to do anything to save the girl. But he wasn't. No. In one room, room 101, he comes face to face with his worst nightmare."

Alfie peered out, trying to see the woman more clearly. He may not have read 1984, but his opinion of Stack and Micky remained the same. They were amateurs who had got lucky. But their luck was about to run out when Bruno's men arrived to collect the coke.

"See, they put a cage around the main guy's face, like the contraption around your head. That's where I got the idea from," Stack moved closer. "Still listening, Alfie?"

He said nothing.

"Anyways, this cage had a rat in it. And the guy knows a hungry rat will chew his face away. And he knows that this particular rat is hungry as hell. So just like that, he tells them anything they want to know and drops the love of his life in it."

Now Alfie got it. They hadn't got a rat. But they had got a weasel.

"Course Bumpy's much more handsome than a rat," Stack said, finishing her sandwich. "And he's far more dangerous. In fact, weasels are banned in Australia 'cause of how deadly they are. But I love them because they're afraid of nothing and no one. And when they get hungry, which is most of the time, all hell breaks loose. They'll attack anything to get food."

Stack leaned into Alfie and touched the base of his neck. "Bumpy would bite here. His little teeth would nibble into the base of your skull and burrow through and then suck your brains out. That's how they kill."

Alfie felt sick to the pit of his stomach.

Stack smirked. "Not that I'm going to do that to you. It wouldn't be very nice, would it? We promised not to kill you if you gave us the numbers to open the safe. But if you don't." She let the threat hang in the air. "Micky's a bit of a Neanderthal. He would have just beaten you to a pulp. But he gave me a chance with you first." She reached for the metal plate. "So, what's it going to be? Do I lift this up and let Bumpy sniff around? Or do you give us the right numbers this time?"

Alfie's heart desperately wanted to believe that Stack was telling the truth. But his head said: "Don't be a schmuck. She's going to kill you anyway."

"One question," he said, his voice still muffled by the weasel, which was becoming ever more agitated.

"What?"

"What's the time?" Alfie yelled.

Stack glanced at her wristwatch. "Seven twenty and thirty-two seconds."

Alfie thought about that. Bruno's men were late, but they would arrive soon, no doubt about that. So should he give these bozos another set of fake numbers and hold on until they come? Nope, that wouldn't work. If the safe didn't open again, the scratchy, whining weasel animal would be allowed out.

"Okay. Four, twelve, seven, six, two, fourteen," Alfie shouted.

"Again."

"Four, twelve, seven, six, two, fourteen."

Stack flicked her head around. "Got that, Micky."

"On it."

In moments Micky was pressing the numbers into the safe's digital pad. Stack hurried over to watch as he yanked open the heavy metal door and reached in. Micky pulled out packages wrapped in blue plastic and embossed with a gold tiger. He piled them up on the floor.

"Alfie. You're a star," Stack yelled as she counted the packages.

Micky took out his Ka-Bar knife. He ran the steel blade along the top of one of the parcels to expose a thin white line of powder. Then he stuck his pinky finger into it and lifted it to his mouth.

"Well?" asked Stack, finishing the count.

"Ace."

"Okay, hold on." She jumped up and walked over to Alfie.

"Just one problem. There are only sixty-eight keys here. There should be seventy. Where are the other two?"

"In the ocean. They fell into the sea," he shouted.

Stack glanced around at Micky, who was walking over to join her.

"Well?"

"Sounds about right."

"So now let me go," Alfie yelled.

"Don't you want us to wait until your friends arrive?"

Alfie frowned. Something was wrong. How did she know about them? Come to think of it, how did she know that two kilos were missing?

Stack glanced at her watch. "They are already over an hour late. Are you sure they're coming?"

Alfie thought about that. Now that was another problem. How did she know they were an hour late?

"These friends. Who are they?" Stack asked.

Should he tell them? Alfie thought. Yes, he decided. It would scare the living daylights out of them.

"Oscar Bruno's friends."

"Oscar Bruno, huh. So, what's your deal with him?"

"We arranged to sell the seventy keys to him. His men are coming to pay us and take the coke, and when they see you here . . ." Alfie paused to let his words sink in. "You do know who Oscar Bruno is, don't you?"

Stack turned to Micky. "You know an Oscar Bruno?"

Micky stroked his chin as he thought about the question. "Yep. Yep. Wasn't he the one who sent us over to deal with Alfie?" he asked.

"What? That can't be right," Alfie said, getting a sinking feeling in the pit of his stomach.

"How do you think we know your name, and that the cocaine was here, and the exact size of the deal? See, Bruno wants the coke, but he's not going to hand over money to some freelancers for it. Our job was to kill you and take the blow," Stack said.

Alfie could feel the blood draining from his face. "No. No way. That doesn't make sense. For a start, you arrived way before the time Bruno fixed. If you had waited, we would have taken the coke out of the safe, and you could have just arrived and killed us. But you didn't. No, you're not with Bruno, and you're fucked."

Micky looked across at Stack. "He has a point there. Why would we turn up early and then have to go to all the trouble of persuading them to open the safe?" He paused. "You tell him, Stack."

"Cause we enjoy our work, Alfie, and just killing someone like you is boring. As I always tell Micky, I enjoy foreplay. And what we got by turning up early is lots of it."

Stack leaned into Alfie. "You're a fucking moron." She reached across to yank the metal plate out of the cage, releasing the weasel.

"Dinner time, Bumpy."

FOURTEEN

IT WAS DINNER TIME FOR DETECTIVE Ramesh Ryan too. He had taken Kate Cassels advice, and she had been right. There was a lot to like about the Sea Castle, the detective decided. For starters, his chair was cushioned and high-backed, allowing him to sit comfortably. One of the detective's pet peeves was how some restaurant seats felt as if they had been designed by members of the Spanish Inquisition. Sometimes too the tables were either too high or too low. You were either peering down at your food or forced to stretch your arms up to reach the plate. But the table was the requisite height and covered with spotlessly clean white linen.

Ryan lifted up the stainless steel knife. It was a good weight, he thought, putting it down. He glanced around. The restaurant decor was a little bizarre, though—a mix of hanging lobster pots and seashells attached to the wall, sitting between framed pictures of Venice canals and gondoliers. Why was it hotels and restaurants loved to put up photos and paintings of other places?

Ryan stared at the menu. The Sea Castle came midway between budget and high-cost. He could only afford to eat at a place like this once a month maximum. For the rest of the time, he ate more cheaply. But tonight was his first night in Barton, so what the heck? But what to choose?

"The trout's very good here as a starter," a voice said.

Ryan turned. The comment had come from one of the two women who sat close to his table. They were the only other customers. Both were about the same age, in their early thirties, but a study in opposites. The woman who'd spoken had long, golden-blonde hair and was dressed in a tight-fitting, low-cut black dress. Gold jewelry hung around her neck while an array of gold bracelets jangled on her wrists. The other woman sported dark curly hair which framed a narrow, ruddy face. She wore a flowing flowered dress and a crystal necklace.

"See, all gone. And it was delicious," The blonde said, pointing to her empty plate that was being collected by the waitress.

Ryan peered at the menu again. The fish was listed in the starters as confit ocean trout served with pickled cucumber, avocado mouse, shaved fennel, pomelo, and tamarind.

"I know it sounds pretentious, but don't let that put you off," the blonde said as if reading his mind. "It really is good." She smiled, an open smile revealing a row of straight, bright white teeth.

"The trout?"

"Yes. Go on. Live dangerously."

"Okay. I think I'll do that. Thank you," Ryan said.

The women exchanged glances. "You're on your own, right?" the blonde said. "And since we're the only other people here, how about you join us? Better than sitting alone."

This was awkward. If the detective refused, he would be insulting their hospitality, and he was brought up to be polite. And it hadn't escaped Ryan that the women were both good-looking. As a single cop who worked long, unsociable hours, the chances of meeting women who weren't in the police force and weren't his colleagues were few and far between. But he had grown used to his own company and actually enjoyed eating alone. So what to do?

The dark-haired woman waved at him. "Please. Come on over."

Making up his mind, the detective stood up and signaled to the waitress that he was moving.

ELLIE SASTRA WAS 'IN MARKETING.' HER friend was Ashley Taylor, who read tarot cards and gave psychic readings. They were celebrating because tomorrow Ashley would be jetting off to Thailand for a two-week holiday funded by a win on the Lotto. The Sea Castle was apparently the place to go on such occasions.

"So, now you know a bit about us, tell us what brings you to our little town, Ryan?" Ellie asked.

The detective hesitated. He was expecting the question, of course, but never knew how to answer it. If he was truthful, it would involve telling them he was a cop. Admitting that in a new social situation rarely went down well. People clammed up as they went through a checklist of what they could and couldn't say.

"I'm just taking a short break from Sydney."

"You upped and left your family?" Ellie asked.

He smiled. The detective knew what that question was all about. "Actually, I'm single, so there's no one to up and leave."

Ellie grinned. "Single, huh. Well, you're at the right table then. Ashley and I are both in that same club."

Ryan's answer had piqued both women's interest, and while he fended off questions about his job, which he explained vaguely was 'in the legal profession,' he answered truthfully about where he was staying. "I'm at the Singing Pelican pub but had to leave tonight because . . ."

"Because Wednesday night is Karaoke night," Ashley said, interrupting.

"Yeah, there's only a certain number of times you can hear 'I Will Survive.'" They laughed.

"Now, have you any recommendations for the main course?"

Ellie had ordered the lamb—described on the menu as two-point lamb cutlets, braised shoulder, pearl couscous, pickled eggplant, yogurt mousse. Vegetarian Ashley opted for the exotically-named star-glazed roast cauliflower with saffron apricots, beetroot emulsion, and pomegranate. Ryan decided he would go for the lamb.

"So, do you know why the Singing Pelican is called the Singing Pelican?" Ashley asked as they waited for their food to arrive.

"Well, the singing bit is easy. I think Johnny Wilson, the owner, thinks he has a good voice. As for the pelicans, I'm betting that he used to like the bird as a kid," Ryan said.

Ellie nodded. "Pretty much spot on. Plus, of course, Johnny thought calling the pub the Singing Pelican would help people remember it."

"It certainly does that." The detective paused. "Sounds like you know him well?"

"Barton's a small town," Ellie said.

"And everyone went to the same high school—except me, of course. I came to live here later," Ashley said.

There was silence for a moment, interrupted by the detective's cell phone ringing. It was Zoe.

THE DETECTIVE STOOD UP. "EXCUSE ME. I'll take this outside." He walked out to the road. "What's up?"

"Sorry to disturb you, but something's come up that I maybe need your help with," Zoe said.

Ryan could tell from the way the constable stressed the word maybe, that this wasn't a call that, given a choice, the constable would have willingly made. What she said next confirmed it. "The Sarge left strict instructions for me to contact you if anything big happened on my watch." Zoe paused. "The thing is there's been a death. Can you come over?"

"Of course. Text me the address," the detective said.

A few moments later, the text arrived in his message box.

"Got it. See you soon Zoe."

Slipping the phone into his pocket, Ryan reopened the door and walked over to the women.

"Sorry ladies, I have to go," he said.

"Really, but you haven't even had your starter," Ellie said, obviously disappointed.

"Unfortunately, something urgent has just come up. But, as you said, it's a small town, so I'm sure we'll meet again."

"I'd like that," Ellie said as the detective hurried out.

FIFTEEN

R YAN TYPED THE ADDRESS THE CONSTABLE had sent him into his GPS. He saw the route took him along the coast road, up and over the hill, and into the area that the police officer had described earlier as where 'old Barton money lived.' Pressing his foot on the accelerator, the detective pulled out of the Singing Pelican car park, passing the teenagers who clustered outside the door smoking and chatting. As Ryan drove onto the main road, he heard the faint tinkling sound of Whitney Houston's 'I Will Always Love You' coming from the pub. The Karaoke night was obviously still in full swing.

Climbing up the hill, the detective opened the window. The moon was full and high in the night sky, shining light on the bay which stretched out below, its waters calm, its beach empty. When the detective's car reached the crest of the hill, the houses started getting larger. Many were set back from the road, protected by high walls and security gates. They probably had swimming pools out back with fabulous views out to sea, the detective mused. His tiny Potts Point apartment would fit comfortably into any of them many times over.

The address Ryan had been given, 149 Sea Cliff Road, was smaller than its neighbors. It was a two-level home, probably built in the thirties. There were no impressive gates or high fencing. It stood on a plot fronted by an unkempt lawn. A narrow brick drive ran from the highway to the front of the home, widening into a large concrete parking area. Zoe's marked police car was already there next to a blue Honda Jazz, and a silver BMW SUV. Ryan parked by the BMW, grabbed a pair of latex gloves from the glove box, and climbed out of the vehicle. He headed for the front door. As he neared, Constable Yang stepped out of the house.

"Sorry to ruin your night," the constable said as Ryan reached her. "I could have handled this myself . . ."

"But the Sarge insisted. I got that, Zoe. So what's the deal?"

"There's a dead man in the backyard. I've called the pathologist, but she hasn't arrived yet." The constable pointed inside the home. "The body's through there. Follow me." She went to step back inside.

The detective shook his head. "No. Not yet Zoe. Aren't you forgetting something?"

"I am?"

"Protective covering?"

The constable held up her hands to show she had white latex gloves on.

"Very good. But what about your feet, and mine too?"

Constable Yang turned bright red. "Oh yes. Sorry." She ran over to her car and opened the trunk as Detective Ryan put his gloves on. The constable returned, clutching two pairs of blue shoe protectors.

"Sorry again. In my defense, this kind of thing doesn't often happen in Barton," she said, handing over one pair of the coverings to Ryan. He slipped the plastic over his boots. Zoe did the same.

"Right, now lead the way," Ryan said. With the constable leading, the officers stepped inside. They walked through the house and out of the back door. Zoe went to continue on but saw the detective had stopped.

"The victim's over there," the constable said, pointing to a body sprawled out on the swimming pool decking next to a small table and chair.

"I know. I always like to get a view of the whole scene first," the detective said, checking out the backyard and its impressive ocean view.

"Okay. Let's go," he said a few moments later.

THE DEAD MAN LAY FACE DOWN, and the detective noted that judging from his muscular arms, he was someone who spent time lifting weights. He looked young, probably in his early twenties, and was expensively dressed—black Fendi sneakers and Prada pants. A padded Moncler jacket hung over the back of a blue plastic chair. A white wife-beater was the only non-designer piece of clothing.

Detective Ryan took a pen from his pocket and, bending down, used it to lift the man's blonde hair off the side of his head. Judging by the tightness of his facial muscles, the detective concluded he hadn't been dead long. A faint white powder mark was visible on the adjacent plastic side table.

"Looks like cocaine," the detective said. "Is that all that's left of it?"

Constable Yang nodded.

"So, get an evidence bag."

Zoe held out two sealed, clear plastic bags. Inside one were traces of the powder. In the other was a rolled-up hundred-dollar bill. "Already done. And I also bagged his wallet and car keys which were on the kitchen table."

The detective smiled. "Good."

"Look, I'm sorry about the shoes. The thing is . . ."

"Who found him?" Ryan said, interrupting. He'd never had time for excuses. What was done was done. Move on.

"His roommate. Mel Knowles. He's upstairs and pretty shook up."

"Did he tell you who the dead man was?"

"Liam Plummer."

"One of the Plummer family you mentioned?"

"He's their only son. And I would have known it was Liam Plummer even if his roommate hadn't told me. He's quite a celebrity in these parts. There are always photos of him in the gossip mags."

"When was he discovered?"

"Mel Knowle's found him about forty minutes ago after coming in from work."

"Did you call Sergeant Acton about this?" the detective asked.

"No. I know it's usual practice if there's a famous victim to call your boss, but . . ." She stopped.

"I understand," Ryan said. And he did. Zoe was trying not to say that informing Sergeant Acton, about finding the body of the son of some wealthy family was not sufficient reason to wake him. He was a police officer whose work ended the moment he left the station.

"So the Plummer son lives here and not with his parents?"

"Yes."

"How'd you think he died?"

"Probably an overdose. The man fell off the chair after snorting the drug."

The detective looked around, his eyes coming to rest on the dead man's jacket.

"Have you another evidence bag?"

Constable Yang pulled out a plastic bag from her pocket. She handed it to the detective. "I thought I'd bagged everything relevant already."

Ryan didn't reply but began checking the victim's jacket. He pulled a small clear bag from one of the pockets and dropped it into the evidence bag. "That's what he carried the cocaine in. He must have opened it, tipped the coke onto the table, and then pushed the bag back into his jacket."

"Case closed then, detective," a voice said from behind them.

Ryan turned to see a short, plump woman in her mid-forties approaching. She wore a mask and hooded blue coveralls. Protective clear shoe coverings had been pulled over her boots, and, like the cops, she wore latex gloves. The woman carried a black 'doctors' bag. Two more women and a man followed behind. All wore the same protective outfits, all grasped cases—the women Gladstone bags and the man a steel camera case.

"Doctor Jen Norman. I'm the pathologist, and this is the forensic team," she said and indicated the others.

"Pleased to meet you all. Detective Ryan," Ryan said.

"The temporary transfer?" Doctor Norman asked.

"The very same. Now I'll leave you all to look at the body . . . constable?" Zoe hesitated.

"Come on. We need to interview Knowles."

"But I've already spoken to him."

"So?" Ryan's manner was often considered brusque, and this time his words came out flat and accusing. He saw the constable flinch. Ignoring her reaction, he turned and headed inside. After a moment, Zoe followed.

RYAN DECIDED TO CONDUCT THE INTERVIEW in the living room. The detective sat opposite the pasty-faced, white-shirted Mel Knowles, the constable next to him, her notebook out and her iPhone recorder on. After going through the preliminaries—time, place, date, those present for the benefit of the recording—Ryan asked the first question.

"So, you're a bartender?"

"I'm a mixologist?" Mel Knowles corrected.

"What's the difference?"

"Well, a mixologist combines elixirs and creates extraordinary cocktails. A bartender just makes great drinks."

"I see. So, where do you work?" Detective Ryan asked.

"In Gosford, at a bar called 'The Little Blue Door.'"

"Gosford? But you don't live there? You live here in Barton?"

"Yep. Gosford's expensive to rent."

"Even on a mixologist's wage?" the detective asked.

"We don't get that much more than bartenders."

"Right."

"And of course, Liam . . ." He stopped and sighed. "I can't believe he's dead. He was so young."

"How old was he?"

"My age. Twenty-four."

"I see." Ryan paused. "You said, 'And of course Liam,' and then you stopped. What were you going to say?"

Knowles hesitated. "I was going to say that, of course, Liam didn't need to work. You know about his family?"

"That they are rich?" Ryan asked.

"Right."

"So, how come you're living here? Surely Liam Plummer didn't need the extra cash from a renter."

"He asked me to live with him." He paused, seeing the questioning expression on the detective's face. "Only as his roommate. Nothing more. He loves . . . loved women."

But he was lonely. He didn't have many real friends."

"You were his friend?"

Knowles nodded. "He used to come into the bar, and we'd chat. We got to like each other. Then a few months ago he offered me a room in this house. He said his dad Charlie had bought this place to knock it down and replace it with apartments. But getting planning permission takes time. Meanwhile, Liam was to live here."

"Seems a shame," Constable Yang said wistfully.

'What does?" Knowles asked.

"I love old properties like this. They have so much character. It's tragic to see them demolished."

Ryan glanced across. Zoe had a lot to learn.

"When did you find Liam Plummer's body?" the detective asked.

"Around ten-thirty . . . but I've told her all this already," Knowles said, pointing at the constable.

"Well, now you're telling me."

"Yes, but is all this really necessary?"

"It's necessary, Mr. Knowles," Detective Ryan said emphatically. "So, when did you leave the club?"

"Just after nine-thirty. It takes around forty minutes to get back here."

"Nine-thirty? That's early for a mixologist to finish, isn't it?"

"I was on the first shift—day into night."

"Okay. So, tell me about finding the body," the detective asked.

"Well, I came in and went through to the pool."

"Why?"

"Because that's where Liam likes to go at that time of night. I wanted to say hi."

"And when you saw his body, what did you do?" Ryan asked.

"I checked his pulse. We're taught all that CPR stuff at the club. It's a condition of employment. Anyway, he had no pulse. And he wasn't breathing. So I knew he was dead."

"What did you do then?" the detective said.

"I called the police. The constable came about fifteen minutes later," Knowles said. "I guessed Liam must have overdosed."

"You weren't surprised?"

"Of course I was shocked. My friend was dead."

"I meant over the coke. The fact that he was taking it."

Knowles stared. "Well, yes. Actually, I was. I never knew he took cocaine—drugs of any kind for that matter. Liam was into weightlifting and exercise."

"That doesn't stop people from taking drugs."

"Maybe not. But I'd never seen Liam taking anything."

"Ever?" the detective queried.

"Ever," Knowles said emphatically.

"So you wouldn't know where he got the coke from?"

"Of course not."

Ryan thought about that for a moment. Then: "Interview over at . . ." the detective leaned forward to check the time on the iPhone. "At 23:35."

He stood up. "Thanks, Mr. Knowles. I'll speak to the pathologist now, and she'll arrange to have the body taken to the mortuary."

That was that for the evening. There was nothing else to do. The detective said his goodbyes to Doctor Norman and her team and arranged to collect the tox, forensics, and mortuary reports when they were completed. Then Ryan and Zoe left and went their separate ways.

SIXTEEN

THE FOLLOWING DAY WAS BRACING. THE chilly wind brushed Ryan's face, cooling his body as he ran. His sneakers were wet and heavy from the water that lapped over them as he jogged along the seashore. But that didn't bother him. He was enjoying himself. It made a pleasant change from slamming his feet down on the hard, uneven Sydney paving stones. He glanced at his Fitbit watch. It was still only six-thirty, and he had been exercising for just under an hour.

Ryan had been taking early morning runs ever since he had joined the police. As a child, he had hated exercise, preferring to spend his time reading and writing, but as he got older, he had put on weight. It didn't happen overnight, but he began to notice the beginnings of a paunch. Ryan's father had been overweight for as long as he could remember, and he'd been diagnosed with high blood pressure before his heart attack. So, when the detective's doctor warned him of his rising blood pressure and weight increase, he decided to do something about it.

At first, Ryan had taken the dieting route, but he loved his food too much for that to work. So, exercise had seemed a reasonable alternative. Ryan rejected ball sports—the camaraderie involved wasn't for him. But jogging suited his temperament. It was a solitary sport and all about endurance, something Ryan had in abundance.

As he ran, the detective mulled over Liam Plummer's death. He had asked Zoe to arrange for Liam's parents to be at the Gosford mortuary to officially confirm their son's identity. With any luck, the preliminary autopsy and toxicology investigation would have been completed when he arrived there.

"Ryan. Yoohoo," a voice yelled from behind, interrupting his thoughts.

The detective turned. A woman was being dragged along by a large, hairy dog and waving at him. It was Ellie Sastra, one of the people he had met last night in the restaurant.

"What are you doing out here at this time?" Ellie asked, reaching him. "No, scrap that. That's a stupid question. You're running, of course." She stopped, and yanked the dog's leash. "Attila, settle down."

Her dog, Attila, had a kind, open face, covered in black, brown, and white hair. He stood around twenty-eight inches tall and must have weighed north of one hundred and sixty pounds. This wasn't an animal you wanted as an enemy.

"A Bernese Mountain Dog?" Ryan asked.

"If you say so. He's not mine. I'm looking after him for a couple of weeks while Ashley, who you met yesterday, is away. I'm under strict instructions to walk him at least twice a day, but honestly, this is my first morning, and I'm already regretting it. He's so strong. He almost pulled me over. I prefer my walks alone."

'How old is he?" the detective asked, leaning down to stroke the animal.

"I think Ashley's had him for a couple of years. Back when she got him, he was just a pup. I don't think she'd bargained on the dog growing this big." She smiled. "Anyway, enough of him. It's good to see you again, Ryan. It's a shame you couldn't stay last night. Did you sort out your urgent business?"

"Yes."

Ellie waited for the detective to say more. But Ryan, like most cops, preferred to receive information rather than offer it up.

Attila yanked on the leash, almost pulling Ellie backward. He clearly wanted to keep walking. "Look, I have to go," she said, "but maybe we could get together sometime."

The detective gave her a quizzical look.

"Not as a date or anything like that, of course, just for coffee or something," she said quickly and reached in her pocket, pulling out a business card. "My details are on there."

Ryan took the card as Attila pulled again on the leash. "Okay, we're going. Enjoy your run."

As they left, the detective glanced down at the card. It had Ellie's company, NorthStar Branding, her full name, Ellie Sastra, and her title, Marketing Director, along with her contact details. In Sydney, Ryan had always had problems meeting women, but things seemed simpler in a town like Barton.

The detective began running again. He had to get changed and have his breakfast before he met Zoe at the Gosford police station. He best hurry.

SEVENTEEN

MEXICAN DAVE WAS IN A HURRY too. He knew how impatient Oscar Bruno was, but he also knew that he couldn't afford to make a mistake. Grasping the Lornet-24 detector tight, Dave swept the device backward and forwards across the dining room wall. The instrument would beep immediately if it found any bugs or surveillance equipment. So far, it had remained silent.

"You finished yet?" Big Jay asked for the fifth time.

Dave bought the device down. "All clean."

"Finally. Stay here. I'll go get the boss."

As he waited, Dave rocked impatiently from foot to foot. Bug-sweeping was his second favorite job. His first was sitting at the monitor desk checking the input from the security cameras dotted all over Villa Bruno. He'd be happy to get back there.

The living room door opened, and Oscar Bruno entered. Big Jay and The Lion trailed behind. The drug dealer had made a speedy recovery. The confused, pathetic figure swathed in a fluffy dressing gown had been superseded by a brand new model. Dressed in tailored gray sweats and a tight black polo shirt, Bruno's brown eyes were now bright, and his colored brown hair was neatly combed. He swung his arms energetically back and forth as he crossed the room.

"Clean?" he asked Mexican Dave.

"As a whistle."

Bruno sat down on the long baroque sofa that was pushed against the far wall. Big Jay and The Lion took up their positions, standing to the right of the couch.

"You can go, Dave. And tell the two outside, they can come in now," Bruno said as he adjusted his substantial butt on the cushions.

"Will do, boss," Dave said, leaving.

BRUNO WAITED IMPATIENTLY. DESPITE OUTWARD APPEARANCES, he was nervous and unhappy. He couldn't seem to snap out of the mood he'd been in since leaving the court. Last night he had eaten alone before going to bed early. This was, as Big Jay commented to all who would listen: "Fucking odd. He should be partying." But his boss was in no mood for celebrations. He was a worried man. He had beaten the rap, but at what cost? He'd got off because of the big bucks he'd paid to the juror. The cops, particularly that Detective Inspector wog cop Ryan, had come perilously close to nailing him. Everyone knew it. And by everyone Bruno meant all his enemies. So, now he needed to set an example. To show his strength—show that Oscar Bruno was back and still very much in control.

Earlier in the morning, while eating his customary bacon and eggs breakfast—eggs over easy, bacon crispy—Bruno had thought about how to send the control message out loud and clear. Maybe he should take a contract out on Ryan? It was criminal folklore that you didn't hit a cop. Perhaps it was time to test that theory? He already knew that the detective was unpopular, so would anyone really care?

THE DOOR SWUNG OPEN, AND STACK and Micky walked in. After the coke had been spirited away, they had been told that Bruno wanted to see them, but they had no idea why. This was the first time they'd been allowed into Villa Bruno's inner sanctum—into the drug dealer's favorite room and one that he had furnished personally with the over-the-top, Italian furnishings so beloved by criminals and the nouveau riche.

Stack and Micky glanced around. The heavy oak dining table boasted impressive carved, ornate legs, as did the red upholstered chairs jammed under it. A chandelier adorned with sparkling crystals threw light on the large, flattering portrait of Oscar Bruno, which hung on the wall behind the table. The Oscar Bruno pictured was at least twenty years younger and considerably better looking than the one currently lounging on the sofa.

The pair reached the center of the room and hesitated, unsure where to stand. Seeing their discomfort, Big Jay pointed to a spot about five yards from Bruno and directly in front of him. "There," he said.

The two took their places

"Big Jay tells me there's a problem," Bruno said, folding his arms.

"Problem?" Stack asked.

"So Big Jay tells me."

Big Jay nodded and peered at the couple. Micky stared back at him. One day, he thought, I'll slit that asshole's throat and feed him to the pigs. "Yeah, well what he . . ." he began.

"Micky," Stack interrupted. That's all she needed, for Micky to open his big mouth. Stack smiled at Bruno. This was as close as she'd ever been to this crusty dick. God, he was old. But that aside, she was quite prepared to take it up the butt to resolve whatever the problem was.

"Problem?" Stack repeated, her voice light and flirtatious.

Bruno looked the teenager up and down. Why was it girls always thought spreading your legs solved any problem? If he wanted, he could take her into the back room and fuck her senseless. Actually, he thought, why bother with the back room. He could do it here. He liked an audience. He paused as he thought about this. Nope. That wouldn't be right. She wasn't his type. She was too skinny. He liked women with a bit of meat on their bones.

"Yes, I said problem. Are you deaf or something?" Bruno said.

"No. I just don't know what could be wrong. We did the job. We brought the coke," Stack said.

"Right," echoed Micky.

"Brought the coke?" Oscar shook his head. "Tell them, Big Jay."

Big Jay had been Stack and Micky's point of contact. The consigliere had taken the job details directly from the boss. He had told them that some freelancers had offered to sell the drug dealer an unauthorized boatload of coke. So the boss had decided to respond in the only way he knew how—by hitting the assholes hard. That's where they came in.

And Stack and Micky had done just that and, as far they were concerned, had done a mighty fine job. But apparently, that wasn't how Bruno saw it.

"You're two keys light," Big Jay said.

Stack gave Bruno her best innocent look. "Oh, that's the problem? Well, see, they told us two packages fell into the water. That's why we're short."

Bruno stared at her. His cold eyes were starting to make Stack feel queasy. "Is that so? Is that how you see it, Micky?" the boss said, turning his gaze to the young man.

"Yeah."

"So, I would be wrong to conclude that you kept those two keys back for yourself," Bruno asked.

"Yeah, 'course."

"We would never . . ." Stack began as Bruno raised his hand.

"Prove it."

Stack glanced across at Micky. How could they prove that?

"But Mr. Bruno . . ."

"I know you told me what supposedly happened to them . . ." Bruno said.

"Definitely happened," Stack said.

"So you say. But in this business, anyone can tell you anything. So I always say—prove it."

Micky glanced over at Stack. He was getting bad vibes about this. "I don't know how we can do that, boss."

"Oh, you don't, do you?" Bruno grinned. Taking their cue Big Jay, and The Lion smiled too. It was hilarious, wasn't it? Stack felt a stab of fear shoot up her spine. This was like being circled by a shiver of Great White sharks.

"See, to prove it, you would need to bring me the two kilos," Bruno continued.

"You have one week to find the missing blow."

Stack saw Micky open his mouth and knew he was about to say something stupid. She yanked his arm. "Don't worry, Mr. Bruno. We'll bring it back to you. Within the week."

Bruno said nothing. His mean eyes followed the pair as they hurried out. He had no doubt that they were telling the truth. But he was still two kilos light. So, they had to find replacement coke somehow. Then the situation would be resolved. But if they didn't? Well, he would make sure that they were killed very slowly and very publicly. It would be just the proof he'd needed to show everyone that Oscar Bruno was back and very much in control. It was perfect. A win-win situation. Bruno felt his mood lift. He felt happy again.

EIGHTEEN

RYAN WASN'T HAPPY. HE HATED DOING what he was about to do. No cop ever relished the thought of facing grieving parents . . . and it never got any easier. The detective arrived in the Gosford mortuary anti-room precisely at the time Constable Yang had arranged. As he had pushed the door open, a man had jumped to his feet. "Finally," he snarled.

It hadn't been the greeting the detective was expecting, but then again, he knew from experience that you never knew how people were going to react in this situation. The detective held out his hand. "Mr. Plummer? Detective Ryan."

The man scowled and ignored the detective's outstretched hand. "Yes. I assumed that."

Charles Plummer exuded wealth and privilege. He was a well-built man in his mid-fifties, with a square face, thick lips, hooded brown eyes, and dyed black hair. He wore a dark blue shirt and striped tie, a blue jacket, and black trousers. People like Charles Plummer had spent their whole lives being in charge, but Ryan knew that death always threw everything into a tailspin.

"You're aware that we've been waiting around for your arrival," Charles Plummer continued.

"I'm sorry, but this was the arranged time."

"Detective, Molly Plummer. Good to meet you." The introduction came from the seated woman. She stood to shake the detective's hand. Molly

Plummer epitomized the type of woman who was referred to as 'a lady who lunches.' A good ten years younger than her husband, she had a narrow, attractive face, thick red lip sticked lips, a botoxed, unlined forehead, and eyes that couldn't hide the fact that they had been filled with tears recently.

"Good to meet you too," Ryan said. "I'm sorry for your loss."

Charles Plummer glanced over at his wife. It was clear from the look that he did not approve of her fraternizing with the 'enemy.' Usually, Molly Plummer was happy to avoid conflict and go along with whatever her husband said and did. But it was her son who was lying on a mortuary slab next door, and today she was not going to put up with her husband's bullying.

The ante-room door opened, and the blue coverall-clad pathologist, Doctor Jen Norman, entered.

"If you are all ready?" she said.

With Charles Plummer leading, they filed into the mortuary. Here: two slabs, one stainless steel and empty, the other containing a body covered with a white sheet, sat in the middle of the room. To the right were a series of steel doors, stacked one on top of the other—storage for the corpses. To the left were shelves, glass-fronted fridges, and two sinks—the equipment and cleaning facilities necessary in any pathology facility.

Molly Plummer reached out to grasp Constable Yang's hand as Doctor Norman waited for permission to lower the slab cloth. The detective noted the move. Clearly, Mrs. Plummer felt happier seeking reassurance from a stranger rather than from her own husband.

"Detective?" Doctor Norman asked.

"Everyone ready?" Ryan asked.

"For Christ's sake, get on with it," Charles Plummer muttered.

"Go ahead," the detective instructed.

Doctor Norman pulled back the sheet. There was an involuntary gasp from Molly Plummer and an odd clucking noise from Charles Plummer.

"Can you confirm that this is your son Liam Plummer?" Ryan asked.

"Yes, yes, it's him," Molly Plummer said, tears welling up.

"Cover him up, for Christ's sake," Charles Plummer said.

Plummer put his arm around his wife and followed the constable out through the mortuary door. Ryan walked behind the group, as Doctor Jen Norman pulled the white sheet back in place.

Outside, Charlie Plummer suddenly stopped and released his grip on his wife. He leaned into Ryan.

"Detective, your assistant . . ." He said, pointing at Zoe.

"She's a Senior Constable, Mr. Plummer, and not my assistant."

"Whatever. She said that you think Liam probably died of some kind of drug overdose. Is that correct?"

"We don't know for sure, but that does seem to be the case."

"Cocaine?"

"We're not sure, but probably."

"Well, that's impossible," Charles Plummer said emphatically.

Ryan stared at him. It was far from impossible. In fact, it was the reason the man had died, but it was neither the time nor the place to have an argument. "Perhaps if you go upstairs with your wife and Constable Yang and fill in the relevant forms, we can discuss this later."

"Detective, that's my son in there. My Son! And I know Liam. He was fit, healthy, and like his family, had absolutely no history of any kind of heart problems. Nor for that matter would he take drugs of any sort!"

"Charles," his wife said, holding out her hand. "Please."

The man ignored her. "I'm giving you due warning. I know my son was murdered, and I insist you open an investigation into who did it." He glared at the detective.

"Come along, Mr. Plummer, we can talk about all this later," Zoe said, putting her arm on his shoulder.

Charles Plummer pushed away the constable's hand. "Don't patronize me. I'm prepared to go over both of your heads. Now take me to your commanding officer."

Charles Plummer looked across at his wife. "Molly?"

"In a moment, Charles."

"Please yourself. Constable, lead the way."

Constable Yang and Charles Plummer headed down the corridor as Molly Plummer took a step closer to the detective. "Take no notice of my husband. He didn't spend much time with Liam. In fact, he barely knew him. I, on the other hand, loved my son and was well aware of his frailties. So, I knew."

"Knew what?" the detective asked.

"That Liam took drugs, lots of them. No one killed my son. He killed himself."

WHILE EVERYONE ELSE WAS UPSTAIRS, Detective Ryan and Doctor Norman ran through the preliminary toxicologist and autopsy reports. And, after taking copies, Ryan left to meet up with Zoe and the Plummers. They were now in the lobby.

Charles Plummer was still angry: "I've had a word with your superiors, and they agreed with me that we've got to get to the bottom of this. My son was murdered. You know it. I know it, and I will make sure that others get to know it too." He grasped his wife's arm. "Molly?"

The two cops watched the couple leave.

"I feel sorry for his wife," Zoe said. "Fancy being married to that."

"We need to visit The Little Blue Door."

"What?"

"Let's go find your car," Ryan said.

NINETEEN

"CHARLES PLUMMER WAS RIGHT ABOUT ONE thing," Ryan said as Zoe drove.

"The pathologist told you that Liam Plummer had been murdered?"

"No."

"What then?" Zoe asked.

"Molly Plummer said that she knew her son took drugs. And Doctor Norman confirmed that Liam Plummer died of a heart attack after taking the cocaine.

"So, it definitely wasn't murder, like Charles Plummer alleged."

"The preliminary tox and the autopsy reports confirmed that Liam Plummer had died of a massive heart attack soon after he had snorted the coke," Ryan said.

"Which proves that his taking the cocaine caused his death."

"Yes, except that as I said, Charles Plummer was correct on one point. It is suspicious that his son died of a heart attack at such a young age. According to the autopsy, Liam Plummer had a strong heart."

"You're going around in circles. Cocaine caused the heart attack."

Ryan shook his head. "It doesn't happen that often with the drugs sold here. Actually, most of the coke is hardly recognizable as such. The dealers cut it with substances like phenacetin, paracetamol, hydroxyzine, diltiazem and levamisole."

"Levamisole?"

"A de-worming medication and by far the most commonly used cocaine adulterant."

"Nice."

"Yes, but the point is that guys like Liam Plummer may think they are taking cocaine, but they are usually snorting many other things besides. That suits everyone—the dealers because they make much more money from it, the doctors, and of course us cops. We don't want bodies piling up in the mortuaries from drug overdoses."

"But Liam Plummer did die of a coke overdose."

"Because of a heart attack," Ryan confirmed again. "But here's the thing. According to the tox report, the stuff Liam Plummer snorted was almost one hundred percent pure."

"Not cut at all?"

"Nope."

"Hell."

"And because of what Molly Plummer said, its odds on her son took the coke voluntarily. So was Liam Plummer given the coke, knowing it was too strong and would probably kill him? If he was, it was murder," the detective said.

"Or suicide."

"Yes, or suicide, though there was no farewell note—nothing. So there's only an outside chance of that. Alternatively, his supplier was unaware of the coke's effects, in which case we're dealing with an amateur. And, unless we find out who that is, there's likely to be more deaths."

"I see," Zoe said, signaled and pulled into the side of the road. "We're here."

She had parked in front of a closed entrance. It was sandwiched between a KFC outlet and a shoe store. Ryan unclipped his seat belt and reached for the door handle. "You still haven't asked why we've come."

"I don't need to. The Little Blue Door is the cocktail bar where Mel Knowles works. So I assume we're here to check up on his alibi."

Ryan smiled. Constable Yang was more intelligent than he had given her credit for.

SOME BARS LIKE TO ANNOUNCE THEMSELVES with flashing neon lights and blingy entrances, but that was not The Little Blue Door's way. The club took a low-key approach. Its owners were obviously relying on word of mouth and the promise of exclusivity to fill the haunt. Zoe banged on the blue door and waited. A narrow metal grid slid open to reveal a pair of brown eyes.

"Yes," said the owner of the eyes.

Zoe held her badge up to the slot. There was a pause and then the sound of chains being released, and a lock being turned. The door swung open to reveal a muscular mountain of a man dressed in a tight-fitting black Tux.

"We've come to see Mel Knowles. Is he here?" Ryan asked.

The bouncer's brow furrowed as he thought about that. "Yep." They waited. The Man Mountain just stared at them.

"Well, we want to see him," Ryan said.

He thought about that too. "Okay. I guess that's fine. Come in." With Ryan in front, the cops squeezed through the open door.

"Follow me," the Man Mountain said, turning to descend stone stairs.

The steps ended in a rectangular lobby, lit by a single hanging shade. A gold wall-mounted arrow pointed right. The Man Mountain and the cops followed its direction, entering a corridor barely wide enough to contain the big man's shoulders. They headed for the door at the end. The Mountain yanked on the handle and pushed it open.

Ryan had been prepared to see a small, cozy space inside. Instead, he'd entered a huge, high ceilinged room. Metal tables, with bar stools pushed underneath, were positioned all along its dank stone walls. A wide stainless steel counter crossed the room at the far end. There was a row of iron stools pushed under it. Backlit shelves filled with liquor bottles sat against the mirrored far wall. The club may not have wanted to announce itself outside, but there were no such inhibitions down here in the catacombs. A massive three-dimensional sign was attached by thick iron chains to the concrete roof. It hung directly above the bar with the words *The Little Blue Door* lit up. Here two men, their backs to them, were stacking bottles onto the shelves.

"He's there," the Man Mountain shouted over the booming rap music. The cops headed for the man that had been pointed out.

"Mr. Knowles," Ryan yelled. Knowles spun around. "Can you turn the sound down?" the detective shouted.

Knowles stepped to the till and pressed a plastic button next to it. The music cut off immediately.

The other barman turned and saw the cops for the first time. "It's okay, Frank, they're here to see me . . . You can go too, Haz," Knowles yelled to the Man Mountain still standing by the entrance.

He leaned across the counter. "Do you want to get me fired," he whispered. "We'll be opening soon, and having you two around isn't good for business."

"Well, if that's the case, perhaps you shouldn't have lied to us last night," Detective Ryan said.

"What?"

The detective knew what was coming next; the denial.

"What do you mean lie? I answered all your questions."

"Of course you did, Mr. Knowles, but that doesn't mean you told the truth. So we can question you here or take you into the station for a more formal interview. Your choice."

The mixologist hesitated. "Okay, look, we can talk in my office." He turned to the other bartender. "Frank, I'm going to leave you for a few moments, if that's all right?"

"No problem."

"Come through." Knowles said to Ryan and Zoe.

He lifted up the bar flap, and the cops stepped behind the counter. The mixologist pushed his hand onto the mirrored glass between the shelves of liquor. A panel swung inward, revealing a small room.

"My office," Knowles said, indicating and signaling for the cops to enter.

A grubby table and four green plastic chairs sat at the front of the poorly lit space. Boxes of spirits were stacked behind. For Ryan, Mel Knowles calling this area his 'office' showed the same sort of misplaced grandeur as when the man had insisted he was named a mixologist rather than a bartender. Knowles shut the panel behind him.

"Take a seat, officers," he said.

The detective swept the dust off one of the chairs and sat down. Constable Yang followed suit. Knowles seated himself on a third chair. "So?" he asked.

"You said you had no knowledge that Liam Plummer took drugs, but that wasn't true, was it?"

Knowles hesitated, weighing up what to say. "Okay, yes, you got me on that. But everything else I told you was."

"So, did you supply the cocaine to him?"

"No."

Ryan leaned back in the plastic chair. The ability to glean whether someone was telling the truth was essential for any detectives' work. Some were good at it; others were not. Ryan was a modest man, but he knew he was an expert questioner. He had replayed last night's interview in his head several times. He remembered the way Knowles' eyes had flickered and moved almost imperceptibly from right to left when he had denied knowing about Liam Plummer taking drugs. It had been a smooth, competent performance but not good enough to hide the lie. Last night Ryan had chosen not to pressure Knowles, deciding to wait until Doctor Norman had confirmed why Liam Plummer had died. Now Mel Knowles stared straight ahead. He wasn't lying this time.

"So why didn't you tell us the truth before?" the detective asked.

"Because . . ." Knowles stopped. "Look, this won't go any further, will it?"

Ryan said nothing. He just waited.

"Okay, well, Liam's mother knew he took drugs. But of course, she couldn't tell her husband." He looked directly at Ryan. "You've met Charlie, right? So you know what he's like?"

The detective said nothing.

"Anyway, Liam knew that if his father had found out that he was doing drugs, he would cut off his allowance. Liam had never worked and lived off the pocket money his father gave him.

"Pocket money?" the detective asked.

"That's what Liam called it, though I wouldn't call a couple of grand a week that."

"And Liam's mother was happy to keep the secret indefinitely?"

"Mrs. Plummer warned Liam that unless he did something about his drug-taking, she would tell Charlie."

"Did Liam agree to give up the drugs?" the detective asked.

"Yes. And to go to Narcotics Anonymous. He went to meetings in Barton."

"Regularly?"

"Once a week. Or at least that's what I told Liam's mom." Knowles took a deep breath. "His mother knew Liam, and I were friends and arranged to meet me a few months ago to offer me what she called a deal." He stopped. "The thing about the Plummers is that everything they do is transactional, although Molly is more subtle about that than Charlie. She agreed that I could go live with Liam rent-free on the condition that I make sure he went to Narcotics Anonymous and that I kept him off drugs. It was a pretty sweet deal."

"So, did he go to Narcotics Anonymous?" Ryan asked.

Knowles squirmed uncomfortably in his seat. "I did what I could; you can't make anyone do anything, least of all a guy like Liam."

"Answer the question," the detective insisted.

"He went from time to time."

"So, when did he last attend a Narcotics Anonymous meeting?"

"Last week. Liam asked me to take him there and wait outside to make sure he didn't leave early."

"So, he was trying?"

Knowles smiled. "As you know, druggies are some of the most manipulative people on the planet. He said he wanted to give up, but then this happens."

"This being he dies?" the detective confirmed.

Knowles went quiet. "Yes."

"So, where did he get his coke?"

"I don't know for sure. A local dealer, I think." Knowles stopped.

"What?" the detective asked, seeing the man's brows furrow.

"Well, Liam had been taking the stuff for years. I don't think he'd ever overdosed. And yet, this time, he didn't just overdose, but the coke killed him. That doesn't make sense, unless . . ."

"Unless what?"

"You know how when you're a kid, and you heard about a sweet that's supposed to be fantastic. You'd get really excited and couldn't wait to try it? That was what Liam was like the other day."

"You think he may have heard about a new coke source?" Detective Ryan asked.

"Maybe—I mean, I'm just saying whatever killed him can't have been what he usually took, can it? This stuff had to have been much stronger."

He looked at Detective Ryan. "Am I right?"

"It's possible."

"Okay. That's everything I know. Now can I get back to work?"

The detective shrugged. "Sure."

He got up and pushed on the panel again, opening the room to the bar. The cops followed. Knowles lifted the counter to let them out.

"One last question, Mr. Knowles. You said Mrs. Plummer's deal involved keeping tabs on her son's drug-taking. But did you ever tell her what was really going on with Liam?" Detective Ryan asked.

"I did my best." He paused. "But apparently, that wasn't good enough. The Plummer woman rang me just now to say that I had to leave the house. That's not fair, is it?"

"I don't think she saw her son's death as being very fair either," Ryan said and walked away.

TWENTY

"It's not fair," Micky said, taking a bite out of the Double Mac. Fair? Sometimes Micky acted just like a little boy, Stack thought, reaching for a chip and absent-mindedly chewing on it. They had been ravenous after their meeting with Oscar Bruno. They knew there was nowhere to eat in a snotty place like Point Piper, so Stack had driven to one of their favorite haunts—the Macca's on Darlinghurst Road in the Cross. After collecting their order, they had sat down at a table in the corner of the restaurant—somewhere they could hold their own 'meeting.' The place was virtually empty. A couple of prostitutes sat at a table yards away, sucking noisily on smoothies and complaining about the lack of business, and a guy with no teeth was nodding off behind them.

"Micky, what's with you? You ever think Bruno was fair?" Stack said.

"I thought he'd at least believe us. I mean, how long have we been working for him? Two years?" Micky replied.

"Right."

"And he still doesn't trust us."

"He doesn't trust anyone" Stack said.

"Ahh!" Micky suddenly yelled, clutching the side of his face and spitting bits of burger onto the table.

"Your tooth again?"

"Yeah." Micky rubbed his hand on his cheek and moved his lips. He had been complaining about the tooth for weeks now but hadn't done anything about it.

"You've got to get it fixed. It's only going to get worse."

"I will. No probs. Soon." Moving his hand from his face, Micky picked up his burger and took another bite, "See, fine," he said, chewing.

"The point is not whether the old bastard is fair or not; the question is where do we get the coke from?" Stack continued.

Micky thought about that. "We could rob someone."

"What? Go in all guns blazing and grab two kilos. That's a lot of coke."

Stack picked up her sausage and egg McMuffin and bit into it. "And even if we could do that, it wouldn't do us any good."

"How so?"

"Cause the coke would probably be Bruno's anyway. He's the major supplier in town," Stack said.

Micky sucked on his thumb. "Yeah. You're right."

He tapped Stack on the shoulder. "Look, there's Eric."

Stack twisted around to view the bird that had just entered the fast-food joint. The Australian white Ibis with its distinctive black head, thin down-curved foot-long bill, black legs and dirty white plumage, is closely related to the African sacred Ibis, but is a very different bird. Sacred it is not! Living all over Sydney and found in all the other big Australian cities too, the Ibis is commonly known as a 'bin chook' because of its habit of rummaging through garbage. Some people were repulsed by the bird's grubbiness and opportunistic nature, but not Stack and Micky. They admired the feathered creature's determination and its talent for survival—familiar qualities they too had in abundance. They had named this particular bird Eric, and he always seemed to wander in when they were eating at Macca's.

"Here, Eric," said Micky, holding a chip out.

Most in the Cross had learned long ago who to approach and who not to approach. Micky, with his wild eyes and frenetic energy, spelled trouble. He was definitely a 'not to be approached' kind of person. But Eric wasn't most people. He was a bird, so he felt no fear when he waddled over and took the food from Micky's outstretched hand.

"I think Bumpy would like Eric," Micky said.

Stack snorted. "Bumpy would rip him to pieces."

Micky frowned. "Yes, I guess you're right," He said as he offered the hungry Ibis another chip.

"Leave him alone. Concentrate. What are we going to do?" Stack asked.

"That's obvious, isn't it. We shoot the asshole?"

"Who? Bruno?"

"Yeah. He can't kill us if he's dead."

Stack stared at Micky. Sometimes she doubted if any part of his brain worked. "What? We just go back and kill him?"

"Yeah."

"His place is like Fort Knox."

"Fort what?"

"Where they keep all the American gold," Stack answered.

"Is that right?" said Micky admiringly. That's one of the things he loved about Stack. She always knew lots of things. "Yeah, I guess that might be a problem."

They stared at each other. What could they do?

"Sleazy Tone," Stack said suddenly.

"You think?" Micky asked.

Sleazy Tone knew everything and everyone in the city. He had his ear so close to the ground it was always in danger of being trampled on. Micky and Stack had first met Sleazy when, like them, he was doing the rounds of the foster parents' homes. "Yes. If anyone knows where to find 2K of coke, it would be Sleazy," Stack said.

TWENTY-ONE

W HEN RYAN ARRIVED AT BARTON'S POLICE station from Gosford, Zoe was already there. After she'd dropped the detective at his car, both had made their own ways back. Ryan knew Zoe would reach the police station well before him because he'd never been a fast driver. But that had its advantages. It gave him time to think and use his 'little gray cells,' as one of his fictional heroes, Hercule Poirot, was fond of saying.

Three vehicles were already in the station car park—two were marked cop cars and belonged to Constable Yang and Sergeant Acton. The other was an old battered silver Honda Civic. The detective backed cautiously into the space next to the Honda. Getting out, he used the key the Sarge had given him to enter the building through the back door. Inside, he hurried up the corridor and into the office.

"RYAN MEET JACKIE STREET, OUR NEW Office Manager," Zoe said as the detective came in. She indicated a round-shouldered woman with wild, unruly hair who sat opposite the constable.

"Good to meet you, Mrs. Street," the detective said, sitting at his desk and noting the computer that was now on it.

"Likewise. And it's Miss, not Mrs. Street. It always has been, and it looks like it always will be. But you can just call me Jackie."

"Jackie came in at short notice," the Sarge said as he entered. He walked

over to Ryan, leaned down, and whispered: "We need to talk—privately."
He indicated the corridor.

The detective got up and followed him out.

IN THE CORRIDOR, THE SARGE BEGAN to talk immediately: "Zoe has told
me everything, and frankly, I'm worried. Explain to me what happened
between Charles Plummer and you."

"Nothing, as far as I'm aware," Ryan said.

"Nothing! Charles Plummer put in a complaint to the Gosford police
about you. Apparently, you didn't believe him that his son Liam was
murdered."

"Correct. I think Liam Plummer died because of an overdose," the
detective said.

"That's what Zoe said you would say. But Charles Plummer doesn't
seem convinced."

"And you believe him?" Ryan asked, realizing precisely what had
happened. Charles Plummer had spoken to a senior officer in Gosford.
Knowing that the man was rich and a frequent contributor to police chari-
ties, the officer had listened carefully and then thrown the ball firmly back
into Sergeant Acton's lap. It was a standard 'cover your ass' procedure.

"Maybe if we go back into the office, Zoe can confirm what actually
took place," Ryan said.

The Sarge thought about this and shrugged. "Fair enough."

RYAN AND ZOE SAT ON THE sofa together as the Sarge pulled up a chair.
The detective was first up. He outlined exactly what had transpired: That
he'd received the results of the postmortem; Molly Plummer's admission
that she knew her son was taking drugs; and the Mel Knowles interview.
Zoe confirmed it all.

Jackie pretended to work as she listened in. The woman had been a
fixture at the station for years but had been 'let go' after budget cuts. This
had come as a terrible shock. Jackie loved her job. True, it was often dull,
but it got her out of her apartment. When Sergeant Acton asked for her to
return, she hadn't hesitated. Now she was determined to stay, but her length
of employment clearly depended on how long the detective remained in

Barton. So, when the cops stopped talking, she listened carefully to the Sarge's reaction.

"Yes, well, I must admit I did have my doubts about the murder. We don't get many murders in this town. The last time was . . ."

"Three years ago, but that was just a domestic gone bad—when the husband knifed his wife in broad daylight. So not much of a case," Jackie interrupted. The three cops swiveled around to view the woman, who had her head down and was typing at her computer.

"Quite," the Sarge said.

"Then there was that hit and run, years ago," Jackie said, looking up. "But the driver eventually turned himself in."

"Thank you, Jackie!" The Sarge waited for Jackie to return to her work. Then: "The point is, I now believe Detective Ryan may be correct. Nevertheless, we need to quickly find the source of the coke. That should help satisfy Charles Plummer and Gosford."

"We?" asked Zoe. "By we you mean Ryan and me, Sarge?"

"No, I mean, we as in he and I."

"Oh." Zoe's face fell.

"Maybe it would be best if the constable and I continued to work together on this. She has been involved from the start," Ryan said quickly. Whatever his reservations about Zoe, the detective knew that working with the Sarge would be a disaster. Ryan had encountered many in the Force like him. For them being a policeman was simply a job, a means to earn a living and not a vocation. They preferred to tread water, avoiding sticking their necks out at any cost.

"Yes, true," said the Sarge, "But . . ."

"And if she was replaced, that would imply that the case had been mishandled don't you think?" Ryan interrupted.

The Sarge thought about that. He had never been a particularly good policeman, but he was a master at survival. If, after offering to work with Ryan, he agreed to step aside and let Zoe partner with the detective, he should be safe from criticism for whatever happened. If the Liam Plummer case was sorted quickly, he would get the credit for his leadership. If Detective Ryan and Constable Yang failed, he could claim that against his better judgment, the higher-ranked detective had insisted on continuing working with the constable. And, unfortunately, things just hadn't panned out.

"Good point. You give the detective all the help he needs, Zoe," the Sarge said.

Constable Yang smiled, relieved.

There was a cough. "If I'm to stay Sarge, you have to get me a proper desk. I can't share with Zoe when she's trying to work on an important assignment," Jackie said, stopping work.

"Another good point," said the Sarge, "But . . ."

"You can get a desk from your cousin at the Singing Pelican. Johnny has lots of unrented rooms at the moment, so losing furniture temporarily should be no problem."

"Okay," the Sarge said, as Ryan absorbed the news that pub owner Johnny Wilson was Bluey's cousin.

"Oh, and since the detective is going to be here for some time, perhaps after he solves this case, he could look into another long-running Barton mystery—the disappearance of Nathan Woodford," Jackie Speed continued. "Eighteen years old, and puff, he's gone."

She looked over at Ryan. "I believe it's what you call a 'cold case', detective?" Jackie said. She watched Ryan's reaction closely. She had sown the seed. With any luck at all, the detective wouldn't be leaving any time soon.

TWENTY-TWO

Ryan and Zoe began their investigation into Liam Plummer's death in earnest over what was left of the afternoon. The dry cleaner reminder was rubbed off the whiteboard board replaced by a photo of the victim. Zoe added the information gathered from Knowles. She also began including salient points from the preliminary toxicology and mortuary reports. Meantime, the detective searched the internet for background on the dead young man. Liam Plummer's social media presence on Facebook and Instagram was limited. He only appeared to make sporadic posts, the last ones being over a week old. But Zoe had been right; the man was a staple of the local newspapers and gossip magazine. They needed little excuse to feature the 'Playboy Plummer.' There were always photos of Liam Plummer attending a whirl of trendy parties while squiring beautiful girls.

After finishing, the detective looked over to Zoe. She was still working at the giant board. Ryan knew he would have to keep a close eye on her—she could and would make mistakes. But he was still happy that he had successfully fought off Sergeant Acton's attempts to ditch the constable.

Ryan moved his gaze to Jackie, who was finishing typing up the previous night's transcript of the Knowles interview. She had surprised the detective with her enthusiasm. She had even brought up the Nathan Woodford cold case—the teenager who'd gone missing years ago.

The back door opened, and a young uniformed cop hurried in. He stared at Ryan before coming over. "You must be the new detective," the cop said, holding out his hand. "Jimmy O'Hagan." He paused. Then: "I mean Constable O'Hagan."

Ryan shook the young man's hand. "Detective Ryan."

Jimmy was as easy to read as a well-written book. He had the classic look of a country boy with his rugged, open face, clear blue eyes, and shock of unkempt blonde hair all packaged in a stocky body.

"Your shift starts at six, Jimmy," the Sarge said, standing. He glanced at this watch. "And as of now, you are sixteen minutes late."

"Sorry, Sarge, heavy traffic," Jimmy said, which Ryan thought was as lousy an excuse as he had heard in a good while. Traffic jams in Barton in the off season were as likely as a cold day in hell.

The Sarge obviously thought that too. He snorted in disbelief and peered over at Jackie. "Now the boy's arrived, you're free to go, Jackie." Looking up, she stopped typing, closed up her laptop, and slipped her jacket on.

"Anything to report, Zoe?" Jimmy asked.

"It's Senior Constable Yang to you. And no, nothing to bother your pretty head over. Just hold the fort here and call me if anything big happens."

By big, Ryan was sure Zoe meant 'anything.' The detective had already got his measure of the country boy. He'd probably come straight from school and been in the Force for a year or so, first as a trainee and then at his present rank. He had been assigned to the Lobster Shift because that's where he could do the least damage.

"Night, everybody," the Sarge said, heading for the door. Jackie left a few moments later, waving as she exited.

"I think I'll be off too," Zoe said. "If that's okay?"

"Fine. I was just going myself," Ryan said.

TWENTY-THREE

B Y THE TIME THE DETECTIVE DROVE out of the station car park and onto the coastal road, the earlier clear, bright weather had vanished. Now the sky was dark and ominous. There was the sound of distant thunder, and large drops of rain began to fall. Ryan flicked on his windshield wipers as he saw a jagged bolt of lightning crack across the horizon.

Living in Britain as a young child, the detective had memories of drizzle constantly falling from the gray London skies. He had longed for a few days of bright sun, but his prayers were rarely answered. Arriving in Sydney, Ryan had been astonished by the weather. Summers were hot and humid, and the sky cloudless and bright, bright blue. Winters were mild and wet— but instead of a steady trickle of water, the rain fell with an intensity he hadn't experienced before. It smashed into the sidewalk and rolled in torrents down the bitumen roads.

The detective turned the steering wheel, following the curve of the road. The storm was moving closer, the rain coming down harder and, the thunder and lightning nearing. He glanced out of the side window. The foaming, seething waves that smashed into the rocks had replaced the calm of the sea.

Ryan pulled off the main road and drove down to the Singing Pelican's car park, the vehicle's bright white headlights cutting through the rain and gloom and illuminating the beach beyond. It was almost deserted, apart from a woman walking her dog. She had obviously miscalculated about the storm.

Parking, the detective released his seat belt, turned off the ignition, reached for his umbrella, and got out. From here he could see that the woman was Ellie, and the dog, Attila.

"You okay?" Ryan shouted to them just as a searing flash of lightning filled the sky, and the animal let out a frightening howl. Attila yanked hard on his leash as Ellie tried to retain control. But she didn't stand a chance. Ryan watched as the canine tore the leash out of her hands and ran away, galloping over the wet sand.

Grasping the unopened umbrella, the detective jumped down onto the beach and ran towards Ellie, ignoring the rain that lashed his face. Reaching the woman, Ryan flung over the umbrella. "Take that. I'll get him." He sprinted after Attila, who was sodden, his fur matted and wet, and his leash trailing behind him.

"Attila, wait," Ryan shouted. "Stay."

The dog turned his massive head to peer at the advancing detective and stopped. Arriving, Ryan reached for the dog. But Attila took a step away. Ryan tumbled forward, his body stretching out, his feet slipping backward. He landed face down on the sand. Looking up, his view was blocked by a large, wet furred head. A pink tongue licked his face. Ryan rose and grasped the dog's leash.

"Are you all right?" Ellie asked as she caught up.

"Sure."

She reached out. "I'll take the dog now."

"No, best I hold onto him, just in case," Ryan said.

"Okay, well, why don't we all go back to my place?"

ELLIE JAMMED THE KEY INTO HER apartment door and pushed it open. "Come on in," she said, turning and signaling to Ryan and a bedraggled Attila. The dog pulled hard on his leash, giving the detective little choice but to follow.

Entering the hallway, the detective unclipped the animal's collar. Attila shook himself, spraying water all over. Then he pushed past Ellie and ran into the living room.

Ellie shook her head. "I should never have volunteered to look after that dog."

"Well, I'll be off," Ryan said, handing the woman the leash and reaching for the open door.

"Don't be silly. I'll get you something to dry yourself with. Come on."

She set off down the corridor. Ryan closed the door and followed.

THE LIVING ROOM WAS CONTEMPORARILY FURNISHED—A long, modern red cloth sofa was pushed against the wall, a nest of stylish glass tables standing to one side of it, with a white wood bookshelf on the other. A Pollack-style oil painting filled with an explosion of colors and shapes hung above the lounge.

Ryan crossed the room to peer out of the windows that stretched across the fourth wall. The storm had already moved on down the coast, and the rain had almost stopped.

"Here, take this," Ellie said.

Ryan turned as Ellie offered him a red and white patterned bath towel.

"Thanks." He rubbed his hair. "You've got quite a view from here."

"It's much better in the day. If you squint your eyes, you can see your place. Those lights are the Singing Pelican's," Ellie said, pointing and moving close. "I bought this apartment because of the view. And since it faces northeast, it gets great light all day."

Ryan touched his hair. It was drier. "Finished," he said, offering the towel back.

"Hardly. You must be wet through," Ellie said, stroking his arm.

"No. I'm fine."

Was Ellie flirting with him? Or was it his imagination? Ryan knew he was a good detective and trusted his instincts when doing the job, but faced with the love question, he floundered, often misreading the most basic signs. When he had plucked up the courage, the woman of his dreams turned into the demon from the dark lagoon. None of his relationships had lasted long, maybe because they were usually driven almost entirely by lust. The sex was great, but after that, what was left?

"Look, the least I can do is get you a glass of wine to thank you for Attila's misbehavior," Ellie said, pointing at the dog, who was now slumped on the floor asleep.

"Well, if you insist."

"Red or white?"

"Red," Ryan said, following Ellie into the kitchen. Here she pulled out a wine bottle from a rack sitting on the black granite worktop.

"I'll open that," he offered.

"No, I'll do it." She twisted the top of the bottle and then reached up to a cabinet, taking out two glasses. She poured the wine.

"So tell me more about yourself," Ellie said, handing over a glass, "You said at the restaurant that you were single. So you've never married?"

"You can tell?"

"It's a guess," Ellie said.

A good guess, though, thought Ryan. "You're right. It's not that I haven't come close. But one or both of us decided that maybe marriage wasn't such a smart way to go. What about you?"

"Well, he was my high school sweetheart, and we discovered too late that things that work for you in your teens often fall apart later."

Ryan took a gulp of the wine. "How long ago did you break up?"

"Three years."

"And no thoughts of remarrying? A pretty woman like you with a fabulous apartment must get lots of suitors."

"In Barton? The talent pool isn't exactly vast. It's more like a puddle actually. Most times, it would be like dating one of my family."

"Oh." He gulped back the last of the wine and put the glass down. "I really should be going."

"You sure?" Ellie brushed his arm again with her hand. She was definitely flirting. What to do? He was only up here for a short time, and things could get hideously complicated. But was he overthinking it?

"Okay I understand," Ellie said quickly, apparently losing interest, "I'll show you out." With Ellie leading, they headed back into the living room and up the hallway. "Do you get any time off on the weekends from detecting, Ryan?" she asked as she opened the door.

"You know I'm a detective?" Ryan said.

"Hasn't everyone been telling you how small a town this is? Yes, of course, a high-flying cop from Sydney. How could I not? Look, if you are free would you like to come to dinner on Saturday?"

"Yes, well . . ." Ryan paused and then took the plunge. "Sure."

"Great."

"What time?"

"Around eight, but I'll confirm by phone."

"Okay. My number is . . ." Ryan began.

"I already have it."

"What? How?"

"You're staying at the Singing Pelican, right?"

Ryan nodded. "Yes."

"There's your answer. Last night after you were all mysterious about what you did, I had to find out more. So I went over to the pub."

"And Johnny Wilson gave you my details?"

"Yes, but he wouldn't give them out to just anyone. The thing is . . ." She stopped. "See, the thing is, he's the high school sweetheart I mentioned. My ex."

"Your ex?"

"Yes, my ex-husband," Ellie said.

TWENTY-FOUR

"MARRIED," MICKY EXCLAIMED IN DISBELIEF.

"Why do you keep repeating that?" Stack asked, exasperated.

"Because I can't believe it?"

"Well, it's true," she said. Like Micky, Stack had found it hard to accept that Sleazy Tone had tied the knot and now lived out in the burbs. But so what? Now, all that mattered was seeing him.

Stack jammed her foot down hard on the accelerator pedal. Her Ford Mustang responded with a throaty roar and accelerated along the flat suburban road. Stack was a petrol head who loved her car. She had only just got the Mustang, and it was way and above the best motor, she'd ever owned. Of course, Micky, being Micky, had almost gagged when he first saw the orange monster. But Stack didn't care. Micky wouldn't know class if it ran over his feet, and the Mustang was pure class.

"So, how close are we?" Stack asked, peering out. They had traveled over twenty miles out from the inner city to Narwee—where Sleazy Tone now lived.

"Take the next left, Balmoral Road," Micky said, looking up from his cell phone. "You sure we got the right address?"

"Yeah. Sleazy confirmed it when I rang him," Stack said. They had visited Tone's old Darlinghurst home but discovered he had moved. The tattooed biker now renting the house was reluctant to pass on Sleazy's new address and cell number, but Micky had soon changed his mind.

Stack took a left into Balmoral Road. "Number twenty-three," Micky said. "It's on this side . . . There." He pointed ahead.

The house in the middle of a street of identical new houses—two-story white-fronted, gray-roofed homes. Stack parked outside.

"God," Micky said and then crossed himself. "This looks like hell."

"It's worse than hell," Stack corrected. "It's the land of real estate agents and telemarketers." She pushed down on the car door handle. "Okay. Let's go."

They walked briskly down the concrete driveway to the front door. Stack pressed the bell. What had Sleazy Tone done? It was hard to believe that an inner-city man who would fuck anything anywhere would end up married and living out here in Dagsville.

The door opened. Stack and Micky gaped at the blonde-haired, twenty-something man, wearing a neat plaid shirt and beige Cargo pants.

"Sleazy Tone?" Stack asked in disbelief.

"Nope," he said. "I told you on the phone it's not Sleazy Tone. It's Tony now. Come in."

Stack and Micky filed past him into a narrow white-walled hallway.

Tony shut the door firmly. "So, what exactly do you want?"

Stack and Micky looked at one another. Maybe an alien had taken over Sleazy's body. It had been a couple of years since they'd seen him last, and he was nothing like the man they had known.

There was the sound of a baby crying upstairs.

"Yours?" Stack asked, pointing up.

Tony smiled. "Russell. He's six months old."

"So, where's the missus?" Micky asked.

"With him," He paused. "Look, I only agreed to see you because we used to be friends."

Used to be, thought Stack. That's nice.

"Okay. I'll come straight to the point. We need to find 2K of blow," she said. "And we thought you could help us."

Tony turned a bright shade of red and shook his head. "Keep your voice down. Fen doesn't know what I used to do."

Used to again? How come everything that came out of Tony's mouth now included the words used to? Stack thought.

"Fen? That's the wife?" Micky asked.

Tony nodded.

"So what did she think you did? Run a monastery?" Stack asked.

"Look, you wasted your time. I'm a different person from the guy you used to know."

"Oh, for fuck's sake Sleazy, quit the act. We're looking for coke, and we know you can help," Micky said, advancing on Tony menacingly.

Stack tapped him on his shoulder. "Take it easy. I'm sure Sleazy . . . Tony, will help us out."

Silence. Tony thought about this. "Two keys?"

They nodded.

"I take it you don't want to pay?"

"Not don't, more can't. We need the stuff quick smart too," Stack said.

Tony took a deep breath. "There is someone. But if I tell you his name, you have to promise not to come back here again."

"You what?" Micky said aggressively.

"Sure, no problem," Stack said, smiling. "If you don't want to see us, so be it."

"And you didn't hear it from me," Tony said.

"No. Course not," Stack replied.

"Mott the Hoople."

"What?" asked Micky.

"Mott the Hoople. That's his name. He deals in those kinds of quantities. He funnels the stuff out to the regions." He stopped, staring at their blank faces. "You never heard of him?"

"This is a one-off for us. Drugs aren't our thing. We're more collection people. Make sure folks meet their obligations, right, Micky?"

"Yeah, right. So tell us about this guy."

Tony explained that Mott was a middleman. But if anyone knew where to source the coke, Mott was your guy. He gave them his address and then added one rider. On Thursdays, through to late Friday, he was usually out and about—uncontactable. So late tomorrow would be the best time to meet up.

"That's all I can give you," Tony said, opening the front door, indicating their time was up.

"It's enough," Stack said.

"Just," Micky said.

They filed out. Tony watched them go.

Stack and Micky had always been crazy, but this—stealing two kilos of coke—was beyond crazy. It was suicidal.

He shrugged as he closed the door. It was their funeral.

TWENTY-FIVE

Jack Breen would likely never have a funeral. And even if he did, there probably wouldn't be much left of his body to bury. It had been an ignominious end for the talented Olympiad who may have won a silver medal for swimming but had discovered too late that this mattered not a jot in a fight with a hundred thousand ton cargo ship.

After he'd dove from The Peggy Sue to find the missing cocaine packages, Jack had felt the water around him boil as the Korean ship started up its engines and turned over its one hundred and thirty-ton propellor. Jack tried to swim away, pushing his feet hard against the swirling water, but he didn't stand a chance. He was dragged back into the colossal rotor, and his face was ripped apart by the ship's massive blade.

Shrimps, crabs, mollusks, and prawns soon discovered Jack's body on the ocean floor. Using their teeth and claws, they ripped the dead flesh and burrowed into the corpse. Here they found what they were looking for—Jack's liver, kidneys, and heart. These were delicious delicacies to be savored. And the meat around his ankles was tasty too. The animals ate through the bone, freeing one of Jack's feet. The foot, jammed into a sneaker, rose quickly to the surface.

Up top, the storm was still raging, turning the ocean into a tempestuous devil sea. The foot and sneaker were grabbed and pummeled by the angry waves. Then, as the water calmed, they floated away, slowly drifting closer and closer to the shore. That's when Barton's famous rip took over. As the winter sun rose, the rip steered the foot and shoe past the town's cliffs and around the bay before unceremoniously dumping it on the beach. And that's where Henry Webster discovered it while taking his little wiry-haired fox terrier, Stevo, for his regular early morning walk.

Soon after, Detective Ramesh Ryan awoke. Looking out the window, he saw a small crowd assembled on the beach. Curious, the detective decided to check out what was going on. He dressed quickly and, as he was pulling on his boots, his cell rang. A breathless Zoe said a mysterious foot and sneaker had been found. Zoe and Constable Jimmy O'Hagan were already on the beach. Could he come too?

Not for the first time, Ryan thought that things in Barton were turning out too much more hectic than he would ever have imagined. But, as the detective opened the door, he vowed to find the time to get down to the job he was really there for.

BY THE TIME THE DETECTIVE ARRIVED, Zoe had already driven metal staves into the soft sand and almost finished setting up an eight-foot protective cordon of tape around the foot. Meanwhile Constable Jimmy O'Hagan was keeping the rubbernecks at bay.

"Morning," Ryan said as he passed Constable O'Hagan and made his way to Zoe. She was attaching police tape to the final stave.

Ducking under the cordon, Ryan bent down to peer at the foot and the gym shoe. He wasn't sure which was more surprising—seeing this on the beach or finding Jimmy O'Hagan there. His shift should have finished a good hour ago.

"What do you think?" Zoe said, kneeling down beside the detective.

"I'm not sure," Ryan said, turning to see two figures dressed in blue coveralls making their way down. One carried a leather bag, the other a silver photographer's case—Doctor Jen Norman and the forensic cameraman. "Looks like the pathologist made it over in good time," the detective said.

Zoe followed Ryan's look. "Yes, but she hasn't brought the full forensic team."

"No need. The foot has probably been in the water for days. They'd find nothing here that they couldn't discover back in Gosford," Ryan said. He moved his gaze over to Jimmy. "I thought Constable O'Hagan had ended his shift."

"He has, but he wanted to help out."

"So miracles can happen."

"Seems so," Zoe said, grinning.

Ryan turned his attention back to the foot and shoe. "So, who found this?"

The constable pointed at a man wearing a flat black cloth hat and a long black waterproof raincoat. He stood with his dog, about twenty yards away and some distance from the crowd.

"Him. Henry Webster. He's here with Stevo every day, come rain or shine. He's a little . . ." she paused, ". . . slow, I guess you'd say."

"But he had the gumption to call the police when he found this. So he's not that slow."

"Detective," Doctor Norman called.

The pathologist and her cameraman had just reached the cops.

"We mustn't keep meeting like this," Doctor Norman said as the cameraman bent down, laid his steel case on the sand, and opened it up.

"We seem to have little choice nowadays," Ryan said, glancing over at the photographer.

"Sorry, you haven't been officially introduced. Benny McNeil. Detective Ryan."

Benny McNeil looked to be in his mid-forties. He had a flat face and dull blue eyes. Wisps of hair pushed out from under his blue coverall hood. He nodded at the detective before continuing to search through his case.

"This it?" Doctor Norman said, taking a step towards the foot while looking around for the best place to put her bag.

"Yes. It was found about an hour ago," Zoe said.

The pathologist bent down to examine the foot and gym shoe close up.

"How long do you think it's been in the water?" Ryan asked.

"Hard to say," the pathologist said, opening her leather bag and producing a metal pointer. She prodded the top of the shoe with it. "There's no sign of adipocere, so the man has been dead for under a month."

"It's a he?" Zoe asked.

"Almost certainly. You don't get many women wearing size 14 black Nike Air Max's. I'd say the guy wearing these had to be at least six-three. Where's the rest of him?"

Ryan pointed out to sea. "Out there somewhere." He glanced at his watch and stood up. "Sorry, I'll have to love you and leave you."

"No problem. We won't be here long. After I bag it, I'll take it back and see if the DNA matches up with anyone in the database," Doctor Norman said.

Zoe stood up too. "I can check as well if any six-foot three-inch males have been reported missing in the last month or so."

"Good. And can you interview Henry Webster, just for the record?" Ryan asked Zoe, before walking off.

"Ryan?" Zoe said, running up behind him. "So, are we dealing with a murder here or what?"

"Murder?" the detective said.

"Yes. I'm guessing that the man was killed at sea, chopped up, and dumped into the ocean."

"I very much doubt that. It's much more likely he drowned."

"But the foot was severed from the body."

"No, it wasn't. The flesh had been bitten away by sea animals—prawns, shrimps, crustaceans, and the like. That would have freed the foot. And it floated off because the Nikes are filled with foam and have gas-filled pockets on the soles, making the foot buoyant."

"Interesting," Constable Yang said . . . And it was. For Zoe working with the detective was proving a revelation. "You going back to the office?" she asked.

"Yep. See you there," Ryan said.

TWENTY-SIX

Even though Ryan told Zoe he was returning to the police station, he wasn't. Not straight away. He was due to attend a Narcotics Anonymous meeting first, but was running late because of the foot on the beach. However, if he had told Zoe where he was really off too, she would have taken it one of two ways. Either she would have concluded that the detective had been hiding a deep, dark secret from her—which he hadn't. Or that he had dumped her, so he could work alone—which he had. Neither would have produced a good response. So Ryan preferred to tell Zoe the little white lie about returning to the office.

The Narcotics Anonymous meeting was already well underway. There were seven of them there. They included thirty-three-year-old Scott Dean. He lived behind the National Park, not far from where Liam Plummer's body had been found. His grandparents had lived in the town since the thirties. On their death, the rambling house had been passed to Scott's parents. His mom and dad had run the local hardware store. When both died from cancer within months of each other, Scott had taken over the property. Living rent-free, with the cash from the business's sale, Scott didn't ever have to work again. And he had spent his days taking drugs. He started coming to Narcotics Anonymous over four years ago when he decided to give up.

Scott enjoyed the meetings. He loved sitting in the old community hall while half-listening to the same stories repeated over and over. And although the organization's name included the word anonymous, and it wasn't cool to admit it, Scott pretty much knew everything about everyone there.

He knew that the fat woman with the long red hair and bloodshot eyes currently holding the floor and referred to as Jean was actually Jean Mildred Collins. She worked part-time at the post office and lived in a rundown apartment close by Roger Beaumont's home. Bald and wrinkled, like an old prune, Roger was now retired and had given up drugs eons ago but loved to come to Narcotics Anonymous for the company.

Then there was the young guy seated two chairs away, Brad Costello. Scott was Costello's sponsor. The twenty-five-year-old with his fit body, black curly hair, and burning brown eyes was most people's definition of a hunk. Scott had met Costello a year ago when he offered his services as a gardener, before becoming his lover, and now—well, who knows?

Jean finally finished speaking. Clapping, Scott nudged his neighbor Ging, who half-heartedly joined in the applause. A tall, bean pole of a man, with a pock-marked face and dirty ginger hair tied into a man-bun, twenty-seven-year-old Ging looked like central casting's idea of a junkie. Ging was the kind of guy that could rub people up the wrong way. He certainly did that for Nancy Kallis. She hated him.

Nancy, a rail-thin woman in her mid-forties with black hair and a triangular mouse-like face, peered around the room as the clapping stopped. "Anyone?" she asked, staring hard at Ging.

"Why are you looking at me?" he asked.

"I'm not. I'm looking around at everyone," Nancy said defensively. A former drug addict like the rest of them, Nancy was the self-appointed chairperson. Narcotics Anonymous meetings weren't supposed to be chaired, but freewheeling gatherings didn't sit happily in Nancy's wheelhouse. She liked order. And when no one had objected, she had taken on the role of chairperson a while back. It had always irritated Nancy that Ging hardly ever said a word. And she had strong suspicions about his motives for coming to the meetings.

"You say you look at everyone, Nancy? So, why do you spend so much time glaring at me then?" Ging asked. "Is it because I'm young and fit, and you're old, wrinkled, and about to die."

"Hey, that's enough," Roger Beaumont said.

"Enough? Enough of what?" Ging said, turning angrily to face Roger.

And it was then, just as the row was about to kick off, that Detective Ramesh Ryan arrived, slamming the door behind him. The argument was forgotten. Everyone swiveled around to view the new arrival.

RYAN RAISED HIS HAND. "SORRY, I'M LATE."

Nancy pointed to an empty seat next to her. "Take a seat . . ."

"Ryan. The name's Ryan," the detective shouted to the room and sat down on a creaky wooden chair.

No one spoke for a moment. Then Roger Beaumont piped up. "Nancy, I didn't think we allowed anyone in late."

The detective tensed. The last thing he wanted was someone making a fuss about him.

"There's no hard and fast rule. It's up to my discretion, and I'm fine with Ryan staying," Nancy said. "So who wants to speak next? Scott?"

"Me?" Scott said as if surprised. "Okay. Well, I've had a terrible week."

"Like you always have," Ging said under his breath.

"I think it's maybe the time of the month, but I seriously thought about topping myself."

"Twelve times," said Ging loudly.

"What?" Scott asked.

In the last week's meeting, you said you'd thought about topping yourself at least twelve times. So, why don't you go ahead and do it?"

"That's an awful thing to say," Jean said, horrified.

"Scott, please go on," Nancy said.

Scott glared at Ging. "Okay. I will."

"And please, no more interruptions," she added.

As Scott talked, Ryan studied the room. The detective was here to follow up on the information given to him by Knowles about Liam Plummer attending the local Narcotics Anonymous meeting. Ryan knew that some used the meetings to distribute drugs—the opposite of what was intended. Someone here could be the supplier of the deadly super strength coke.

Scott finished his speech, and then Brad Costello had his turn. With time running out, Nancy closed the meeting. The room emptied quicker than a melting snow cone in hell. Only the chairperson remained. Nancy came over to the detective, as he knew she would. A new recruit in such a small place is always welcome.

"So, Ryan, this your first time at Narcotics Anonymous?" Nancy asked.

"No, not really. Look, if it's okay with you, I'd like to pick your brains?"

The woman beamed with pleasure. "I'm all yours."

"A guy called Liam Plummer was a regular here, right?"

Nancy's smile faded. "You do realize that we call this organization Narcotics Anonymous for a reason. So I obviously can't answer that question." She looked hard at the detective. "Who exactly are you, and why would you want to know that?"

It was time to own up. The detective produced his ID.

Nancy studied it. "A cop! You know you're required to declare yourself."

Ryan raised his hands. "All I want is some help. Liam Plummer died yesterday from an overdose. He had taken some super strength coke."

"Yes. I read about that in this morning's paper."

"So, you'll understand that we must find the source of this drug as quickly as possible."

"That's no excuse, detective. People come here to speak their minds and not to have the police spying on them." She indicated the door. "I'd like you to leave and not come back."

Ryan hesitated. Perhaps he had made a mistake, but it was the only lead he had.

"Okay, I'm going," he said, pulling out a business card. "But please take this. It's my cellphone number. If there's anything you remember about Liam, let me know." Ryan headed for the door.

"Detective?"

He stopped and turned. "As you obviously are aware, Liam Plummer attended meetings here." She hesitated. "Some people strike up friendships at Narcotics Anonymous, something I encourage. However, I always found Liam and Ging, the thin, pale young man, an unusual pairing."

"They were friends?" the detective asked.

"Apparently. Even though they didn't have much in common—except for these meetings, of course."

"Do you know where Ging lives?"

Nancy frowned. "That's all I'm prepared to say. You're a detective, so detect."

TWENTY-SEVEN

Ging took a long drag on the cigarette. Where was this guy? It was bad enough getting up early for the meetings but having to hang around outside the ugly-assed building was the pits.

He took a deep breath. People didn't understand how difficult his work was. He knew what they thought. How tough can it be to be a drug dealer? They had no idea. Sure it was lucrative, but the risks were high too.

The big glass entrance doors slid open. The Indian guy he had been waiting for strode out. Ging walked towards him, his hand raised. "Hey." The man stopped.

"I didn't introduce myself back there, Ryan. My name's Ging." He offered the detective a cigarette.

"No. I gave up."

"Oh yeah. When?"

"Yesterday."

"Good luck with that then," Ging said, smiling and slipping the pack of smokes back into his pocket. "I haven't seen you around. Are you new to Barton?"

"I've only been here a few days."

"What do you think of it?"

"I like it."

"So, why are you in town?" Ging asked.

"I'm doing this and that. You know how it is?" He smiled at Ging.

"Anyway, got to go." See you around."

Ryan walked off slowly. It was now or never, the detective thought.

Ging hesitated. What was the worst that could happen? Well, he could be a cop. But he knew all the local cops by sight. None of them were brown-skinned.

"Hey, hold up."

The detective waited for Ging to catch him up.

"I forgot to say is that if you ever needed anything, I'm your man," Ging said.

"Anything?"

"Yeah, anything."

"Like?" Ryan asked.

Was this guy for real? Ging thought. He leaned in close. "You know . . . coke . . . loobs . . ."

"Oh right," Ryan said and reached behind under his jacket.

Ging saw the move. Fuck, the guy was a cop! He went to run as the detective stuck out his foot while yanking out a pair of cuffs.

Ging tripped and fell forward onto the concrete. The detective reached down and pulled the dealer's arms back, clipping the cuffs over his wrists.

WHILE RYAN LOADED GING INTO HIS car, readying to take him to the station, Kate Cassels finished applying her mascara and preparing for work. She pushed the blush brush back into the tube and dropped it into her purse before gathering up her parker and slipping it on. She peered into the full-length mirror bolted onto the side of the closet door. The green of the coat perfectly matched her eyes and made them pop; and her makeup evened her skin tone and hid the pimple that had chosen today to come out. Kate's ripped blue jeans and black blouse, cut to enhance her breasts and reveal as much of her stomach as was decent, completed the look. Not bad, not bad at all, Katie girl, she thought. That should get those tightwads at the pub tipping generously—not that that would make working there much more palatable.

Today the thought of going into the pub was making Kate gag. But she knew she shouldn't complain. She had to remember how lucky she was. She was young, pretty, and had a cheap place to live—somewhere she had made even nicer. Kate had painted the room, choosing an 'ocean air' blue color. Then she had stuck old retro album covers on the wall. This, along with the gray dove quilt and the succulents she had bought to line the sill, gave the room a bright, homey feel . . . which reminded her.

Kate stepped over to the window and prodded the soil in the plants one by one. They were all still moist. *Good.* What had the old guy at the nursery said? *These are easy to keep. Just water them once a week, and you can't go wrong. Bullshit.* Three of them had died almost immediately.

It was time to go. Kate stepped out of the bedroom onto the landing. Here things weren't so great. Scott Dean's house was the antipathy of all those glossy house and garden magazines that Kate loved to read. He had done pretty much nothing to the enormous house since his parents had died. All the wallpaper was peeling, and the paint was grubby and chipped . . . and no work had been done in the kitchen and bathroom for close to a decade.

As she headed down the stairs, Kate again tried to think positively. Johnny may have been an asshole of an employer, but at least he didn't mind when she took time off for an audition. And to be fair, he had also introduced her to Scott. When she put out feelers for somewhere to rent cheaply, Kate thought that Johnny would offer her one of his pub rooms. But apparently, that was asking too much! Instead, he had suggested Kate contact Scott who he said had plenty of space in his house and wasn't so much interested in the rent as needing someone to keep him company, adding quickly that Scott was, of course, gay—and then bingo, Kate and Scott had hit it off straight away.

Kate reached the bottom of the stairs and stopped. What was that noise? Someone crying? It came from what Scott called his study—the room where he spent so much of his time. Walking across the living room and reaching the study door, she hesitated. Scott was obviously having an awful day today. But what to do? If Kate had been a callous woman, she would have just left. She really wasn't anywhere nearly as brutal or uncaring as she pretended to be, so she knocked hard on the door. "Scott. You okay?"

Hearing no answer, Kate pushed open the door. She hated the study. It was full of brown wood furniture and piles of old newspapers and books.

If Kate had spent as much time in here as Scott did, she was pretty sure she would be just as depressed as he was.

Scott sat at the desk, his hands over his head, sobbing.

"What's up?" Kate asked, weaving past the garbage littering the thread-worn carpet. She put her arm around Scott's shoulders. He lifted his head and pressed it into her stomach, his shoulders shaking. "It's no good, Kate. I can't go on."

"That's ridiculous. Of course, you can," she said.

That produced more tears. "Everyone is always so dismissive. You, Brad—everyone."

"I'm not being dismissive. I know you're depressed, but we all have our down days," Kate said.

"No one goes through what I've been through. If I had the strength, I would top myself, right here, right now."

"Now you're being melodramatic."

"Am I? Is that what I'm being?"

Kate stared at him. "Scott, I have to go. I'll be late for work."

He moved his head up and wiped away the tears. "You're always busy, busy, busy—too fucking busy for me."

"That's just not true. And it's hurtful you saying that. Every time I ask you what's wrong, you just tell me I wouldn't understand."

Scott looked at her and then lowered his head onto the desk. Kate shrugged and headed for the door.

"What if I was to tell you why I'm like this all the time?" Scott shouted to her back.

Kate swiveled around. "What?" she asked.

"Sit down and hear me out, please. I need to talk to you about something vital."

TWENTY-EIGHT

In Interview Room One, Detective Ryan was trying to get Ging to talk. The drug dealer sat opposite Ryan and Constable Yang and next to his lawyer Malcolm Morgan-Brown, an overweight man in his mid-fifties. Ging was peering up at the fluorescent lights and saying nothing.

The fat lawyer cleared his throat. "So, detective, what exactly do you intend to charge my client with?"

Ryan shuffled the notes in front of him and then looked across at the constable. She had put her iPhone on the table, next to a small plastic bag filled with white powder.

"Constable, show Mr. Morgan-Brown will you please?" Ryan said, indicating the container.

Constable Yang picked it up. "This bag was found on your client, Ginger Watson," Zoe said.

"Allegedly. And what's the charge?" the lawyer asked.

"No charge yet. And as you can see, we aren't recording anything yet. At this stage, we just wanted to have an informal chat with Ging. Frankly, your presence here is a bit premature," Ryan said.

"I'll decide what is and isn't premature. My client called me asking me to represent him, and that's what I'm doing. Now, if there is no charge—Ginger," the lawyer said, getting to his feet.

Ryan stared at the fat man. He had expected some fifth-rate jerk to come in to defend the small-time, dumb-fuck drug dealer—not Malcolm

Morgan-Brown. Sergeant Acton and Zoe had frowned and breathed in deeply on hearing the name. They'd explained to Ryan that the lawyer was a partner in Ansen, Morgan-Brown, and Phelps, a top-tier law firm from Gosford—a big fish, coming, at a moment's notice, to represent a minnow. That would suggest something else—that there was a sophisticated drugs operation operating around here, and someone was prepared to pay out to protect it.

"I would stay if I was you," Detective Ryan said to the lawyer and his client, both of whom were now standing. "Ginger Watson did offer to sell me drugs, and we did find that packet on him," Ryan said. "There's no allegedly about that. I'm sure too that when we get the toxicology report on the powder, it will confirm that it's coke. Possession of the stimulant is a criminal offense under Section 10 of the Drug Misuse and Trafficking Act 1985 and carries a maximum penalty of two years in prison. That said, if your client is cooperative, then I'm sure we can come to some arrangement. So please sit down and let's talk."

"What the fuck do you mean cooperative? I'm not talking about anything with you. I'm no snitch," Ging snarled.

"Ginger," Morgan-Brown said, waving to his client to retake a seat. "Cooperative? How so?"

"I'm investigating the death of Liam Plummer," the detective said.

"Charles Plummer's son?" the lawyer asked.

"Yes. He appears to have died from a heart attack caused by overdosing on coke. Liam Plummer went to the local Narcotics Anonymous, and, as I understand it, he was friends with your client."

"Yeah, I knew him. Everyone knew Liam. He was a nice guy. But what I want to know is how come a cop can turn up at a Narcotics Anonymous meeting without announcing himself? That's entrapment," Ging said.

"Your client's quite the lawyer," Detective Ryan said amiably. "But I would advise him to quit making allegations that he can't prove. He has no evidence that I hadn't previously arranged to be at that meeting, does he?"

Ging was about to reply, but Morgan-Brown interrupted quickly. "Ginger, please." The lawyer turned back to Ryan. "You say Liam Plummer overdosed on coke?"

"Yes. Coke that could have been supplied by your client."

"You saying I sold Liam coke?"

"Ginger!"

"I'm sure that's very provable," said Ryan.

"Don't say anything," the lawyer warned. "Go on, detective."

"If, after we carry out a tox report on the white power found in your client's possession, it turns out to be too low of a concentration to have caused the death of Liam Plummer, then we could come to a deal."

"What kind of deal?"

"I would need Ging to find out who is distributing this high-concentration drug."

Morgan-Brown nodded. "If you could just give me a few minutes alone with my client." The officers stood up and left the room.

"DO YOU THINK HE'LL GO FOR it?" Zoe asked as she closed the interview room door behind her.

"Yes. If Ging didn't supply coke from the same batch that killed Liam."

"And you don't think he did?"

"No." Ryan reached to open the door. "Come on, we've given them enough time."

The cops reentered the room, and Malcolm Morgan-Brown and Ging waited for them to take their seats. Ryan leaned forward, his elbows on the desk. "Well?"

"One question. When exactly did Liam Plummer overdose?" the lawyer asked.

"Last night," the detective said.

Morgan-Brown looked across at Ging. "That coke had nothing to do with me," he said.

"Then that deal sounds perfectly acceptable," the lawyer said.

"I'll give him three days," Ryan said, standing. "And I expect him to come back with confirmable details."

Morgan-Brown nodded. "OK, Ginger?"

"Yes."

"So, Ginger can go now?"

"He can," Ryan said.

Malcolm Morgan-Brown heaved his considerable bulk up from the chair. "Come on," he said to his client.

"Constable, can you show them out, please."

The two men followed her out, as Ryan sat back down.

"WHY DID YOU DO THAT?" ZOE said, after returning to the interview room.

"Do what?" Ryan asked.

"Let that piece of garbage off so easily."

"Ging is a small-time loser, but he's not an absolute idiot. No drug dealer would choose to sell his clients ninety percent plus pure coke. They'd never make the kind of money they do unless they cut it. In fact, I'm willing to bet that the tox report will confirm that there is very little coke in that pack of white powder," the detective said, indicating the bag on the desk. "So Ging has two reasons to find out who is stupid enough to sell coke of that quality. Firstly, I'm damn sure he doesn't want to spend time in jail. Secondly, whoever is the big boss controlling the drug supply up here, and I'm damn sure that's not Ging, well they will want the same question answered."

"I see," said Zoe.

"And can you get a sample of Ging's coke down to Gosford for analysis," Ryan said, standing.

"Before you go, detective, I have a bone to pick with you. I thought you told the Sarge we were going to be working together."

"We did, just now."

Zoe shook her head. "Yes, but you went to the Narcotics Anonymous meeting alone."

"I'm going to go there with a uniformed cop? Yeah, that would have worked."

"You could have explained that to me, though."

Ryan knew this would happen. He shouldn't have overpromised. It was time to show his teeth. "What are you, Zoe, a child? I'm a detective, and you are a constable. I'll decide if, where, and when we work together.

Ryan marched out of the room, leaving an unhappy Zoe behind.

TWENTY-NINE

F. OPENED THE RICKETY IRON GATE and stepped into Scott Dean's garden. It backed onto the National Park and provided a perfect backdrop for the property. In the off season it was deserted. So, F.'s entry was unobserved—which is what he wanted it to be.

F.'s backpack slipped off his shoulder as he pushed away an overhanging branch. Centering the pack, he stepped onto what remained of a narrow concrete path. The garden was a jungle and surrounded by high overgrown hedges, providing perfect privacy from the neighbors.

Arriving at the back door, F. twisted the handle. As always, it was unlocked. F. flicked on the light as he entered the kitchen. The single bulb barely illuminated a room that had seen much better days. A filthy gas stove stood in the center of a row of dilapidated floor and wall cabinets. The old blue striped wallpaper was peeling, revealing crumbling plaster underneath. A scratched, dented white fridge hummed loudly in the corner.

F. walked across the space and through the open door into the living room. "Scott, where are you?" F. yelled as he threaded his way past cardboard boxes overflowing with old magazines and papers. Reaching the study door, F. knocked loudly. "Scott?"

"Come in," a muffled voice answered.

F. levered the metal door handle down and leaned against the heavy door. It reluctantly opened. Inside, Scott sat behind the large wooden desk.

"Take a seat," Scott said, indicating one of the two worn armchairs. F. took his backpack off, dumped it on the floor, and sat down.

"Good of you to come at such short notice," Scott said.

"Of course. I'm always here for you," F. said. "What's up?"

"I've made a decision."

"Oh, really," F said, pretending to be surprised.

"I have to go to the police."

Scott waited for a reaction. F. kept quiet.

"I've been thinking about doing it forever. I just can't go on lying to myself—to everyone." Scott searched F's face. "So, how do you feel about that?"

F smiled. "I'm happy." He wasn't, of course. It was unfathomable. The man had inherited this fabulous house that he'd let go to rack and ruin. He had more than enough money to never have to work again, and yet over the years, he had sunk into a deeper and deeper depression.

"Happy?" Scott repeated. Had he heard right?

"Let me tell you a secret," F. said and reached down to open the backpack. "I expected this."

Scott grinned. F. was so intuitive.

"That's why I've brought something to celebrate," F. said. He placed a bottle of Glenlivet whiskey on the table. "Your favorite tipple."

"You really don't mind?" Scott asked.

"No." F. reached down again into the backpack and produced two plastic tumblers.

"But I thought you'd be mad at me."

"Well, I'm not," F. said, twisting the bottle cap open and pouring the whiskey into the beakers. "Bottoms up." He handed a tumbler to Scott, who greedily slugged the alcohol back.

"We're friends, right?" F. said.

"Always. "

"So how can one friend enjoy seeing another suffer?" F. asked.

Scott took another gulp of the whiskey. "You're right. They can't." He stared at F, "Aren't you drinking?"

"Sure." F. lifted the glass to his lips and then stopped. "Who else have you told about this decision?"

"No one. Just you."

F. poured more whiskey into Scott's glass and stood up. "Do you mind? I need to use the bathroom."

"Go ahead." F. walked out of the room, closing the door behind him.

THIRTY

"CAN I HAVE A WORD, DETECTIVE?" Sergeant Gary Acton asked Ryan as he returned to the office from the interview room.

"Certainly," the detective said as the door opened behind him, and the constable came in.

Ryan turned to her. "Zoe, while I speak to the Sarge, can you put all of Ging's details on the whiteboard, please," he said.

She hesitated. She was furious at Ryan, and now he was acting as if nothing had happened. She considered disobeying him—but he was the senior officer. "Will do," she said coldly.

"We can talk outside," the Sarge said to Ryan, taking a pack of cigarettes out of his uniform pocket and picking up a newspaper from his desk.

THE SERGEANT AND THE DETECTIVE STOOD at the front of the cop station. Ryan watched the policeman, waiting as he lit up a cigarette.

"Are Zoe and you OK?" the Sarge finally asked.

"Fine. I didn't know you smoked."

"I know, it's a disgusting habit. Zoe's always going on about how I should give up." The Sarge paused. "You've never smoked?"

Ryan shook his head. The detective hadn't spoken to Sergeant Acton since he returned with Ging, but on the way to the interview room, he'd been aware of tension in the air. Had he somehow offended the cop, as well as Zoe?

The Sarge took a long drag on the cigarette and indicated the newspaper he was carrying. "Did you see this?"

"No."

"Well, take a look." The Sarge handed it over.

The detective glanced down at the bold headline on the front page. "Famous family's son drug death disaster," it read in bold black type. "Exclusive." Ryan skimmed the copy. After finishing, he handed the newspaper back to the Sarge. "Nice."

"'Nice? I've been fielding questions about this all morning. I want to know how they got the story? Did you give it to them because they seem to know a heck of a lot about Liam Plummer's death?"

"No, I didn't, Sarge. I suspect most of the copy came from Plummer's roommate Mel Knowles. He seems the kind of guy who would be willing to make money out of a friend's death. But the news was inevitably going to be leaked by someone."

"Inevitable? Is that what you think? The local rag breaks the story, and you come out with something like that. Now I understand why Sydney was so willing to send you up here!"

Ryan stared at the man. He knew what was up. "Did Charles Plummer speak to you this morning?"

"Yes, as a matter of fact, he did. He wanted to know how come his family's private affairs were spread all over the local rag."

It was as the detective had thought. The Sarge's quest for a quiet life had been blown apart. He needed someone to blame, so Ryan, the out of towner, was the chosen culprit.

"Unfortunately, if you are a wealthy high profile family and your son dies of a drugs overdose, you have to be prepared for the information to come out. Maybe it's not such a bad thing either. At least now the public is aware of this new deadly coke," Ryan said.

The Sarge opened his mouth to say something and then changed his mind. He turned around and headed back inside. Ryan watched him go just as his cell phone rang.

"Yes," he said, answering.

"Hi, it's Ellie . . . Ellie Sastra."

"Oh, hello."

Ellie picked up on the hesitancy in the detective's voice. "I haven't rung at a bad time, have I?"

"No. Not at all."

"Well, I was thinking . . . would you like to come around for dinner tonight?"

"Tonight?"

"Yes, I know I said Saturday and I know it's short notice, but I figured why not give it a try."

Ryan thought about the offer.

"Of course, if you're not free, we could make it some other time," Ellie said.

"No. I'd love that," Ryan said, the decision made.

"Eight-thirty then?"

"Perfect."

"See you later."

Ryan clicked off the phone. Things were happening rapidly on the Ellie front. But he had no problem with that . . . none at all.

THIRTY-ONE

F. HAD NO PROBLEM EITHER. Things were going exactly to plan. He peered at Scott Dean, who lay sprawled out in the office chair. His eyes were open, staring straight ahead.

F. unbuttoned the left arm of Scott's shirt with his gloved hand. He rolled it up, stopping when he almost reached the paralyzed man's shoulder. Letting the arm fall, F. leaned forward and whispered into Scott's ear. "Hey buddy, I know you can hear me, so let me tell you what's happening. The whiskey was laced with Georgia's Homeboy, GHB. And you know what that does."

Moving away and bending down, F. pulled out a roll of paper towels and an empty plastic bag from his backpack. He ripped off a sheet of paper and mopped up a small pool of spilled whiskey from the desktop. Unzipping the plastic bag, he pushed the sodden paper into it and added the empty tumbler that had fallen onto the carpet. Sealing the container, he dropped it and the roll of paper towels back into the rucksack.

Next, he opened a pouch on the side of the pack and pulled out a second plastic bag filled with white power, along with a metal tablespoon and a syringe. He placed these on the desk before returning to the backpack and taking out a small water bottle. He put this on the desk, too, before removing a lighter from his pocket. Satisfied that everything he needed was in place, F. unzipped the plastic bag containing the white powder. He tipped the drug onto the spoon and then poured a few drops of the bottled water on top. Picking up the lighter, he flicked the wheel, igniting the gas. Carefully lifting the spoon, F. held the flame under the coke and water and watched as the mixture fused. Then he placed the spoon and the lighter onto the desk and grabbed the syringe. He held the needle over the spoon and pulled back the plunger. The heated mixture filled the needle barrel. Holding the syringe with his gloved hands, F. moved around to the back of the desk. He lifted Scott's exposed left arm, jammed the needle in, pressing the plunger down. Scott's body shook, and his eyes closed.

"Sweet dreams," F. said quietly, pulling the needle out. Then he leaned over the comatosed man, reached for his right hand, lifted it and spread the thumb and index finger apart. He placed the needle between them and squeezed. Releasing the hand, F. watched as the syringe fell onto the floor. Moving around to the front of the desk, F. picked up the spoon and studied the position of Scott's slumped body before placing the bag containing the remaining traces of the coke and spoon carefully just in front and to the right of the man.

His work complete, F. took a step back to study the tableau. Yes, that all worked. He lifted the pack up and slung it onto his back. Time to go.

"Bye, buddy," F. said, turning to leave. Murdering Scott had proved both satisfying and surprisingly easy.

ONE MILE AWAY ELLIE DIPPED THE WOODEN SPOON into the tomato sauce, lifted it, and sipped the liquid. It had thickened up well but didn't quite have the flavor she had hoped for. She reached for the saltshaker, held it over the steel saucepan, and turned the grinder. The large white flakes dropped into the red stew. She stirred and tasted the tomato pasta mixture. *Better.*

Her cell rang. Picking it up, she listened for a moment. "Good," she said, her voice giving no indication of the elevation she felt with the news. Clicking off the phone, she returned to the cooking.

Ellie had spent time deciding what to cook for Ryan. She didn't want to make a dietary blunder. Ellie hadn't asked but knew Indians were often vegetarians. She had finally plumped for the spaghetti dish with no meat in it.

Ellie glanced at her watch. The first test of any man was whether he was punctual. Fifteen minutes to go. Should she trust that he would turn up on time and start cooking the spaghetti now, or should she wait? Ellie opted for a compromise. She opened a kitchen cabinet and pulled out another steel pan. Ellie filled it half full of water before sprinkling in a generous helping of salt. Then she placed the pan on the stove and turned the burner on. Ellie gave the sauce one more stir before lowering the heat a notch. Rubbing her hands over her apron, she stepped out of the kitchen. Time to put her warpaint on.

KATE TURNED THE KEY AND PUSHED open Scott Dean's front door. She had been on a double shift, but luckily her replacement Chris had arrived early to relieve her. She was exhausted. One barmaid or barman per shift wasn't enough. And tonight, Johnny wasn't around to help either. It was as if he had lost interest in the pub.

Kate's footsteps echoed on the wooden boards as she strode down the hall. Her head was still buzzing with what Scott had told her before she had left for work. After he had spoken, it was as if a huge weight had been lifted off him. Scott had sworn Kate to secrecy, but she wasn't sure she could keep the revelation to herself.

Reaching the living room, she looked around. Scott wasn't there, but she could see the light spilling out from under the study door. Kate hesitated. Scott never worked this late. Perhaps he had forgotten to turn the study light off.

"Scott," Kate shouted as she walked across the dirty purple carpet to the study door. She knocked on the door. "You there?" There was no reply. She grasped the brass handle and turned it to the right. Pushing the door open, she took a step into the room, stopped, and stared. She screamed. Her loud blood wrenching cry echoed around the house.

AT THAT EXACT MOMENT, RYAN PUSHED OPEN Ellie's apartment's entrance door and stepped into the marbled lobby, a bottle of red wine in hand. He strode across the glossy polished tiles to the elevator and pressed the button. A bell dinged, and the lift door opened. He stepped in.

The elevator control pad could have been designed by NASA. Ryan found the four-floor button and pressed it. A hushed women's voice sang out: "Going up." Then, as the elevator rose, figures on the monitor indicating time, speed, and floor appeared in circles on the monitor.

Ryan straightened his tie and ran his hands over the lapels of his blue suit, careful to brush away any stray traces of dandruff. It never made a good impression to arrive looking as if you had just been in a snowstorm.

The elevator bell dinged. "You have arrived. Good luck," the elevator voice said.

Good luck! Why? Because he had made it in one piece? Mystifying. Ryan exited and headed down the corridor. Reaching Ellie's door, the detective took a deep breath and pressed the bell. The door swung open almost immediately.

Ryan tried not to stare. Ellie looked sensational. Her long blonde hair cascaded over her shoulders, flowing over the top of a beige blouse that was cut to reveal a hint of cleavage. The tanned skin around her neck was broken by two gold chains intertwined with a set of gold medallions. A wide ivory-colored leather belt wrapped around the bottom of the shirt, and below this, a pair of taupe-colored trousers hugged tight to her long legs. The ensemble was completed with flesh-colored high heels.

"You look . . . good," Ryan stuttered.

"You too," Ellie said smiling and leaned forward to kiss him on both cheeks. "Come on in."

The detective entered the apartment, and Ellie closed the door behind him. "Is that for me?" she said, pointing to the bottle of wine.

He nodded and handed it to Ellie before following her down the hallway into the living room.

He took a deep breath as he entered. "Something smells good."

"Oh, it's just a little soupçon I slung together. Please. Take a seat."

He sat down on the sofa next to a slumbering Attila.

"Now tell me about your day," Ellie asked.

Ryan was about to reply when his cell rang. "Yes," he said, answering it. It was Zoe.

"I'm sorry to disturb you, but there's been another incident," the constable said.

"I'll finish up," Ellie mouthed and headed back to the kitchen.

"An incident?" Ryan asked.

"A drug death," Zoe said.

From the coke, the detective instantly thought. *Shit.* They had to find the source quickly. "Who?" he asked.

"A man called Scott Dean."

"Scott? The only Scott, the detective, knew of in this town was the one he'd seen at the Narcotics Anonymous meeting. It couldn't be the same person, could it? "Text me the address, and I'll come straight over," he said and stood up.

"You're leaving?" Ellie said, hurrying back from the kitchen. "Sorry, I couldn't help but overhear."

"Yes. I'm really sorry, but something urgent has just come up." The disappointment etched on Ellie's face said it all.

THIRTY-TWO

DETECTIVE RYAN, CONSTABLE YANG, AND KATE CASSELS stood by the study door, looking across at Scott Dean. He was slumped on the desk, his head down, wedged between the piles of paper. The detective had immediately recognized the man. It was the same Scott he had seen just a few hours ago at the Narcotics Anonymous meeting. Back then, of course, he had been very much alive.

Ryan pulled down his white gloves, so they fitted snuggly on both hands. He had already slipped on overshoes outside. The detective had been pleased to see Zoe had put on gloves and shoe coverings too. She was learning fast.

"This is how you found him?" Ryan asked Kate.

"Yes." She paused. "I came in, saw him, and screamed. Then I called the police."

"That's all you did?"

"Yes."

"This was where you were standing?"

"Yes."

"So, why did you scream?" the detective asked.

Kate shook her head. The man was obviously dumb. "Why do you think?"

Ryan turned his gaze to Scott. "Well, from here, all I see is a man wearing a dirty blue sweatshirt, with his head resting on the desk. He could have been asleep."

"Oh. I see. You would make a good actor the way you think things through," Kate said.

The detective ignored the comment. "Please answer the question."

"Screaming was a reflex action. After that, I walked over to the desk and saw all the drug stuff and thought that maybe Scott was just nodding."

"You knew that was drug paraphernalia?"

Kate stared at the detective. "Are you're trying to trick me?"

"What?"

"Because I know about that stuff." She pointed at the spoon, lighter, and coke bag on the desk. "You think that because I know about it, I maybe had something to do with Scott's death. Perhaps I was taking drugs with him?"

"It's a possibility."

"No, it's not," Kate said indignantly. "I would never push a needle into my arm."

The detective said nothing.

"Oh, for god's sake. I was on a double shift at the pub today and only got back here at around ten."

"OK. Well, let's return to the living room. There are more questions I need to ask you, and we'll be more comfortable there."

Kate rolled her eyes. "Must we?"

"It won't take long, and it's always best to get these things done before people start to forget," the detective said.

They filed out of the study. Kate slumped onto the living room's dirty brown sofa while the detective and Zoe sat on the shabby armchairs opposite.

"Before we start, I want Constable Yang to record our conversation if that's all right?" Ryan said.

"Yeah. That's fine."

Zoe produced her iPhone, placing it on an old rickety coffee table. She pressed the screen and nodded to Ryan. "Interview with Kate Cassels with Detective Ramesh Ryan and Constable Zoe Yang," he began before giving the date, time, and location. "Ready?" he asked as he finished.

"Yes."

"After you entered the study, when did you decide that Scott Dean was definitely dead, Kate?"

"When I checked his pulse."

"You know how to do that?" the detective asked.

"I learned it when I played a nurse. If I take on a role, I think it's essential to become the character. I'm a method actor, detective, and . . ."

"And how long ago did you find Scott dead?" Ryan asked, interrupting.

"About forty-five minutes ago. Then I called the police and the constable, and you arrived."

"And you live here?" the detective queried.

"I have a room upstairs. Scott offered it to me for a reasonable rent a couple of years ago. Of course, it would have been easier if Johnny . . ." Kate pulled a face, ". . . well if Johnny had let me rent one of his spare rooms. I mean, that would have been simpler, but he wanted top dollar. He's the meanest man I've ever met. There was one time . . ."

"Right," the detective said quickly. "So why did you go into the study?"

"What?"

"You said you had just done a double shift?"

"Yes."

"So you must have been tired. Why not go straight to bed?" Ryan asked.

"Well, I saw the light was on, and that was pretty unusual at that time of night," Kate said.

"But it wasn't that late?"

"No, but Scott's become more and more depressed recently and taken to going to bed early. So I didn't expect him to be up and went into the study to check."

"Check on what?" the detective asked.

"I don't know. Just to see what Scott was up to." She paused.

"Go on," Ryan said.

"I was worried about him."

"Why?"

"Because of his depression."

"Would you consider Scott Dean, a good friend?" the detective asked.

"No. I mean, don't get me wrong. I like . . . liked Scott. And I did care about him. But he is . . . was a difficult man to get close to." She sniffled and wiped her eyes with the back of her hand.

Ryan watched, not saying anything. Then: "Do you know of any friends or relatives that should be informed of his death?"

"I know his parents are dead. They left him this place. And he never mentioned any other relatives. He was a bit of a loner." She paused. "There is Brad, of course."

"Brad?" the detective said.

"Brad Costello."

"Who's he?"

"He's Scott's friend."

Ryan listened to the way Kate pronounced friend. There was an aggressiveness in her tone.

"Friend?"

"He and Scott had a fling, but that seems to have run out of steam."

"How long did this fling last?"

"A few months."

"How did they meet?" he asked.

"He came around pretending to be a gardener."

"Pretending?"

"If you look at the state of the garden, you'll know what I mean. I think Brad targets lonely gay men like Scott and lives off them. But Scott got wise to him, and anyway, I think the lust had gone. I think now they only saw each other occasionally, mainly at Narcotics Anonymous."

"You know about Scott attending the meetings?" Ryan asked.

"Yeah. He was open about his drug-taking. But I thought all that was behind him." She paused. "Obviously not, though."

"And Brad Costello?" the detective said.

"I think he went to the meetings to keep Scott company. He was no druggie. I'll give him that."

"Do you know where Brad Costello lives?" asked Ryan, now remembering the good-looking young man that had exchanged glances with Scott at the Narcotics Anonymous meeting.

"I don't think so . . . Oh wait."

She reached into her pocket, pulled out her phone, and scrolled through her contacts. "Scott did give me Brad's address once."

"Why did he do that?" the detective asked.

"It was when Scott first met him. I think he was proud that he had a handsome young boyfriend, even one as manipulative and mercenary as

Brad. I think Scott wanted to give me the information to prove that he and Brad were close."

"So, did Brad Costello move in here?"

"No way. There was part of Scott that was totally innocent, romantic, and susceptible, and another much tougher part. He was always very aware of gold diggers like Brad . . . Ah, here it is."

The constable stood up and took Kate's phone, and sent the contact to herself.

"I think that will do for now," Detective Ryan said. "Interview over at 23:15," he said.

"So, can I go to bed now?" Kate asked, standing and yawning.

"You can't stay here," the detective said, "at least not for a day or so. Not until we've checked everything out."

"But I have nowhere else to go."

"Nowhere?"

"Nope—except, well, it's off season, so Johnny has plenty of empty rooms at the pub, but . . ."

"Constable, can you ask him?" Ryan said interrupting.

Zoe nodded. "Of course. What do you think, Kate?"

She smiled. "Yeah, that would be good. It would be more likely to get a result."

"That's settled then. Go get yourself a change of clothes," the detective said.

"I'll only be a few minutes," Kate said, heading for the stairs.

The cops watched her go. "There's no need to tell Johnny Wilson what's happened, Zoe. Invent some story about Kate needing to move because of a small fire in her room or something. And tell her not to blab about Scott Dean's death either."

"OK," Zoe said, standing.

"When are the pathologist and forensics team due to arrive?"

"Soon. I called them after I called you. I don't think Doctor Norman's seen so many deaths in Barton in such a short time." Zoe paused. "Nor have I, as a matter of fact. The Sarge is going to blow a fuse."

"You think?"

"I know. Do you want me to come back after I've dropped off Kate?"

"No. I can take it from here. See you in the office tomorrow," Ryan said.

Zoe hesitated. She was keen to hear Ryan's take on Scott Dean's death. "It seems a pretty open and shut case, don't you think? "she said. "The guy was a known drug addict."

"I'm ready," Kate shouted as she ran down the stairs carrying a small weekender case.

Ryan held out his hand. "House keys, please, Kate."

The woman frowned. "But . . ."

"You'll get them back. I just don't want anyone wandering in and out at the moment."

"Right." She reached into her pocket and dropped the keys into the detective's hand.

"Thanks. And do you know where Scott kept his set?"

"I'm not sure. Can I go now?"

"Yeah."

The detective watched the two women go before returning to the study.

WHEN RYAN HAD FIRST JOINED THE POLICE, he'd hated the idea of being alone in a room with a cadaver. But he had soon realized that if he was ever to follow in the footsteps of the great detectives, he had to accept death, learn from it, and enjoy its presence. The bodies he saw now were usually people to whom the Grim Reaper had come suddenly and unexpectedly. Their contorted limbs, twisted bodies, and screwed-up faces were silent witnesses to how they had met their final end.

The detective carefully avoided the piles of paper cluttering the floor and squeezed behind the desk. He stared at the remnants of the heated drug that remained on the spoon. A small clear plastic bag with traces of white powder inside lay close by, and a lighter was lined up next to it. The syringe was on the floor, presumably having dropped from Scott's hands. His death did appear to be an open and shut case—an accidental overdose or maybe even suicide.

Ryan moved back around to the front of the desk to re-examine the scene, studying it carefully. The front doorbell rang once and then several times more. Forensics?

THIRTY-THREE

THERE WERE FOUR OF THEM OUTSIDE Scott Dean's front door, all dressed in blue cloth helmeted coveralls, blue shoe covers, white face masks, and tight white gloves. Ryan recognized the pathologist Doctor Jen Norman and the photographer Benny McNeil, but not the other two. From what little he could see of their faces, they appeared to be identical twins.

"Everyone come in. Please follow me. The body's in the study," Detective Ryan said.

"You're sure keeping us busy," Doctor Norman said as she walked by the detective's side, "Two deaths in Barton in the last few days, along with a washed-up foot. Sergeant Acton will not be pleased."

"So, I've been told," the detective said as they all entered the study.

"Before we get started, I realized I haven't officially introduced everyone, detective. Benny, you already know," Doctor Norman said. "The photographer nodded to Ryan. "And the ladies are Fiona Gardner and Annette Banks. Before you ask, yes, they are identical twins."

The women smiled at Ryan, their eyes sparkling. "Lovely to meet you, detective," one of them said. "I'm Fiona."

"And I'm Annette," said the other.

Doctor Norman clapped her hands. "Shall we?" The group began to unpack their tools. Like any experienced team, few words were exchanged. Each knew what they had to do. Benny MacNeil took pictures, and the twins began dusting items for fingerprints. Meantime the pathologist put her hands on either side of Scott's head and lifted it.

"TOD?" asked Ryan, staring at the man's face, which had already taken on a ghastly greenish tinge.

"You don't honestly expect me to answer that question, now do you?" the doctor replied.

"It was worth a try."

"Detective, since this is a small, junk-filled room, I would appreciate . . ."

"Just going," Ryan said, raising his hand. "One last question. When will you have the preliminary findings?"

"Tomorrow, possibly. I'll let you know," Doctor Norman said.

"The tox report needs to be completed tonight."

"What? No way. Not with the amount of work you've generated."

"It has to be done," the detective insisted.

Doctor Norman peered at him quizzically. "What aren't you telling me?" She waited.

"It's just a hunch," Ryan said.

"Oh, I see. One of those famous detective's hunches. I'm sorry, that hunch business won't fly. You need to be more specific."

"If I did, it could influence the result. But I really would appreciate it if you could get the preliminaries done overnight."

Doctor Norman screwed her face up. "I don't know, detective. I'll try, but I can't make any promises."

Ryan smiled. "Thanks. Do your best." The detective pulled open the study door. It was time to leave. Hopefully, he would know by tomorrow if the coke was from the same source as the drug that had killed Liam Plummer.

Ryan turned back as a thought occurred to him. "By the way, any news yet on the foot?"

Doctor Norman shook her head. "What do you think I am, a miracle worker?"

"Of course, but . . ."

"You had to ask?"

"Right," said Ryan smiling. "Goodnight."

He walked out of the room, closing the door quietly behind him. There was always a struggle between a pathologist and a detective. The detective wants forensics to come up with results quickly. But a pathologist who buckled under the pressure would often produce a shoddy report. Stubbornness was a plus rather than a minus in the close-knit world of medical examiners.

THE DETECTIVE OPENED THE FRONT DOOR and stepped out. The east wind whipped across his face as he walked down the gravel path. Unfastening the metal gate, he felt drops of rain on his face. The storm had passed, but its remnants remained.

Ryan turned left out of the gate and headed to his car. The dead man's house was one of the few double-story houses on the street. Most homes were old-fashioned, one-floor fifties-style bungalows, probably bought years ago and now worth a lot of money.

The detective unlocked the car door, climbed in, and clicked on his seat belt. The sound of the engine turning over broke the silence of the street. Ryan released the hand brake and headed off.

THIRTY-FOUR

The following day the wispy-white morning clouds tracked slowly over the blue sky while the sun's warm orange rays bounced over the back of Ryan's jacket as he pushed the key into Scott Dean's front door. Opening it, the detective strode down the hallway, into the living room, and across to the study. Blue police tape stretched out across the room's half-opened door, blocking the entrance. Ryan ducked under it and entered. Scott Dean's body had been removed, along with the drug equipment and the coke baggie. A thin layer of white fingerprinting dust had settled over the desk. Everything else remained untouched.

The detective had woken up keen to get to work but first had taken his early morning exercise. Splashing through the glistening pools of water and the soft, moist sand was so much more fun than pounding the uneven, cracked pavements of Potts Point. The run also held out the tantalizing prospect of bumping into Ellie and Attila on their morning walk. But there was no sign of the woman, and Ryan decided that was probably just as well. He didn't need distractions today.

Looking around the study, Ryan readied himself. It was time to get to it.

Sergeant Gary Acton knew he should get down to work too but was finding it hard. He couldn't take his eyes off the big whiteboard. Until a few days ago, it contained nothing but a reminder about his dry cleaning. How things had changed. Now it was filled with photos of dead men and drug dealers. Zoe was just pinning up a picture of Scott Dean, and that was upsetting. The Sarge had known Scott for years. Though they had never been close, they had gone to the same school.

"Do you have to put that there Zoe?" he asked.

The constable, her black marker pen in hand, was just about to write out Scott Dean's name and the date of his death below the photo. "Sorry, Ryan told me to do it."

"I guess you must then." The Sarge was beginning to wish he'd never heard the name Ramesh Ryan. So much had changed since his arrival, coinciding as it did with a sudden and inexplicable spike in carnage rates. Of course, the Sarge couldn't really blame Detective Ryan for the spate of recent premature deaths. It wasn't his fault that Liam Plummer and Scott had died violently only days apart, nor that the foot of an unknown man had suddenly washed up on Barton's beach. And yet—it did still seem to be one heck of a coincidence.

"Where is the great man anyway this morning?" The Sarge asked.

"Taking another look around Scott's place," Zoe said, continuing to write on the board.

"But I thought you said it was an open and shut case. The poor guy just overdosed."

"That's what I think, but Ryan's the detective, and maybe he has other ideas."

Other ideas! Jeez, the Sarge thought. He really wished things would return to normal. Usually, nothing much ever happened in Barton, and that was the way he liked it. Clearly, that wasn't the case for Zoe, though. Today she was positively glowing.

Sergeant Acton had always known that the constable was ambitious and wouldn't want to stick around for long. And now that the town had become death central, that ambition had become ever more apparent. Of course, he had bought this on himself by opening his big mouth and asking for a detective. What was he thinking?

The Sarge turned to glance over at Jackie. She was busy typing up Kate Cassel's interview. Jackie had already proved to be a real asset in clearing the backlog of filing and paperwork. The woman looked over at the policeman and smiled.

"I knew Scott's mom, you know," Jackie said.

The policeman ignored her, but Zoe took the bait. "You did?"

"Yes. She was such a nice woman. Dead now, of course," Jackie said, returning to her typing. Zoe frowned. She had hoped for more—perhaps some gem that she could pass on to the detective? But what she heard was another of Jackie's famous non-sequiturs. The constable glanced across at the large, white-faced clock on the far wall. Detective Ryan had been explicit when he had phoned her this morning. She was to collect Brad Costello from his home and ferry him around to Scott Dean's home by eleven. But on no account was she to mention to Costello anything about Scott's death.

She would set off for Costello in half an hour.

RYAN CHECKED HIS WATCH. He had still heard nothing from Doctor Norman. The detective had thought about calling her but knew that would be a waste of time and might annoy her . . . and he needed the pathologist working with him, not against him.

The detective grasped the rusty handle and pulled the back door open. He stepped out on the concrete path and peered out at the tangled mass of overgrown bushes, shrubs, and trees. Scott may have secured his front door, but there was no such security at the back of the property.

The detective stepped back into the kitchen and peered at the calendar stuck to the battered fridge door. Its presence suggested some sort of order, which was odd considering all the chaos in the house—the piles of papers, the cardboard boxes, and the other flotsam and jetsam. There was obviously a small part of the late Scott Dean's mind that had occasionally strived for structure.

Ryan knew about hoarders. As a child, he had lived close by an old woman who had the disease. The first time he'd entered her home, tempted by an offer of candies, he had been astonished by the great mounds of 'stuff' that filled the place. His mother had gone crazy on hearing where he'd been and banned him from going there ever again. But Ryan liked the woman. He had ignored his mom and visited her regularly, happy to accept the candies on offer. Like her, Scott Dean had almost certainly had an obsessive-compulsive personality disorder. It was the most common illness associated with hoarding and often was accompanied by depression—something Scott seemed to have had in spades.

The weekly Narcotics Anonymous meetings were marked up on the fridge calendar. The letter F was written in another space for last Wednesday. There were several other markings for F. Maybe it was a reminder to Scott to buy more food? He opened the fridge door, gagging with the smell. If this was the case, the dead man hadn't followed through. His fridge was empty except for a rancid carton of milk and an unopened vacuum-packed bag of ground coffee. Closing the door and taking out his phone, Ryan took photos of the calendar pages. He was a stickler for recording anything he couldn't adequately explain.

Ryan had spent the previous hour exploring the large house and eventually discovered the two items he had been looking for—Scott's iPhone and his laptop. Neither had been particularly easy to find. The phone was in the study, hidden under a pile of papers. The computer lay under Scott's bed, rammed between two overflowing cardboard boxes. Both devices were locked, so they were currently useless to him.

The front doorbell rang. Ryan headed back into the living room and down the hallway. He opened the door to discover Zoe and a tall, handsome young man outside.

THIRTY-FIVE

"**B**RAD COSTELLO," ZOE SAID BY WAY of explanation.

Ryan nodded. "Yes, we've met. Come in," he said. The pair stepped into the hallway.

"So you were at . . ." Costello said and stopped, presumably remembering that Narcotic Anonymous meetings were supposed to be just that—anonymous.

"Yes, Mr. Costello, I saw you there. Detective Ryan," Ryan said, offering his hand. "Thanks for coming."

"Mr. Costello can't stay long," Zoe said as Ryan closed the front door.

"I've got a gardening client this morning," Costello explained as they set off down the hall and headed for the living room. "What's this all about anyway. Constable Yang wouldn't tell me anything except that you wanted to see me on an urgent matter. Coming from a police officer, that was an offer I couldn't refuse," he said, grinning.

Ryan didn't reply. Instead, on entering the dining room, he indicated the sofa. "Take a seat."

Costello remained standing, scanning the room. "What's that for? Has there been a burglary here or something?" he said, his eyes alighting on the police tape.

"Please sit down," Ryan repeated.

Costello ignored the detective. "Scott, Scott, are you there?" He shouted.

"Mr. Costello. Please. A seat."

Costello finally sat down on the couch.

"I'm afraid that Mr. Dean . . . Scott . . . is dead," Detective Ryan said.

Zoe stared at the detective. What was he thinking? There were better ways, more sympathetic ways, to break the news?

"Dead," Costello said, his face whitening. "No, that's not possible."

"I'm afraid it's true," the detective said.

Costello burst into tears. Zoe bent down and put her arm around him to comfort him.

"How? How did it happen?" he asked through the veil of tears.

Ryan had been studying the man from the moment he'd entered the house. Bringing a suspect to a dead man's house was unusual, but it was a technique the detective had used before. Guilty people often give themselves away when they are faced with the results of their actions. They do it with a subtle eye movement, or some other form of body language, as they struggle to pretend that they know nothing. But Costello had asked the question so many forget if they have foreknowledge of death—How? And at that moment, the detective decided that Brad Costello was innocent of any involvement in Scott Dean's death.

"I'm not at liberty to tell you that at this time," the detective said. "All I can say is that he died last night."

Costello flicked his gaze from the detective to the constable.

"Drugs? Was it because of drugs?" He waited.

The cops said nothing.

"I know he was depressed, but . . ." His voice trailed off as he thought about this.

"Mr. Costello, we need to interview you," Detective Ryan said.

"You do? Why?"

"It's standard procedure for anyone close to a person who suddenly dies."

"It is?" Costello said.

Ryan nodded.

"In that case, fine, go ahead."

"Do you mind if the constable takes notes and we record the conversation, Mr. Costello?" Ryan asked.

"Why?"

"Standard procedure again."

"OK," he said, resigned.

Zoe took her arm off Costello's shoulder, stood up, and produced her phone. She placed it on the coffee table before sitting in an armchair opposite a pad in hand. Ryan took a seat too.

"Interview with Brad Costello," Detective Ryan began, giving the usual details before asking his first question. "How long did you know Scott Dean?"

Costello lifted his hand and ran it through his long hair before brushing it off his handsome face. "Around a year. We were in love, you know." He smiled wistfully. "We met when I knocked on his door looking for work."

"What sort of work?"

"I'm a landscaper, and his garden was crying out for help."

"And he agreed to hire you."

Costello smiled. "Yes. Just on a casual basis. To get things tidied up a little."

"Which you did?" the detective asked.

"At first, yes. But it was obvious that Scott . . . well, you know."

"Know what?"

"Scott and I had an instant attraction." He stopped. "I can't believe he's dead." He started to cry again.

Ryan waited. Then: "You mentioned that you knew he was depressed. Do you know why?"

"Why does anyone get depressed?" Costello said. "I'm not a psychologist—or is that psychiatrist? Whatever. Anyway, he never talked about a reason. All I know is that when he met me . . ." He paused for a long moment to think about it, a smile breaking on his face. "I think I stopped his depression—for a while anyway."

"But you and Scott drifted apart?"

"What? Who told you that?" Costello asked.

"Kate Cassels."

"She said that? When?"

"Last night. She was the one who found Scott," the detective replied.

"So, even when she discovered he was dead, she still had time to bitch about me. That woman is a piece of work."

"Is what Kate Cassels said true?" Ryan inquired.

"Of course not. She's just a jealous bitch. I wouldn't trust anything coming from her. She was afraid Scott would ask me to live with him, and she would be thrown out. Which she would have been the moment I moved in."

"But Scott didn't ask you to come to live here?"

"No. But he was going to. I'm sure of it. Like I said, we are . . . were . . . in love."

He started to tear up again. "So what's going to happen to him . . . his body . . . now? Can I see him?"

"He will be buried after we complete the autopsy," the detective said.

"Autopsy?"

"Again, standard procedure for a sudden death." Ryan paused. "Did Scott have any living relatives?"

"Not that I know of. His mom and dad both died years ago, and he had no brothers or sisters."

Costello suddenly stood up. "Look, can I go now? I really feel shattered."

"Of course."

"Interview ended," the constable said into the iPhone. Then she scooped the cell back into her pocket.

"Constable, can you take Mr. Costello home?

"No problem. Shall we?" The constable walked to the door. Costello followed.

"One more question," Ryan said. Costello stopped. "Do you know the passwords for either Scott's iPhone or his computer?"

"What? No. Of course not." He frowned. "Why would you want those?"

"Standard procedure again," the detective said. Zoe glanced at him. There was no part of the standard procedure that explained that question.

"Thanks for your help," Ryan said. "It's much appreciated."

Costello nodded and followed the constable up the hallway and out of the house.

THIRTY-SIX

F.'s BLACK SUV WAS HIDDEN BETWEEN a large white truck and a sedan, but he could still see Scott Dean's house. He watched as the uniformed cop and Brad Costello came out, got into the marked police car, and drove off.

F. had planned to just drive by and check the scene out. Then he had seen the detective's car parked outside. That's when he'd pulled up. Why was he here now? Maybe he was just being thorough and looking around the house for one last time. That made sense. But if that was the case, why had the uniformed cop turned up with Costello? Of course, everyone knew Brad and Scott were having an affair. Perhaps the detective thought Costello had something to do with Scott's death? He smiled. Oh yeah, that would be it. He was worrying for no reason.

F. turned the ignition key, and as he did, his cell pinged. F. was someone who had to check out anything new on his phone immediately. Picking the device up from the center console, he peered at the screen. There was a text. *"I know why you did it and have the proof. Await further instructions about payment."*

What the hell did that mean? He typed back quickly. *"Who are you?"* and pressed send. The message disappeared and then reappeared with the words: *"Service no longer available."* Then he tried calling. He got the Service Discontinued message.

Whoever had sent the text had either used a burner phone or posted the text through an app specializing in transmitting anonymous messages. Either way, it wasn't likely that he would ever be able to find the sender.

F. spun around. Was there someone watching him? He couldn't see anyone. Could someone have seen him last night at Scott's? No. Not possible. He had been thorough. He had checked. So what was this all about? He typed a number into the keyboard, put the phone to his ear, and waited.

"Bean. We have a problem," F. said into the phone.

"What kind of problem?"

"Not on the cell. Meet me in one hour. The usual place."

"OK."

F. dropped the phone back into the console, turned the car wheel, and moved his foot from the brake to the accelerator.

AT THAT VERY MOMENT, RYAN CLOSED THE FRONT DOOR and walked up the narrow pathway. He was holding two plastic evidence bags containing Scott's iPhone and laptop. As the detective opened the front gate, a black SUV drove past. The detective didn't notice the vehicle. He was too deep in thought. Doctor Norman had just called. She said she had the preliminary tox and autopsy results but needed to go into the details with him personally. Could the detective come down to Gosford? "Of course. No problem," Ryan had said. "And can you also arrange for an IT person to be there when I see you?"

Doctor Norman hadn't asked the detective why. She already knew the answer.

Ryan unlocked his car, climbed in, and carefully placed the evidence bags on the floor. He hesitated before starting the vehicle up. The detective had a decision to make. Should he call Zoe? Ryan took his phone out of his jacket pocket and dialed the constable's cell.

"Yes," she said.

"It's Ryan. Have you dropped Costello off yet?"

"Just now."

"And did he say anything else about Scott Dean?"

"No. He was pretty shook up."

Silence.

"Ryan? You still there."

"Sorry. Can you meet me at the pathologist's lab in Gosford?"

"Doctor Norman's completed her report?"

"Yes."

"OK, see you there," Zoe said.

THIRTY-SEVEN

WHEN THE DETECTIVE ARRIVED AT THE MORTUARY, the IT man was already waiting. "The name's Cyrus Woods. And you are Detective Ryan, right?" he said the moment Ryan entered the lab.

Cyrus Woods was no malnourished, pale-faced adolescent—the usual caricature of a computer geek. Standing well over six feet and in his mid-twenties, he was big and beefy with a mop of curly ginger hair that poked down from under a black baseball hat. For a cop, Woods was more than casually dressed. He wore a blue denim jacket over an open-necked red and black checkered shirt, black trousers, and blue Nike sneakers.

"Just to confirm. You are Gosford's resident computer expert?" Ryan asked.

"Yes. Of course." He stopped. "I know I don't look much like a cop, and even less like someone who knows something about computers but—how does that old saying go—don't judge a book by its cover?"

"Well can you open these?" Ryan said, offering Woods the evidence bags containing Scott Dean's laptop and phone.

"I take it you don't have the passwords?"

"Nope."

"Whose are they?"

Ryan looked across at Scott's body that lay naked, sprawled out on the stainless steel table in the center of the room. "His."

"So I'm guessing he's not going to help us much?"

The door opened, and Zoe came in. "Sorry, I'm late." She stopped as she noticed Cyrus Woods. He was staring at her.

"Can I help you?" she asked.

Woods reddened. He may not have looked like a geek, but he certainly acted like a geek around a pretty woman.

"This is Cyrus Woods, Constable Yang. Our technical whizz," Doctor Norman said quickly.

"Good to meet you." Zoe offered her hand.

The IT man shook it. "I'm sorry about staring, but . . ."

"Yeah. Whatever. Can we get on with this, please?" Ryan interjected.

"No problem," Woods said, regaining his composure. "The thing is, Apple has made it difficult to open these machines without a password. But it's not impossible. It depends to a certain extent on how diligent your dead man was about uploading the updates. And it would help too if I knew a few basics like the man's full name, his birth date, the school he went to, the area he lived in—those sorts of things. You'll be surprised how often people use basic and easily available information for their pass-words. Only a few weeks ago . . ."

Ryan held up his hand quickly. "We'll get those to you. How long will this take?"

"I don't know. A day or so."

"And if you can't do it?"

"Then I'll have to go direct to Apple for help. That usually takes weeks, but I may be able to hurry them along." He stopped. "Anything else?"

"No," the detective said.

Woods went to pick up the evidence bags.

"The computer and iPhone will need to be dusted first," Ryan said.

"Of course. Doctor Norman?" Woods asked.

"I'll organize it and get them up to you."

"Fine. I'll be back in touch," Woods said, leaving the room.

"I'll dig up that information he asked for if that's alright?" Zoe asked Ryan.

"Go ahead." The detective turned his attention back to Doctor Norman. "So?"

"Let me show you." The pathologist went to Scott Dean's body and pointed at his left arm. "See, there. That's the puncture mark where the needle was injected. Soon after, his heart would have started to race, and he would have begun to sweat and hallucinate. Then oxygen starvation occurred, which would have stopped other vital organs like the heart and the brain. At that point, even if someone had somehow managed to get his heart started again, he would still have been a vegetable. Brain damage is irreversible."

"So an overdose. And the coke?" the detective asked.

"It was from the same batch as the stuff that killed Liam Plummer."

"That's what I suspected."

"But his death isn't that straightforward. I looked down this arm, his other arm—all over his body actually, and there were no other syringe puncture marks. Not one. Either old or new. Of course, that doesn't mean that he hadn't taken coke before. His body showed signs of damage because of past drug use. The blood vessels to his heart were over-dilated and weakened. This probably caused him chest pains and shortness of breath when he was alive. There was also lung and bowel damage associated with high coke usage. But he had snorted the drug rather than injected it."

"That doesn't rule out that he could have used a syringe just this once as an experiment," Zoe said.

"No, it doesn't. And the dusted prints in the preliminary forensic report all belonged to Scott Dean, no one else. However, finding Gamma-Hydroxybutyrate in his bloodstream suggests someone wanted to incapacitate him before sticking the needle in his arm."

"Gamma-Hydroxybutyrate?" asked Zoe.

"The date rape drug. It takes a short time to kick in, leaving the victim incapable of defending himself. And if Ryan hadn't insisted that we complete the tox examination overnight, we would probably have never found it. GHB is usually only traceable for around eight hours. So, that's a big tick for you, detective."

"And for you too, Doctor, for getting it done so fast. Where's the tox report?" Ryan asked.

Doctor Norman pointed to a small pile of binders on a metal side table. "Over there."

"Can I take a copy?" Ryan asked, walking over.

"Of course. But please remember these are only preliminary results."

"I understand." The detective picked up the file.

"So, WHAT DOES ALL THIS MEAN?" Zoe asked Ryan as they left the room.

"Now we know that Liam Plummer and Scott Dean used coke from the same batch but for different reasons," Ryan said. "I believe Liam Plummer chose to take the drug. His death was an accident. But Scott Dean only had one puncture mark on his body, so it's improbable he would have suddenly taken the drug by syringe. Someone used GHB to incapacitate the man, knowing that its traces would disappear quickly. Then coke was injected into Scott Dean's arms, and he overdosed."

"So?" Zoe asked.

"He was murdered."

THIRTY-EIGHT

FORTY MINUTES LATER, RYAN PULLED UP OUTSIDE Scott Dean's house. Zoe had already arrived and was waiting for him. Before they'd left Gosford, Ryan had explained to the constable that since they were now dealing with murder, they now had to scour the property for clues. The detective got out of his car and slipped on his protective gloves as Zoe walked over. She, too, had put gloves on. The officers headed down the path to the front door.

"How are we going to do this?" the policewoman asked as Ryan pushed the key into the lock and turned it.

"Together, room by room. We'll start in the study."

"How can anyone live like this?" the constable said as she followed the detective through to the living room, trying to avoid the piles of papers and garbage. "This is like an obstacle course. And the smell seems to have got worse. I don't know how Kate survived here."

"I think she spent most of her time in her room," the detective said.

"She could have cleaned up a bit."

"Scott wouldn't have let her. Hoarders don't want anyone touching their stuff." They reached the open study door and together unhitched the blue crime scene tape before entering the room.

"I'll look through everything on the desk and in the drawers if you go through the garbage on the floor," Ryan said.

The constable crouched down. The closer she got to it, the more pungent the smell. Finding anything here was going to be a daunting and unpleasant task.

"So, what exactly are we looking for?"

"Scott was targeted. Therefore, he was killed for a reason. Actually, one of four L reasons—Love, Lust, Location, or Loot. I'm not sure yet which applies here, but I do know that whoever killed him did their damnedest to make it look like an accident."

"And they had to have access to that batch of strong coke."

"Correct," Ryan said as he picked up a pile of papers from the table, brushing away the thin layer of fingerprint dust that had settled on them. "What we need are details that tell us more about Scott."

"Right." Zoe hesitated. "There's something I still don't understand. What made you think Scott had been murdered in the first place? You insisted that the body be checked overnight for poisons or toxins. Did you know they would find GHB?"

"No, of course not. I'm not that smart."

"But everything was set up to look like an overdose. Why did you think Scott hadn't just taken the drug himself and died?"

Ryan put down the sheet of paper he was holding. "Look around you. What do you see?"

"This is a trick question, right? Like the ones, they ask at the academy? What do I see? I see mess and garbage, and I smell a horrible stench from things that have probably been rotting for weeks."

"Yes, there's that. But there also isn't much order. The killer's problem was that they weren't a hoarder, so they didn't think like a hoarder. The whole drug paraphernalia, the syringe, the spoon, the baggie, and the lighter were neatly set out. That's just not how Scott would have done it. And now it's time to catch the bastard who killed him, so let's keep searching."

FOR THE NEXT SEVERAL HOURS, THE detective and the constable examined everything in the house carefully. It was dull, boring, and unpleasant. And it was hard for Zoe to resist the temptation to clean up as she went. But Ryan was clear. Leave everything as you found it, except anything that could be important or unusual, which they would bag. Despite this, when the constable did find a vacuum cleaner in the wardrobe in Scott's bedroom, she was tempted to start using it. She pointed at the cleaner. "Look at this."

The detective poked his head from under the bed. "A vacuum cleaner?"

"Yeah. And it looks fairly new. So someone at some time cared enough about tidying up to buy one." She went to grab the machine.

"Zoe!"

"I know. I know. No time to clean. Back to work! You're no fun detective, are you?"

Ryan wasn't sure how he could become a 'fun detective' or indeed if he wanted to be one, but the search certainly wasn't fun. There was one silver lining, though. Scott had only reached stage two of the hoarding process—the second level associated with the disease. The final level, level five, involved fire hazards, rotting food, and at least four too many pets. It was a godsend that Scott didn't have any animals. That would be beyond unbearable. But given twenty more years, Ryan had no doubt that he would have ascended to become a top-of-the-line hoarder.

By the end of the search, they had filled three boxes of potentially helpful material—a mix of old bills and bank statements as well as newspaper cuttings, diplomas, and photos. Ryan believed there wasn't necessarily a 'smoking gun' in any of it, but only further examination would confirm exactly what they had. That could be completed more comfortably at the station.

The cops carried the boxes outside, putting them into the trunk of Zoe's car.

"I'll follow you back," Ryan said, as his stomach rumbled noisily.

"Why don't we get some food first?" Zoe said, hearing the sound.

"Maybe that would be best."

THIRTY-NINE

IT WAS ONLY A SHORT DRIVE to Ma Jefferies Fish and Chip Parlor. As the officers settled at a table outside, a large middle-aged woman wearing a jaunty blue and white cardboard hat appeared from inside, handed them menus, and introduced herself as Ma Jefferies.

"Get you, folks, some water—still, sparkling, or tap?" she asked.

They opted for tap, and as the woman went to get it, they studied the menu. The usual suspects were there—battered fish and chips, salt n' pepper squid and chips, calamari, and fish cocktail.

"I know, I know," Zoe said, anticipating the detective's reactions. "This place is emptier than a banker's heart at the moment, but that means nothing. We're in Barton in the off season. And the menu doesn't look special but wait until you taste the fish. It's so fresh you'll swear it's still alive."

"There you go," Ma Jefferies said, returning with the carafe of water and glasses. She took their orders—two servings of the battered fish and chips.

Zoe lifted the carafe and poured water into the glasses. "You know more bodies are piling up than were around after the shoot-out in OK Corral. And it all started when you arrived."

"What are you saying? That I'm some sort of representative for the Grim Reaper?"

"Of course not. But it does seem strange."

Ryan lifted his glass and took a sip of the water. "I'm as surprised as you are. I thought this place would be dead." He smiled. "Sorry. Excuse the pun."

Zoe hesitated. Then: "I know you're the detective, and I'm just a lowly constable, but there's something I've been meaning to ask, and maybe it has to do with the deaths. Why are you here, really? And don't give me that BS about the Sarge asking for a detective."

"He did, and my Chief Inspector obliged."

"Two battered fish and chips," Ma Jefferies said, returning and offering them sets of cutlery wrapped in blue striped napkins, before placing the plates of steaming food down. "Enjoy," she commanded and left.

Neither Zoe nor Ryan said anything for the next few minutes. They were too busy eating. The fish was so fresh it crumpled in Ryan's mouth. The chips were thick and crinkly and cooked just the way the detective liked them.

"Good?" Zoe asked finally.

Ryan nodded enthusiastically. "Exactly like you said."

"So go on, tell me. Why are you really here?" Zoe said, leaning back in her chair.

Ryan pushed his empty plate to one side: "I messed up a court case, and Sydney's biggest drug dealer got away. After that, my boss decided it was best for my health to leave town for a while."

The detective raised his hand, signaling the server over. Ma Jefferies headed out. "The bill please?" Ryan said.

The woman nodded, and quickly scooped the plates up. The cops waited until she retreated back inside.

Then: "Your boss thought the guy could come after you? Is that likely? Those bastards are usually not that dumb as to come after a cop," Zoe asked.

"I'd been on the dealer's trail for a couple of years now. And my snooping cost him millions of dollars. He wouldn't have been happy about that." He turned to see Ma Jefferies approaching. She held a crockery plate with the bill in one hand and a credit card machine in the other.

Zoe reached into her pocket. The detective shook his head. "My shout," he said, scanning the bill and tapping his credit card over the machine.

"Great food. My compliments to the chef," Ryan said.

"Thanks," the woman said and walked away . . .

"This is one to put in my phone under Best Chippie," the detective said, standing. "Now, let's get back to the station."

Zoe stood up too. "No need both of us making the trip. I'll take the boxes in, and you go get yourself a shower. I'll see you tomorrow."

Ryan thought about that for a moment. It made sense.

"OK. Thanks."

"Thank you for the meal," Zoe said.

They headed for their cars, which were parked next to each other across the road.

"By the way, Ryan, you must come around for dinner with Louise and me," Zoe offered as she opened her vehicle door. "I cook a mean veal schnitzel."

"I may take you up on that," Ryan said as he pressed the remote on his key fob and heard his car door click open.

EIGHTY MILES AWAY, STACK PRESSED THE KEY BUTTON and locked the door of her orange Ford Mustang. She had just parked on the New South Head Road in Double Bay—an inner-city suburb that real estate agents like to call Sydney's "Little Europe. "

Micky adjusted his backpack as they waited for a gap in the traffic. Seeing one, they headed across the street to a four-level nondescript office block. The name "The Emporium" was stenciled in big letters across its glass entrance door. It was the place Tony had told them they would find Mott the Hoople—in a suite on the ground floor.

Entering the lobby, the pair circled around the empty reception desk and passed the elevator stack before reaching a corridor that ran along the back of the building. "Left or right?" Micky asked. Stack shrugged. She had no more idea than he did. And anyway, the whole place felt wrong. What kind of a drug dealer worked out of somewhere like this?

"Left then," Micky said decisively. They walked past white doors, numbered five, six, and seven before they reached the one with a small brass letter eight on it.

Micky gave Stack the thumbs up. "Told you it was left."

"So you did, smart ass," she said, knocking.

Silence.

Micky hammered. *Still there was silence.*

They looked at each other. Had Tony sold them a pup?

Stack went to knock again, just as the door opened to reveal a middle-aged man with thinning, mousey-colored combed-over hair, a fat face, and thick glasses.

"Can I help you?"

"We're looking for Mott . . .," Stack said and hesitated.

"Mott the Hoople. Yeah, that's me."

"Tony gave us your address."

"Tony?" Mott said puzzled.

"Sleazy Tone," said Stack.

"Right . . . And you are?"

"Here to see you," Micky said, pushing past Mott.

Stack smiled apologetically. "Sorry. I'm Stack, and the rude guy's Micky."

"I guess you better come in then, too," Mott said.

Stack entered. Mott closed the door.

The office was small, with a low ceiling and dirty off-white walls. A credenza desk with a glass top stood in its center. Chipped and scuffed, it had seen better days. A line of cell phones was spread over the desk. A pile of unmarked cardboard boxes sat on the floor next to it. Micky leaned against a round-armed sofa sitting against the wall.

"Take a seat," Mott said, indicating the couch.

"Micky?" Stack said, sitting. She tapped the sofa. Micky yawned and placed his backpack down before sliding into the seat.

"So, how is Sleazy?" Mott said.

"He likes to be called Tony now," Stack said.

"You don't say."

"Apparently. The thing is, we're here because we're looking for coke, and Tony said you're the man that can help."

"Coke? You mean as in the drug cocaine?"

"Exactly. Can you help?"

"That's a very unusual request," Mott said, stepping behind his desk and bending down out of sight. There was the sound of a drawer being opened. Micky reached into his backpack and pulled out his Glock 19, a suppressor attached to its barrel. Mott reappeared and stared at the gun that was now pointed directly at him.

"Hands up," Micky said.

"Really?"

"You heard me." Mott raised his arms.

"That what you just got" Stack asked. "An LM-8 bug detector?" she said, peering at the small black plastic box Mott held in one hand.

"Right in one, young lady. It's just a basic precaution in case you are what they used to call back in the day 'carrying a wire.'"

"What's he talking about, Stack?"

"He thinks we might be working for the cops."

"Oh, yeah. That's going to happen," Micky said.

"Ain't that the truth," Stack said. "OK, put the gun down, Micky. Let the man do his thing." He lowered the weapon as Mott walked back around the desk and across to the pair.

"Do you mind standing?" Mott said.

Stack rose and motioned to Micky to get up. Mott quickly and efficiently moved the device up and down the pair.

"Clean."

"Of course we're clean," Micky said, watching as Mott returned the device to the drawer, pushed the metal swivel chair from behind the desk, and positioned the seat in front of them.

"Could you?" Mott asked, indicating the couch. They sat down again.

"So coke? How much do you require?" Mott said, lowering himself into the chair.

"Two keys," Stack said.

Mott whistled.

"Sleazy said you could get it," Stack said.

"Did he now? And did he tell you what I do?"

"He said you organize drug shipments," Stack replied.

"The important word in that sentence is organize. I'm a coordinator, an arranger for the movement of the drugs from A to B. That means I don't touch the drugs. I don't even see them." He pointed to the phones. "Those are my only points of contact."

"Burner phones?" Stack asked.

"Changed daily." He pointed to the boxes. "That's a few months' worth." He stopped. "Look, I think Sleazy may have just wanted to get rid of you."

Micky glanced at Stack. Was he telling the truth? Had they been suckered?

"I see," Stack said. "So we're expected to believe that you have no access to any coke?"

"Yes. It's the shipping end that's involved in transporting the material. That's Sleazy's domain."

"Sleazy still works with you?"

"That's how we know each other."

"See, that's a lie, right there," Micky said, standing. "Sleazy's retired."

"That's what he said? Well, it's not true. Tone is very much in the game."

Micky took a step forward and pushed his Glock hard against the side of Mott's head. "I think you're lying."

"Seriously?" Mott said.

"Micky! Cool it," Stack said. "So you're saying we should go back to Sleazy and get the coke from him?"

"Definitely not. Unless you want to die?"

"Die? Why would we die?" Stack asked.

"Because Sleazy and I work for the same man. Robbing him would almost certainly lead to you being hunted down and killed."

"And that person is?"

"Oscar Bruno."

"Fuck," Micky said.

"I take it you know of Mr. Bruno?" Mott flicked his head towards Micky. "Young man, please?"

Micky reluctantly stepped back, removing his gun from Mott's head.

"But we're finding the coke for Bruno," he said.

"So, you want to rip off his cocaine and then return it to him? And you think Mr. Bruno wouldn't notice?"

Silence. Then: "What are we going to do, Stack?"

"I don't know. Let me think."

"Maybe I can help?" Mott said.

"You've just told me you can't get us the coke," Stack said.

"No. I said that the coke I deal with comes via Mr. Bruno. But, and this is a real piece of luck for you, I've spoken to a contact in just the last half hour who informs me that one of his dealers has reported a problem.

Apparently, cocaine that has nothing to do with Mr. Bruno has just appeared in my contact's bailiwick."

"What?" Micky asked, totally confused.

"Rogue coke."

"Oh. Right."

"Now there is something you could do that would win both of us brownie points with Mr. Bruno. Are you up for it?"

"Do bears shit in the woods?" Stack asked.

FORTY

RYAN WASN'T CONSIDERING BEARS and their toiletry habits. He had Scott Dean's death on his mind. Trying to find who it was who had killed him was a challenge dear to his heart. The investigation—the clues, the chase, making the invisible visible—were what Ryan lived for.

So it was a happy detective that entered the Singing Pelican that afternoon. Inside were the usual smattering of regulars—bolted to their high-backed wooden chairs, their hands locked around dimpled glasses, nursing their beers, and staring forlornly into space. Ryan waved to Johnny and Kate, who were working behind the bar. He didn't want to stop and chat. The detective's skin itched from the dust and grime in Scott Dean's place. He desperately needed a shower.

"Ryan," Johnny shouted as the detective hurried across the room. "Hold on a moment, would you?"

Pushing up the bar counter, the pub owner strode over to Ryan. "Why didn't you tell me?" he demanded as he reached the detective.

"Excuse me?"

"I'm one of Scott's oldest friends, and you didn't say anything."

The detective peered over Johnny's shoulder. Kate had her head down and was busy drying a wine glass, avoiding Ryan's eyes. "Kate told you?"

"Yes . . . Kate," he shouted and motioned for her to join them. "She did. But don't blame her. She didn't want to say anything. Last night she made up some lame excuse about needing to move out of Scott's for a short time because of a gas leak. I didn't press her because it was late. I assumed she had just had a fight with him and had been chucked out. Scott has . . ." he paused. ". . . had a temper, you know. Anyway, this morning I pestered her until she told me the truth."

"Sorry, detective, I probably shouldn't have said anything," Kate said, arriving.

"Yes, you should. I had every right to know," Johnny said, raising his voice.

The detective glanced around. A few of the regulars had started to take an interest in the conversation. "It's probably best if we go somewhere more private to discuss this," he said.

Johnny took in the people watching. "You're probably right. Follow me."

He walked back to the bar. The detective and Kate followed. Pulling the counter up, Johnny motioned them through.

"Hold the fort Kate," the pub owner said, bending to grab a metal handle on the floor and lifting up a wooden cover to reveal a set of stone stairs.

"Go ahead," Johnny said to Ryan.

The detective went down the stairs and entered a concrete-floored stone-walled cellar. Steel beer barrels were pushed together on one side with plastic tubes inserted into the top of each keg. The tubes were affixed to the wall and ran up to the ceiling, taking the beer on its journey to the bar above. Wooden shelves to the left were filled with wine and spirit bottles. Six stainless steel kegs stood opposite.

"We can sit there, "Johnny said, joining Ryan and pointing to a small metal table.

The men walked over, and Johnny pulled out one of the three green plastic chairs from under the table. "Please sit down," he said, reaching over to remove a black leather briefcase from the seat.

"I would rather die than be disgraced," The detective said as he sat.

"What?" Johnny asked, looking around for somewhere to put the attaché.

"It's my family's motto. What's yours?" Ryan asked, pointing to a coat of arms embossed on the top of the case.

"You know about coats of arms?" Johnny said, putting the case on the table next to an ashtray overflowing with cigarette butts. "Most people know nothing about them."

"My dad had me read all about our clan when I was a kid."

"Really. Well, the Wilson's motto is Semper Vigilans. Always watchful. And as you can see, our coat of arms is a brown belt circling a red lion." Johnny took a seat, reached for the ashtray, and quickly placed it on the floor. "Look, I want to know why I heard about Scott's death from my bar person and not from the police?"

"We inform relatives rather than friends first."

"And you couldn't make an exception in this instance?"

Ryan shook his head. "That's just not allowed."

"Anytime?"

"No, sorry."

Johnny thought about this for a moment. "OK, well, I still think you could have bent the rules and told me . . . but excuse reluctantly accepted." Ryan went to stand, and Johnny put up his hand and the detective's arm.

"Kate said Scott died from an overdose. Is that right?"

"I can't discuss that at the moment, sorry."

"Why not?"

"The investigation is still ongoing."

"Well, let me help you. Over the past few months, Scott had gotten more and more depressed. He just sat around and moped. I tried to jolt him out of it, but . . ." Johnny paused. ". . . obviously, I didn't do enough."

"How often did you see him?" Ryan asked.

"Once, or twice a month." Johnny thought about that. "I know I should have done more, but you know. Life happens."

"How long had you known him?"

"Since school. As a kid, though, Scott was very different from what he is . . . was . . . today." He stopped. "I called him yesterday, you know. I offered to come around, but he put me off." He paused. "Do you think if I had . . ."

"I don't think it would have made any difference," the detective said. He stood up. "I really do have to go." He brushed his suit, and a pile of dust rose into the air. "I need a shower."

The two men crossed the room and climbed up the stairs single file before entering the bar. Johnny pulled up the counter break to allow the detective out and leaned in close.

"There is one other thing I've been meaning to mention . . . Ellie."

"Ellie Sastra?" the detective asked.

"My ex-wife. You've been seeing her, apparently."

"Not exactly seeing her, but . . ."

"I think she's keen."

"She told you that?"

"I may be her ex, but we are still friends. Anyway, what I want to say is, I have no problem with it."

"It?" the detective said.

"You know. She's a lovely woman and quite a catch." He paused. "Though not for me, of course," Johnny smiled wanly.

"Right," Ryan said. He didn't quite know how to respond, so he indicated upstairs. "I better go. That shower beckons."

FORTY-ONE

GING WAS WAITING FOR THE CALL. His contact had told him someone would ring around this time. Nervous, the drug dealer decided to relax. He pulled out a wad of notes from his pocket and detached a single bill. Placing it on the kitchen table, he peered at the face of a mustached man, Sir John Montash—engineer, soldier, builder, and civic leader. Ging stroked the note flat and turned it over to stare at the portrait of the opera singer Dame Nellie Melba. They were the people he loved most in the world because they adorned his favorite note, the hundred-dollar bill.

Ging rolled the note into a cylinder. He placed one end to his nose, touched the white powder, breathed in, and vacuumed up the line. Ging moved the cylinder to the next strip of coke. He snorted it up before moving on to demolish the final line.

The hit was immediate. Now Ging felt invincible. He could do this. He was King of the World. Ging knew the euphoria he was feeling wouldn't last long. Coming down was a bitch, but not bad enough for the drug dealer to ever consider giving up. Coke was Ging's drug of choice, but this hadn't always been the case. At thirteen, he had developed a taste for marijuana . . . but he'd got bored. Weed didn't cut it for him anymore. He had gone on to experiment with Molly, Amphetamines, Ice, and Oxycontin, before settling on Bernie's Gold Dust, The Bug Bloke, Flake—Cocaine.

Ging rocked backward and forwards. He remembered what that smug bastard lawyer said when he had left the cop station. "Ginger, that's a great deal I got you." Great? BS. What did he know? In TV cop shows, the local dealer always has an encyclopedic knowledge of the area's drug scene. But that wasn't the case for Ging. He had his small elite group of locals to supply and hadn't the time to worry about who his competitors were.

Ging had always seen himself as a cut above those others. Despite his scruffy, down-at-heel look, the drug dealer was no poor kid from a broken home. The only boy in a family of four, he had a loving mother and a serial entrepreneur father who had done his best to spend 'quality' time with him. Ging loved his dad and had inherited a strong business acumen from him, and leaving school, he had decided on drug dealing as a career with promise. Ging had driven down to Sydney to seek out a permanent source of drugs. 'The business,' as he grandiosely liked to call it, had taken off rapidly after that.

Now Ging was rich enough to afford expensive clothes, a flash car, and to buy an upmarket apartment. But he hadn't done any of that. Ging wasn't stupid. He knew that his middle-class clients wouldn't appreciate him showing off. He dressed down, drove a bashed-up Toyota Yaris, rented a modest, older-style one-bedroom apartment, and hoarded his money. But his world had come crashing down outside Narcotics Anonymous, where he knew he'd behaved like an idiot.

Ging's cell started to vibrate. He waited for a moment before picking it up. "Yes," he said.

"You're looking for somebody and something?" a menacing voice asked.

"Yes. Can you help?"

"Sure. We're coming up."

"Where shall I . . ." Ging began.

"We know where you are. We'll find you."

The phone clicked off.

Ging stood up. What the fuck was that all about? His paranoia shot off the chart. Who exactly were 'we'? And what were they going to do when they came up? He should have never agreed to find Liam's other supplier. It was dumb. Maybe he should make other plans?

Ryan was unaware of the drug dealer's dilemma. He was concentrating on a more mundane matter—his washing. He filled a green cap up with liquid soap and poured it into the compartment marked 'washing powder.' Then he slotted three dollar coins into the money box and pressed the button marked bright colors. There was a brief hesitation before the appliance's motor turned on.

Satisfied, the detective returned to sit on the wooden bench. After his much-needed shower, Ryan hadn't had any choice but to go to the launderette. He had to wash his dirty clothes and clean his underwear and socks so he would have something to wear tomorrow.

The cold wash would take forty minutes. Then the detective had to unload the wet clothes into the drier. That would take another forty minutes. He could go back to the pub in between, but Ryan had decided against the trip. He would stay put.

Since his days at the Police Academy, the detective had always used launderettes. He liked them. They were warm and cozy and an ideal place to think. And at that moment, the detective was thinking about Johnny Wilson and what he had said about his ex-wife. Although Ryan accepted that this was a small town, the speed with which the news about Ellie had gotten around was unnerving. And Johnny had used the word 'seeing'—a euphemism for dating. True, Ryan had agreed to have dinner with Ellie, but that wasn't really a date, was it?

"Ryan?"

The detective came out of his revelry. Ellie stood at the launderette door, Attila by her side. "Do you mind if we join you?"

Ryan tapped the bench. "Take a seat."

"Sit, Attila," Ellie said to the dog as she sat down.

"Doing laundry is a pain, don't you think?"

"No. I like it"

"You're a strange man."

"Do you mean that in a good or a bad way?" Ryan asked.

"Good, of course, every time. There's nothing wrong with a bit of strangeness."

"That's all right then. Did you know I was here?"

"No. I saw you when I was passing with Attila. He was pining for a walk."

Ellie looked down at the dog. "I think Attila misses Ashley but she'll be back soon, thank god." Ellie rubbed the top of Attila's head. "No offense." She moved closer to Ryan and whispered: "Truth is, I'm more of a cat woman."

"Me too," Ryan said. "So, have you heard from Ashley?"

"Just once. She rang to check up on Attila. She said she was having a great time. She's so lucky. I'd love to go to Thailand."

"You've not been?"

"No, never. And you?"

"Nope."

"So, maybe one day we could go together," Ellie said.

Ryan frowned.

"Relax, I was just joking," Ellie said.

Silence, as they both listened to the sound of the washing machine. "I'm glad I saw you tonight. I heard the terrible news about Scott."

"You did?" Ryan couldn't believe it. Everyone seemed to have heard about Scott Dean's death.

"This is a small town," Ellie said, reading his reaction.

"So everyone keeps saying."

"You know Scott, Johnny, and I were all in the same year at High School? Hearing about someone you went to school with dying is distressing. Of course, Johnny will be much more affected. He was Scott's only real friend."

"What about Brad Costello?"

"The gardener?"

"Yes."

"Johnny believed he was a gold digger, not a real friend," Ryan said.

Attila started to whine. "Shh . . . It was a drug's overdose, wasn't it?"

"What?"

"That killed Scott? Can't say I'm surprised. He had a history of taking drugs."

The dog barked. Ellie rolled her eyes. "OK, OK, We're going." She stood up. "Sorry." She tugged at Attila's leash. "Look, I'd love to cook another dinner. Hopefully, this time things will work out better."

"Yeah, I'm sorry about rushing off."

"Not your fault. So are you up for that?" she asked.

Ryan hesitated. Then: "Sure. Let me give you a ring when things get less hectic."

Ellie pulled a face. "Don't be like that. If you don't want to, just say."

"No, that's not it. I definitely want to have dinner. I'm just really busy at the moment."

"Of course. OK, well I'll wait for your call. Come on, Attila." She tugged at the dog's leash and headed for the door.

FORTY-TWO

IT WAS THE START OF ANOTHER FABULOUS DAY. The sun's golden rays kissed the white tops of the waves and bounced along the fine beach sand. But Ryan was oblivious to nature's beauty as he hurried from the pub to his car, his feet crunching on the coarse pebbles.

The detective was in a mood that he characterized as being 'impatiently determined,' but others saw differently. Few in the police had Ryan's unswerving resolve to solve a case, and most found it challenging to cope with his intense focus. The fact that Liam Plummer and Scott Dean's deaths were only a matter of days old was irrelevant to the detective. He still hadn't found the source of the coke, nor had he any idea about the identity of Scott Dean's killer.

Getting into his car, Ryan flicked the ignition, released the brake and, pressed his foot hard down on the accelerator pedal. It only took him fifteen minutes to reach the station, and arriving, Ryan traced the blacktop driveway to the rear car park. He was surprised to see that Zoe's car was already there, next to Jackie's old white Ford Fiesta. So they were just as anxious as him to get to work.

The detective used his key to enter the rear door. He hurried down the corridor and opened the office door. Jackie stood in the far corner, her back to him, pouring water from the kettle into an ugly green tea pot.

"Morning, Ryan," she said without turning. "Tea?"

"Yes, thanks. Where's Zoe?"

"In Room One."

"I'll go see her." Ryan reentered the corridor and went into the interview room. Here the constable was spreading the contents of one of the boxes from Scott Dean's house over the table.

"Morning, boss," Zoe said, looking around.

"You're bright and early."

"I wanted to get a head start."

Ryan nodded, pleased. "Right, well, I better get down to it too."

He flipped open the cardboard lid of the second box and peered in. Although Scott's home was packed to the gunnels with 'stuff' that the hoarder had accumulated, little had looked to be of much use.

The interview room door swung open, and Jackie Street came in. She carried a plastic tray with two blue mugs, a spoon, and a chipped blue and yellow striped sugar bowl on it. She carefully placed the tray on the small table at the far end of the room. Jackie handed one of the mugs to Zoe. "There you go. White. No sugar."

"Thanks."

"And detective, your tea's there." Jackie indicated the tray. "I don't know how many sugars you take, so you'll have to sweeten it yourself," she said and peered over Zoe's shoulders. "Is that an article about that boy's disappearance?" Jackie pointed at a yellowed newspaper cutting the constable was holding.

"Yes."

Jackie looked closer and read the date. "Two thousand and six. How time flies."

"I remember when Nathan Woodford vanished," Zoe said.

"You do? From all that time back?" Ryan asked, looking up.

"Of course. Even though I was only eleven years old, it was big news in Barton. It was so exciting what with the search and the school being turned upside down. It must have been even more momentous for Scott, though. He would have been the same age and in the same year as Nathan Woodford. I guess that's why he has all these newspaper cuttings of the case," Zoe said.

"I mentioned the boy's disappearance the other day, detective, remember? The great Barton mystery," Jackie said. "I was working here then, along with the Sarge and his boss Sergeant Harry Robinson." She shook her head. "There were police looking for Nathan everywhere. The beach, the cliffs. I'd never seen Sergeant Robinson work so hard—not that that was difficult." She paused and crossed herself. "I shouldn't say that. It's not good to speak badly of the dead."

"Sergeant Robinson died?" Ryan asked.

"Five years ago. Heart attack. Personally, I think it was this case that killed him. He couldn't prove what we all knew, and I think that played on his mind."

"What was that?"

"That the boy's father killed Nathan Woodford."

"The police said he was a runaway," Zoe said.

"That's what the police put out. But soon after, Woodward's father left Barton and never came back. And Nathan Woodford hasn't been seen since."

"That's hardly conclusive," Zoe said.

"You believe what you want to believe, constable. But I know the truth," Jackie said, tapping her nose as she made for the door and left.

"Is there a picture of the Nathan Woodford in any of that material?" Ryan asked.

The constable shuffled through the cuttings and picked one up. "That's him," she said, indicating a grainy black and white photo of a thin-faced spotty boy with unruly light brown curly hair and sticky-out ears wearing thick, black-rimmed glasses. Nathan Woodford, aged eighteen, was captioned underneath.

Ryan shuffled through his box and sighting a photo picked it up. Two teenage boys, dressed in identical blue tracksuits, their backs to a swimming pool, were pictured. Gold medallions hung around their necks.

"That's Nathan Woodford too, right?" Ryan said, offering the picture to Zoe and indicating the boy on the left. "And the other one's Scott Dean."

"Yes. I think so.

The detective took the photo back and looked at it again. "Not only did they go to the same school at the same time, but they were both in the diving team."

"How do you know that?"

The detective pointed to the red and white straps attached to the medal-lions. "See, they have Beach High Diving Team printed on them."

The door opened, and Jackie reappeared. "I'm sorry to interrupt you, Ryan, but there's something I forgot to mention. I must have had a senior moment. Kate Cassels' has been holding on the phone for you in the office."

"Tell her I'll call her back, can you?"

"She says it's urgent."

Ryan sighed. "OK. I'm on my way."

THE DETECTIVE PICKED THE PHONE UP from Jackie's desk. "Hi, Kate. How can I help?"

"I was wondering if I could go back to Scott's today," Kate said.

Clearly, the detective thought, he and Kate Cassels had different defini-tions of the word urgent.

"No, I'm sorry, but that's out of the question. The investigation is ongo-ing. It'll be a few more days before you can return home. But don't worry, I'll definitely let you know when we're finished."

"Oh. OK. I guess Johnny will be happy for me to stay a few more days. Thanks."

The phone clicked off and then rang again almost immediately. Jackie picked it up. "Barton Police Station," she said and listened.

"It's for you. Kate again," Jackie said, handing the phone back to Ryan.

"Yes," the detective said, now annoyed.

"There's something I should have mentioned earlier. Brad Costello and I witnessed Scott's will."

"Really." Now that was exciting news. "When?"

"A couple of months ago."

"Would you know the exact date?"

"No. Sorry."

"If you could try and remember it, that would be useful."

"OK, I'll try."

"Well, thanks for that," Ryan said, putting down the phone.

The Sarge came in. "Morning, everyone," he said, walking over to his desk and unbuttoning his heavy black overcoat.

"Ryan, I've been thinking it would be good . . ."

"Sorry, Sarge. I've got to go. Tell Zoe I'll be back later, but meantime, she's to list everything in the boxes," he said and headed for the door.

The Sarge watched him leave. "List everything in the boxes," he repeated, slinging his coat over his chair. "You know there used to be a time, not so long ago, when I was in charge of this office, Jackie. But that was before I got promoted to Detective Ryan's messenger boy."

FORTY-THREE

BACK IN SYDNEY, STACK HAD A DIFFERENT PROBLEM. She was concerned about Bumpy's health. The weasel's eyes didn't look good this morning. Green fluid was seeping out of them. His food bowl had hardly been touched since yesterday. Weasels usually eat about forty percent of their body weight every day, so that wasn't good.

Stack had delayed departing for Barton while she tried to work out what, if anything, was wrong with her pet. Searching the internet, she had found that weasels are susceptible to far more diseases than she had ever imagined. Her little cute fur ball could apparently get infections with names like tularemia, canine distemper, murine, and sacrcosporidiosis. If Bumpy wasn't a weasel, she would have been able to take him to a vet, but since the animals are illegal in Australia, that wasn't an option.

Micky had been his usual helpful self. Any warmth she'd felt towards him after their marathon fucking session last night had disappeared when, on finally waking up and hearing about Bumpy, he'd volunteered to shoot the animal to put it out of its misery.

And of course, being a man, Micky had to have bigger problems than her pet. He said that whatever pain Bumpy felt, his was much worse. His tooth was throbbing, so shouldn't Stack be more concerned about him? And anyway, wasn't it about time they left?

Stack had to admit Micky had a point. Not about his tooth—she'd first told him to get it fixed weeks ago—but about getting going. Sick weasel or no sick weasel, it was time they were on their way. So, grasping Bumpy's cage tight, Stack locked the apartment door and headed for the elevator with Micky in tow.

EIGHTY MILES AWAY, RYAN HAD ALMOST REACHED Scott Dean's home. On his way over he had rung Costello, who had confirmed Kate's story about witnessing Scott Dean's will. Costello hadn't remembered exactly when that was but said he would try to recall.

Arriving at the house, Ryan slipped on a pair of white gloves, unlocked the front door, and entered. He was angry about forgetting to ask either Kate or Costello about a will. The detective had assumed Scott hadn't been organized enough to have one . . . but he had been wrong.

Ryan sat down on the couch. A thick layer of dust flew up. He and Zoe had combed the house. If the will had been in plain sight, they would have seen it; so Scott Dean must have found a first-class hiding place for it somewhere in the house.

The detective stood up and scratched his neck. The room was already making him itch again. So, where would Scott have concealed the will? Here, in the living room? Not likely. No one usually hides essential items in a space that's so accessible; ditto the kitchen. And he'd already decided the study had been more than well enough searched—so maybe upstairs?

The detective climbed to the first floor. There were four bedrooms on this level. Kate lived in one, the room directly opposite the landing. Ryan couldn't see Scott hiding anything important there. There would be a problem with access. Two of the other three bedrooms were empty, or at least no one seemed to use them. Scott just hoarded garbage in them. His will might have been hidden in one of those. But it was much more likely that if it still existed, it was in Scott's own bedroom. Here he could get it at any time, and the room wasn't somewhere anyone else could enter unless invited.

The oak wood floorboards groaned as Ryan hurried down the corridor. Reaching the main bedroom, Ryan turned the handle and pushed. The hinges grated as the door partially opened, its path blocked by a heavy, rusty iron fan.

Squeezing through, the detective stepped onto the threadbare carpet. A king-sized bed took up much of the space in the room. An old-fashioned brown wooden dressing table sat in front of the windows, its top covered with debris—a white plastic fan lying on its side, a sidelight, its bulb broken, and several empty plastic water bottles. Filthy, moldy thick yellow flock curtains framed the ugly piece of furniture.

A stand-alone wooden closet, its doors opened wide, stood opposite. The detective peered in. A long metal pole ran from one side of the closet to the other. Piles of dirty old clothes covered its carpeted floor, partially obscuring a newish, bright red vacuum cleaner, the brush and plastic hose jammed into its squat body.

Ryan removed the garments from the cleaner. The vacuum was still in pristine condition. The words Electrolux and Silent Performer were printed across the vacuum. A handbook had been jammed under it.

The detective pulled out the book and opened it. "As the name suggests, this vacuum features a Silent Pro System resulting in minimal noise, while the washable HEPA filter works to clean your floors with incredible efficiency," he read. Incredible efficiency would definitely be needed in this place, Ryan thought, closing the book.

Zoe had commented on the machine when she had seen it during the search yesterday. "So someone cared enough about cleaning to buy one of these," he remembered she'd said. That someone could only have been Scott. And thinking about it again, that was more than a little odd.

Ryan pulled out the hose from the cleaner before twisting the device around and lifting the red lever with the word 'open' printed across it. There was a white bag inside.

The detective carefully unclipped the front of the bag, lifted it up, and pushed two fingers through the cardboard-covered opening. He felt something inside: a roll of paper. He pulled it out and unspooled it. The words: "This is the Last Will Testament', came into view. They were written in an old-fashioned font at the top of the first page, followed by the name Scott Hartford Dean. He scanned the three pages of the document quickly. Then he called Zoe. She was to text over Brad Costello's address to him and to meet him there.

FORTY-FOUR

BACK IN SYDNEY, OSCAR BRUNO STEPPED out of the mansion. Despite donning a thick overcoat, the drug dealer shivered in the cold as he gazed around. Spotting him, a casual observer may have thought that he had stepped out to admire the magnificent bay view. Nothing could be further from the truth. Bruno wasn't communing with nature. He was there because he was paranoid.

Bruno's paranoia had started after he had killed his father. Oscar Bruno Senior was a petty criminal, who after his wife died in a car crash, had vowed to bring up his ten-year-old boy and namesake with loving care— or as much loving care as he could muster. Afraid of a jail sentence and separation from his son, Bruno Senior had even thought about abandoning his life of crime. He hadn't—burglary was so much easier than working on a construction site. So, while unable to give up thieving, Bruno's father tried to steer young Oscar away from this career path . . . and he had succeeded. His son had no intention of spending his life in penny-ante criminality. He had set his sights much higher. This is why Bruno Senior had to die, knifed to death, his mutilated body later buried in one of Sydney's stunning national parks.

Bruno had never had any feelings of shame or remorse about murdering his father. It was just something that had to be done. But in doing it, the criminal had begun worrying in earnest about treachery and the possibility that in the future, others could be as disloyal to him as he had been to his dad.

Bruno had taken his father's severed head as an offering to big-time gang boss Raymondo Stantarni. It had been the nineteen-year-old's way of proving that he would do anything for Signore Stantarni if the crime leader would just give him a chance.

It took a lot to impress Stantarni, but impressed he was, and he took young Bruno under his wing, awarding him the position of bodyguard and general muscle. Bruno was prepared to do everything he was asked in that role, including maiming, shooting, and killing.

Bruno's loyalty was rewarded by his promotion to capo and then Raymondo Stantarni's consigliere. His ascension up the criminal ladder taught him that you can never be too paranoid. Indeed if Stantarni had been a little less trusting and more obsessively anxious, then he might have lived longer. Bruno's unsuspecting boss was sent to hell by a man he believed was loyal to him. Riddled with bullets, Signore Stantarni was left bleeding to death outside his mistress's Elizabeth Bay apartment.

Bruno had led the late Stantarni's crime gang ever since, assiduously weeding out those who were too keen or too ambitious. He always used their deaths to solidify his rule, personally torturing and mutilating the suspects before putting them out of their misery.

So, the drug dealer never trusted anyone or anything anymore. And even though Mexican Dave regularly swept the mansion for bugs, Bruno had decided last night that from now on, he would only discuss delicate operations outside—like the one he wanted to talk to Big Jay and The Lion about now.

THE TWO BIG MEN WERE WORRIED SICK about meeting their boss. As the highest-ranking gang members, they coordinated drug deals, prostitution, and sex trafficking—the meat and potatoes of Bruno's empire. But that didn't mean they were safe.

"Do you think this is about those fucking morons Micky and Stack?" The Lion asked as Big Jay yanked open the heavy reinforced back door.

"Why would it be?" the big man queried, though, in truth, he knew there were plenty of reasons why. The young pair had seemed to be the boss's new favorites until the other day, that is, and the discovery of the missing coke. After that debacle, Big Jay and The Lion had expected Bruno to tell them to take the kids on a drive. Instead, he had given Stack and Micky a week to return the blow. Later the big men had privately voiced concern that maybe the boss was getting soft. Now though, they were thinking that maybe their conversations hadn't been as private as they had thought. Maybe someone had overheard them criticizing Bruno. And that notion was scary as all hell.

"Hi, boss," Big Jay said as they approached Bruno.

Silence.

"Cold out here, isn't it?" The Lion said, keen to get the conversation going.

Silence

"So, what's this all about?" The Lion said, trying again to engage his boss.

Bruno enjoyed these moments. He never let any of his men feel comfortable around him. He waited a little longer before turning to face them. "What do you think of that 'lost' coke?"

Big Jay shrugged. "It was unfortunate."

"Unfortunate? Two kilos. They lost me two K!"

"I didn't mean that it was right. It was a shit show," Big Jay said hastily.

"So, what do you think about me giving them a week to find the stuff and return it?" Bruno asked.

The Lion glanced quickly at Big Jay. He knows! "Good decision, boss."

"Yeah, great," echoed Big Jay.

"It was bad, real bad," said Bruno.

Big Jay and The Lion said nothing; how to reply to that?

There was a long pause. Then: "Not sure what you mean by bad," Big Jay said.

"I mean, it was the wrong decision. I should have had them iced there and then," Bruno said.

"Yeah, but you can still do that, boss, when they come back," The Lion said.

"With or without the two Ks, if you want to," Big Jay said.

"Right," said Bruno. Pausing, he made a movement with his mouth. It was intended as a smile, but it was the kind of look a shark would have given if it had ever tried to grin. "Yep, I'll deal with them when they return, which they will." He paused again: "Anyway, enough of that. That's not what we're out here for."

Big Jay and The Lion froze. If it wasn't for that, then what was it for?

"What do you know about Detective Inspector Ramesh Ryan?"

"The wog detective?" Big Jay said.

"Right."

"He's just a cop."

Bruno stared at Big Jay. "He's an excellent cop, though, otherwise how could he have got me into court."

Big Jay glanced at The Lion. Then: "Yeah, 'course, boss. But you still beat the rap." He paused. "Easily."

"No, it was close. And now I have to go around pretending I'm some kind of retard. He did that." Bruno paused again. "So, I want to kill him."

The two gangsters couldn't believe what they were hearing.

"Kill him, boss? But he's . . .," The Lion said.

"I know. And you don't kill them," Bruno said, interrupting. "But what about a corrupt cop that gets shot up in a drugs deal that goes wrong. What about that cop?"

Big Jay and The Lion smiled.

"Great idea, boss," The Lion said.

"OK, so I want you two to find him and bring him back here. I can set it up as if he's taking a kickback for letting me go free, and he got greedy and bang bang. No one will give a shit. One dead corrupt cop who isn't liked much, so I hear, him being a wog and all."

The two men were impressed. Their boss was, as always, brilliant.

"Leave it to us," said Big Jay.

"Yeah, we're on it," The Lion said.

They turned to go.

"Don't you want to know where to find him?"

"He's a Sydney cop, isn't he? Big Jay asked spinning around. "So Sydney."

Bruno shook his head. "No."

"What?" The Lion said, confused.

"Well, you're right. He does usually work here, but he's not here at the moment. He's been reassigned to a little shit hole on the Central Coast that goes by the name of Barton. That's where you'll find him. So off you go and bring the bastard back," Bruno said. "But don't hurt him. That's for me to do."

FORTY-FIVE

As Big Jay and The Lion were digesting Bruno's astonishing order, the intended kidnappee, Ryan, stood by his car outside a residential complex, completely unaware of the plans for his future.

The detective took out a clear plastic evidence bag from his jacket pocket. The bag contained the will he had found at Scott Dean's home. He handed it to Zoe. "Put these on," Ryan said, giving her a pair of gloves. Slipping on the mitts, Zoe pulled the papers out and quickly skimmed through them.

"What do you think? Ryan asked.

"Looks genuine," the constable said, carefully replaced the will and returned the bag to Ryan before taking off her gloves.

"I'll deliver it to Gosford for fingerprinting later. But first, let's go see Costello," Ryan said, walking to the apartment block's entrance. Zoe followed.

Inside they waited for the elevator. "You know this was an early Charles Plummer. He built it in the mid-eighties," Zoe said, pressing the elevator button again.

"And you know this because?"

"Plummer's a famous colorful identity around these parts, so every cop knows his history."

"A colorful identity, huh. I guess that's one way of describing him," Ryan said as the elevator door slid open and the cops stepped in. Zoe pressed the button for the third floor, and the elevator rose slowly before shuddering to a halt. The doors creaked open to reveal a dimly lit hallway. On the wall opposite, tarnished brass arrows pointed left and right. The cops turned left, following the direction marked for the apartments numbered 28 to 33. They stopped in front of unit 33.

Ryan rapped on the door and waited. Zoe had made the appointment with Brad Costello after the detective called her, so he was expecting them. The small spy hole went dark. Then the door opened.

"Come in, come in," the young man said, pulling the door wide. The officers stepped through, straight into the apartment's living room.

"Welcome to my humble abode," Costello said, motioning around.

An enterprising estate agent would probably have called the studio cozy and bijou. Ryan, however, would have offered up different adjectives—cramped and gloomy came to mind. A single bed was pushed against the far wall. It was covered with a patterned quilt—a vintage block print of evergreen trees dotted on a creamy background. A white-framed circular metal side table sat next to it. A black cell phone lay on the table. A gray fabric two-seater was positioned close by, filling much of the rest of the room. A rectangular coffee table, supported on thin, wooden legs, stood opposite.

"Sit down, please, officers," Costello said, directing them to the sofa. "Tea . . . Coffee . . . Something stronger?" Ryan and Zoe shook their heads as they struggled to make themselves comfortable on the couch.

"I'm fine," said Zoe

"Me too."

"You don't know what you're missing," Costello said as he plunked down on the only other seat—a red armchair. "Now Constable Yang said you wanted to meet urgently, so I'm assuming there's something more you want to ask about poor Scott, detective?"

"There is," said Ryan.

"OK, but before you start, there's something I have to tell you." Costello took his phone from his pocket. He scrolled through it. "You asked me, detective, if I could try and recall when Kate Cassels and I had signed Scott's will. Well, it was on a Tuesday, 5th June." He turned the phone's screen towards them. "See there."

"That's a great help. And actually, we're here because of the will. We have a few more questions about it," Detective Ryan said.

"I see." Costello paused. "Have you found it yet?"

"We're still looking. But can you tell me when Scott Dean mentioned he wanted you to witness the document?"

"The night before. So that would be the 4th June. He said that Kate Cassels would come to his study the next morning and I should be there too. Of course, that wasn't a problem. I was spending most days at his home, so I only had to go downstairs."

"Kate Cassels mentioned that neither of you saw what was in the document," the detective said.

"Yes. Scott was very secretive. The will was folded so that we could only see what we had to sign."

"Do you know where he kept it?"

"No idea," Costello said.

"Oh . . . Kate Cassels didn't know either," Detective Ryan said.

"I'm not surprised. Why would he tell her?"

"Why'd you say that?" asked the detective.

"Don't get me wrong, it's not that Scott and her didn't get on. But their relationship was strictly as a landlord and a tenant. He didn't even tell me, and we were very, very close." Costello started to snivel. "Sorry, it's just . . ." He reached into his pocket and dabbed his eyes with a tissue.

"And what about Kate Cassels and you?"

"You know what I think about her. She used any opportunity to name-call me in front of Scott." He paused. "I'm sorry, but I really don't like that woman. Ask me another question, please."

"That's it. That's all we need to know." Ryan glanced across at Zoe, and they both stood up.

"You could have asked me any of that over the phone."

"I'm old-fashioned. I prefer face-to-face meetings," Ryan said.

"How quaint. And that's definitely all you need from me?"

"For the time being," the detective replied.

"Well, I'm always available," Costello said, standing. "Shall we?" He indicated the door.

They made their way out, and as Costello reached the entrance, he swiveled around.

"There is one thing. I just can't stop thinking about it. Do you believe Scott knew he was going to die?"

"What?"

"Well, his sudden need to complete his will, where did that come from? Maybe he knew he was about to go?"

"What are you implying?" the detective asked.

"This is difficult to say," Costello said, lifting his hand to his eyes to wipe another tear away. "Was it suicide—the overdose and all? "

He waited for a reply, but neither officer obliged.

"Here's what I think. Scott knew. He definitely knew." Costello opened the door. "I had mixed emotions when he told me he wanted me to be a witness on his will. I was so proud, but I was also upset. I hid that, of course, and made a joke of it. I said something like I hoped he wasn't thinking of dying."

"And what did he say?"

"He said, of course not. But that's not the way things turned out, was it?"

The cops stepped out into the corridor.

'Thank you again, Mr. Costello," Detective Ryan said.

"Like I said, don't hesitate to contact me if you need anything more."

Brad Costello watched the cops walk down the corridor to the elevators before finally closing the apartment door.

"THE WILL WAS WITNESSED ON THE day he said, fifth of June. So that checks out," Zoe said as the elevator arrived and the doors opened.

"Yes, it does," Ryan said, stepping into the elevator and pressing the button marked G. "How are you getting on sorting through the Scott Dean boxes?"

"I've cataloged most of the material, but I'm not sure if any of it helps. You're the detective, though, so maybe there's something I'm missing," Zoe said.

The elevator reached the ground floor, and the doors slowly opened. "I did notice that most of the material you chose was from when Scott was at school. Why was that?"

"That appeared to be the most interesting period of his life," Ryan said, walking out into the foyer. Zoe followed.

"You're right. It was as if Scott's life ended when he left school," the constable said, as she struggled to keep up with the detective. "Actually, even back then, by Year 12, he wasn't doing as well. The teachers wrote in their reports that he didn't seem to be trying anymore. Up until then, he was an A-plus student."

"See, so you did find something interesting," Ryan said as he pushed open the front entrance door. His cell rang. Zoe stopped as the detective reached into his jacket pocket, took the phone out, and clicked it on. "Detective Ryan."

"Cyrus Woods, from Gosford. The IT guy."

"Yes."

"I've managed to crack the passwords for Scott Dean's laptop and phone, so you can come over and collect the devices."

"Fantastic. Will do. I'll be there in about half-hour," Ryan said.

He turned to Zoe. "The IT man's found the passwords for Scott Dean's laptop and phone."

"That's good. By the way, I sent him over the information he asked for—birthdate, address. That stuff."

"That probably helped. I'll go see Woods and also put Scott Dean's will in for fingerprinting."

"I'll follow you over," Zoe said.

"No. No need. I'll see you back at the office."

"OK," Zoe said, disappointed. One moment the detective needed her the next, he didn't. What was that all about?

FORTY-SIX

RYAN HAD NO IDEA WHERE CYRUS WOOD'S OFFICE WAS, nor it, appeared, did the burly uniformed Sergeant at Gosford's police station's front reception.

"Who?" he asked.

"Cyrus Woods. He's in your IT department."

"Oh, he is, is he? And you are?"

"Detective Ryan." Ryan showed the officer his ID.

The Sergeant did a double take. "Yeah, right. Detective Ryan. You're the new guy in Barton?"

"Yes."

"The Sarge told me about getting a detective. Said you came from Sydney." He stopped suddenly, swiveled around on his chair, and shouted. "Steve, can you come out here."

A chubby uniformed cop in his late twenties walked into view.

"Detective Ryan here needs to get to the IT department to see a guy called Cyrus Woods. Ever heard of him?"

"Sure."

"Oh . . . New is he?"

"No, Sarge, he's been working here for a couple of years."

He shook his head. "No one ever tells me anything. So, can you take him over there?

"OK."

The young cop introduced himself as Steve Major and led the detective through a confusing maze of corridors. As they walked, the cop peppered Ryan with questions about being a detective. Major said he would love to be one but knew he would have to have a few more years in uniform before applying. His enthusiasm and ambition lifted Ryan's spirits.

"Here we are," Constable Major said, stopping in front of a nondescript brown door with the words IT printed in its center. He knocked but got no answer, so turned the door handle, and went in. Ryan went in after him.

The room was dark, lit only by two dimmed flush-mounted squares of fluorescents. A long desk ran the length of the back wall, butting onto closed white blinds. Two chairs were pushed under the table. Both sat in front of large Apple desktop computers. A man, his back to them, peered at one of the devices' screens.

"Visitor," Constable Major said.

Cyrus Woods spun around.

"Detective Ryan."

Ryan glanced around the room. "They don't give you much space down here, do they?"

"We're the forgotten men." Woods reached over to tug at the shutter cord. The blinds opened to reveal a red brick wall. "We don't even get windows." He pulled the cord, and the blinds closed.

"OK. I'll be off then," Constable Major said. "You think you can find your way back?"

"I should be OK." Ryan reached into his pocket. "Can you do me one more favor? Get this to forensics?" He offered the cop the clear plastic evidence bag containing Scott Dean's will.

"No problem," Constable Major said, taking the item.

"Tell them it's for the Scott Dean case and needs to be fingerprinted. And say I would really appreciate it if they could make it a rush job."

"OK," he said and left.

Ryan turned his attention back to Woods. "So, you found the passwords?"

"Yep. The laptop and phone are in there, ready to go." He pointed to a plastic bag that sat on the desk.

"Thanks." Ryan paused and then put the question to Woods he knew he was waiting for: "So, how did you find the codes? Did you use any of the information you asked Zoe for?"

Woods's face lit up. "Good question. And no. I didn't need it." For the next few minutes, Woods described in detail how the 'magic' had been achieved. Like anyone who loved their work, the IT guy assumed that Ryan was as interested in it as he was—and being more-or-less a Luddite, the detective understood little of what was being said. From what he did grasp, Scott Dean hadn't updated his software. This had produced something called "insufficient traffic layer protection," allowing "unvalidated redirects and forwards" and 'cross-site request forgery' amongst other things.

"All of this meant a hacker could easily utilize the weaknesses. Then it was just a matter of checking where on the device he had stored the codes," Woods said.

"You knew he had done that?"

"Of course. The fact that Scott Dean hadn't updated the devices meant he had no idea about security. They were in a file rather obviously called Passcodes. I've messaged your cell with the codes for both devices."

"Impressive. Good work. Thank you," Ryan said.

Woods's face broke into a broad grin. Most cops had little understanding of technology, and even fewer ever offered thanks to IT wizards like Woods. So he was happy to receive any sort of acknowledgment.

"I've got another favor to ask. Do you mind if I stay here for a while so I can search the devices before I leave?" Ryan asked.

"No, go right ahead. Use Kavia's space, he's off ill today."

"Right."

Woods handed the detective the bag with the laptop and cell in. "It's a shame Kavia couldn't be here. He really wanted to meet you."

"Oh, that's unfortunate," Ryan said and meant it. The Australian police force made a lot of noise about expanding its cultural recruitment, but the results had been tepid at best. A cop was still more than likely to be white. So, the detective understood why a man called Kavia would enjoy meeting someone with his colored skin.

"If Kavia's ever in Barton, he should pop into the station. It would be good to say hello."

"Great. I'll definitely tell him that," Woods said as Ryan sat down and took Scott Dean's cell phone out of the bag. He carefully placed it on the desk before reaching for his own phone.

"Don't bother," Woods said. "The code's 2251."

Ryan typed in the numbers. The cell opened.

"Worked?"

"Yeah."

Scott obviously hadn't made much use of the phone. He had none of the leading social media apps—Facebook, Twitter, Instagram, or Snapchat. His phone contact list was short and consisted mainly of the numbers and names of various local restaurants—probably for takeaway and delivery food orders. There were few personal numbers, and some of these were out of date—Scott hadn't even bothered to delete the numbers for his dead parents. All but one of the recent calls were for food deliveries. The only personal call was a local one made in the afternoon of his death. The detective assumed this was from Johnny ---- the call the pub owner had told him he'd made to Scott. Ryan dialed the number on his own cell.

"Detective Ryan?" a voice said.

"Johnny Wilson?"

"Yes."

"You have my number on your phone?" the detective asked.

"Of course. I make a note of all my guests' contacts on it. How can I help?"

"You have. Just now."

"What?"

"I'll explain later. But thank you."

Ryan clicked off his cell and returned to scrolling through Scott's iPhone. The photo library was empty. A few dates were highlighted in the phone calendar and included Narcotics Anonymous meetings and references to Brad Costello. But these became less frequent. The letter F was printed in some of the squares. Ryan remembered that he had seen this written up on the calendar in Scott's kitchen and assumed it stood for food.

Ryan put the cell down and pulled the laptop out of the bag. He opened it up.

"His name is the username and the password is Armstand 18," Woods said, without looking up from his computer.

"Thanks," the detective said.

"Usually a guy like that puts in his mother's name or the name of his dog or something similar, but Armstand? That's a strange one. I did a bit of checking . . ." Woods looked over at Ryan. ". . . not that I wanted to tread on anyone's toes. I was just interested."

"No problem. So?"

"Armstand is a term used in competitive diving. There's something called the Armstand Dive, where the diver puts his hand down on the board, flicks his legs in the air, and then dives. I'm guessing this guy was a diver."

"Yes. When Scott was in high school. Year 12. The eighteen in the code was probably chosen because that was his age then."

"I just thought it was a random number choice. I guess that's why you're the detective and I'm not," Woods said, returning to his work.

Ryan typed in the username and password on Scott's computer. The screen cleared, replaced by the Home page. Like Scott's phone, the laptop looked to be little-used. And the detective could find nothing personal on it. He never appeared to email, and the main files had titles like electricity and gas. Although Scott may have been a hoarder, it was evident that he liked to keep tight control on his money. He had page after page of bills as well as monthly copies of his bank statements. Looking through the most recent statement, Ryan saw Scott had about twenty thousand in his check account and several hundred thousand in a bank savings account—presumably inheritance left to Scott by his parents. The detective had hoped that the devices would give some kind of clue to Scott Dean's killer, but so far, he had found nothing of value—that was until he opened a file entitled future. As he studied the only document in the file, there was a knock on the door.

"Come in," Woods called out. Two women entered. "Yes," Woods said.

"We're here to see Detective Ryan," the woman on the left said.

Ryan raised his hand. "That's me."

"Forensics, detective" the woman said by way of introduction.

We brought you the material," the other women said.

"Oh, thanks," Ryan said. He recognized the women. It was the twins. But he had no idea which was which.

"Annette," the one on the left said.

"And Fiona," the other chimed.

"Yes, of course," Ryan said.

The forensic twins, out of their shapeless blue hooded protective overalls, looked very different. Annette wore pressed black pants banded by a black leather belt with a silver metal buckle. A creamy-colored blouse was tucked tight into her trousers. Over it, she wore a fitted black jacket. Her blonde hair was loose and long, draping her shoulders. Fiona had on a gray-fitted trouser suit. Underneath the coat, she wore a white ribbed blouse with a white bow at the collar. Her blonde hair had been pushed up onto her head and bunched into a beehive.

The detective took the clear bag containing Scott's will from Annette. "And the report too," she said, handing Ryan a manilla envelope.

Fiona offered the detective a second brown envelope. "This is the breakdown of the coke sample for Ginger Watson your constable sent us."

The detective pulled a single page out of the first envelope and glanced at it. "This all?"

"There wasn't much to see," Annette said.

"And that cocaine sample definitely didn't match the make-up of the coke associated with the deaths of Liam Plummer and Scott Dean. It's full of additives," Fiona said.

The detective stroked his chin. "Thanks, ladies. You've been a great help."

"That's our job," Annette said, smiling at the detective and revealing sparkling white teeth. She glanced across at her sister.

"Anyway, anything else you need, don't hesitate to ask," Fiona said. They turned together and left the room.

As the door closed behind them, Woods turned back around. "I've never seen that before," he said.

"What?" the detective asked.

"Such a rapid turnaround. And then delivering the results to you personally. That's impressive." Woods stared at Ryan. "You knew, though, didn't you?"

"Knew what?"

Woods shook his head. "Suit yourself." He returned to working on his computer.

The detective wouldn't admit it, but Woods was right. Ryan did know. Although not handsome in the league of movie stars like Brad Pitt, or George Clooney, the detective was aware that he had an attractive face that women found pleasing. And he wasn't above using that knowledge to move an investigation forward. He could have returned to Barton but had chosen to stay in the IT office to examine Scott's laptop and phone, hoping that the twins would quickly complete the fingerprint report on the will and bring the results to him . . . and they had done just that. The Ging coke analysis was an added bonus.

Ryan slipped a pair of white evidence gloves from his pocket and pulled them on. Opening the evidence bag, he took out Scott Dean's will, photographed it with his phone, and sent it to Zoe's cell. Then he dialed her number and waited.

When the constable answered, Ryan asked her to arrange for Brad Costello to come into the Barton station within the hour. "Tell him that there are a few loose ends that need to be tied up," he said.

"What if he can't make it at such short notice?"

"There won't be a problem if you say that it's about the will that we've now found. Put him in Interview Room One."

Ryan also told the constable to call a woman named Nancy Kallis. "Her contact details are in the will I've just sent to your phone."

"When do you want her to come in?" Zoe asked.

"In the next hour. Just say we need to confirm a few details on Scott Dean's will. You can put her in Interview Room Two.

"Can I tell her Scott is dead?"

"Yes, definitely. And that he died of an overdose."

"And you're sure she'll be available?"

"Absolutely no doubt. But, and this is important, you have to call Brad Costello first and then leave it for at least ten minutes before you contact Nancy Kallis. And don't let them see each other.

"But . . ."

"Please, trust me on this. And one more thing. Can you print off two copies of the Scott Dean's will that I've just sent to you?" the detective asked.

"OK," Zoe confirmed before Ryan rung off.

The detective slid Scott Dean's laptop and phone back into the plastic bag and stood up.

Woods glanced over. "You off?"

"Yes. Thanks for all your work and for letting me use the space."

"No problem."

Ryan walked to the door. "And remember to pass my message onto Kavia."

"Will do," Woods said.

FORTY-SEVEN

As Ryan was leaving for Barton, Stack was about to return to Sydney. She jammed on the Mustang's brakes and spun the car around.

Micky awoke with a start. "What the fuck," he said, looking around. "What you doing?"

"We're going back," Stack said, pressing her foot hard down on the accelerator.

"Why?"

"Are you deaf? Can't you hear that?"

That was high-pitched screaming and wailing coming from the weasel's cage on the back seat.

"Oh yeah. What is it?"

"It's not an it. It's Bumpy. I think he's dying."

"Let him die then."

Stack couldn't believe what Micky had just said. "You're a bastard, you know that? Bumpy's my friend." She thought about adding that he was more of a friend than you cluck nuts but thought better of it.

"Sure, he's your pal, but we need to find that coke. Our lives depend on it. So let's go on."

Stack flicked her head around and glared defiantly at him. "No."

Micky would appear to be the alpha in the couple's relationship to the casual observer, but that was not the case. For Stack, Micky had two positives going for him—he was OK to work with most of the time and was good in bed. But he also had a long list of negatives, including being childish, impulsive, mean, stupid, and unreliable. So although she quite liked the man, that was about it—nothing more.

On the other hand, Stack knew that Micky loved her—really loved her. She would often catch him staring at her with big, droopy eyes—like an ugly, lovesick monkey. And he was always going on about how they were the perfect couple. He even once said that they should get married and have kids—which was such a horrifying thought Stack had had nightmares about it for days.

"Stack, we should continue on," Micky said.

"No," she repeated. And then she used her old but consistently successful line: "You do want me to be happy, don't you?" She paused, waiting for his reaction. He was softening but was not there yet. "It's not fair in his condition, Bumpy has to bounce around in the car. He'll be more comfortable at home, and I can look after him there . . . Please." Now one final push: "Tomorrow he'll be better, and we can come back up, OK?"

"Tomorrow?"

"Definitely." She gave him one of her patented 'shucks' looks that always melted the poor sucker's heart.

"Oh, all right," he said.

BIG JAY AND THE LION HAD A DECISION TO MAKE TOO, and they decided that the Crescent Hotel would be the place in which to make it. Not just was the pub a discreet place to meet in, it was also lunchtime, and they were hungry. Of course, when you are both over six foot four inches tall and weigh well over two hundred and fifty pounds, food is rarely far from your mind. So, it was with a sense of relief that the two men hurried into the bar.

The Crescent Hotel, slap bang in the heart of Kings Cross, was a favorite for both men, though its charms were not immediately obvious. The hotel was poorly lit, and the regulars were not what anyone would describe as being 'of good standing.' They were old school Crossers—stubborn miscreants for whom the gentrification of the area signaled its demise. Imbued with an Australian sense of stubbornness, the pub was one of the few places Big Jay and The Lion still felt at home.

The big men made for the middle booth and collapsed on the padded black leatherette seats. From here, both had a clear sight of the bar, and for Big Jay, the door outside to the left. The Lion had the diagonally opposite view to the entrance door to the right; so they had all entrances and exits covered. The men were regulars here, though they usually came in on different days. They didn't have to wait long for service. Hilda Floris, a fixture in the pub for over twenty years, had seen them enter and immediately poured two schooners of beer before coming over.

"What's it to be gentlemen? The usual?" she said, placing the beers on the table. "Rib eye steak, well done for you?" she asked, addressing The Lion.

"Thanks, Hilda."

"And the same for you?" she said looking at Big Jay.

"You got anything like a salmon burger?" Big Jay asked.

"A salmon burger?"

Hilda and The Lion stared at Big Jay. They both lived in a world of unchanging constants—a place where you always knew where you stood. To throw a salmon burger into the mix was tantamount to tipping the world on its axis.

"Sure, we can do that," said Hilda after a long moment, her face wrinkling as she tried to regain her composure. "I'll get those orders for you." She headed back to the bar.

Big Jay picked up his beer and tapped his substantial gut. "Got to think of my figure. Maybe you should consider that too?"

It was a masterly retort. Big Jay had faced head-on the shock of the salmon burger and then parried with an attack.

"Nah, I'm fine." The Lion tapped his stomach too. "It's taken me years to get this. I wouldn't want to lose it now." He paused. "Besides, being skinny wouldn't be good for my brand—yours neither."

The reply was said almost as a throwaway, but Big Jay didn't like it—not one bit. What was The Lion on about, 'his brand'? Where the fuck had he got that from? Some New Age marketing book? Was he saying that losing a few pounds was somehow wrong?

"Yeah, maybe. But I want to give it a go," Big Jay said.

The Lion smiled. "Whatever."

Silence. Then: "So, what do you think?" Big Jay asked.

It was the question they had come to answer. Decision time. They had to talk about the job they'd been given.

Big Jay and The Lion had roles in Bruno's gang akin to C-suite executives of a large corporation. Big Jay's domain was drugs—gak, heroin, weed. The Lion was in charge of anything that involved women, men, and children—strip clubs, massage parlors, prostitution, and sex trafficking. Under normal circumstances, what they were about to do would have been way below their pay grade. Kidnapping, bashings, and torturing were usually assigned to lowly gang members, but this job was exceptional.

"I think we should motor up tomorrow. I've got things to wrap up here," The Lion said.

"Me too. Lots of things. So no hurry," Big Jay said, slurping a mouthful of beer.

Decision made, it was time to eat. Detective Ramesh Ryan's kidnapping would have to wait until the next day.

FORTY-EIGHT

Detective Ryan had no idea about his proposed kidnapping nor indeed that it had been postponed for a day. Scott Dean's will was the only thing on his mind, as he arrived at Barton Police Station. Seeing the car park was now completely full, Ryan pulled up on the main road. Grabbing the bags containing the electronics, Scott's will, and the forensic report, he hurried into the building.

Inside, The Sarge and Jackie sat working. Zoe stood by the printer, slipping papers into a blue folder. "Afternoon," they all chorused as the detective came in.

"Hi," Ryan said, placing everything he was carrying onto his desk.

"I've put Nancy Kallis in the second interview room. Brad Costello hasn't arrived yet, but he's agreed to come," Zoe said.

"How was Miss Kallis?"

"Upset. She was shocked when I told her about Scott Dean's death."

"She hadn't heard?"

"No."

Ryan pointed at the blue folder Zoe was grasping. "Copies of the will?"

"Yes."

"OK, let's go see her. And bring those duplicates with you."

Nancy Kallis sat sipping a cup of tea in Interview Room Two. Her eyes were teary, her red lipstick smudged, and her black hair disheveled.

"This is Detective Ryan, Miss Kallis. He wants to talk to you about Scott Dean's will," Constable Yang said as the cops entered and sat down opposite the distraught woman.

"Yes, I know the detective," Nancy Kallis said, reaching for her small black clutch bag and retrieving a scrunched-up tissue to dab her eyes.

"You've met?" Zoe said, glancing at Ryan and thinking: Why hadn't he mentioned that?

"It was at a local Narcotics Anonymous meeting. He was there . . ."

"For research," Ryan said.

"Yes, research," Nancy Kallis agreed. "Scott was there that day too. He was a regular. I knew him well. We were very close." She paused. "Constable Yang said it was an overdose?"

"Yes," Ryan said.

"Tragic."

"Are you surprised?" Ryan asked.

The woman sighed heavily. "We're all human. All fallible."

Nancy took a gulp of tea.

"Had he lapsed before?" the detective asked.

"Not in the past few years. And I would have known. As I said, I was a very good friend . . ."

"So why do you think this happened now?" Ryan queried.

"I can't really explain it. Of course, Scott had been depressed for a long time, but I thought that Brad . . ."

"Brad Costello?"

"Yes. Meeting Brad was a help. Scott was so much happier after that."

"Brad Costello knew that you were close to Scott?"

"Of course."

"But he didn't tell you about Scott's death?" the detective asked.

"No," Nancy said hesitantly.

"Why do you think that was?"

Nancy sniffed. "Well, just between you and me detective, Brad and I hadn't been getting on that well recently. I think he was jealous of my relationship with Scott."

"And that's why he didn't inform you of his death?"

"I assume so," Nancy replied.

The door behind them opened, and Jackie poked her head around. "Your other visitor has just arrived. I've put him in One."

"Thank you, Jackie," Ryan said as she closed the door behind her.

The detective indicated the blue folder Zoe held. "Could you give Miss Kallis a copy, please, constable?"

Zoe offered Nancy Scott Dean's will. "Please read through it," the detective said as he stood up. Taking her cue, Zoe did the same, picking up the blue folder as she did.

"Excuse us. We'll be back soon," the detective said.

Outside, the two cops headed up the corridor.

"What's going on, Ryan?" Zoe whispered. "Why didn't you say you'd met Nancy Kallis before? And why didn't you put Brad Costello and her together? He's the Executor, so shouldn't he explain about her being the Beneficiary?"

"All in good time," Ryan said, opening the door to Interview Room One. Inside, Brad Costello sat at the table.

The detective and the constable took their seats opposite.

"Thanks for coming in at such short notice," Ryan said.

"Like I told you earlier, anything to help. So, what's all this about finding Scott's will?"

"Constable?" Ryan said.

Zoe opened the blue folder again and handed another copy of the will to Costello.

"We found it this morning," the detective said. "Please read it through."

The cops waited as Costello skimmed over the document. After finishing, he looked up.

"Scott made me the Executor?"

"That's what it says. You didn't know?"

"No. As I told you before, Scott didn't let us view the will when Kate Cassels and I signed it."

"So, are you surprised?" the detective asked.

Costello thought about that. "I'm surprised he didn't say I was to be the Executor, but I am the obvious choice."

"And what about Nancy Kallis being the sole Beneficiary?" the detective said.

"They were very close. Nancy had known Scott for a year—through the Narcotics Anonymous meetings—and she was a good friend too. Thinking about it, she too is an obvious choice."

"But you get nothing?" the detective asked.

"Money was never the reason for my relationship with Scott, despite what others said. Of course, I'm a little disappointed, but at least Scott recognized my talents and made me his Executor." He stopped. "I guess in that role, I should contact Nancy to tell her that she's the Beneficiary."

"Actually, you can tell her right now," Ryan said.

"She's here?"

"Yes. Knowing what was in the will, I took the liberty of arranging for her to come to the station. She's reading through it at the moment. I'll go get her," the detective said.

He stood up. Constable Yang moved to follow.

"No, constable, you stay with Mr. Costello. I'll fetch Miss Kallis in."

Ryan left, made his way back down the corridor, and entered Interview Room Two again. On his entry, Nancy looked up.

"Is this for real? I'm the Sole Beneficiary?" she said, waving the copy of the will.

"That's what it says. How do you feel about that?"

"Surprised. But then again, I am probably Scott's oldest friend."

"Brad Costello said something like that too about you."

"Brad Costello?"

"Yes, he's here. You can meet him."

Nancy Kallis pushed herself out of the chair, clutching her bag in one hand and the will in the other. As she went to follow the detective, her phone rang.

Stopping, Nancy opened her clutch bag and took her cell out.

"Hello?" She listened for a moment. "Yes, he's here. I'll put him on."

Nancy offered Ryan her phone. "It's for you."

"Me?"

"Someone from the office got our numbers mixed up."

Detective Ryan took the phone. "Hi, Jackie . . . yes . . . yes . . . Wait a moment, can you."

"Can you go into the main office, the one you first went into? It's through the door at the top of the corridor. I'll come after I've finished this call," the detective said to Nancy.

The detective waited until the woman had left the room.

"Thanks, Jackie. She's on her way. Bring her to Interview Room One in about five minutes," he said before ending the call.

The detective waited for a few moments more before leaving the room. He stopped outside Interview Room One. Using Nancy Kallis's phone, he searched for and pressed the most recent call listed. The detective held the cell close to his ears.

"Nancy? "a voice said at the other end.

Hearing this, the detective turned the handle and opened the door.

"Hello, Mr. Costello," the detective said into the phone while looking across at Brad Costello, who also had a cell to his ear.

Ryan held up his phone. "I got your number from the recent calls list on Nancy Kallis's cell. You rang her forty minutes ago, and the call lasted five minutes."

"So?" said Costello.

"So, you contacted Nancy Kallis before you came to the station."

"What of it?"

There was a knock on the door, and Jackie and Nancy came in.

"Miss Kallis, please take a seat next to Mr. Costello," the detective said.

Nancy hesitated and then sat down.

"Thanks, Jackie," the detective said. Jackie left the room.

"My phone," Nancy said, holding out her hand.

Ryan ignored her request. "Miss Kallis, you told us you didn't know about Scott Dean's death because Mr. Costello hadn't told you about it. And yet you spoke to him just forty minutes ago. Please explain."

Nancy hesitated as Brad Costello shot her a warning look.

"I'm waiting," the detective said.

"I forgot."

"You forgot that Mr. Costello spoke to you and undoubtedly told you that Scott Dean was dead? But both the constable and I just witnessed your Oscar-winning performance in the other room." He paused. "That's not going to fly when you go to trial."

"Trial?"

"Of course."

"Don't say anything," Costello snarled.

"On the other hand, if you admit the truth, here now . . ." The detective waited.

"What would happen then?" Nancy asked.

"Maybe we could cut you a deal."

Nancy hesitated.

"For god's sake, he's lying. He's just trying to trap you," Costello said.

Ignoring him Nancy pointed at Costello. "It was all his idea."

"Shut up. For god's sake bitch, zip it."

"Who you calling a bitch?" Nancy shouted back.

" Can't you see what he's trying to do, idiot?" Costello said.

"You're calling me an idiot?" Nancy raised her hand to slap him.

Detective Ryan grabbed her arm and pulled her back. "You have a choice too, Mr. Costello. You can either admit exactly what part you both played in forging Scott Dean's will and write statements to that effect. Or . . ." He let the words hang heavy in the air.

"Or what?" Costello asked defiantly.

"Or I'll charge you both with Scott Dean's murder."

"Murder? You didn't tell me he was murdered." Nancy said to Costello.

"Because he wasn't," Costello said.

Detective Ryan looked from one to the other. "You have my word that Scott Dean was murdered. And who were the people who had the best motive to commit that murder? The detective paused to give them ample time to think about this. "Both of you, of course! The people named in that forged will. You murdered him for his money."

"That's ridiculous. I had nothing to do with Scott's death," Costello said.

"Oh, so you have an alibi for the night of his death?" the detective said.

"I was at home."

"Alone?"

"Yes."

"Oh, that's right. I asked you that the other day. You have the interview record, right Constable Yang?" the detective said.

"Yes," the constable replied.

"Unfortunately, Mr. Costello, that's no alibi."

"But it's the truth."

"I hope for your sake the jury sees it that way," said the detective.

Nancy looked from Costello to the detective. "Did you kill him, you bastard?"

"Of course not."

"Can you take Miss Kallis next door, constable?"

Constable Yang took the woman's arm. "Come along," she said, leading Nancy to the door.

"I had nothing to do with any murder," she shouted back at Detective Ryan. "Nothing."

As the door closed behind the two women, Brad Costello slumped back in his chair. "I want a lawyer."

"Of course. But an attorney won't do you much good. Scott Dean was murdered. And I can prove that you and Nancy Kallis conspired to profit from Scott Dean's death by creating a forgery of his will. So what better motive for killing Scott?"

Costello stared at him. "We didn't do it. You know that."

"It's not what I know or don't know; the real question is what will a jury believe?"

There was a long silence. Then: "Hypothetically, if someone is convicted of fraud, what kind of sentence are they looking at?" Costello asked.

"Ten years maximum. But if, hypothetically, that someone admits the crime and accepts guilt, there's usually leeway on the sentencing. Of course, hypothetically again, if there are two people involved and one admits everything first and implicates the other, then that first person would likely get the reduced prison term," the detective said.

Again, there was a long silence. Ryan waited. This was the moment of truth.

"I want to make a statement," Costello said.

FORTY-NINE

After Costello's confession, Nancy crumpled like a pack of cards. She signed a statement detailing her part in the scheme to rip off Scott Dean's estate. When the detective had both statements admitting guilt, he charged Nancy Kallis and Brad Costello with forgery. Then he released them, informing them that their court date would be confirmed later. Constable Yang was to accompany Costello home.

Returning to the office and carrying the two signed confession documents, Detective Ryan was feted like a conquering hero. The Sarge slapped the detective on his back. "I knew I'd made the right decision bringing this man in," he said to Jackie as he put on his overcoat, pushing his arms down into its sleeves. "A celebratory drink for everyone?"

"I don't mind if I do," said Jackie, slipping on her pea-green jacket.

"Not for me," Ryan said. "Zoe's due back soon. I'll wait for her."

"Very well. But if you change your mind, we'll be at the Royal. It's just up the road," the Sarge said, opening the door for Jackie.

"Before you go, Jackie, can you tell me the passcode for the printer."

"Bluey," she said.

"Thanks."

Ryan waited for the door to close behind them. Despite their excitement, he knew the case wouldn't be a slam dunk until Zoe returned, hopefully with what he needed. Meantime Ryan opened Scott Dean's laptop using the passcode Cyrus Woods had found. He attached the office printer to the computer. Scrolling through, he found the file marked Future and sent the document in it to the printer.

As the machine spat out the printed pages, the door opened, and Zoe returned. She waved a document in the air. "Got it," she said, offering it to the detective. Ryan quickly scanned through it.

"Everything in order?" The constable asked.

"Yep, the document you just gave me, the original will, is exactly the same as the will I found on Scott Dean's laptop."

"Why do you think Brad Costello kept Scott Dean's original will?"

"He needed it to be able to copy Kate Cassels's signature."

"Right," Zoe said and looked around the office. "Have the Sarge and Jackie gone?"

"Yeah. The Sarge was very happy. Even slapped me on the back."

"Doesn't that piss you off? You know he's been bad-mouthing you ever since you arrived," Zoe said.

"I'm guessing he thought I would make his life even easier, but it hasn't turned out that way. So you can't really blame him."

"You're very forgiving."

"I'm just a realist. It's what I expected." Ryan picked up Brad Costello and Nancy Kallis's signed statements. "Can you make sure that Jackie makes copies of these and files them, please?"

"Will do," Zoe said, taking them.

"How many?"

"In Sydney, the magic number is ten," Ryan said.

"It is in Barton too."

"So from the moment you found Scott Dean's will on his laptop, you knew the one with Brad Costello on as the Executor was a fake?" Zoe asked.

"That and the fact that the forensic report revealed that there were no fingerprints on Costello's fake will. He'd got the first bit right—using gloves to avoid putting his own prints on the document, but he should have realized Scott Dean's prints should have been on the will too."

Zoe shook her head. "How dumb is that?"

"Costello may have been stupid about that part, but he got some things right."

"What besides making an accurate forgery of Kate Cassels signature?"

"Yes, besides that, Costello knew about the back door to the house being open all the time. That's how he sneaked in. And he was smart enough to find the hiding place for the will. I'm assuming that Scott Dean inadvertently revealed it to him. That's the thing about grifters, they're always on the lookout for the main chance. And Costello didn't make the obvious mistake of naming himself as a Beneficiary. He knew all kinds of alarm bells would go off if he had have done that."

"In Nancy Kallis's statement, she said they were to split the monies from the sale of the house and anything else fifty/fifty. Do you believe that?" Zoe asked.

"No. Costello would have double-crossed her."

"You think?"

"Yeah. For sure. Costello's a greedy bastard."

"But not a murderer?" Zoe said.

"No."

"Even though forging the will gave him all the motive in the world to kill Scott Dean?" she asked.

"Murdering someone isn't easy. I knew Costello didn't have the killer instinct."

"So all that talk about charging them with it was bull?"

"I had to get them to admit to the forgery. Without the threat of a murder charge, we may not have got Nancy Kallis or Brad Costello's statements."

"But there was evidence. What about the phone call?"

"True. But any competent defense lawyer would have produced a plausible story to justify it."

"So why did Brad Costello choose Nancy Kallis?" Zoe asked.

"Being a skilled grifter, Costello had worked out that Nancy Kallis was barely scraping by and had dubious moral values. He knew she would go along with the plan."

"Did you know Costello would call Nancy Kallis just before she came into the station?"

"Brad Costello's whole plan was done on the fly after he found out about Scott Dean's death. He returned to Scott's house, stole the original will and later returned to replace it with the new forged copy. But Costello is a control freak who trusts no one. Although Nancy had agreed to the whole scheme, when he was called into the station, he rang Nancy to make sure she was completely up to speed."

"And once they both arrived at the station, it was just a matter of letting them dig their own graves," Zoe said as she placed all the folders on Jackie's desk.

"Exactly."

The door behind them opened, and Constable Jimmy O'Hagan came in carrying three pizzas.

"So, what are we celebrating?" he asked as he put the boxes down.

FIFTY

ZOE HAD CALLED JIMMY, MENTIONED A CELEBRATION, and asked him to pick up pizzas on his way into the station. And, while Ryan chewed on the thick, cheesy dough, Senior Constable Zoe Yang gave the rookie constable a summary of the day's news.

"Two deaths and then the bad guys being arrested . . . all in one week. Wow. This place is really hotting up," the rookie cop exclaimed, his mouth full.

For the next few minutes, all were quiet as they demolished the food. After that, it was time for Ryan and Zoe to leave. And by then, the country boy cop was whistling happily to himself. It was quite a transformation from the young, sullen man on offer last night. But Ryan knew Jimmy's good mood was unlikely to last. The late shift in a small-town police station consists of long periods of boredom followed by more languor. It's a far cry from how police work is portrayed in movies and on T.V.

OUTSIDE, THE DETECTIVE PULLED UP the faux fur-lined hood of his parka to protect himself from the icy wind. He had only put on his padded blue jacket at the last minute this morning when he'd seen a cold snap with plummeting temperatures forecast for the evening. Ryan hated the cold weather, and when, like now, the barometer suddenly dropped, it reminded him why he could never live anywhere that had a 'real winter.'

Climbing into his car, the detective turned on the heater. Cool air pumped out of the vents before being replaced by gusts of warmth. Only then did Ryan unzip his jacket, flick on the indicator and drive off.

As he headed for the Singing Pelican, the detective's mind wandered. Who could have wanted Scott Dean dead? Nancy Kallis and Brad Costello were clearly not the murderers, but what about other Narcotics Anonymous members? They all had extensive experience with drugs and most probably still knew where to get them. So could the murderer be one of them?

Ryan jammed his foot on the brake. He'd almost driven past the pub. The detective twisted the steering wheel hard to the right and went down to the crowded car park, searching for a space. Finally finding one, he reversed and switched off the ignition just as his cell rang. It was Zoe.

"I teed up the appointment for nine-thirty tomorrow morning. Is that okay?" the constable asked.

"No problem. How did she sound?" Ryan asked.

"Surprised. She wanted to know what this was all about. I told her what you asked me to say—that a new detective was working with us, and he wanted to catch up on the case. "

"And?"

"And she sounded excited. I hope we haven't got her hopes up too high, and she thinks we're going to tell her something new about her son. Maybe we should have just been straight and told her the truth. That we wanted to see her about a will and would explain more when met?"

"No. Any mention about any will needs to be done face-to-face, not over the phone. And Kate Cassels has to be there too," the detective said.

"Will you deal with that?"

"Sure. Oh, and by the way, Zoe, I forgot to mention that I was given the report on Ging's coke sample when I was down in Gosford. It's definitely not the same batch of coke from the one that killed Plummer and Dean."

"Right."

"Can you follow up with Ging's lawyer and see how he's getting on?" Ryan said.

"Will do. And I'll drop by the Pelican tomorrow morning to pick Kate and you up."

"Sounds like a plan. See you then," the detective said.

Ryan jammed the phone back into his jacket pocket, zipped his parker up, and pulled his jacket hood on before getting out of the car. Ignoring the freezing wind, he strode towards the pub, his feet crunching on the gravel.

Opening the pub door, noise and heat assailed the detective. A wood fire, its flames leaping high, crackled in the old-fashioned stone fireplace.

Kate, a tray of drinks in hand, was weaving through the crowd. A young guy mixed drinks behind the bar. Johnny stood on a small plinth dressed in a black tuxedo, white shirt, and bow tie in front. "Okay, settle down," Johnny said but was ignored. The chatter continued. "Quiet, please. I need your attention," he shouted. This time the talk subsided.

"Thank you." Johnny reached back onto the bar counter, picked up a hideous plastic pink bird, and held it up. "Just a reminder that you're playing for a truly priceless award—the right to win Piper the Trivia Pelican. So the stakes are high." There were whistles and catcalls as Johnny put the Pelican back.

"Okay. Okay," The pub owner yelled. "Now you've got five minutes to answer the questions. Good luck." Pens were grasped. Heads were lowered. Papers were filled.

Ryan took off his hood and unzipped his jacket before walking over to Kate, who had stopped to unload a tray of drinks. "Evening, Kate," he said, shouting over the noise.

"Hi."

"Got a moment?"

She glanced across at the bar. Johnny had joined the young bartender and was busy pulling beers. "Sorry, duty calls." She hurried back to the counter. Ryan watched her go before following her to the bar.

"Evening, detective. A nippy one tonight, huh. What can I get you?" Johnny said as the detective arrived.

"Nothing at the moment. I just need to take Kate away to have a word, if that's okay?"

"No can do, we're too busy."

"It'll only take a minute. It's to do with Scott."

Johnny placed two full schooners on Kate's tray. "Scott?" He frowned. "So she can return to his house now, can she?"

"No, not yet. And it's not about that. But it's important," the detective said.

Johnny hesitated and then shrugged. "Okay, but be quick."

"Thanks," Ryan said to Kate and pointed to the stairs. "Over there? It's quieter."

Kate left her tray on the bar and walked with him to the steps.

"You've got quite a crowd tonight," Ryan said as they stopped.

"It's Trivia Night—one of Johnny's money-making ideas. It's not usually as chaotic as this, though. Terry was due in tonight to help Johnny and Chris out, but he didn't turn up."

"Okay, I'll make this fast then. Are you free tomorrow morning for a couple of hours?"

"Why?"

"We've found Scott's will, and you're named as the Executor."

Kate stared at him. "Me? For real?"

"Yes, for real. I want you to meet the Beneficiary. Constable Yang will pick us up from here at nine."

"Who is the Beneficiary?"

"A Mrs. Woodford."

"I've never heard of her."

"Kate, I need you now," Johnny shouted.

The detective glanced around as the agitated pub owner approached. "I'm sorry, but you've had your minute."

"Ryan needs me tomorrow morning," Kate said.

"No way. That's your shift."

"It's police business," Ryan said.

"What?"

"I'm the Executor of Scott's estate," Kate said.

"So you found the will?" Johnny asked.

"Yes," Ryan confirmed.

"That's good. But like I said, Kate's working then. And she should be working now."

"I don't want to pull rank. But as I said, this is police business," Ryan said.

"And I'm trying to run a business," the pub owner said, turning. "Kate, come on."

"Ryan wants me to meet the Beneficiary," Kate said.

"Who is it?" Johnny said, interested. "Me?"

"No. Someone called Woodford."

Johnny pulled a face, obviously disappointed.

"That information's confidential, Kate," Ryan said. "Like I said, this is part of an important ongoing police investigation."

"Sorry. My bad." Kate turned to face Johnny. "You could put Chris on in the morning instead of me. He'd love a double shift tomorrow. He needs the cash."

"Don't we all," the pub owner said, sighing heavily. "Okay. Seeing as its police business. But now let's go, Kate."

Ryan watched as the two returned to the bar. Kate picked up her drinks tray and headed back into the crowd. Meantime Johnny climbed back onto the plinth. "Right, everyone. Time to find a winner."

FIFTY-ONE

THE NOISE FROM THE ROOM BELOW FADED as Ryan climbed the stairs. Reaching the landing, he turned and strode down the narrow corridor. Reaching his door, Ryan searched for the key. The parka was a great coat for keeping him warm, but its numerous pockets were a problem. Searching through them, the detective finally found the key and pushed and turned it in the keyhole. Grasping the worn brass handle, Ryan shoved the door open and stepped into his room.

Inside was bitter cold. The detective switched on the overhead light and hurried over to the gas fire. Like most things in the room, it was vintage but hopefully still worked. The detective ran his hands over the fire's silver metal surrounds, searching for the pilot-light button. Finding it, he pressed hard. There was a popping sound, and the creamy white element lit up. The detective felt heat beat against his legs and watched for a moment as the blue flames danced. Satisfied, Ryan slipped his coat off, folded it carefully, and placed it down on the sofa before walking over to the window. Grasping the thick curtains, the detective yanked them closed, blocking out the frosty black sky.

Since arriving in Barton, Ryan hadn't spent much time in his room. He had been way too busy. Tonight the detective had no plans to go out but felt guilty, like a schoolboy playing hooky. He was midway through the investigation—still searching for answers. But he knew he shouldn't fill every waking hour working. From time to time, he had to pull back. That would allow space for his mind to wander—something Ryan knew was a necessary part of his thinking process.

The detective headed across the room into the tiny kitchen. He flicked on the overhead spots. Cats and swinging were words that had come to mind when Ryan had first viewed the narrow space. Scratched and marked white countertops sat above old white wooden cupboards. On one side, one top was broken by a battered stove with two old hot plates and a grubby silver metal sink. On the other side, a vintage white refrigerator separated the Formica. Three off-white cupboards hung above it. The detective had already checked through these. There wasn't much to see—just the basics, a collection of cups, plates, bowls, a frypan, and three saucepans. But there was no coffee-making equipment.

Coffee was the detective's Kryptonite. Without three or four cups a day, he transformed from Dr. Henry Jekyll into Mr. Edward Hyde. For the most part, Ryan was content to drink more or less any sort of coffee—as long as it was brownish and hot, it did the trick. But the detective needed to have at least one premium brewed cup daily to satisfy his craving.

Ryan knew that any room rented on a police per diem would rarely if ever, supply the items he needed. So, when he went away, he always packed his 'coffee kit'—a French Presse, a coffee grinder, and a bag of beans, along with a large carton of long-life milk, to be used if he hadn't time to buy ordinary milk. All of this had been unpacked on Ryan's arrival. Now the detective was looking forward to a piping hot cup of coffee. But to make the brew, nothing could be left to chance. Ryan first filled up the kettle and switched it on. Then he took out a large spoon from the cutlery drawer, along with the beans and the grinder. Next, the detective searched through the cups. He chose the only one without a chip. It was yellow and embossed with a graphic of a bird, its mouth wide open—a singing pelican. Then the detective took out the milk from the fridge, placing it on the kitchen top. After that, he spooned the beans into the grinder and switched it on.

Despite the many recent technological advancements in kitchen equipment, the coffee grinder had been left out of the list of must improve. It remained an irritatingly noisy piece—which was why Ryan didn't hear his phone ringing until after he turned off the machine.

He hated interrupting the sacred coffee-making process midway, but the caller showed no signs of giving up. Sighing, Ryan walked back into the living room and retrieved the cell from his jacket.

"Detective Ryan."

"Evening Ryan." The voice was husky and deep and sounded to Ryan as if its owner needed to clear his throat. It was Detective Rob Headley calling from Sydney.

"How can I help you, Headley?" the detective said, walking back into the kitchen.

Ryan and Detective Headley had never been bosom pals, so it was a surprise that he had followed through on his offer to call. The only time they had worked closely together was on a big case a year ago. Then both had been part of a four-man squad set up after a hot tip about a drugs delivery to Oscar Bruno, but the investigation had fizzled out. The drop had never materialized, and soon after, the informant had disappeared.

"I just wanted to check up on you," Headley said.

"In an official capacity?" Ryan said as he spooned the ground coffee into the Presse.

"No, as a friend. How are you getting on?"

The detective reached to turn the kettle off before pouring the boiling water into the cafetière.

"You really want to know?" Ryan pushed the press plunger down slowly.

"Course. Being sent away was pretty brutal—Barton, right?"

"Yeah."

"Well, I was born in a small town, and I live in a small town, and I'll probably die in a small town."

Ryan shook his head. "Are you singing?"

"I thought that song would be appropriate. John Mellencamp. 'Small Town.' Know it?"

"No."

"How old are you—thirty-eight, thirty-nine?"

Ryan ignored the question as he poured the hot brewed coffee into the cup.

"Before your time, I guess. Before mine, actually. But it's a great tune," Headley said.

Ryan tipped milk into the mug and took a sip of the coffee. It was perfect.

"So do you?" Headley asked.

"Do I what?"

"Need some help?

Ryan thought about that. Irritating as he was, maybe Headley could be useful.

"Do you know of any recent drug drops?" Ryan asked.

"What? Since you've been out of Sydney?"

"Yes."

"There's always drugs coming into the city, you know that."

"By sea." Ryan said and waited.

"I did hear that Customs intercepted a suspicious Korean tanker off-shore a few days ago."

"And?"

"They found nothing."

"Could you find out the day, time, and exact location of the interception?" Ryan asked.

"Why?"

"Just a hunch. "

"A hunch, huh. You're a man of mystery. That's all you're going to give me?" Headley said.

"For the time being."

There was silence. Then: "Okay, I'll text you the information." Headley paused.

"You are okay in Barton, though, right?"

"I'm coping."

"And they put you up in a good place?"

"The Singing Pelican," Ryan replied.

"What?"

"It's a pub."

"Nice. Someone's got a sense of humor." Headley stopped: "Anyway, it was good to talk, man. Hasta luego."

The phone clicked off. Ryan took another sip of coffee and stared off into space, mulling over the unexpected call.

FIFTY-TWO

WHEN THE DETECTIVE GOT UP THE NEXT DAY, the room was frigid again. He immediately turned on the gas fire to the maximum before drawing the curtains and peering out. The weather hadn't improved. In fact, it had gotten worse. Outside was dark and oppressive. The black clouds were low. Rain pelted down. Monstrous waves smashed into the steep black cliffs, and thick layers of spray leaped high into the sky.

Seeing the conditions, the detective decided to give his regular run a miss. He took a quick shower and got dressed in his heaviest clothes. But on a day like today, he would need all the help he could get to keep warm, so Ryan walked across to his suitcase and opened it.

Being facetious, the detective had hung up his clothes and shoes immediately on his arrival. Then he had taken his toiletries out and unpacked them in the bathroom. His case was now almost empty. Ryan had left something behind, though—a black cashmere scarf. He could have hung it up, but he hadn't. Ryan had left one item in his suitcase in the superstitious belief that it warded off the chance of him permanently remaining in the town. Though he liked Barton, the detective had no intention of staying there any longer than necessary. Sydney was his home. That's where he belonged.

The detective peered at the scarf. If he took it out, nothing would remain in the suitcase. *Scary.* Was he really prepared to do that? But he needed the scarf today. What to do?

Ryan went to the closet. Inside, his clothes were arranged on the hangers in color order. The detective unhooked a thin blue shirt. Closing the door, he returned to the case, placed the shirt in it, and took out the scarf. Voila—one piece out, one piece in—problem solved, a crisis averted.

Now he had an important Sydney call to make. He reached for his cell and dialed. Half an hour later, the conversation was still ongoing when he heard beeping on the line. Seeing the number, the detective hastily wrapped up the exchange. It was his mother.

"Ramesh, is that you?" Mumta said, sounding unhappy.

"Yes. Of course."

"What took you so long?"

"Mom . . ." about to say more, Ryan stopped. There was no point. Mumta expected her son to be on an instant call back. When he had joined the police, he had told her that there would be occasions when he wouldn't be able to answer if she rang. She had agreed that yes, she supposed there would be those occasions, though, for the life of her, she couldn't think of any of them offhand. However, she would bear that in mind, so, when, in the middle of his first extensive training exercise, his mom rang, he ignored the call. And then he missed the next call, made just five minutes later, and the next one five minutes after that. Six calls and messages later, he finally gave in. He had rung her back. After that, Ryan accepted it was in his interest to answer his mom's calls immediately.

This morning Mumta only had two subjects on her mind. When her son was coming home to Sydney? His 'I have no idea' didn't go down well and led to a twenty-minute rant about how the Australian police were taking him for granted. Then she moved on to the weather.

"The Central Coast has a terrible forecast for today. What's it like there now? Rainy?"

"Yes"

"And bitter cold."

"I think so."

She sighed. "That's why you should be back in Sydney."

"Mother . . ."

"I know. You're there for your work. But promise me that you'll keep warm and dry in that godforsaken place."

"I promise. I have the gas fire on," Ryan said.

"So you're warm?"

"Yes."

"What about when you go outside?" Mumta asked.

"I have a heavy jacket."

"Not enough. What about a scarf?"

"Yes. I've got one of those."

"Then wear it," Mumta said.

"Yes, mother."

Mercifully the conversation had finished soon after, and his mother had rung off.

Ryan checked the forecast on his phone. The temperature had dropped considerably since yesterday. He put his parka on and wrapped the cashmere scarf around his neck. After switching the gas fire off, Ryan left, locking the door behind him.

As he walked along the corridor, he heard people talking below. That was odd. Every other morning no one had been around. This was normal in most pubs. Owning a bar involved working late nights, so the staff didn't usually come in until about ten or ten-thirty.

Today though, as he climbed down the stairs, Ryan could see Ellie and Johnny sitting, nursing cups of coffee and chatting. Attila lay on the floor. His head was down, and his eyes closed. There was a metal water bowl by his side.

Ellie waved as she sighted Ryan. "Morning."

"Up late?" Johnny said, turning to watch the cop approach.

"I gave today's run a miss. It looks bad out there."

"Lucky you, I had no choice. I had to take the dog out." Ellie said, shaking her wet hair. Water droplets fell onto the detective's jacket as she looked him up and down. "I see you've dressed for the weather."

"Yes, I suppose you being from . . ." Johnny began.

"Sydney," Ellie said, interrupting.

"Yeah, Sydney. That's what I was going to say . . . you probably expected it to be different up here, which is why you bought some heavy clothes. But to be honest, it's much worse weather than we usually get at this time of year."

"Climate change," Ellie said definitively.

"Must be," Ryan agreed, sitting down. "What brings you here, Ellie?"

"That's down to Attila. I promised I'd bring him here while Ashley was away. She comes in with the dog every morning for his biscuit."

"The Old Mother Hubbard I give Atilla," Johnny said.

"That's nice," Ryan said.

Ellie smiled at her ex-husband. "He's a real softie underneath all that macho bluster."

Ryan glanced from one to the other. The exes still appeared to have a reasonably friendly relationship.

"You should come in more often now you're looking after Ashley's dog," Johnny said.

"I have a job to do. I'm only in now because it's my 'work from home day.' Most times, I can't sit around gasbagging with you," Ellie said.

"Ashley did, and she works too."

"Being a yoga teacher isn't a full-time job," Ellie said, giving her ex a menacing look. The pub owner stood up hastily. "How about I get you a cup of coffee, Ryan, on the house, of course."

"Thanks. That would be great," he said.

Johnny walked off to the bar. Ellie watched him go. "That free coffee offer must have hurt. It's one of the many reasons Johnny and I split up. He makes Ebenezer Scrooge look like a big spender." She took a mouthful of her drink. "It's great to see you, by the way."

"You too."

They sat in silence for a moment. Then: "Johnny said something about Scott Dean's will and Kate Cassels."

Ryan said nothing.

"I'm not saying anything untoward, am I? Only he told me that Kate was named as the Executor and that you're both going to see Julie Woodford this morning."

"He told you that?"

"Don't frown. You know that in this town, what one person knows, we all know." She paused. "Odd, though. I mean that Scott Dean leaves his house and money to Julie Woodford. I didn't think they even knew each other."

"You talking about the will?" Johnny said, returning with the coffee. He placed the cup in front of the detective. "I've put milk in, but no sugar. Is that okay?"

"Fine, thank you."

"Scott should have remembered you too. You were his friend after all," Ellie said.

"It's no problem. I didn't expect anything." Johnny said and looked around as the door opened behind him and a large, bald man wearing a brown long Driza-bone coat entered.

"Morning, Johnny."

The pub owner stood up. "Hi, Jim." He glanced across at Ryan. "You know Ellie, of course."

"Hi Jim," she said.

"But you haven't met Ryan. He's staying here," Johnny continued. "Jim, meet Ryan . . . Ryan, meet Jim."

"Good to meet you," the detective said.

"You too."

"Jim runs the company that picks up my empty beer barrels. He collects them every week."

The detective turned as he felt a blast of cold air behind him. Zoe came in, her puffer jacket glistening with rainwater. "Morning, everyone. Detective, you ready?"

"I am. But Kate isn't down yet."

"Did you open up the back?" Jim asked Johnny, ignoring the constable.

"No, sorry. I forgot," Johnny replied.

"I come here every week, and you forgot?" Jim sighed. "Look, no biggy." He held out his hand. "I'll take the keys and do it myself."

"No, I'll come with you. I want to make sure you take the right ones," Johnny said.

"So first you forget I'm coming and then don't trust me to do my job." Jim smiled. "Don't worry, I won't make off with any of the full barrels."

"Easier if I go with you," Johnny insisted.

Jim shrugged. "Please yourself. Lead the way."

Ryan watched as Jim followed Johnny to the bar and opened the counter up.

"Where is that woman then?" Zoe asked, glancing around.

"Johnny's always complaining she leaves things to the last minute," Ellie said. She leaned in close to Ryan. "To be honest, Kate's wearing out her welcome here. Do you know when she'll be able to go back?"

"I'm not sure. Soon I hope," Ryan replied.

"I'm no detective, but you seem to be taking an awfully long time on a simple drug overdose case."

Ryan said nothing.

"I best be going," Ellie said and bent down to clip the leash back on Attila's collar. The dog rose and stretched out his hind legs. "What do you think, Zoe? Scott Dean's death and then this strange will. It's hard to make sense of it all."

"I'm just happy we have the best detective in the country to help us out. He couldn't have come at a better time," Zoe said.

"Spoilsport. You're as bad as Ryan. I can't get any gossip out of either of you," Ellie said, reaching for her raincoat hanging behind her chair. "Now, don't forget to give me a call about that dinner," she said, as she slipped on her coat.

"Will do," Ryan said.

Zoe glanced at Ryan.

"Come along, Attila," Ellie said, yanking on his leash. "Bye, you two."

"Okay, everyone. Sorry I'm late, but let's go," a voice shouted from behind. It was Kate, hurrying down the stairs.

FIFTY-THREE

"HI," BIG JAY SAID AS HE opened the passenger door of the white Hyundai iLoad van, the rain dripping down his face. The Lion scowled. Big Jay was running late, and he wasn't pleased.

"What's got your knickers in a twist?" Big Jay asked, settling into the passenger seat.

"I've been waiting over twenty minutes."

"So? You delayed the pickup by an hour."

The Lion stared at his companion or "Mr. Salmon Burger," as he had now decided to call Big Jay, though not to his face, of course. He could be touchy. "Well, we're not going to arrive until this afternoon, and the drive up looks like it will be terrible." The Lion pointed through the windshield at the rain cannoning down.

"If you'd rented an Australian car instead of this slant-eyed piece of shit, you'd cruise through it," Big Jay said.

The Lion clenched his fist. He had no idea why Oscar Bruno had insisted they go up together. "Shall we use your motor instead?" he said, already knowing the answer to his question.

"You what?"

"Maybe we should use your Ozzie supercar?" The Lion asked. He loved needling Big Jay. The big man drove Australia's fastest production car—a Holden HSV GTSR W1. It was his pride and joy and totally unsuitable for the job they were about to do. "Well?"

Big Jay said nothing.

Sensing victory, The Lion checked over his companion's clothing. Big Jay was an Australian who believed that it was perpetually summer and dressed accordingly. Today he was kitted out in a black zip-up hooded sweat, black stretch Chubby shorts, and white Nike Air Max sneakers.

"That's what you're wearing?" The Lion asked, looking Big Jay up and down.

"You got a problem with that?" Big Jay said, taking in The Lion's winter wear of a heavy leather padded jacket, black cargo pants, and boots.

"It's fucking freezing out there. But please, yourself," The Lion said, turning up the heating. "And where's your bag?"

"What do I need a bag for? I've got everything I need here," Big Jay said, flipping up his sweatshirt to reveal a SIG Sauer P226 stuffed down the front of his shorts."

"We might have to stay overnight, that's what," the Lion said.

Big Jay scrunched his face. "No way. We pick up the schmuck and return today."

"If you say so," The Lion said, jamming the accelerator pedal down and pulling out onto the main road.

UNLIKE BIG JAY AND THE LION, Stack and Micky weren't going anywhere, at least not at the moment. Stack grasped a small cross made of popsicle sticks and watched Micky shovel soil onto a tiny grave. He patted the earth down and looked back at the woman. She nodded. Yes, he was finished. He had done an excellent job.

Stack bent down to thrust the cross into the dirt. "This is thanks to my friend Bumpy the weasel who in his short life brought joy to both of us before his sudden death from unknown causes last night." She sniffed mournfully. Tears appeared in her eyes. Crossing herself, Stack stood up. "Say something," she said, nudging Micky in the ribs.

There was silence as Micky thought about that, then: "Okay, well, Bumpy and I might not have always seen eye to eye." He stopped. That was a stupid thing to say. Of course, he hadn't seen eye to eye with the weasel, the animal was ten inches high, and he was over six feet tall. "Despite all of that, I got on well with him, and I know he loved Stack, so that's all good. It's a shame that he had to die now so we couldn't leave earlier, but then I guess you can't decide when you're going to keel over, can you? Anyway, goodbye Bumpy." He started to lift his right hand up and then decided that maybe saluting the animal was a bit much. He glanced across at Stack. "Okay?"

"Good, except for that bit about leaving earlier."

"Oh. I thought I was saying something nice there," Micky said.

Stack's lips tightened. Trying to get Micky to empathize was futile. But at least he'd helped to dig the grave. And with the brief ceremony, she felt some closure.

After finding the animal dead in his cage in the morning, there was no way she could have just rushed off. And since the park was at the back of her apartment block, she could visit the grave regularly.

"Can we go now?" Micky said.

"All right." Bumpy or no Bumpy, Stack was enough of a realist to understand that if they didn't get up to Barton soon, their lives could end as abruptly as the weasel's.

Back in Barton, Senior Constable Zoe Yang pulled up outside the wooden slatted fence of Julie Woodford's bungalow. The constable was proud of her driving skills, but even so, had driven cautiously on the way over. The car's wipers had struggled to overcome the torrential rain, making visibility difficult. The roads had also started to flood, so aquaplaning was a real possibility. But at least it had been warm in the car. Zoe had the heater on full blast. Like Ryan, she hated the cold.

The constable switched off the ignition. "So, any more questions?" Ryan asked, looking around at Kate, who was clutching Scott Dean's will.

"I just have to read out the bit from this that says who the Beneficiary is and what she gets?" Kate asked, holding up the will.

"Yes," Ryan said. The young woman looked nervous, which was hardly surprising. A twenty-three-year-old is rarely asked to be the Executor of a will. But it appeared Scott had trusted Kate, though apparently not enough to reveal to her why he had decided to leave his entire estate to Mrs. Julie Woodford.

"There is one other thing you should know before we go in. Mrs. Woodford hasn't been told about the will."

"What?" Kate said, astonished.

"Her son disappeared years ago. The case was never officially closed. So, she may be under the impression that we are here to see her about that," Ryan said.

"Under the impression? Why didn't you tell her the truth? Tell her about the will?" Kate asked.

"We don't give out those kinds of details over the phone," the detective replied.

Kate took a deep breath. "I don't know . . ."

"It'll be fine," Ryan said. "I'll explain exactly why we are here before you read out the relevant section."

"So shall we?" Zoe asked.

Kate nodded. She went to reach for the handle before changing her mind. "Do you think this Mrs. Woodford will want to sell Scott's house?"

"Maybe," said Ryan.

"So then I'd have to leave?"

"If she did sell it, yes."

"Good. That'll give me the push I need to go to L.A.," Kate said as she climbed out and flicked open her umbrella. The others joined her, and, with the detective leading, they walked across to the gate. Ryan opened it and moved aside to let Kate and Zoe go through. Following behind, he glanced around at the garden. Even though it was winter, it was full of color—the yellow and reds of banksias, the white and pinks of camellias, and the blue-greens of grevillea's. And the shrubs were artfully arranged, filling soil squares dotted around the lawn. Julie Woodford obviously had green fingers.

Arriving at the front door, Zoe pressed the bell and waited. After several moments it was opened by a well-groomed, slim women in her fifties with brown, shoulder-length hair, cut in a bob. It framed a thin harassed face, hang-dog eyes, and a prominent nose. "Come in. Come in," Julie Woodford instructed eagerly.

Kate deposited her umbrella in the stand by the door, and Mrs. Woodford shepherded them along the hallway and into the living room. This room, like the hall, was painted white. A large three-seater beige cloth sofa was pushed up against net-curtained windows. It sat at ninety degrees to a smaller matching two-seater. The sofas were separated by a wooden coffee table. A round wooden dining table stood at the opposite end of the room, four padded fabric-covered chairs pushed under it. A large glass vase filled with pink carnations sat on the table. A funnel-shaped vase of red roses rested on the top of a white dresser close by. Except for the flowers, there were no personal touches in the room—no photos, no ornaments, and no paintings or mirrors on the walls.

"So who's who?" Julie Woodford said as they all stood awkwardly by the door.

"I'm Detective Ryan. Mrs. Woodford."

"Please call me Julie. Mrs. Woodford makes me sound like I'm a hundred and eight."

"I'm Constable Yang, Zoe. I rang you yesterday."

"Right. It's good to put a face to the voice."

"And I'm Kate Cassels, the Executor."

"Executor?" Julie hesitated. "I thought this had something to do with Nathan?"

"No, actually, it's about a will," Ryan said.

It was like a balloon had been pricked; the life seemed to drain from Julie Woodford's body. "Oh." She glared at Zoe. "I thought you said that was why the detective wanted to see me?"

"Well, yes, I said that Ryan would like to meet you. He's new here. But we've also come about a will."

"Whose will?"

"Scott Hartford Dean's," the detective said.

"Scott Hartford Dean." She twisted the name around her tongue, testing to see if it fitted. "Then you've come to the wrong place. I don't know anyone called Scott Hartford Dean."

"Perhaps if we could sit down?" Ryan said.

Julie hesitated, fighting between a desire to ask them to leave and being a polite host. Good manners won the day.

"Sorry. Of course. Please." She indicated the couches.

Ryan and Kate chose the three-seater. Zoe sat on the two-seater. Julie remained standing. "Before we start tea, coffee, anyone?"

"Not for me," Ryan said.

"Likewise," said Zoe.

"Kate?"

"No, I'm fine."

"Well, you're easy guests," Julie said, taking a seat next to the constable.

"This won't take long," Ryan said. "Kate?"

Kate took out the copy of the will from her pocket and spread it out. She explained that this was the Last Will and Testament of Scott Hartford Dean and then read out the information about Julie Woodford being the Sole Benefactor of the estate.

Ryan watched closely. If Julie was expecting this, then she deserved an acting award. Her face showed surprise, then incomprehension, and finally confusion.

"And you're absolutely certain that the Julie Woodford mentioned here is me?" she asked when Kate finished.

"The Benefactor is a Mrs. Julie Woodford who lives at this address," Zoe said. "There are no other Julie Woodford's here, are there?"

"No. So I'm the Sole Benefactor? How strange."

Julie turned to Kate. "Do you have any idea why my name is in that will?"

"Sorry. No."

"What's your connection with this Scott Hartford Dean?"

"I rent a room in his house."

"And he chose a young woman like you to be the Executor?. . . Not that that's a problem. You seem very capable," Julie added hastily.

"It's my first time. And you're right. It's daunting."

Julie glanced across at Ryan. "And since you are here, detective, I take it Mr. Scott Dean died in . . ."

"He overdosed," Ryan said.

"How old was he?"

"Just thirty-three."

"That young?" Julie said, thinking. Then: "So what happens now?"

"There are a few technical details we have to clear up first, but after that, Kate can organize a lawyer, and you'll have papers to sign," Ryan said. Silence, as Julie thought about this.

"Well, now that's over, is it okay if I go?" Kate asked eagerly.

"Sure," Ryan said. "Constable, can you drive Kate home, please?"

Zoe gave the detective a quizzical look. Was he trying to get rid of her? She hesitated.

"Constable," Ryan repeated. Zoe and Kate stood up.

"Thank you for your time, Julie," The constable said and waited for Ryan to join them.

"I'll stay for a few more minutes, if that's okay, Julie. This is a good opportunity to find out about your son's case."

Julie smiled. "Of course."

"Zoe, if you could pick me up after you've dropped off Kate."

"Will do," the constable said, remaining poker face while trying to hide her fury. What about all that talk about being a team? Obviously, that was so much B.S.

"Let me show you out," Julie said and led the constable and Kate into the hall.

Ryan heard Zoe thanking Julie for her time before the front door closed.

"I will take you up on that offer of a cup of coffee, Julie," the detective said on the woman's return.

JULIE'S KITCHEN, LIKE THE LIVING ROOM and the hall the room was a soulless space, spotlessly clean but with no notes or photos on the fridge or cookbooks on the marbled countertop.

"So, you're new to Barton, detective?" Julie said, switching the kettle on.

"Yes, very new."

"But you know about my son Nathan?" she said, opening a wall cupboard and taking out a jar of instant coffee.

"I know he went missing fifteen years ago and that the police investigated his disappearance."

Julie grasped two blue mugs from a shelf and put them next to the kettle before sliding the cutlery drawer out and picking up a teaspoon. "Strong or weak?"

Ryan couldn't stand instant coffee. He had never understood why it had the word coffee included in its title. Instant sludge would be a better name. But needs must. "Strong."

"Me too," said Julie, tipping two heaped spoons of the granules into the cups. "Sugar?"

Ryan shook his head. "No."

"Me neither," the woman said as she opened the fridge door, reached in, and brought out a milk carton. "You know I was really excited when your constable rang. I thought maybe you had something new to tell me about Nathan." She paused. "You don't, though, do you?"

"No. I'm sorry that that wasn't made clear. We just came about the will." He paused. "You didn't ask the question that most people ask."

"Which is?"

"How much?"

"Oh, yes, sorry. I suppose it was the shock. So you tell me, how much?"

"He has a big house and some money in the bank."

"So quite a lot."

"Yes. Quite a lot."

"Oh."

"You don't seem very excited."

"Is that rude of me?" Julie asked.

"No. Just unusual."

"This Scott Hartford Dean. Who is he?"

"Your son Nathan and Scott were both in the school diving team."

"Really. So there was a connection."

"Yes."

Julie thought about this. "What do you know about Nathan?"

"Nothing really," the detective replied.

"Oh, in that case . . ." Julie paused. "I want to show you something. Please follow me."

She led Ryan out of the kitchen, through the living room, and into the hallway. She pointed to a door opposite.

"That's Nathan's room." Julie opened the door and switched on the light. Ryan entered the room, stopping to look around. The place wasn't so much an homage to Julie Woodford's son, more a living, breathing time capsule of a teenage boy's room in the mid-noughties. The single bed was unmade, the blue quilt slung halfway across as if someone had just got up and flung it back. One wall had been painted black, and the others gray. All were plastered with posters of movies stars—Cate Blanchett, Kate Winslett, and Charlize Theron; exotic cars—Bugatti's, Ferraris, and Lamborghinis; and a picture of an orange sun rising over a crystal-clear blue ocean. An Ikea closet filled part of one wall. Its door was open, boy's clothes spilling out. The room's bright blue curtains were closed. A desk with an old-style Apple computer, an open notebook, and a pen on top sat beneath them. Two framed photos were positioned on one corner of the desk.

"This is how he left his room the day he disappeared." Julie said. She peered at the detective. "Crazy, right?"

That wasn't what Ryan was thinking. He had seen rooms like this before, rooms to which a son or daughter had never returned. And the detective had met the parents—people barely living. He knew Julie still wasn't prepared to give up hope—not before she knew for certain what really happened.

"This is why I didn't ask about the money. I hardly slept last night, imagining what you might tell me. I had two scenarios. The first was that Nathan was alive. You had found him, or at least knew where he lived. The other was that you had found his body. Either way, it would have been closure. And I would have given every cent I had in the world to get that."

"I'm sorry, not telling you really was unforgivable," the detective said. He walked across to the desk and picked up a framed photo of a geeky-looking boy with long unkempt brown hair and wearing black-framed eyeglasses: Nathan Woodford. His mother stood proudly next to him, her arms around his shoulders.

"He loved this photo," Julie said, coming up behind. "That's me, by the way."

Ryan had recognized the younger Julie Woodford, but she had aged badly.

"Let me show you something else." She pulled open the drawer under the desk, reached in, and pulled out three medals. One was silver, the other two bronze.

"Diving medals. I never knew why Nathan didn't hang these up on the wall. I guess he wasn't as proud of them as I was."

There was the distant whistle of a kettle. Julie carefully placed the medals back into the drawer and closed it. "Best make you that cup of coffee, now."

FIFTY-FOUR

"YOU REMEMBERED," THE DETECTIVE SAID AS Julie poured hot water into the cups.

"What?"

"When you picked up the diving metals, you remembered, about Scott Hartford Dean."

"Yes. You're right," Julie said, surprised. "I did remember who he was." She picked up the carton of milk.

"Just a dash, please," Ryan said.

Julie poured a lick of milk into each mug and stirred the liquid with the spoon. "Back then, Scott Hartford Dean was just called Scotty—which is why I didn't make the connection. He was the star of the diving team, the one who always won the gold medals. Nathan was never that determined. I think my son only did it for the girls. There was always a few that hung around the divers." She stopped to watch as Ryan picked up a cup and took a sip.

"Well?"

"Very good." It was a lie. The coffee was undrinkable.

"So why would Scotty leave everything in his will to me? It just doesn't make sense.

"Maybe it has something to do with Nathan's disappearance?"

"No," she said emphatically. "Everyone knows who was responsible for that."

"Who?"

"His father, of course."

FIFTY-FIVE

THE LION AND BIG JAY HAD reached the outskirts of Barton. It had been a slow drive. There had been flooding on the roads, causing tailbacks. But despite Big Jay's dire predictions about The Lion's car breaking down, the Hyundai had successfully navigated its way through the water.

Coming up, they had kept their conversation neutral, talking about the usual—football and women. Business, their business, was off the table. They had ignored the elephant in the room—Oscar Bruno. Loyalty was all-important in a criminal gang. Rarely did anyone question the decisions made by the boss. But this was a unique situation. They were on their way to kidnap a cop and bring him back to Sydney to be killed—a genuinely seismic event! If the man they'd been tasked to capture hadn't been the detective, they knew Bruno would have chosen someone else to do the job. But for such an important task, why send up monkeys when you had the organ grinders? It made sense. But there was a lot that didn't, and that was the problem.

Over the years, crime has changed. It has become far more corporate. Big Jay and The Lion may have dressed like thugs and may have talked like two casual acquaintances shooting the breeze, but this was not who they really were. They were strategy men, adept at analyzing schemes and policies and working out ways to maximize profit. But looking and talking the way they did was an advantage—people constantly underestimated them—not each other, though. They were both well aware that each was not who they seemed. Each knew that the other man was horrified about their boss's plan for Detective Ramesh Ryan.

But they had spent their lives working with Bruno. The company had been hugely successful under his guidance, its profits growing year-in-year-out. So both were unwilling to admit to any reservations out loud. For now, they accepted that their boss was still more intelligent than them and that the order to kidnap and kill the cop was a shrewd decision; so they were still going to bring the detective back. Of course, to honor Bruno's wishes, they first had to get to Barton's police station, and this, according to the G.P.S., was just a few minutes' drive away.

A FEW MILES AWAY, DETECTIVE RYAN AND Julie Woodford sat in the living room drinking lousy coffee while explaining what had happened the day Nathan disappeared.

"Paul, his father, came around in the morning, and they had a fight," she began. "We'd split up months before. I couldn't take his moods and his temper anymore. Anyway, he came by wanting to make amends."

"Paul wanted to get back with you?"

"Yes, but Nathan wouldn't even let him in the house. They had a big row. They were shoving one another and swearing. I tried to break them up and calm things down. Finally, Paul stormed off."

"And Nathan went to school."

"Yes." She took a sip of coffee. "When Paul was living with me here, they got on well. But when he left, they started to butt heads. It was both of their faults—Nathan's teenage testosterone kicking in and his father's drinking. Plus, I think Paul wanted his son to become a carbon copy of him. But Nathan was more sensitive. Shy. Particularly around girls."

"Did he have a girlfriend?"

"No . . ." She stopped. ". . . though he did mention someone he liked, and who he thought liked him." Julie clicked her fingers. "What was her name?" She shook her head. "No. It's gone. I'm getting more and more senior moments." She stared into space before pulling herself back. "The evening after the fight, Nathan didn't return. He didn't ring me either. I had no idea where he was."

"Did he often do that?" the detective asked.

"No, never."

"Did you go to the police when he didn't return?"

"There would have been no point. I knew the police would have just told me to wait. They would say that Nathan would turn up. And he was eighteen by then—an adult. Plus, it was a Friday night too, so there was no school the next day. I didn't want to look like an over-anxious helicopter mom," Julie said.

"But Nathan didn't come back that night?"

"No."

"When did you inform the police?" Ryan asked.

"The next day. I told Paul then too."

"How did he react?"

"He was strangely pleased. He said it was a good thing that Nathan had finally cut the apron strings."

"And the police?"

"They gave me the 'boys will be boys' speech and said that he was probably with a girl somewhere. Besides, they were swamped because there had been a big storm in the night, and many properties were damaged. It was still raining heavily the next morning."

"When did they start to look?" the detective asked.

"Not until the Sunday. They checked that he had left school as usual on Friday, but Nathan vanished into thin air after that."

"So, what did the police think?" Detective Ryan asked.

"At first that he had run away after the fight with Paul."

"Did you think that had happened?"

"No way. And as time went on, I came to believe that Paul knew more than he was saying. And the police thought that too eventually," Julie replied.

"They thought he had something to do with Nathan's disappearance?"

"Yes, but they didn't have any proof. Paul said he was home alone Friday night, and they couldn't prove or disprove that."

"And what about you?" he asked.

"Paul had such a short fuse, and he really held a grudge. That morning Nathan humiliated him in front of me. I think he confronted him again that night," Julie said.

"And."

"Maybe he punched Nathan, and he fell and hit his head or something. I don't know."

"So what about the body?"

"Paul was a truck driver and worked up at the local quarry. You can put two and two together."

"Did the police search the quarry?" the detective asked.

"Yes, but they never found a body."

"And you never heard from Nathan again?" Ryan asked.

"No." Julie said.

"What did you do?"

"I went crazy at Paul. I accused him of murder. He cried and claimed, Nathan going had nothing to do with him. And then he left."

"He left Barton? Where did he go?" Ryan asked.

"No one knows. My husband was always talking about us moving to England, so maybe he went there," Julie replied.

"But didn't the police try to stop him?"

"How could they. They had no proof. If I'm honest, nor did I."

Ryan's phone rang. He reached into his pocket to retrieve it. "Hello." He listened. "Constable Yang's back," he said, clicking his phone off. "I should go."

JULIE WOODFORD AND DETECTIVE RYAN WALKED down the hallway. She was quiet now, thinking about her son.

"I was admiring your garden on the way in. It looks great," Ryan said, attempting to lighten the mood. "I noticed all the beautiful flowers inside too."

Julie smiled. "It's the only thing I really enjoy doing nowadays. And it's one advantage of working at a florist,"

"Oh, did we take you away from your work?" the detective asked.

"No, it's fine. I told them I would be late in today."

She opened the door, and Ryan stepped out before turning to face her. "I promise I'll look into Nathan's disappearance. The fact that Scott Dean left everything to you must have something to do with it."

"You think?"

"Of course. You didn't even know the man. But he knew Nathan," he said.

Julie nodded. "Thank you."

Ryan smiled. He could feel her pain. Shivering, he hurried to the constable's waiting car, eager to get out of the rain and the bitter cold.

"Do you want me to take you to the station?" Zoe asked as Ryan slid into the seat next to her.

"No. Back to the pub, please. I need to pick up my car."

Zoe pulled out into the road.

Ryan glanced across at her. "I'm sorry," he said.

"What for? There's nothing for you to be sorry about."

"There is. I know I said I would try to make sure you worked with me, but the truth is that sometimes it's just easier for me to do things alone," Ryan said.

"Of course."

"You mean that?"

"Of course means of course. You're the detective; I'm just a constable. I'm grateful that I'm able to work with you and understand that there are times that this just isn't possible, but . . ." She stopped.

"Go on."

". . . but I hate dishonesty. That's one reason I became a cop."

"You're saying I'm dishonest?" Ryan queried.

"I'm saying that if you had told me that you were going to talk to Julie Woodford without me being there, then that would have been fine. You've had years of experience and knowledge when it's best to do those kinds of things on your own, but please let me know ahead of time."

Zoe was the second woman that morning that had mentioned dishonesty to Ryan. Julie Woodford had been upset too. She was expecting the detective to be meeting her about her missing son Nathan and not about a will. But he had deceived her for a reason. He needed a face-to-face to see for himself how she reacted to the news that she had inherited money from Scott Dean. The only connection between Julie Woodford and Scott Dean appeared to be Nathan Woodford, and he had vaguely thought that maybe together they had had something to do with the teenager's disappearance.

Now though, Ryan knew that was nonsense. He glanced across at Zoe. "You know I came up with Kate in your car for a reason."

"Which was?"

"I wanted you to see how she reacted on reading Scott Dean's will, and I needed your input."

"Then why haven't you asked for it yet?"

"Because you haven't given me a chance," Ryan said.

"Oh."

"So?"

"I think Kate maybe knew what was in the will already—who the Beneficiary was, and that she was the Executor but . . ." The constable hesitated as she signaled, pulled off the main road, and headed down to the Singing Pelican car park. ". . . but she is an actress, so it's hard to gauge."

"That's my opinion too," Ryan said.

"Good."

"And I'll try to be more honest with you in the future."

"Good too," Zoe concurred.

The constable parked outside the Singing Pelican.

Ryan hesitated before getting out of the car. "One more thing. Do you know where the paperwork for the investigation into the Nathan Woodford case is?"

"All those records are up at the station."

"That's what I figured. I want to look through them. But, in the spirit of honesty, I want to do that on my own and not at the office. It's too distracting back there."

"So?"

"I'll collect the material from the station and bring it back here to read."

"Sounds like a plan. I'll see you there," Zoe said as Ryan opened the car door.

FIFTY-SIX

THE PROMISED SECOND TEXT HAD FINALLY arrived. F. again went through the motions of trying to trace the caller and got nowhere. They'd used an untraceable burner phone again. He read the message two more times, memorizing every detail. Then he had phoned Bean and read out its contents.

"So, what do we do now?" he asked.

"We pay the money."

" I was thinking that maybe we just ignore it."

"They could go to the cops if we don't hand over the ten thousand."

"But perhaps this is just the start. Maybe they'll keep asking for more."

"I said we pay the money, not any more money."

"Right, but . . ."

"Just listen for a moment. They want you to put the cash in a briefcase, wrap it up like a parcel, address it with the details they gave you, and then leave it at the Gosford store?"

"Yes."

"So they're stupid amateurs. What kind of a half-assed plan is that?"

"Agreed, unless . . ."

"Unless what?"

"Unless they've worked out some way of escaping undetected."

"That's possible."

"Why don't I plant a tracker in the case?"

"You don't think they'll be expecting that?"

"Maybe. Maybe not."

"No. Too risky. If they find it, they'll know we double-crossed them. Who knows what they would do then? You watch who comes for the pickup, take photos, and then, if possible, you follow them and get the money back."

"And if they do something we haven't thought of?"

"Then you have the photos, so we can find them. We know they probably live in Barton, so how difficult can that be?"

"And what happens then?"

"When?"

"When we know who it is?"

F. heard Bean take a sharp intake of breath.

"Do I have to spell it out?" There was a click as Bean ended the call.

Big Jay and The Lion had a plan—a simple one. They would wait as long as necessary. The Lion had parked the silver Hyundai down the road from the Barton Police Station

They had only been parked a short time before they saw the detective arrive. He had parked his green Ford Focus on the main road before hurrying into the station.

"That's him, right?" The Lion had asked.

"'Course. How many Indian detectives can there be in this shit hole?"

"I'm betting he'll come out for lunch," Big Jay said, slumping back in his seat.

"Yeah," The Lion agreed.

Per the plan, they waited, though that wasn't as easy as it sounded. Neither Big Jay nor The Lion enjoyed sitting around. They both had limited attention spans and got bored easily, so it was a relief when the detective reappeared.

"Hey," Big Jay said, nudging The Lion. "That's him."

The Indian detective had stopped outside the station doorway to button up his raincoat before heading to his car. Moments later, the vehicle pulled away.

The Lion waited for a few moments before following. Neither Big Jay nor he was sure what would happen next. If, as they hoped, the detective was going for lunch, then they might be able to grab him outside the restaurant.

The detective's car turned left and then took a right turn. Ahead The Lion saw the familiar golden arches of McDonald's

"What do you think?" asked Big Jay quietly.

"Yes, possible."

And the possible became a definite as the Ford Focus signaled and drove around the back of the fast-food restaurant.

The Lion released his foot from the brake, pushed it down on the accelerator pedal, and followed. The detective had parked in the middle row. The Lion reversed directly behind the detective's car.

Big Jay opened the glove box and removed two masks. Both were hideous. One was the face of a frightening-looking clown—gray-faced, with massive sharp teeth, red lips, a red nose, black mascaraed eyes, and tufts of red hair. The other was a ghoul with a gray skull, rotten teeth, half a nose, and scary eye sockets. They had been chosen for maximum shock value. If anyone came out of Macca's and witnessed the kidnapping, their attention would be on the masks. The kidnapper's height, their weight, and whatever else they were wearing would be ignored.

Big Jay handed the skull mask to The Lion and then peered into the side mirror. The detective had joined the short line and was waiting to order. "One camera," The Lion said as he checked the building out through his side mirror.

"Fine."

Neither man was much worried about that. The Lion had a spare set of stolen plates in the back. Once they were on the road, they would take the originals off and replace them with these tags, so, if the camera did record anything, the cops would have different plate numbers. Their van had been rented with fake ID, and it would be torched the moment they completed the job.

Inside the restaurant, the detective had been handed a bag of food. He made for the back door.

"He's coming out," Big Jay said.

Both men reached for their weapons—Big Jay's SIG Sauer was stuffed down his shorts, and The Lion's Remington 870 pump-action shotgun lay on the floor next to him. The men had checked and loaded the weapons while waiting outside the police station. They were tense. There were still so many things out of their control—things that could go wrong.

Big Jay made the sign of the cross while The Lion took three deep breaths trying to calm himself. Then the men slipped on their masks. The Lion opened the driver's door and stepped out. Big Jay jumped down. He slid open the van's side door, watching as The Lion set off.

The Indian detective quickly walked to his car. He held the food bag in one hand and was searching in his raincoat pocket for his keys. Finding them, he pressed the auto-key fob. The car doors unlocked.

As the cop took a step forward, he heard the unmistakable sound of a shotgun being racked and felt the pressure of a barrel being pressed hard into the back of his neck. He froze.

"Drop the keys here," The Lion said, his open hand sliding in front of the detective.

The man obeyed instantly. He would do whatever he was asked.

"Now turn around and go to the open door where the clown is standing."

The detective did what he was told and walked towards the man in the clown mask.

"Get in," The Lion ordered.

Big Jay helped him along, pushing the detective hard from behind. The man sprawled forward, his body pitching onto the floor. Big Jay and The Lion jumped into the back of the vehicle. Big Jay picked up the bag of food and closed the side door while The Lion raised the Remington and smashed the weapon's wooden butt hard down onto the detective's head.

The Lion was an expert at cold-cocking. He knew how to use just enough force to knock a man unconscious but not enough to do any permanent damage. The detective would awake with one heck of a headache but nothing more. That was the way Bruno would want it. The drug boss had specifically said he didn't want damaged goods delivered.

So far, the kidnapping had gone like clockwork, but the men knew that time was ticking on. They had given themselves four minutes. Two minutes had already passed. Ripping off their masks and putting down their weapons, they worked quickly and efficiently. Big Jay pulled out a roll of gray duct tape and plastic clips from a bag sitting behind the passenger seat. He tossed the ties over to The Lion. Then Big Jay took a switch knife from his pocket, released the blade, and cut a strip of the sticky sheet off. He pushed the unconscious detective's face up and slammed the tape over his mouth, making sure that his nose was well clear so he could breathe. Next, he wound the duct tape around the detective's ankles before slitting it with the knife. Meantime The Lion yanked the detective's arms behind him and slid one of the black hoops over each of his hands before pulling the two ties tight.

Big Jay closed the switchblade and dropped it back into his pocket before retrieving a brown hessian sack from behind the passenger seat. "Ready?" he asked. The Lion nodded and moved to the right of the prone detective. Big Jay remained on the left. Together they each grasped one of the detective's arms, yanking him up and slamming him hard against the vehicle's side. Then in one fluid movement, Big Jay jammed the bag over the unconscious cop's head. At the same time, The Lion unbuttoned the detective's raincoat and removed his .38 Smith and Wesson from its holster belt. He handed the weapon to Big Jay, who stuffed it in his pants. Continuing to check the man's pockets, The Lion found his wallet, iPhone, and an ID badge. He pushed the wallet and badge into his pocket and dropped the iPhone to the floor before stomping on it hard. Big Jay shoved the detective back onto the floor while The Lion picked up a heavy black waterproof sheet from behind the seats. The men unfolded the cover and dropped it on top of the cop.

The Lion checked his wristwatch and grinned. "Three and a half minutes. Not bad for a couple of oldies."

DETECTIVE RAMESH RYAN HURRIED UP THE station corridor. "Afternoon, detective," the Sarge said, coming out of the bathroom and pushing open the office door. He allowed Ryan to enter in front of him. The room was empty.

"Before you ask, Zoe and Jackie are still in the Evidence Room digging out the reports you wanted," The Sarge said, sitting at his desk. "It's strange though, isn't it?"

"What is?" the detective said, peering at the updated whiteboard.

"Scott leaving all his money to Julie Woodford. Is that why you want to see the investigation into her son's disappearance?"

"I think there could be a connection."

"I don't see how. Everyone knows who did it."

"Did what?" the detective said.

"Killed Nathan Woodford."

"So you think he was murdered?" Ryan asked.

"Must have been. Otherwise, why didn't Nathan Woodford come back to see his mom? No, he was definitely killed. By the father."

"That's what the investigation found?"

"'Course not. My predecessor, the late and great Sergeant Harry Robinson, wasn't about to put down in writing something that he couldn't prove. But he knew it was the father. He told me himself."

The door swung open, and Jackie and then Zoe entered. Both carried cardboard boxes.

"Let me take one of those from you," the detective said, grabbing a box from Jackie.

"Bit of a mess down there, Jackie?" the Sarge asked as Zoe put down her carton on the detective's desk.

"A complete dog's breakfast. We were lucky to find anything."

"I think everything there needs to be scanned and digitized. You up for that Jackie?" the Sarge asked.

Jackie certainly was. But it was not wise to look too keen around Bluey.

"I don't know if I have time. I'm only supposed to be here for a few more weeks," she said.

"I'm sure we can find the budget to cover any extension," the Sarge said.

"In that case, put it on the list," Jackie said, returning to her desk.

"I'll be taking this material home, if that's okay, Sarge," Ryan said, indicating the box he was carrying.

"Suit yourself. Oh, and by the way, one of your lot came by earlier looking for you."

"One of my lot?" Ryan said.

Sergeant Acton hesitated. The detective's tone indicated that maybe he hadn't phrased that too well.

"I mean a detective. Name of Karcan, or something like that." He moved papers around on his messy desk before finding what he was looking for. "Here." The Sarge handed Ryan a business card with Gosford Police Station's number, address, and a name: Detective Kavia Gupta.

"I told him you would be in soon, but he didn't want to wait. He said he'd just popped by on the off-chance, and he'd try again another time."

The detective said nothing, annoying the Sarge. Cops are nosey; it's a part of their DNA. The other detective had been equally circumspect about why he wanted to see Ryan.

"So, what's all that about?" the Sarge was forced to ask.

Ryan could have said that because Kavia was brown-skinned like him and had wanted to bond and exchange information about the prejudice he faced in the police force. But he was confident that answer wouldn't be well received. "He's from the Gosford I.T. department and may have wanted to pass on some additional information."

"There's a thing called the phone for that."

"Some people prefer to say things face-to-face."

"I'll take the other box out to your car, then shall I, Ryan?" Zoe asked, interrupting.

"No. It's fine. I'll take them out one at a time."

"That's crazy." She picked up the remaining box from the desk. "Where you parked?"

"At the back," Ryan said, giving in.

Zoe looked out at the rain from the rear station door. "It's easing."

"But it's still bloody cold."

She smiled. "We both sound so British, talking about the weather all the time."

They walked out of the station and over to the detective's car. Ryan pressed the key fob and opened the trunk.

"There's something I wanted to ask you," Zoe said. "I know it's none of my business, but this morning Ellie Sastra and you . . . well . . ." She stopped.

"What?" Ryan asked, placing his box in the trunk.

"Well, she's a bit of a heartbreaker," Zoe said putting her box next to his. The detective slammed the trunk shut.

"And you know this because?" he said.

"Because I'm a cop and a woman who lives in a tiny town.

"And I'm a big boy who lives in a big city, so I think I can handle myself."

"Yes, of course, you can," the constable said quickly. "Have fun with the reports," Zoe said, walking away.

Ryan got into his car. The constable was starting to sound like his mother.

FIFTY-SEVEN

RYAN PASSED AN ORANGE MUSTANG SPEEDING in the opposite direction as he drove back to the Singing Pelican. He took no notice of it. The detective was keen to read the reports. And, in the Mustang, Stack and Micky were too preoccupied with finding Ging to care about the detective in the other car.

It hadn't been a good trip up. Stack had spent the entire journey more or less silent. She was thinking about Bumpy. She had never felt this way about an animal before, and his death had affected her far more than she would ever have believed.

Micky, being a man, had assumed that Stack was quiet because she was annoyed with him. He had made a few delusory attempts at conversation, and when these failed, he had done what he always did in these situations. He ran his hand up and down her leg, muttering, "maybe we should stop for a few minutes." Sometimes this worked, sometimes it didn't. In this case, it didn't. It failed spectacularly.

Stack grabbed his hand and slapped it down on his leg. "Leave me alone. I'm driving," she'd said, and that was the end of that. Micky had spent the rest of the ride in silence too. The impasse was only broken when they had driven into Barton. Neither was impressed.

"This place is a shit hole," Stack said, looking around.

"No. This is no shit hole; it's a fart hole." Micky said, and Stack's face broke into a smile.

"You feeling better now?" Micky asked, confident that his juvenile humor had won her over.

"I was never ill. I was just thinking about things."

This was a novel concept for Micky. "What things?"

"Bumpy if you must know."

"Oh." What was it with that animal? Micky thought.

"So, how close are we?"

Micky studied the map on his cell. "Ging's place is about twenty farts from here."

Stack smiled and shook her head; so the ice had been broken. Bumpy had been forgotten. But Micky's toothache hadn't. He'd been trying to ignore the throbbing pain the whole trip, but as the car hit a bump, he screamed, "Ahh,"

"Your tooth again?"

"Yeah," Micky said, putting his hand up to his mouth.

"Before we see Ging, we've got a job to do. We're going to get that fixed."

DETECTIVE RAMESH RYAN HAD A JOB to do too but was finding it difficult to raise the enthusiasm. He glanced at the gas fire's flickering orange flames before turning to peer at the police report on the desk. It was part one of a five-part investigation into Nathan Woodford's disappearance. Ryan knew the cardinal rule of any police inquiry—the less you know, the more pages you fill. If there had been a definitive conclusion, then only one report would have been written.

His phone pinged. He glanced at it. It was a text from Ellie asking if he wanted to meet up for dinner.

Ryan sat back in his chair. The message had reawakened his annoyance with Zoe. Ellie was none of her business. She was a beautiful, single woman, and he was a single man. So what if they wanted to take things further?

"I've got some work to finish tonight. But how about tomorrow night?" he texted back to Ellie.

The reply came almost immediately: "Yes. Let's do that. Have a good evening."

So, that was that.

From below, he heard a voice testing a microphone. One, two, three was repeated several times . . . karaoke night again at the Singing Pelican, and they were setting up. Before long, the music would start, and things would get noisy. Ryan really needed to get on with his reading. He had procrastinated enough.

The detective stared at the coat of arms on the front page of the report. The emblem showed a soaring brown wedge-tailed eagle carrying a scroll with the word *Nemesis* on it. Above the bird was a smaller white circle, with a red cross and yellow stars on each stave and a yellow dragon in the middle—the St. Edward's Crown.

Two tram lines surrounded the eagle and the St. Edward's Crown. The words New South Wales Police Force were printed between them. A green wreath formed the final layer of the insignia. It was broken at the top by the crown of the Queen of England and by the Latin words: Culpam Poena Permit Comes at its base.

The badge was designed to impress; but Ryan had reservations about including the Nemesis banner, with its blunt message of vengeance and punishment. The Latin motto—in English, "Punishment follows closely upon the heels of crime"—didn't leave room for subtext either.

Penance and revenge were essential to any society, but Ryan believed the cause, the why of a crime, was crucial too. In his opinion, there were few evil people. The majority attempted to be law-abiding but sometimes failed. The detective saw his job as being about finding out why good people did terrible things. Only then was it time to consider their punishment.

He turned the front page over and began to read. The late Senior Sergeant Harry Robinson's name was typed at the top, along with the name and address of Barton Police Station. Robinson was identified as the investigator. Below was the name and address of the person who instigated the investigation—Julie Woodford—and the date she had reported the disappearance of her son Nathan Woodford.

Sergeant Robinson was obviously a stickler for detail and was meticulous about writing up the investigation's progress step by step. There was extensive detail of the limited places initially searched—excused in the report by the heavy rainstorms hindering progress. It wasn't until day two that Julie Woodford was interviewed by Sergeant Robinson. The Sergeant noted that search parties made up of Barton volunteers and police had been organized by day three.

Short interviews with Nathan Woodford's school friends painted a picture of a boy who was a loner, with no close friends, male or female. None of the students said they had any plans to see Nathan Woodford over the weekend. The diving club was his only extra-curriculum interest, and here Scott Dean was noted as one of its members.

Ryan's phone vibrated. He reached for it, happy to take a break. It was a text from Detective Rob Headley. The message detailed the information Ryan had asked him for. A Korean vessel named the Chong San had been boarded by Customs before Ryan headed for Barton. Headley had given the coordinates when the ship had been found. Ryan quickly checked these on his phone. The boat was some five miles off the coast and directly east of Sydney.

He rang back the detective: "Hi, Ryan here."

"Did you read the text?" Headley said.

"Yes."

"So, is that information of any use to you?"

"Could be. I'm not sure yet. You talked to the people who did the raid, right?"

"Yes," Headley said.

"And what did they say?"

"They had had a pretty solid tip about the ship and acted on it immediately. Although the customs didn't find anything, they were sure they had just dropped off a large drugs consignment."

"Right."

"So, is this something to do with your work up there?" Headley asked.

"It could be. I'll tell you more if it comes to anything. But thanks again. Much appreciated."

The detective clicked the phone off before calling Zoe.

"Hi, Ryan. I'm glad you rang. About what I said . . ."

"Don't worry about that. Could you follow up something for me?"

"Of course," she said.

"Can you check the current ocean patterns with the coordinates on that day? I'll message them over to you. Then I need you to work out how likely it is that a package dropped from there would be dumped on Barton Beach."

"That's quite an ask, Ryan."

"I know . . ."

"But luckily, I do know a local fisherman who can help me with that," Zoe said, interrupting.

"Great."

"I'm guessing you'll want that answer A.S.A.P.?"

"Exactly," Ryan said.

"By the way, about the foot, I've also checked up on missing persons. No one fitting the description you gave me has been reported missing recently, though that doesn't mean all that much. Sometimes it takes weeks before a missing person appears on the lists," Zoe said.

"Okay, well keep on it," the detective said, and hung up before quickly typing up the promised text and sending it to the constable. Then he stood, stretched, and walked over to stare out of the window. Lightning cracked the dark sky. Rain pelted down, hurling itself against the glass, while waves punched and kicked the steep black cliff rocks below. Tonight wasn't a good night to be out and about.

FIFTY-EIGHT

THE LION WISHED HE WASN'T OUT AND ABOUT, but as he told Big Jay: "What our Lord and Master commands, so we provide." Their lord and master was, of course, Oscar Bruno, and now they were on their way back to him with Detective Ramesh Ryan . . . but Bruno didn't know that yet. Being cautious, neither man wanted to jinx their plan by announcing that the job had been successfully completed too early. They would make the call to their boss after they had changed the van's plates.

A lightning bolt flashed across the sky, illuminating the road ahead and revealing a narrow track running off the road and into the dense forest.

"That's it?" Big Jay asked.

The Lion nodded and swerved into the drive, throwing Big Jay to one side, his shoulder knocking hard against the car window. There was a low, muffled groan from the back. Big Jay spun around and, lifting his flashlight high, pointed the beam at a black mound.

"He okay?" The Lion asked as he maneuvered the van along the narrow dirt track they had checked out on the way up.

"Couldn't be better," Big Jay said.

The Lion reached into the glove box for his flashlight as his phone vibrated. Picking the cell up, he stared at the phone screen.

"You coming?" Big Jay said, pushing open the passenger side door.

"Sure." The Lion dropped the phone back into his pocket and climbed out.

Both men were protected from the full force of the storm by the tree canopies. The dense forest dampened any car noise from the road, so it felt like they were miles away from civilization—totally private.

Big Jay gripped the side door handle and yanked it open. Jumping in, he grabbed the tags and tools. "Who was that on the phone?" he asked as he worked.

"Just a text, with the cop's address. Apparently, he's staying at a pub called the Singing Pelican."

"Bit late for that, isn't it?" Big Jay said, taking the new plates and a screwdriver offered to him.

"Yeah. I guess." The Lion frowned. "There is one thing, though." He took the phone out of his pocket and clicked it on. "It says he drives a Ford Focus."

"So. He does have a Ford Focus."

"But according to this text, it's blue." He offered the text up to Big Jay to read. "Wasn't he driving a green Ford Focus?"

WHILE THE LION AND BIG JAY were trying to figure out what was going on, Ryan fought to keep his eyes open. He yawned and pinched his arm as his head lolled forward. Downstairs the music had got ever louder. He could hear Lizzo's "Truth Hurts" booming out from below. Maybe it hadn't been such a good idea to read the reports in his room. He shook his head and pulled it up. He had to focus.

According to the document, the police were still convinced Nathan Woodford was just a runaway by the fourth day. By then, Ryan had read more than enough to get a measure of Sergeant Robinson. He fell into the 'more than my job's worth' category of cops—those who had joined the police because it was a secure job, which, if you kept your head down, you could leave with a reasonable pension. Robinson didn't want to believe that Nathan Woodford had been murdered. Nor did the boy's mother, Julie Woodford.

Ryan turned the page: day five. Sergeant Robinson had finally got around to formally interviewing his own deputy—Constable Gary Acton. Reading through the notes, it showed that the Sarge had been on foot patrol the night Nathan disappeared. He confirmed that he had seen

Nathan's father, Paul Woodford, walking along the beach in the middle of the storm—something he had noted was "unusual."

The detective stretched, trying to wake himself up. Then he flicked back through the pages to read Sergeant Robinson's first interview with Paul Woodford. It had covered the main points—where the man was on the night—home alone, he said; when he was told his son was missing—the next day by his wife Julie from whom he was separated.

Ryan forced himself upright and picked up his phone. What was wrong? Was he ill? The thumping music didn't help either. He dialed. Answering the call, Constable Jimmy O'Hagan was keen to talk.

"Hi, detective. How's it going? A nasty old night out there, right?"

"Yes, Jimmy, I wonder . . ."

"I bet the ocean's good and rough."

"Yes. Jimmy . . ."

"I'm glad you called. I meant to ask, do you think there's any chance of you putting in a word for me to get a transfer to Sydney?" Jimmy said.

"Can we discuss that some other time? I need your help," Ryan said.

"You do?" The country boy sounded surprised.

"I need Sergeant Acton's cell number. Have you got it?"

"I think so." There was the sound of papers being rustled. "Sorry. I'm sure I saw it somewhere."

"Maybe on his desk?" the detective said.

"Oh, right."

Jimmy's chair squeaked as he stood up. After a few moments, he was back on the phone. "You were right. Got it." He paused. "The Sarge doesn't like to be disturbed at night, though, not unless it's an emergency. Is this an emergency?"

"The number, Jimmy."

There was a brief pause. "Can you tell the Sarge you insisted?"

"The number."

Jimmy reeled off the Sarge's cell. Ryan clicked off the phone and redialed quickly. He was feeling really sick—like he was going to vomit.

"Sarge," the detective said when the call was finally answered.

"Who is this?"

"Ryan."

"Oh, hi detective. What's up?"

"I've just read your interview with Sergeant Robinson about the night that Nathan Woodford vanished."

"Oh yeah."

"You saw the father, Paul Woodford, on the beach that night."

"Yes."

"Where were you when you spotted him?"

"That was years ago, Ryan."

"It's important."

There was a long pause. Finally: "From memory, I was on the road about a hundred yards away. Paul Woodford was on the beach, walking away from me. But you must have read that in the report." Ryan could hear the irritation growing in the Sarge's voice, but he didn't care.

"Was that the first time that Sergeant Robinson had been given that information?"

"I guess."

"And how did he react?" Ryan asked.

"For Christ's sake, Ryan, can't we discuss this tomorrow? It's a cold case."

"No. Strike while the iron's hot. That's my motto."

There was a long sigh. It clearly wasn't the Sarge's maxim. "I think that what I'd said got Harry thinking. It was after that that he put Paul Woodford in the frame."

"Because it contradicted what Nathan's father had said about being home alone?"

"Yes. Then you'll see in the second interview with Paul Woodford that he admits to fighting with his son the day he disappeared. Another big red flag."

"A flag that sent the message to Sergeant Robinson that Paul Woodford killed Nathan," Ryan said.

"A bit of a leap, I know. And Harry couldn't prove it. There was no body, and all the evidence was circumstantial, so he wasn't willing to charge him. And then Paul Woodford left town. Again that could have been a coincidence, but it smelt to high heaven."

"There's no mention at the time of Scott Dean being a suspect?"

"No. Why would there be?"

"I don't know about back then, but he has just left his estate to Nathan's mother, which, as we discussed, doesn't really make sense."

There was a silence. "I see what you mean."

Ryan put his hand to his head. He really wasn't feeling well.

"Sarge, I've got to go. I'm feeling a bit under the weather," the detective said, clicking off the phone and standing up. The room swayed, and his head hurt. Coffee, he needed coffee. Ryan walked towards the kitchen, but as he did, he began to rock.

He had to open the door and let some air in. Ryan reached for the handle, turned it, and pulled. The door didn't move. He shook it. Was it locked? How could that be? He tried again. The same result. Locked? Okay, so where did I put the key?

The detective tried to think. It must be in his coat. Taking tentative steps forward and lurching from side to side, he went into the bedroom and reached the closet. He pulled the door open and stuffed his hands into the coat's front pockets: nothing. Where had he put it? Maybe in an inside pocket. He yanked the parka off its hangar and tried again. His hand gripped a metal key.

Must get back. Ryan's eyes were closing. He forced them open. This was no time to sleep. He lurched as he left the bedroom and, reaching the front door, tried to line the opener up with the keyhole. He kept missing until finally, summoning all his strength, he jammed the key in.

Ryan leaned his head against the wood. If he just closed his eyes for a few moments . . . He shook his head hard, pulled open the door, and fell forward. The music now was so loud. He vomited onto the carpet. The swirling colors of the sick and reds and blues of the carpet mixed and mingled.

"Help. Help," the detective shouted, his voice cracking. Sleep, his mind told him.

He stumbled forward. The hallway appeared to be never-ending. If he could only make it to the stairs. Just a few more steps. He pushed his hand out to grip the banister and missed. Falling forward, he twisted, spiraled down, and smashed his head against the bottom of the stairs. *Darkness.*

FIFTY-NINE

W**HAT HAD JUST HAPPENED? OR MAYBE** it hadn't just happened. Perhaps it had happened a while ago? Detective Kavia Gupta tried to remember and ignore his throbbing head. He had been about to get in his car, then someone had stuck a gun in his back—a man wearing a skull mask and carrying a shotgun. There was another one too—a clown.

He had done what they had asked. And then? He opened his eyes. What was that? It looked like meshing. It itched his nose and his face. The detective's I.T. training involved thinking coolly, calmly, and logically. Someone had put something over his head. And there was something weighty lying on top of his body too. Conclusion: A heavy cover had been thrown over him.

He tried to move his arms. They had been yanked behind him. His hands were tied. He tried to separate his legs. They were bound too. He could feel something over his mouth. He licked it with his tongue. *Tape.*

The weight above him suddenly moved away. The mesh hood was yanked off. A man bent down and forward, close to his face—so close he could smell Big Mac on his breath. The man jammed a phone on the side of the detective's face. "See, different," the man said.

BIG JAY SQUINTED AT THE IPHONE that The Lion held up against the cop's face. There was a photo of Detective Ramesh Ryan on the screen. Ryan was brown, and he had a handsome asymmetrical face, a small nose, and thick lips. The other man was brown too but had much cruder features: a large nose, small eyes, one of which was half closed—a lazy eye.

"Detective Kavia Gupta," The Lion read from the ID badge he had pulled from his pocket. "Two Indian detectives in one small town. A fucking miracle." He paused. "A good job we didn't call the boss."

Big Jay knelt down next to Kavia and ripped the duct tape off his mouth.

"Are you Detective Kavia Gupta?" He asked, his voice raised.

"Kidnapping, a cop, is a serious offense," the detective said.

Big Jay glanced across at The Lion. "Smartass here thinks he's telling us something we don't already know."

Kavia started to shake. Of course, they knew, and yet they weren't afraid—so these guys were aware of precisely what they were doing. Then he had another thought—an awful thought. He had just seen them.

"Look," the cop began but was interrupted by the duct tape being slapped back over his mouth.

"Up you come," Big Jay said. The men picked the policeman up and threw him out of the open door onto the wet ground. Moments later, a 9 mm slug shattered Detective Ravia Gumpta's skull.

BACK IN BARTON, ZOE HAD DECIDED to drop by the Ging's apartment on her way home—on the off chance that he was around. She'd rung the drug dealer's lawyer, Malcolm Morgan-Brown, first to tell him that the results had come back on the sample of Ging's coke and that it definitely wasn't from the same batch that they were looking for. In fact, it was stuffed with so many additives that even calling it coke was a stretch. Pleased, the lawyer had assured Zoe that Ging would have something to say soon about the consignment of coke that had killed Liam Plummer. Constable Yang, however, didn't trust defense lawyers—or any lawyers for that matter. So she had decided to check on progress with the man himself.

Zoe parked her car outside Ging's art deco apartment block, and headed to the door. She pressed the buzzer for Unit 101 and waited. Getting no answer, she tried again, but still nothing. As she was about to leave, accepting that 'dropping by' a drug dealer's home perhaps wasn't such a brilliant idea, the front entrance door opened and a young woman came out.

"Ma'am, do you mind leaving that open?" Zoe said. The woman stopped, taking in the constable's uniform. She held the door, too, as Zoe eased past.

Inside, surmising that unit 101 was probably on the first level, the constable decided to take the stairs rather than the elevator. Arriving on the first floor, Zoe pushed open the fire door and stepped into the corridor. There were six apartments on this level.

Checking the numbers, the constable saw that Ging's unit was at the far end. As she neared it, she stopped. Like all in his profession, Ging had a healthy respect for security. A deadbolt lock is the most common and effective way to secure a front door. A bolt inside the cylinder moves sideways and pushes into the frame when the key is turned, locking the door. The rectangular metal strike plate keeps the bolt secure and should stop it from ripping through the structure if force is used on the door. Those who are really security conscious can add a cam lock—a device with a cylindrical base with a keyhole and a metal piece known as the cam. This sits perpendicular to the end of the base. When the key is turned, it moves the cam up or down. Zoe knew Ging had fitted both these locks because there were two large, jagged holes in the door, reminders of where they had once been.

The constable reached for her holster and pulled out her Glock. She had never had to use her gun before; Barton wasn't that sort of town—well, not until the arrival of Detective Ramesh Ryan. Zoe looked at her outstretched hand. It was shaking. She was scared—petrified.

The constable looked back. Either everyone was out, or they had learned that interfering in Ging's business was not good for their health. They would be of no assistance.

She listened. There was only silence. Maybe whoever had been here had gone? One thing was sure though, Ging hadn't let them in. So where was he and what to do?

Zoe could follow the police handbook and call for backup. But who would arrive first? Constable Jimmy O'Hagan! Useless! Or the Sarge—but he would take at least thirty minutes to make it here. There was Ryan too, but she had tried to call him twice earlier with the information he had asked for. He hadn't picked up. Ging, though, could be dying inside the apartment. She had no choice. She had to go in.

Lifting her leg, Zoe drove her heavy black boot hard into the door. It swung open.

"Police," she shouted, pushing her gun out.

Silence.

There was a closed-door at the end of the hall. Breathing deeply, Zoe stepped forward, stretched out her left hand, and turned the handle. Swinging the Glock around, she checked the living room. *Clear.*

She swiveled to her left. An open door revealed a bathroom. Stepping in, she scanned the space with her gun. *Clear.* Reentering the living room, Zoe lifted her hand to brush the sweat from her face and stared through an archway into the adjoining kitchen. It looked to be empty too.

Taking a deep breath, the constable advanced. She walked past the sink and fridge to the open door at the back. Peering through, Zoe stepped onto a metal landing. She glanced up and down the fire escape stairs that ran at the side of the building.

There was no one, nothing.

Taking a step back, Zoe reached to holster her gun. And that's when her portable radio squawked. The sound made her jump, and she dropped her weapon onto the kitchen floor. Bending, she picked the gun up before taking out the radio and pressing its side.

"Yeah."

"Yeah? No, I don't think that's right. Shouldn't I give you my call sign, and you give me yours?"

"What the fuck, Jimmy? What is it?" Zoe said, her heartbeat gradually slowing.

"Just got a call in. Ryan's down."

"Down? What do you mean down? Someone shot him?"

"No, I mean he fainted and is unconscious at the Pelican. An ambulance has been ordered, but . . ."

"Okay. I'm on my way."

Zoe was out of the apartment block, into her car, and driving away in a matter of minutes. It was just possible that if she hadn't been in such a hurry that she may have noticed the orange Ford Mustang parked up the street.

"THE COP'S GONE," SAID MICKY, STATING the obvious. "Do you think Ging set us up?"

"No way. He ran to save his skin."

"So, what next?"

"I don't know. Maybe we could have caught Ging if you hadn't gone to the dentist."

"I didn't want to go. You made me."

"Cause you've been moaning on about the pain for days. And the tooth's fixed now?"

"Yeah."

"I think you were scared to go," Stack said, knowing she was pressing his buttons.

"Fuck you."

"That's nice."

"So what now?" Micky asked.

"We find somewhere to stay tonight and get onto it tomorrow. By then, I'll have worked out what to do."

"Sounds like a plan."

Yeah, and how is it it's always up to me to come up with one, Stack thought, as she pulled out into the road. Micky was so useless.

SIXTY

JOHNNY WILSON, KATE CASSELS, AND CHRIS, the barman, stood front and center of the silent, shocked crowd. They watched as two paramedics grasped Detective Ramesh Ryan's arms and legs and gently placed the unconscious man's body onto the gurney, coordinating the clipping of the black belts around the detective's legs, waist, and shoulders. Then they positioned Ryan's head on the thick yellow padding at the end of the stretcher.

"He looks terrible," Kate whispered to Johnny.

They watched as the medics grasped the gurney handles. Waving for people to let them through, the ambulance men headed for the Singing Pelican's door.

As they made it outside, a cop car, its siren blazing, and lights flashing came into view. Speeding, it swung off the main road and headed for the parked ambulance. Behind, the crowd spilled out of the pub as the medics carried the stretcher to their vehicle. They hoisted the gurney onto a wheeled stretcher which stood at the mouth of the ambulance's open doors. Using more belts, they locked the portable gurney and the stretcher together. The conjoined contraption was pushed into the vehicle as the police car pulled to a halt close by. Its lights were switched off, and its siren silenced, Constable Yang jumped out and ran to the ambulance. She leaned into the vehicle and saw the medics had fitted a mask on the detective's face and turned on the oxygen supply.

"What happened to him?" the constable asked.

"Carbon monoxide poisoning," one of the medics as he stood up.

"So, how bad is it?" Zoe asked as the ambulance man jumped down next to her.

"The good news is he opened his eyes after we started administering the oxygen. But they'll have to do tests to work out how much of the monoxide he took in," the medic said, closing the vehicle's doors. "At the minimum, he needs to be hospitalized and fed with oxygen for at least the next twelve hours. He pointed at the pub: "He was poisoned in there by leaking gas. If I was you, I would get everyone out and have the place locked up immediately."

Leaving the constable, the medic climbed into the ambulance. Moments later, the vehicle, it's siren blaring, took off.

SIXTY-ONE

WHILE ZOE WORRIED ABOUT THE POSSIBILITY of Ryan dying, Stack was also thinking about death—her death—which was becoming increasingly likely if she didn't manage to return two keys of blow to Oscar Bruno soon. Maybe, she thought, coming to Barton on the off chance that they could find a stash of this supposed stolen coke hadn't been such a good idea—particularly now that their only point of contact, Ging, had vanished.

Stack leaned against the motel bed board and scrolled through her phone. What was the name of the guy that they had been told had over-dosed? Liam . . . Liam Plummer? That was it. She touched a link and, a local newspaper article popped onto the screen. Stack slowly read it, her excitement growing. Finally, there was something worthwhile.

"Hey, come take a look at this," Micky said, as she begun to read the news report again.

Stack glanced up. Micky was standing at the bathroom door. Sometimes . . . no, make that most times . . . he was a major pain in the butt. Couldn't he see she was doing something?

"You have to see this," he said.

"Micky!"

"Please."

He was obviously not going to leave her alone.

Stack rolled off the bed. "This better be good," she muttered.

"It's good, alright. Come on."

Stack peered into the bathroom.

"There," Micky said, pointing at the toilet.

"I think I've seen one of those before," Stack said, turning to leave.

"No, this is what that guy at reception was on about. Watch." Micky pressed an illuminated yellow button on the keypad next to the lavatory. A jet of water shot up from the side of the bowl. "That's to clean your bum. This one here, that's for you. It gives you a cunt clean," Micky said, pressing another lit button. Water streamed directly up.

"Great, huh?" And that's not all." He grabbed Stack's hand and stuffed it down into the toilet bowl.

"Micky let go," Stack said, struggling to free herself.

Micky ignored her and touched one more button. A jet of warm air caressed her hand. "And that's for drying your butt."

Stack smiled. Actually, the toilet was pretty cool and certainly not what you expected to find in a cheap motel.

Micky began to pull at Stack jeans.

"What you doing?"

"Let's try it out."

Working with Micky meant fucking regularly. Stack didn't mind. He was a handsome enough guy. But tonight, she wasn't really in the mood. Her mind was racing over what she had just read. The article had outlined how Liam Plummer, apparently a celebrity up here, had died after taking some new batch of super-strength coke. The journalist had obviously got most of her information from Liam's roommate—described as a mixologist who worked in a Gosford bar named The Little Blue Door. Stack was pretty sure there was no such thing as super strength coke—just blow that had fewer additives. And saying that the drug had 'just arrived' could mean that it was some of the coke that had fallen into the ocean—after all, Barton had a beach, right?

"Stack," Micky said, still trying to remove her pants.

Stack slapped his hand. "Hold up." She unbuckled her belt and let her jeans drop to the floor.

Micky's trousers were off in seconds too. This may have been a cheap motel in a fart house town, but things weren't all bad, he thought.

ON THE OTHER HAND, THINGS WERE NOT LOOKING GOOD for Detective Ryan. He lay motionless in the hospital bed. His eyes were closed, and an oxygen mask was strapped over his colorless face. A monitor was hooked up to him, along with infusion and syringe pumps. Zoe watched on as a nurse wrote down metrics from the machine.

"How's he doing?" a voice said from behind.

Zoe swiveled around. It was the Sarge.

"As well as can be expected, I think," she said. "Thanks for coming."

"You think I was going to stay at home?" the Sarge said, staring down at the detective.

"I could kill Johnny for what he's done to Ryan," the constable said.

"You told me the gas people thought the poisoning came from a gas fire leak. So it was an accident."

"Yeah, but he should have replaced that fire years ago."

The Sarge grunted. He agreed with Zoe. Bluey knew how tight his cousin Johnny could be. He turned his attention to the nurse. She was re-attaching the clipboard to the end of the detective's bed. "So the good news is Ryan will recover, right?"

"Neither of you should be here," the nurse said.

"But he will get better?" the Sarge asked.

The nurse pointed at the name tag pinned to the front of her uniform. "What does that say?"

"Nurse Swan."

"Nurse right? I'm not a doctor. Doctors give a diagnosis."

The Sarge frowned. He had gone to all the trouble of putting on his uniform so everyone could see he was a cop, but this woman clearly had no respect for the police. "Look . . ."

"Perhaps it would be best if we left Ryan alone, Sarge?" Zoe said.

"I'll go as soon as the nurse answers my question."

"According to the doctor," the nurse said, emphasizing the word doctor, "he's been lucky. If he'd been exposed to the gas much longer, he would have suffered permanent brain damage."

"So there's no brain damage?"

"The doctor won't know for certain until tomorrow. That'll give him time to get oxygen back into his bloodstream. Now can you both leave, please?"

"THERE'S NO POINT IN WAITING. THE cop isn't going anywhere tonight," Big Jay said as he climbed back into the white van.

"And you know this because?" The Lion asked.

"When was the last time you heard of a patient being released in the middle of the night?"

The Lion nodded. "Good point." Despite or maybe because of his bulk Big Jay had the knack of getting people to talk. That's how they had first discovered that Detective Ryan had been rushed from the pub to the local hospital.

After killing, burning, and burying the other Indian detective deep in the woods, the big men had high-tailed it back to the Singing Pelican. They were anxious to move the job along after their disastrous mistake. Though they hadn't talked about it, it weighed heavy on the men. They were professionals. It had been insanely stupid to assume that because the man they had kidnapped was around the same age as Detective Ryan and brown-skinned, he was the guy they were looking for. They should have checked the photo on the phone and his ID. That would have only taken a few seconds.

"I guess we come back tomorrow. Meantime let's find somewhere to stay," The Lion said, pressing his foot on the accelerator.

SIXTY-TWO

THE SUN HAD ALREADY BURNT OFF the early mist, so it appeared the cold snap had passed. The better weather looked set to wash away any memories of yesterday—at least that's what Stack hoped as she watched the grill slide open. Bloodshot eyes peered out. "Yes?"

"We've come to see Mel Knowles."

"We're not open. Go away."

Stack gave Mr. Bloodshot Eyes one more chance.

"We're friends of Mel's. We really need to see him."

"I couldn't care a less if you're the fucking King of England we're closed."

Stack shrugged and moved aside. Micky lifted his 9 mm Glock and thrust it hard against the grill.

"Open up fuck butt, or you and your brains are going to go their separate ways."

There was the sound of chains and locks being released. The door opened.

Micky pulled his gun up, pointing it under the chin of the man-mountain who stood in the doorway.

"Okay, big boy, where's Mel Knowles?"

"Downstairs."

Micky swung his gun hard into the Mountain's stomach. He grunted and bent forward. Micky lifted the weapon's butt, bashed it hard into the man's head, and as he fell to the floor, lifted his leg high and drove it into the man's groin. The force carried the Mountain up and forward.

"You first," Micky said, pushing the man hard. He tumbled down the stairs, his head smashing onto the concrete below.

F. STARED OUT OF THE CAR windshield at the innocuous blue and white store with the large front window a hundred yards down. If he had brought his binoculars, he could have made out the sign above the window that read "Hey Danny" in a thick black font, and below that, in smaller letters 'Parcel Pickup"—but he had forgotten them. It was unfortunate but not the end of the world. He lifted the Canon 35mm camera to his eye. He would use it to see the bastard who picked up the parcel.

Looking through the viewfinder, he saw a young guy enter the store. Could that be the blackmailer? If so, he was right on time. F. adjusted the camera's focus. Someone else had just come in, too—an older guy wearing a black cloth jacket and flat duckbill cap.

The first guy had been handed his parcel. He held it above his head. It was the signal F. was waiting for. "Got you," F. said and rapidly took photos. He put the camera down on the passenger seat and climbed out of his car. Catching the bastard was going to be simple.

The blackmailer, the parcel under his arm, opened the store door. If he turned right, he would walk away from F. Left, towards him. The guy turned right, strolling away seemingly without a care in the world. He marched down the hill towards the sea. F. would soon catch him if he could just cross the road. A stream of fast-moving traffic blocked his path. Frustrated, F. turned and ran down the street, across from the man holding the parcel under his arm.

F. drew parallel. The traffic thinned, and seeing a gap, F. sprinted across the road. The guy spotted him and started to run. It was a race, one that F believed he could win. He may have put on a few pounds since leaving school, but he had always been a good sprinter. On the other hand, the man was finding the going difficult.

F. got closer and closer. Finally reaching the guy, he put his hand on his shoulder and twisted him around. "Give me the parcel," F. ordered and snatched at it.

"Okay, easy," the man said. "You want it; you can have it." He handed the package over. "What's in it anyway?"

"You don't know?" F. said, peering at the man. In his mid-thirties, he had a pock-marked face, dull brown eyes, a large nose, and long unkempt black hair that reached to the top of a dirty white T shirt. F. had never seen him before.

"You go to Narcotics Anonymous?"

"What"

"Narcotics Anonymous."

"No, man."

"So, how do you know Scott?"

"Who's he?"

F. released the man and tore at the brown paper, dropping it onto the pavement. He pulled out a hard-sided case. Kneeling down, he placed the valise on the concrete and flicked open the two metal catches. Using one hand, F. cautiously lifted the lid. The case was filled with fine brown soil.

"Where's my money?" F. asked

"What? The weirdo said you would give me another fifty bucks once you'd opened the case. But I had to make you run for it. He said it was a joke," the man said.

F. stood up rapidly and grabbed the guy by the throat. "Which weirdo?

"Hey, easy." The man gasped for breath. "The one in the store with me. He saw me begging and gave me the first fifty bucks to pick up a package. He came into the shop too. Told me to hold the parcel up. After I did that, he exchanged it for the one he'd just collected.

"Fuck," F. yelled and ran back to the store. It was empty. Reaching into his pocket, he pulled out his iPhone and opened it. Whoever the black-mailer was, they may have thought that they were brilliant, but they were wrong. He was smarter.

SIXTY-THREE

SITTING UP IN BED, RYAN WATCHED as the doctor placed the stethoscope on his chest. His oxygen mask was gone, and all the measures and monitors had been unclipped earlier. Papers had been signed, and now all he needed was the say-so from this doctor, and he could leave.

The doctor pulled the stethoscope away, and the nurse handed him a clipboard. "Remarkable. You're a very lucky detective," the doctor said, writing on the board. "How do you feel?"

"Great. Raring to go." Ryan actually felt like a pneumatic drill was buzzing inside his head, but he wouldn't tell the doctor that.

"I think if you really want to, you can leave, but please take it easy for the next few days. Your body's taken a major hit."

"So, that's your all clear?"

"Yes. Get dressed, and you can go."

THE SMALL WHITE DOT ON F.'s iPhone screen was bright and clear. The car he was following was about a quarter of a mile away and traveling at high speed, but F. wasn't concerned. The tracker signal would remain strong if he didn't let the vehicle get too far ahead. Then, when they stopped, he would have them.

They had made a fool out of him with that package swap, but F. consoled himself that at least he'd ignored Bean's advice and put a tracker in one of the rolls of bills. Soon he would have the money back, and just as importantly, he'd know who it was who had tried to blackmail them.

F. looked down at the iPhone. The dot was stationary now. The car had halted on the main Gosford road on its way back to Barton.

F. turned right. The dot still wasn't moving. Had the car stopped at the lights or parked? Well, he would know in the next minute or so. F. hadn't worked out the fine details yet of what to do next, but he agreed with Bean. There was only one way of shutting a blackmailer up permanently.

F. stopped at the end of the road and looked right and left. The main road was busy, and he had to wait for a minute before crossing and traveling north. F. glanced down at the dot on the map. It hadn't moved. It was looking like the guy had parked.

He pulled out to overtake and then slotted in behind a caravan being towed by an SUV. In the summer, scores of campers blocked the streets, and F. hated being stuck behind them. But he had the bastard now. There was no hurry.

The SUV and caravan reached the crest of the hill and began their descent. Checking his mirror, F. accelerated, pulled out, and speeded past.

Ahead he saw cars braking as they neared traffic lights. He slowed. There had been an accident in the intersection. A black Honda Accord had been speeding over the lights and had maybe taken a chance on an amber signal, and the guy in the red Toyota pick-up had probably done the same and driven into the vehicle's side.

He glanced at his cell as he advanced towards the two crashed cars. The dot had stopped on the map somewhere around here. In fact, now his car was almost in precisely the same position as the dot, which meant—the blackmailer was in one of the crashed vehicles!

SIXTY-FOUR

"H E'LL BE OUT SOON," BIG JAY said.

"How do you know?" The Lion asked.

"Because of that," Big Jay said, pointing out of the van window.

That was a cop car. It had just pulled up outside the Lady Vale Hospital. A uniformed woman officer had gotten out and gone into the building. "She was here last night, and today she's come to pick him up."

"She could just be checking up on him," The Lion said.

Big Jay shook his head. "No way. He's leaving."

"If you say so."

Silence. Then: "Good choice, by the way," Big Jay said.

"What was?"

"The Paradise whatever. I liked it. Did you try those buttons on the toilet?"

"No"

"I did."

"And?"

"The motel guy was right." Big Jay chuckled. "Now I've got the cleanest butt in all of Australia."

The Lion grunted and reached his hands up, trying to stretch his back crippled by last night's bed. Sleeping on the thin motel mattress listening to his compatriot snoring and wheezing in the other bed had meant he didn't get much sleep, and now he was in a terrible mood.

"Hold on. That the cop?" Big Jay asked

The Lion pulled his arms down and reached for his phone in the central console. He checked a profile photo on the cell against the tall, well-built brown-skinned man with the uniformed cop exiting the hospital.

"That's him."

He pushed the phone over to Big Jay, who peered at the photo and nodded. "Definitely."

"WHERE TOO, RYAN?" ZOE ASKED AS the detective slid into the passenger seat.

"The Pelican."

"You sure?"

"It was just a gas leak. It could have happened anywhere."

"But it didn't. It happened there and almost killed you."

"Don't exaggerate."

"I'm not. And anyway, the pub's closed while the leak's checked out."

"Well, I have to go back to collect my clothes. I also need my car," Ryan said.

Zoe sighed, turned the ignition on, and pressed down on the accelerator. The car moved off.

A few moments later, a white van pulled out of the car park opposite and followed at a safe distance behind.

SIXTY-FIVE

RYAN STARED OUT AT THE PUB. There was police blue and white tape around the front entrance of the Singing Pelican. "Do not Enter" notices were plastered on the bar windows.

"Like I told you, we shouldn't go in. It could be dangerous," the constable said.

"You told me they'd found the leak? Wasn't it from the gas fire in my room?"

"Sure, that's what the local gas man said, but there's an outside possibility that it could be from somewhere else. A Gosford crew will be over later to do a complete check."

"Those guys love drama. Come on," Ryan said, reaching for the door handle and climbing out of the car.

Behind, he heard the crackle of Zoe's radio and watched as she picked it up and listened. Moments later, she lowered her window.

"Ryan. Sorry I've got to go. There's been an accident. I'll see you back at the station. Remember though, just pack your things quickly and get out of there."

As the police car headed off, Ryan walked over to the pub entrance and pried off the tape. He tried the door. It was locked. Taking a credit card from his wallet, he slid it into the crack between the door and the frame and moved it up and down while turning the handle. Ryan heard the lock cylinder click and the latch release. Johnny was evidently too stingy to buy a decent lock.

The detective stepped inside the pub, closing the door. Chairs and stools had been knocked over. Half-filled glasses had been hastily abandoned. The air smelt of sweat and alcohol.

Ryan walked across to the stairs, the wooden steps creaking as he climbed. He had told Zoe he had just returned to collect his clothes. That was one reason, but not the only reason.

Reaching the landing, the detective turned and walked to his room. He was in luck. The door hadn't been locked. Inside, almost everything was just as he had left it—the boxes on the floor, a report left open on the table. The stone fireplace the gas fire had sat in was now empty, the heater removed, its connection pipe sealed.

Retrieving his phone from his pocket, Ryan switched on the flashlight and squatted down to examine the chimney. He waved the beam around the stack. The bricks were black. He ran his index finger across the stone and peered at the grime—coal dust, deposited long ago when open fires had burnt in the grate. He pointed the beam up the center of the shaft. It was blocked by a closed black metal damper door. Ryan pushed his arm up, reaching as far as he could. He still couldn't touch the lever that would allow him to unlock the flue. He would need a long, hooked pole to do that, and he didn't have one.

The detective edged back out of the hearth, turned the flashlight off, and stood up. He brushed the dust off his jacket and thought about what he had found. With the damper door shut, there would be no ventilation, so invisible, deadly gas fumes would flow back into the room. Zoe had been right. He was lucky to be alive!

The phone vibrated in his hand. He glanced at the number on the screen before answering.

"Yes, mom."

"Oh, thank god. I've heard nothing. Not a word."

"That's not true. I know Zoe told you I was in the hospital overnight, but not to worry. And I'm fine."

There was a long pause. "Well, yes, the constable might have said something like that. But since when have people who stay overnight in hospital been fine? And then I didn't hear anything from you."

"Because I was asleep."

"Not this morning."

"No, but I did try to call you. You didn't answer," Ryan said.

"I was doing my yoga."

"So? You can't have been that worried."

There was a pause. "I thought you said you were staying at a nice place. A nice place doesn't have gas leaks."

Outside Ryan heard a wooden floorboard groan. "Mom, I've got to go. I'll call you later. But don't worry. I'm fit as a fiddle now."

Ryan clicked off the phone, putting it on the table as he reached for his holstered Glock. He listened. Had he really heard something or just imagined it?

He crept to the door, turned the handle, and opened it slowly. Peering out, he looked left and right: no one, nothing.

Feeling stupid, Ryan holstered his gun and then set about collecting his clothes and toiletries and packing them into his suitcase. It didn't take him long. He was soon ready to go.

Opening the door, his case in his hand, Ryan stepped out and stopped. His brain was obviously not working well today. He had forgotten his cell. He turned around and reached for the door handle.

"Put the case down and move away from the door," a voice said from behind. He felt the pressure of a weapon pushed into his back.

Ryan raised his arms. He felt, rather than saw, someone, reach forward, unclip his holster, and remove his Glock.

So there were two of them—one behind and another to his side.

"Turn slowly," the one behind ordered.

The detective swiveled around. A big man in a heavy coat pointed a shotgun at his stomach. Another even larger man stood adjacent. He was dressed as if he had just been for a jog around the block—in a sweatshirt, shorts, and sneakers. This man held Ryan's Glock in one hand and a SIG Sauer P226 in the other. He pointed both of them at the detective. Ryan recognized the men. They were part of Oscar Bruno's gang.

"What's your name?" The Lion asked.

The detective said nothing.

The Lion drove his fist into Ryan's stomach. The detective winced.

"Well?"

The detective still said nothing.

Holding the shotgun with one hand, The Lion reached into his pocket and brought out his phone. He searched the device and turned it around to show a screen with Ryan's photo on.

"That's you, right? Detective Ramesh Ryan?"

The detective didn't speak.

Big Jay stuffed Ryan's weapon into the top of his shorts and patted him down with his free hand. He pulled out a black leather wallet from the detective's inside pocket and flicked it open to reveal a police ID card in a plastic insert.

"Detective Ramesh Ryan," Big Jay said, reading from the words printed to the right of Ryan's photo. He tossed the wallet to The Lion, who caught it with one hand, and glanced at the picture before stuffing the wallet into his trouser pocket. "It's him," The Lion confirmed. "Move," he ordered, pressuring the shotgun trigger.

The detective turned. This was no time to play the hero. "Where are we going?"

"Now he can talk," The Lion said. "Just keep walking, butthead."

The detective continued on down the corridor, the men behind him. Suddenly, from below came the sound of a single gunshot and a horrifying scream.

"Stop," The Lion whispered, jamming the shotgun into Ryan's back. Big Jay crept past the detective and, keeping close to the wall, ran to the landing. Here he halted and waited.

Silence.

Big Jay glanced back at The Lion and pointed his finger down before descending the stairs.

"Go," The Lion whispered to Ryan.

Together they quietly walked to the landing. "Stop." The Lion waited. He was beginning to worry. Where the heck was Big Jay?

SIXTY-SIX

BIG JAY APPEARED AT THE FOOT of the stairs. Relieved, The Lion released his breath. "Well?"

"Come on down," Big Jay said.

With the detective ahead, The Lion descended the stairs to join his compatriot.

"It's someone we know," Big Jay said.

"Who?" The Lion asked.

Big Jay moved his head, and The Lion followed his gaze. A man and a woman stood behind the bar.

The woman waved cheerily. "Hi," she said. She seemed chilled, too chilled for someone who was facing two armed men. She leaned in close to the man next to her. He was cradling a gun and tapping his foot impatiently. "Micky, be nice," the girl said.

"Hello," Micky said, pulling his face into what he obviously imagined was a smile. Ryan hadn't seen either of them before, but they appeared to know the two big men.

"Who's he?" Micky asked, pointing to the detective.

"What's all the shouting about, Stack?" The Lion said, ignoring the question and addressing the girl.

"Take a look."

"Go," said The Lion, prodding his shotgun into the detective's back. The three men walked across the room with Big Jay leading, Ryan behind, and The Lion covering him at the back.

Stack pulled up the bar counter and waved the men through.

The cellar flap was open. In the room below a figure was sprawled out on the floor face down in a pool of blood.

"Is he dead?" The Lion asked.

"Nope. Not yet anyway."

"Who shot him?"

"Me," Micky said. "He was making a run for it."

Stack shook her head. "Yeah, but what use is he to us now?"

"Should I have just let him go?" Micky asked.

"I'm not saying that . . ." Stack said.

"Shut up both of you," Big Jay said, swinging his gun around and pointing it at the pair.

Micky lifted his Glock and aimed at Big Jay's heart. "Go ahead, big boy."

There was an ominous sound of The Lion's pump-action shotgun being primed. "Put the gun down, dick."

"Oh, for Christ's sake," Stack said. "Enough of this macho shit." She stared at Ryan, a look of recognition flashing across her face."

"I know you. You're the cop that tried to put Bruno away."

"He is?" Micky said.

"Yeah. I'm right, aren't I?" Stack asked the big men.

"Never mind that. Who's that down there? "The Lion said, pointing at the wounded man in the cellar.

"The guy who owns this place. Johnny something. He's been dealing coke. Bruno's blow," she said.

"And you know this because?" Big Jay asked.

"We had a 'talk' with a guy in a bar, whose friend overdosed. It's the two keys of coke that came from the ship."

"So, where is it?" The Lion asked.

"Well, he would have told us if Micky hadn't blasted him."

"I told you . . ." Micky began.

Big Jay put his hand up. "Enough." He turned to The Lion. "We've got to go. We've wasted enough time here."

Ryan felt the shotgun rammed in his back. "After you, detective."

"DETECTIVE? SO I WAS RIGHT, RIGHT?" Stack said triumphantly as the men headed out. She tapped her forehead. "I've got an excellent memory for faces. Right, Micky?

But Micky wasn't listening. He was staring down at Johnny Wilson's body. "You could be right. Maybe I was a bit hasty."

Stack leaned across and kissed him on his cheek. "That's what I love about you. If you make a mistake, you own up." She paused. "'Course now he can't tell us where he's hidden the blow. And we've got nothing to take back to Bruno." They stared at each other, both thinking about what that meant.

"Let's run for it," Stack said.

"What's the point? He'll find us." Micky paused. "I'd like to put a bullet in that bastard's brain."

"Me too. Not much chance of that, though." She stopped. "Do you think they're taking that cop back to Bruno?"

"I'm not sure? Perhaps they're just going to shoot him."

"No. They could have done that here. They're taking the cop to Bruno," Stack said, her mind made up.

Micky smiled. "What for? A cup of tea or something?"

"Something like that," Stack said, grinning. She paused. "I've got an idea."

Micky smiled. He always liked Stack ideas. "Yeah, what?"

"What if we could find something to take back to Bruno that he really, really wants?"

"Yeah, well, that was supposed to be the coke. But we haven't got it."

"But if we got something else? And then, when we're close to him, pow pow. No more Oscar Bruno."

SIXTY-SEVEN

Big Jay and The Lion bound Ryan's hands with plastic ties, taped his ankles together, slapped duct tape over his mouth, and yanked a hessian sack over his head. After slamming the detective face down onto the van's floor, they slung the heavy waterproof tarpaulin over him.

Ryan had considered fighting back but decided against it. It was improbable that he would overcome two armed professional criminals who were watching his every move. The detective, however, anticipated that once he was bound, they wouldn't watch him as closely. That was when he would have his best chance of escape.

Bang! The truck suddenly leaped up as its front wheels smashed in and out of a pothole.

The men's decision to drive back to Sydney on the smaller badly-maintained rural roads helped too.

"Hey, watch where you're going, will you?" Big Jay yelled as Ryan used the distraction to roll over onto his back. Now came the tricky bit. The detective slowly raised his bound arms, bending them and keeping them close to his body. He practiced bringing his hands back down. After a few tries, Ryan was ready. He raised his arms up as high as he could and waited for the vehicle to hit another pothole.

The minutes passed. Maybe he should take a chance and do something now? That's when the truck's front wheels hit another crater in the road.

The vehicle bounced up. Seizing the moment, the detective yanked his arms down, pulling them apart.

"Jeez," Big Jay shouted as the plastic ties split, freeing the detective's hands. "If you can't drive, I'll do it."

"Fuck you. And isn't it time you checked out the cop?" The Lion said.

Hearing this, Ryan rolled to his right and clasped his hands tightly together. Moments later, the side of the tarp was pulled up. The detective sensed someone peering in. Then he felt the weight of the tarpaulin dropping back into place.

"He's fine." Silence again.

The detective freed his hands, bending his fingers backward and forwards to get the blood flowing. Satisfied, he tore the sack off his head with one hand. With the other, he ripped the duct tape from his mouth and breathed in deeply. It was still dark under the tarp, but now, with the sacking off, Ryan had eyes on the tape that was wrapped around his ankles.

He bent, reaching his arms down while moving his legs up. Running his hands over the strapping, Ryan searched for the edge of the tape. Finding it, he pulled, slowly unraveling the binding. With his ankles free, Ryan dropped the tape onto the floor and stretched out his legs. What to do now? The odds were still the same—two against one, and they were armed. But the men had their backs to the detective, and both were relaxed, confident that Ryan remained firmly tied. So he had the element of surprise on his side.

The driver, The Lion, would have his shotgun close by. It was most probably propped up against the van's door, next to his leg. The other man, Big Jay, had two pistols—the SIG Sauer and Ryan's Glock. They would probably be stuffed into the top of his pants.

The driver was the weaker link of the two. It would take him more time to reach for and raise his weapon. And he would need to keep control of the van. If Ryan could pull him back, the vehicle would lurch. Big Jay would take a few seconds to grasp what was going on, giving the detective time to grab the shotgun and shoot the big guy. It was risky, but it could work.

Suddenly the tarp was pulled away. Light poured in. The detective rolled around. Too late! Big Jay leaned over the back of the passenger seat, pointing a SIG Sauer P226 at his head. "Shit. He got free."

"What?"

"I said he was about to jump us—weren't you, you bastard?" Big Jay said, his gun jamming hard into Ryan's head. "So he needs to be taught a lesson, right?"

"What?" The Lion said.

"Didn't you hear me? I said this . . ."

"Those two morons, Micky and Stack, are behind us," The Lion said, interrupting.

"You sure?"

"Sure, I'm sure. I think they've been following us."

Big Jay, his gun still aimed at the detective, turned to peer through the side mirror.

"I see them. Let them overtake."

The Lion slowed.

"So, shall I teach this cop a lesson?" Big Jay said.

"I don't see that Bruno would have a problem with that as long as . . ." The Lion begun. "Oh, fuck!"

A shot rang out. The driver's side window disintegrated, sending shards of glass flying.

"What the . . ." Big Jay said.

There was another shot, and The Lion's body jerked, falling forward over the wheel.

Ryan jumped at the distracted Big Jay, knocking his gun up, releasing it from the big man's hands. Simultaneously the van careered out of control, hitting the curb and launching high into the air before spinning around. Its roof bashed onto the ground, and the vehicle skidded upside down towards a line of trees.

The detective fell back, his head crashing against the floor. Big Jay fell forward, onto the dash.

Bang. The truck plowed into a huge eucalyptus tree and rolled back onto its side before coming to a halt.

THE LION GROANED, FORCING OPEN HIS eyes. He'd never been shot before. Someone had once told him it didn't hurt. They were wrong. It hurt like hell.

Big Jay slowly opened his eyes. He leaned against the center console, which was now sticky and thick with The Lion's blood. The upside-down vehicle had tilted, the passenger side was suspended way above the ground. Big Jay crawled forward, his hand outstretched. He felt like he'd just done twenty rounds with Mike Tyson. He grasped the door handle and levered himself up.

Lying on the floor behind the passenger seat, Ryan felt the truck shake as Big Jay moved. He turned his head, searching for the big man's gun. There it was! The SIG Sauer had slid away and lay against the back door of the truck.

SIXTY-EIGHT

S TACK SKIDDED TO A HALT, PARKING the Mustang on the main road.
"Drive closer," Micky instructed.

"It's better here. Safer," Stack said.

"Don't you think they're all dead?"

"I hope not. We want the cop alive," Stack said.

"Yeah. Right."

"Pass me my gun."

Micky leaned forward, opened the glove compartment, and pulled out a SIG P365. He handed it to Stack.

The pair got out of the car. Stack came from the driver's side as Micky climbed out of the passenger door. They walked cautiously towards the truck. As they neared its passenger door opened and a big man dropped down onto the ground. He sprinted for the tree cover.

"Big Jay?" Stack asked.

"Yeah." Micky grinned and raised his Glock. "I'll go get him.

"Okay. I'll find the cop."

MICKY MOVED OFF, FOLLOWING BIG JAY'S trail. He knew Stack would be okay. He had pumped two slugs into The Lion, so he was either dead or very close to death. Assuming the cop was still alive, he would have been tied, gagged, and bound. So he would pose no problem for Stack.

Micky stopped at the tree line and listened. He could hear Big Jay crashing through the woods like an enraged bull elephant. He grinned. The big man obviously hadn't spent much time in the country—but Micky had. One of his foster families had lived in the boondocks. They'd taught him all about hunting, shooting, and fishing. He'd never liked fishing but had enjoyed the hunting and shooting bit.

He grinned. This was going to be fun.

Ryan wasn't thinking about fun. He was thinking about surviving. With Big Jay gone, only The Lion remained. He was dying, but that didn't mean he was harmless. The man's shotgun would be close by where he now lay. You didn't need much strength to pull a trigger. And assuming Stack and Micky had shot him—which was pretty much a certainty—they would now be on their way over. So the odds had worsened. Two and a half against one. The detective crawled toward the Sig.

Big Jay had decided that an ambush was his best option. Sprawled out, his head hidden behind a thick, rotting tree trunk, he pointed the detective's Glock, waiting for someone to appear. Big Jay didn't like using other people's guns, not until he had tested them out. Trusting your life to someone else's weapon wasn't ideal. But beggars couldn't be choosers. And in his haste, he had left his own gun, his SIG Sauer, behind.

Killing had always come easy to Big Jay. He knew that The Lion felt the same way, and although he didn't really like the man, he had developed a grudging respect for him on this trip. Of course, The Lion had just made a mistake, a big mistake. He should have realized earlier he was being followed. Now he was either dead or about to die. No point in thinking about that, though. Big Jay had a job to do. He had to kill both those little bastard kids, which should be a piece of cake.

Big Jay twisted on the ground, trying to make himself comfortable. He could hear birds singing and the leaves rustling in the light breeze. Even though he didn't usually like the country much, out here felt peaceful and relaxed.

There was a whistle—low and piercing. It came from behind. Big Jay swiveled around, his gun raised, ready to shoot, but he was too slow, far too slow. The first bullet from Micky's gun burrowed into him, hitting his stomach and ripping it apart. The second slug drove into his skull, sending fragments of loose bone spinning high into the sky.

RYAN HEARD THE DISTANT ECHO OF the shots just before Stack spoke. "That's my man Micky. He's finishing off Big Jay. He'll be on his way back now."

The woman was more intelligent than the detective had given her credit for. She was outside the truck, figuring out who was still alive inside.

"You there, Lion? You big fat twat," Stack yelled.

Silence.

"I guess not; otherwise, you wouldn't be smart enough to keep quiet."

Silence.

"So that just leaves you, cop. I daresay Micky thinks you're all thrust up like a Christmas turkey. I don't think so, though. I think you're one heck of a smart cookie. And a smart cookie could get out of any knots those failed boy scouts tied. So I'm not coming in. No, I'm waiting here for my man. And, if you're as bright as I think you are, you'll have already worked out that you won't be able to shoot both of us."

Ryan said nothing. He began to slide towards the steel bulkhead. He was betting on Stack appearing at the driver's window but knew that even if she had moved around to the passenger window, he had that covered too.

"Now, don't make this difficult. I don't want to kill you," Stack shouted.

Ryan listened carefully. The woman's voice had moved closer and came from the driver's side. So, to get a clear line of fire, she would most probably take a position by the shot-out window. He raised his gun, ready.

But there was no Stack. No gun. Just the clunk clunk of a weapon being loaded.

He pulled himself around as the back doors were flung open. Ryan pointed his weapon at Stack as she aimed her gun at him. A draw.

Or it was until Micky appeared, behind and to the left of the girl, his Glock aimed at him. And the crazy man was just itching to shoot.

"Micky, don't," Stack warned. "Put your gun down, cop, and we won't kill you. Otherwise, all bets are off."

Ryan weighed up his options. He could take out Micky, but Stack would definitely shoot him in the time it took for him to swing his gun back to her. Alternatively, he could shoot Stack, but he had no doubt that trigger-happy Micky would have pumped out a shot by then.

Ryan put his gun on the floor. "Okay, I'm coming," he said, praying he had made the right decision.

"Good choice," Stack said. "Now stand up, walk over, and jump down."

Keeping close to the right-hand side of the truck, trying to keep Micky's gun as far away from him as possible, the detective stepped towards Stack. The man and woman moved their weapons around, following his path— and that was when they made their first big mistake. Following him meant they had to take their eyes off the front of the truck—and that was where, not moments ago, Ryan had heard a weapon being locked and loaded.

What happened next happened fast. The shotgun's deafening blast reverberated inside the truck. The detective threw himself against the van's side as Stack's body was lifted off the ground and flung back, blood pouring from a gaping hole in her belly. A hideous apparition rose at the front of the Hyundai. He grasped a smoking sawn-off scattergun and was readying to fire again.

"Fuck you," Micky screamed out. He twisted the Glock around and shot at the blood-stained vision, the bullets pummeling into the man's body— but that was Micky's second mistake. The Lion was now definitely dead, but Micky had forgotten about the detective who was still very much alive.

Ryan dived to the floor, grasped the SIG Sauer, and fired. The slug tore into Micky's right leg. He screamed out in pain and fell backward, releasing his gun as he joined the dead Stack on the ground.

It took the detective just three seconds to reach the yelling man and one more second to pistol-whip him into unconsciousness.

SIXTY-NINE

Ryan had taken no chances. He had first checked Stack's pulse. She was definitely dead. Moving on, he'd used the duct tape from the van to gag and tether Micky. The man may still have been unconscious and bleeding from the leg, but that didn't mean he was powerless. He would deal with the wound after he'd found the cell.

The detective had left his own phone at the pub, but there was one cell that he really wanted to find. Climbing back into the van, the detective advanced. The vehicle swayed a little as he walked but held steady.

Ryan carefully pulled himself over the bulkhead and dropped into the passenger seat. The Lion's phone was exactly where he thought it would be—in the gray plastic container in the Hyundai's central console. So far, so good, but now Ryan needed to open it, which meant things would get messy.

Cell in hand, the detective clicked the console top closed and leaned over to stare at The Lion's lifeless body. The big man's head had fallen back onto the steering wheel, and the rest of him was crunched up below, hemmed in by the driver's seat. Miraculously The Lion's face was unscathed, but Micky's bullets had shredded his body, leaving dark red, gaping holes. Blood still spurted from them.

Swallowing hard, Ryan reached one hand behind the man's head, levering it forward while clicking the phone's switch with his other hand. The screen came to life, revealing the time and date and a photo of a smiling Lion, his arm around a black-haired, bearded man in his twenties.

Seeing the picture, Ryan felt a pang of remorse. So there was at least one other person who would be cut up about The Lion's death. But the detective comforted himself that the young man in the photo was not innocent. Anyone who chose to involve themselves with a murderous bastard like The Lion had to be aware of what he did for a living.

Twisting the phone around and pushing The Lion's head forward, he waited, unsure if this would work. After a moment, Ryan turned the phone back around. *Bingo.* The face ID had registered, and the cell had opened on the home screen. Holding the cell, the detective crawled back over to the passenger seat. He pressed the green phone icon at the bottom of the screen, tapped the keypad symbol, and typed in a number. After several moments There was a click.

"Zoe?" he asked.

"Ryan? Is that you?"

"Yes."

"Thank god. I almost didn't answer. I didn't recognize the number. Where are you? There's an all-points bulletin out for you."

"You need to send an ambulance to the Singing Pelican; Johnny is . . ."

"It's been done, Ryan."

"What?"

"The crew who came around to check the gas leak found him."

"And?"

"He's going to have surgery but should live. So, where are you?"

"Hold on." Ryan flicked back onto the home screen and pressed the green and blue 'Find My' symbol. Opening it, he selected the People tab, then chose 'Share my location.' He entered Zoe's name and number before sending the message.

"You should be able to find me now. I'm about thirty minutes out from Barton on one of the smaller roads on the way back to Sydney."

"Right. Got it. So what happened?"

Ryan summarized the events to a silent Zoe.

"That's incredible. And you think it was this drug dealer, Oscar Bruno, who sent them to kidnap you?"

"I'm sure of it."

"But you're definitely all right?"

"Yes. Look, put a call into my boss in Sydney, Chief Inspector Dan Dudley. Ask him to send a team over here along with an ambulance. There's one alive and three dead."

"Shit, I'll have to tell The Sarge everything too, though god knows what that will do to his heart. We may need another ambulance for him." There was a pause. "Anything else?"

"No,

"Okay, see you soon."

Ryan heard Zoe's phone click off. Now that job was completed, the detective had another task for The Lion's iPhone. He jabbed the green 'Messages' symbol on the home screen and scanned down the list of incoming texts. There were a few short cryptic messages mailed from the same number. There was also a photo of the detective. It had been sent a couple of days ago. Ryan took a screenshot of it, emailing it to his own phone. Scrolling down, he found another message detailing his Singing Pelican location and the tag, color, make, and model of his car. He took a screenshot of this, too, and also emailed it to himself.

Job done; Ryan shoved the phone into his pocket and grabbed The Lion's raincoat from the vehicle's well. Then he jumped out of the passenger door. Ryan walked along the side of the van to the back. Here everything was as before. Stack was still very dead, and Micky was still unconscious. But his face was now a deathly shade of white. Micky was a murderous sociopath, but Ryan didn't want him to die. Faced with the possibility of a life sentence, the man maybe could be turned.

The detective rolled the raincoat up and pressed it on Micky's wounded leg before jamming his knee on the cloth and leaning his weight onto it. It would help to stem the flow of blood, but it wouldn't stop it completely. A professional tourniquet would need to be applied by a medical professional to do the job correctly.

Ryan remained where he was for what felt like an eternity. He listened to Micky's heavy breathing. Occasionally he heard the sound of a car speeding past . . . but no one stopped. Where was everyone?

SEVENTY

IT WAS A TOSS-UP AS TO who arrived first: Zoe's cop car, the ambulance, or the Sydney cops. They came in a cacophony of sound and vision—of flashing lights and screaming sirens. All wanting to know: What? Where? Why?

After medics had spirited Micky Docker away and everyone had set to work, Ryan briefed Chief Inspector Dudley in his car. Dudley listened as Ryan outlined precisely what had happened.

"Well, you've made a right mess here," the Chief Inspector said as the detective concluded. He rubbed his chin and turned to watch the work. Tape had been placed around a wide area, centering on the van. Fingerprints were being dusted, photos taken, and evidence collected—all part of the seven S's: Securing and gathering evidence, separating the witnesses, sketching the scene, scanning the scene, and searching for evidence.

The Chief Inspector seemed relaxed, relishing being there. Ryan had seen this before. Cops who had utilized their political skills to scale the slippery promotion ladder may have won the battle but lost the war, realizing too late that the fun was really all about doing 'real' police work in the field.

"And how close are you to tying up the rest?" Dudley asked, turning back.

"Almost there, Sir."

"Good."

"So can I go back to Barton with Constable Yang now? Ryan asked.

"You'll write up a full statement about this there?"

"Yes, Sir."

"Two days maximum, okay? Then I want you back in Sydney," the Chief Inspector ordered.

"Thank you, Sir," The detective said, reaching for the car door and pulling it open.

"By the way, Ryan, well done. Missing all those flying bullets was quite a feat." Dudley paused. "Maybe they should call you Teflon Ryan instead of me."

"I didn't know they called you that, Sir," Ryan said, getting out.

SEVENTY-ONE

CONSTABLE ZOE YANG PULLED INTO THE Singing Pelican's car park. She reached across to shake Ryan awake. The detective had fallen asleep half an hour ago, soon after the constable had updated him on Johnny Wilson's situation. She had told him that the pub owner would probably be unavailable to talk to until late tomorrow. The constable also relayed that she had collected the detective's suitcase and everything else from his room . . . and she had returned his phone.

"We're here?" Ryan asked, yawning.

"Yeah. But can't this wait? You've had an unbelievable day."

"No. Sorry. I want to do it now."

Zoe sighed. "Okay, but you never said what we are looking for."

"It's a surprise."

The constable shook her head. "A surprise?" The detective still appeared to relish keeping information back from her.

"You coming?" Ryan said.

The constable answered by opening the car door. They walked over to the pub. Its door was still festooned with blue and white police tape. Warning notices remained plastered over the windows.

Ryan and Zoe freed the sticky tape barricade, entered the pub, and headed for the bar. Lifting the counter flap and stepping through, the officers took off the police tape strung across the open cellar entrance.

"You first," Ryan said, allowing Zoe to lead.

THE ONLY INDICATION THAT ANYTHING UNTOWARD had happened in the basement was a dark red bloodstain soaked into the sandstone in the middle of the room.

"Right. Now, will you tell me what we're doing here?" the constable asked.

"I want to find the coke."

"Coke? You never mentioned anything about coke being down here." Was Ryan ever going to stop playing games with her?

"Sorry, I thought I had. Johnny Wilson was dealing."

"And you know this because . . .?"

"Because it was the reason he returned here today even though the pub was all shut up. It was also why Stack and Micky came to the hotel. Someone told them about Johnny dealing cocaine. And I think that someone was right."

"Which someone?"

"Mel Knowles."

"The roommate? But we interviewed him—twice. He never said anything about Johnny."

"Well, we weren't using Stack's and Micky's persuasive techniques. Johnny was down here in the cellar when those two arrived. Seeing them, he panicked, ran for it, and, well, the rest you know."

Zoe gazed around the room. "So assuming, just for a moment, you're right. You think the cocaine is still here somewhere?"

"Yes. Definitely. Johnny didn't have time to pick it up before Stack and Micky arrived. The question is where?"

Ryan took a step forward and tapped the top of each of the six kegs lined up against the far wall.

"These are all full barrels. They supply the beer upstairs. It wouldn't be practical to store coke in them." He stepped across to the kegs standing upright opposite. "The empties," he said. "The coke's in one of those."

"How could you possibly know that?"

"You remember when we were waiting for Kate and that guy Jim arrived to collect the empty barrels?"

"Yes."

"He was surprised when Johnny insisted on coming with him to collect those kegs. Jim said something about Johnny still not trusting him."

"I remember."

"I think Johnny didn't trust Jim because he was worried that he would mistakenly take away the empty barrel that contained the coke."

Zoe tapped the top of the nearest empty keg. "But this one still has its lid and that thing on," she said, pointing to a metal valve that protruded through the center of the top.

"That thing is called a beer spear."

"Well, whatever it's named, taking the lid off and the beer spear out to source the coke would be far too time-consuming, surely?" Zoe said.

"You're right." The detective kneeled down. He viewed the shiny empty barrels from this new angle. They were all perfectly in line. He stood up again and looked over the top of the containers. Then the detective strode down the line to the third barrel. "There's more space between this container and the one next to it."

"So?" the constable said, joining him.

"So that could mean something—or nothing."

Ryan rolled the barrel out of the line before running his hand over the metal at the base of the container. His fingers passed back and forth over a tiny bump in the alloy. The detective grasped it and pulled, opening a rectangular metal cover. The flap was about ten inches long by eight inches deep. Now that the covering had been pulled out, the detective could see directly into the interior of the barrel. Pulling his phone from his pocket and clicking on the flashlight, he pointed it into the darkness. "Take a look."

Zoe bent down. "The coke is hidden in here?"

"I think so." Ryan pointed the flashlight down to the bottom of the barrel. Rows of plastic bags were piled one on top of the other. "You got gloves on you?" the detective asked.

The constable reached into her pocket and handed Ryan a pair.

"Take photos with my phone, please," Ryan said, handing his cell to the constable before stretching one of the gloves over his hand. Then, as Zoe took pictures, he opened and closed the secret compartment.

"This wouldn't have taken him long to make," Ryan said as he reached into the barrel and pulled out a small clear plastic bag filled with fine white powder.

FORTY MINUTES LATER, THEY HAD PUT all the cocaine into the trunk of Zoe's car. The constable volunteered to take the drugs into the office and take a sample to Gosford for analysis. There was no doubting that Johnny was dealing, but there was still the question of whether this coke came from the same source as the powder that had killed Liam Plummer and Scott Dean. With any luck, they would know the answer by tomorrow.

SEVENTY-TWO

THE NAME OF THE MOTEL—"PARADISE FOUND"—vastly overestimated the allure of the detective's new lodgings. The rundown single-story motel formed an L-shape around the parking lot, virtually empty because it was off season. So Ryan had no problem pulling up directly in front of his room.

The constable had given Ryan the name and address of the motel she had booked for him before they parted. But Zoe warned him that although the place was clean and within budget, it was no Ritz-Carlton. She was right.

Ryan pushed the key into the paneled door of room seven. Turning the handle, he entered and walked down the short corridor past the bathroom on the left, the fridge, and the closet on the right. He dropped his suitcase down.

Looking around the room, the detective gave the place a C plus, multiple points being deducted for the ugliness of the blue and green swirly carpet. A queen-sized bed was made up with white sheets. White pillows lay against the bed's upholstered headboard. Thin white towels had been left at the bed's base. A large colored framed photo of the Roman Colosseum hung over the bed. A walnut-colored desk ran along the opposite wall. Two chairs had been pushed under it. A flat-screen TV was mounted above the desk.

Ryan opened the suitcase and quickly unpacked the clothes in the closet, hanging them up in color order—lights to darks. Then he set up his coffee-making apparatus next to the kettle and put his laptop on the desk. Finally, he unpacked his toiletry bag in the bathroom before closing and stowing the case.

Satisfied everything was in order, the detective removed his shoes. He stretched out on the bed. A wave of tiredness swept over him as the phone rang in his pocket. He weighed up whether to answer it or not. He had only spoken to his mother yesterday and wasn't due to have another call this soon, so it was unlikely to be her. Of course, if Mumta had known that he had been kidnapped, she would be ringing morning, noon, and night. But she was never going to find that out, not from him, not ever!

The cell continued to ring. Reluctantly the detective answered it. It was Ellie.

"Hi Ryan, are we on for tonight?" she asked.

So much had happened he had forgotten entirely their arrangement for him to come over to dinner tonight. "Sorry. Can we have a rain check on that?"

"Sure." There was a pause. "Actually, that's good for me. Not because I don't want to see you. I do. But with all that's going on with Johnny—you know about that?" It was a metaphorical question which she answered herself. "Of course you do; you're a detective."

"What exactly do you know?" Ryan asked.

"Just that Johnny's in hospital after being shot, which seems incredible in a place like Barton." She started to quietly sob.

"You okay?"

"Not really," she said, trying to stifle the tears. "What exactly happened?"

"Have you asked him?"

"No, not yet. Johnny's only just come out of surgery, and they won't let any visitors in to see him until after four o'clock tomorrow." She paused. "Can't you tell me something?"

Ryan felt uncomfortable. He always found it challenging to repeat the line about not saying anything because he was a police officer. "No, sorry. You're going to visit him tomorrow?"

"Yes," Ellie said.

"So, how about we meet up in the hospital cafeteria, say around three-thirty? We can talk then."

"Yes. Good idea. Thank you."

"So, see you tomorrow?"

"You're on." She paused. "By the way, there is one piece of good news. Ashley's back, so Attila's out of my hair now. I don't know how I could handle the dog and this at the same time. Anyway, bye for now."

The phone clicked off. The detective lay back on the bed. Ellie hadn't mentioned anything about the detective having to overnight at the hospital after the gas leak at the pub. Of course, she may not have known about that. But was that likely? Ryan sighed. He had a habit of misreading signals from women he was attracted to. He was thirty-eight and a capable detective, but he never knew if a woman liked him or just wanted to be friends. He ran his hand over his face and stood up. No point in dwelling on that, though. He had work to do.

Ryan spent the rest of the evening writing up a detailed report of the day's events. The police force has become increasingly bureaucratic, and most of the form-filling had little to do with actually arresting and jailing criminals. The detective, though, knew that this was one instance when writing up a report was more than helpful—it was essential; completing it now meant that details of the day's tumultuous events were still fresh in his mind.

Two hours later, he finished. He could finally sleep.

SEVENTY-THREE

RYAN GAZED OUT OF THE MOTEL WINDOW as he sipped his coffee. The detective had slept surprisingly well. Cheap motels usually gave Ryan the creeps. The thought of all the people who had slept on the same mattress leaving their disgusting germs and disease upset him, but escaping death two days in a row has a habit of concentrating the mind. That worry felt trivial now.

Eager to start the day and knowing he had a tight schedule, Ryan set off for the station soon after. He arrived at almost the same time as Zoe. The constable was just entering the building as Ryan turned into the car park and pulled into a vacant space next to a beaten-up Honda Civic. Constable Jimmy O'Hagan sat inside the vehicle, readying to leave, but on seeing the detective, he rolled down his sedan window. "Morning, Sir."

"Morning Jimmy," Ryan said, getting out of his car.

"I heard all the news, wow! You okay?"

"I'm fine," Ryan replied.

"Thank goodness. All this makes you think, doesn't it? I mean, we could be here one minute and be gone the next," Jimmy O'Hagan said before rolling his window up, waving a cheery goodbye, and reversing out.

Jimmy was supposed to wait until at least one police officer had arrived at the station to take over. Technically the constable had done just that, however Ryan would have liked to have seen a little more enthusiasm from the young police officer. He appeared to have slipped back into his old ways.

By the time Ryan reached the office, Zoe had already made coffee for both of them. She handed him a cup. "Just to update you, I've checked on Johnny. The surgery went well, apparently. They've put him in an induced coma and are thinking of bringing him out of it later today."

The constable's information confirmed what Ellie had told Ryan last night. "So we'll definitely have to wait to speak to him," Ryan said. He sat down at his desk and opened his laptop just as the Sarge and Jackie arrived.

"It's good to see you," Jackie said after hugging him.

"It would take more than a few bad guys to put Ryan down," The Sarge said, shaking the detective's hand vigorously while looking around the room for agreement. "I would have rung last night, but Zoe thought it best if we leave you alone for a bit. Let you get some rest." He stopped. "So, how are you feeling?"

"Fine. Did Chief Inspector Dudley's office contact you?"

"No," the Sarge said.

"Yes, they did, Sarge. Last night. I put the note on your desk," Jackie said, pointing. "There it is."

The Sarge picked the form up and read it through quickly. "So you have to go back to Sydney? That's a bit sudden. There's hardly enough time to organize a leaving party."

The Sarge sat down in his chair. "Okay, fill me in. What's the update on F.?"

Ryan looked bemused. "F.?"

"Johnny Wilson. Fisty. That's Johnny's nickname. He got it at school because he was always fighting."

"I think he's going to be okay," Ryan said slowly, thinking about what had just been said.

"That's good. That's good," The Sarge offered. "He was shot in the back, right?"

"You tell the Sarge, Zoe, you found him."

She smiled. "Okay, well, from what we know . . ." She stopped and glanced over at Jackie.

"What?" Jackie asked, seeing the look.

"Nothing," Zoe said quickly.

"Oh, I get it. I've been working in this office for more days than you've had hot dinners, constable. No one's ever questioned my ability to keep the information confidential. But since you don't trust me, I'll go powder my nose." She strode across the room, closing the door nosily behind her.

There was a stunned silence, broken by the Sarge. "Don't worry about Jackie; she'll get over it. And it's true, she can be a bit of a blabbermouth. So, go on, tell me the news."

"Ryan thinks that Johnny Wilson was shot because they were looking for cocaine," Zoe said.

"Coke? That's garbage. There's no way he would have anything to do with coke."

"We found over a kilo of the stuff in an empty barrel in his cellar last night. I've put it in the evidence room."

"Fisty's a drug dealer?"

"Looks like it," Zoe said.

The Sarge tried to process the news. "There's no way. You must have made a mistake."

"There's no mistake. And Johnny may be involved in much more than that too," Ryan said quietly.

"More? What more exactly?"

The detective hesitated. Maybe it wasn't wise to say anything else; not to the Sarge, not now. He was a cop, but he was also Johnny's cousin. "Nothing we can prove at the moment, so best not to talk about it," the detective said, as the back door clicked open and Jackie returned.

"Everyone finished?" she said huffily and, not waiting for an answer, went to her desk. After that, they all returned to their work. Ryan checked over his statement; Zoe wrote coded updates on the whiteboard; Jackie typed furiously, and The Sarge sorted through papers on his desk while furtively looking up at the detective.

Ryan saw the glances. "Can I help you, Sarge?" he said finally.

"Well, there was one other thing." He peered across at Jackie. "And I don't have a problem with anyone hearing this." He paused. "The thing is, Ryan, you asked me about the night that Nathan Woodford went missing. You know I told Sergeant Harry Robinson that I saw Nathan's father walking on the beach?"

"Yes."

"Well, there was one other thing, something that maybe I should have mentioned at the time." He stopped. "Not that it was relevant. I mean, everyone knows that Paul Woodford killed his son. Sergeant Robinson was definitely of that opinion even though he couldn't prove it in a court of law."

"What do you want to tell me, Sarge?"

"You have to understand I'm only throwing this out there for the sake of completion."

"What?" Ryan asked.

"And bearing in mind that it has nothing to do with Nathan Woodford's disappearance."

"Sarge?"

"Okay." He took a deep breath. "That night, there was a massive storm. That was in the report, right?

Ryan kept quiet.

The Sarge continued: "So I was surprised to see Scott Dean mooring his boat. He must have been out fishing with Fisty despite the weather."

"Johnny Wilson was on a boat with Scott Dean the night Nathan Woodford disappeared?"

"Yes," the Sarge said.

"And you're just mentioning this now, fifteen years later?" Ryan asked.

"Well, it had nothing to do with the boy's disappearance, did it?" The Sarge said defensively. "I'm just saying it for the sake of completion. But we all know who did it, don't we? His father, Paul Woodford."

SEVENTY-FOUR

As Detective Ryan absorbed this new information, Kate readied to leave the Gosford Medical Hospital. Although her body still ached all over, there was no way she was going to stay there a moment longer. She couldn't remember much about the accident—only that she had accelerated through an amber light and another vehicle had suddenly appeared on her left, clipping the back end of her car, and sending it spinning.

After that, things had moved fast. Kate had been groggy but conscious when she had been rushed into the ER. The nurse had passed her onto a doctor, Dr. Chan, who had told her how blessed she was, though apparently not as blessed as the other driver, who had emerged from the crash unscathed.

Kate had been sent for test after test. This had taken all day and had constantly interrupted her attempts to get through to the car rental company. Everything had come back negative, but Doctor Chan was adamant Kate had to stay overnight "just in case."

Awake and up early, she had finally managed to speak to someone at the rental company—the manager, Mr. Grendal Walters, a pompous man who had told Kate that yes they had found her briefcase, but no it wasn't with them anymore. Since she hadn't been in touch, they'd dropped it off last night at Barton Police Station. "Oh, and by the way, could she come by the office to fill out the details of the crash?" Putting down her phone, Kate swore that was never going to happen.

The news about the briefcase was beyond annoying, but as she pulled on the oversized man's jacket and the baggy heavy trousers, her mood had brightened. The briefcase wasn't lost. She knew where it was. And now she would get it back.

As Kate left the hospital, Ryan got the call he had been waiting for. He listened as one of the twins, Fiona, confirmed that the tests showed the coke sample Zoe had dropped off was definitely from the same batch as the drug that had killed Scott Dean and Liam Plummer. The detailed information was all in the toxicology report. This had been completed rapidly 'because it was for him.' Then he was transferred to the pathologist, who also wanted to speak to the detective.

"Busy morning? Doctor Norman asked.

"Looks that way. What's up?"

"It's about the foot, and the sneaker washed up on the Barton beach. Unfortunately, we haven't found a DNA match."

"Oh," Ryan said.

"What about your constable? Has she discovered anyone in the missing person lists?" the Doctor asked.

"No. Not yet." He paused. "Do you know how long the foot had been in the water?"

"Up to seven days. I can't be more precise."

Four days ago, the Korean boat had been intercepted by the Customs. Of course, it could just be a coincidence, but the detective wasn't a great believer in coincidences.

"Okay, I'll pick up the report."

"Zoe," Ryan said, putting the phone away. "Come with me."

"I didn't want to get into who should and shouldn't hear this. So I thought it best if we talk somewhere more private," Ryan said as they entered Interview Room One. The detective then quickly updated her on the information he had just received about the cocaine.

"So, that means that Johnny's coke was from the same batch that killed Liam Plummer and Scott Dean."

"Exactly. And it could have come from a Korean ship."

"Those were the coordinates you gave me? Of that ship?" Zoe asked.

"Yes."

"Well, I haven't had time to tell you yet what I found," she said.

"Which is?" Ryan asked.

"You asked me whether it was likely that a package dropped at those coordinates would be dumped on Barton Beach."

"Yes."

"It is likely. Highly likely. So the packages that came from the Korean ship were filled with coke?" Zoe asked.

"I think so. The same cocaine Johnny used to kill Scott Dean," Ryan replied.

"Wow. Hold on. Do you think Johnny murdered Scott? That's a huge leap, Ryan. Why would Johnny kill Scott? You told me there were four principal reasons for murder—love, lust, loathing, or loot. I can't see any of those working in this case."

"Well remembered," Ryan said, pleased. Zoe would make a damn good detective one day. "I don't know for certain yet, but one thing I do know is that Johnny thought I was getting too close to finding an answer to that question."

"How so?" Zoe asked.

"Because he tried to murder me with gas," Ryan replied.

"You're blowing my mind, Ryan. You sure? Wasn't the leak just an accident?"

"I checked yesterday. The flue in the chimney had been closed, so the carbon monoxide would flow back into the room. And when I had tried to get out, the door was locked too. Luckily I found my key, but twenty more minutes and I would have been dead. Of course, there's nothing I could use in a court of law, not until I speak to Johnny."

"You think he'd admit everything to you? Just like that?" Zoe asked.

"That depends on the evidence we say we already have."

"But you don't have any. Not really."

Ryan peered at Zoe. The constable still had a lot to learn.

There was a knock on the door, and The Sarge came in holding a black leather briefcase.

"Sorry to interrupt. This was delivered last night by a car rental company. Jimmy hid it under a pile of papers, and Jackie just found it. I had a few words with the lad, and it won't happen again. Sorry."

Ryan took the briefcase and turned it around. There was a red and brown coat of arms embossed on its front. The detective laid the case on the desk and flicked the catches open. It was filled with rolls of fifty-dollar bills.

SEVENTY-FIVE

KATE TRIED TO IGNORE THE BURLY bearded Uber driver. He hadn't stopped talking since he had picked her up at the hospital. He had rambled on and on about the weather—warm for this time of year; Sport—how the Bunnies had had a great win last night; and taxi driving—how being a gig worker was a pain in the butt.

It was almost impossible to think, and she really needed to do that. She wanted to go through what she would say at the station. The cops weren't going to allow her to just pick up the briefcase and leave. They would want to know where the money came from. The trick was to keep any explanation simple, mundane, and believable.

"We're here," the driver said as he pulled up in front of the police station. Kate reached to open the door.

"Miss can I ask you something?" the driver said before she could get out.

Kate held her breath and prayed he wasn't going to ask her for a date.

"Go ahead," she said.

"Your clothes. Is that some kind of new fashion, or what?" the driver asked.

Damn, Kate thought, the idiot wants to know if I'm a dyke. She tugged at her men's linen jacket. "Yeah, it's this year's look. What do you think?"

"Very . . . nice."

"Have a good day," Kate said and quickly stepped out of the vehicle. As the car took off, she pushed open the door of the police station and strode confidently into the lobby. It was deserted. Kate pressed her hand down hard on the brass bell on the front desk. She waited. A uniformed cop appeared. He rammed his cap on as he walked across.

"Morning. How can I help?"

Kate knew the cop. He was Johnny's cousin and came into the pub occasionally. "Sergeant Acton, right?" she asked.

"And you are Kate? Kate Cassels? You work with Johnny?"

"Yes."

"So what can I do for you?"

Let the show begin, Kate thought. "I believe my briefcase has been left here. Do you have it?"

"Case you say? I'm not sure. Please take a seat. I'll go check."

The cop returned a few minutes later, all smiles. "Good news. We do have it."

"Fantastic," she said.

"But before we can hand it over, you'll need to fill out a form."

"No problem."

"My assistant Jackie will take you through to where you can complete the document. Please go to that door," the Sarge said, pointing.

Kate stood up and walked across as the Sarge reached down to press a small white button on his side of the desk. The office door buzzed. Kate pulled it open to reveal a smiling middle-aged woman. "Kate Cassels?" the woman asked. Kate nodded.

"Please follow me," Jackie said. She led Kate across the empty office, through another door, and into a corridor before halting in front of a door marked Interview Room One. She knocked.

"Coffee?" Jackie asked as they waited outside.

"Thank you. White, no sugar," Kate said.

"Come," a voice said from inside. Jackie opened the door and indicated for Kate to go inside.

Two police officers were seated at a wooden desk in the middle of the room. Kate's briefcase sat in front of them. She smiled. Kate recognized both cops immediately.

"Detective, constable. We must stop meeting like this," Kate said, now completely relaxed.

Ryan stood up and held out his hand. "Good to see you, Kate. Please." He indicated the chair on the opposite side of the desk. "And you remember Zoe, of course?"

"Hi, Kate. Nice to see you again."

"Likewise," Kate said, taking a seat. This was going to be like taking candy from a baby.

Ryan tapped the top of the case. "So, this is yours?"

"Yes. I thought I'd lost it in the accident, but luckily the car rental company bought it here."

"Accident?" Ryan asked.

"It's a long story."

"We'd love to hear it. But I have a favor to ask first. Could Constable Yang record our conversation? We need to have something on record to show that we didn't hand the briefcase over to just anyone."

"But wouldn't all that information be on the form?" Kate asked.

"We do need a little more than it requires, bearing in mind what's inside the case." He turned it towards Kate and flicked open the locks, pulling the top back to reveal the rolled fifty-dollar bills. "Yours?"

"Yes."

"So, is recording this okay?" Ryan asked, closing the briefcase and swinging it back around.

Kate hesitated. She could object, but if she had nothing to hide, why wouldn't she allow it? "Fine," Kate said.

"Good," Ryan said, nodding to Zoe, who produced her iPhone, and turned the recorder on the device. "So tell us how the briefcase ended up here?"

"Well . . ." Kate began explaining the rental car, the accident, and how the case had gone missing while in the hospital. She tried to add as much detail as possible, believing that the more she supplied, the more believable the story became.

"Are you all right now?" Zoe asked, concerned.

"Yes. I'm fine. Just a few aches and pains." She waited. The cops said nothing. "Now, can I sign the form and take my briefcase?" Kate asked finally.

Zoe glanced across at the detective, who nodded.

"Sure." He reached into his suit jacket, produced a single-page document, and carefully placed it on the desk. He was about to push it over but stopped. "Sorry, I forgot. Before we do that, I need to tell you that we're almost ready to release Scott Dean's body. So in your capacity as Executor, this is a heads-up that you can start organizing his funeral."

"That's great. After we've finished here, I'll begin making the arrangements."

"Fantastic," Ryan said. "Now the form."

He picked it up and then put it down. One more question: "Did Scott Dean keep much money around the house?"

Kate stared at him. She saw where he was going. "You think I stole this money from him?"

"It had crossed my mind," Ryan replied.

There was a knock on the door, and Jackie came in with a cup of coffee. She placed it in front of Kate.

"There you go."

"Thank you."

They waited until Jackie left.

Then Kate took a sip of the coffee. "Of course, I didn't take it from Scott. It's from my savings. After the funeral, I plan to go to Hollywood to try my luck."

"So you took your savings out for the trip?"

"Yes."

"Exactly when and where did you get the cash?" Ryan asked.

"From my bank. The NAB. Yesterday."

"In Gosford?" the detective said.

"Yes."

Kate began to feel queasy. If they were to check, they would discover her bank account rarely had more than a hundred dollars in it.

Ryan flipped open the locks on the case, opened it, and reached in. Placing his hand under a bundle of bills, he grasped a tiny round think black plastic disc and held it aloft. "Do you usually carry a tracker with your money?"

A tracker, Kate thought. That bastard Johnny had put it in with the cash. "I put it in there as a safeguard. In the event, the cash was stolen."

"Really." Ryan replaced the tracker and closed the case. "Good idea." He pushed the form over and took out a pen from his pocket, rolling it over to her.

"There you go. Your name, address, etc.," Ryan said.

Kate started to fill in the document, not quite believing that there were no more questions.

"Oh, one more thing, Kate. Aside from the cash, is this briefcase definitely yours?" Ryan asked.

"Of course."

"Strange that."

'What is?" Kate asked.

He flicked the closed case around. "See that?"

She peered at the shield he was indicating.

What was it? Kate hadn't noticed it before. What to say? "Oh, that. That's my family's arms. I had it embossed."

She waited. Had the detective believed her?

"So you and Johnny are related?"

What? What was he talking about? "No."

"I think you must be. I saw this same coat of arms on a briefcase in Johnny's office. Actually, on this case." He stopped. It was time to go for the jugular. "Kate, you're lying. We found coke in Johnny's cellar. He was dealing. We found cocaine from the same batch in Scott's veins. That's what killed him. Johnny murdered Scott Dean, and if we offered him a deal, he would confirm that you aided and abetted him in the killing."

"What are you talking about? I had nothing to do with killing Scott nor with dealing coke," Kate said, alarmed.

"No. But you have Johnny Wilson's briefcase, packed full of money. So, where did the cash come from? Certainly not from your bank."

Ryan waited. In the cat and mouse game of a police interview, there comes a tipping point where the suspect throws in the towel or demands a lawyer. If Kate asked for an attorney, all bets were off. Ryan may never be able to discover the truth.

"Well, what's it to be? We charge you with murder, and you go down with Johnny Wilson. Or you tell us honestly how you got those funds?"

Kate looked from Ryan to Zoe and back. She released her breath. "If I admit where I got the cash from, will you let me go?"

"Co-operating early is one way to lessen any sentence." There was a long silence.

"I got the money from Johnny. I was blackmailing him."

SEVENTY-SIX

"I STILL THINK YOU SHOULD HAVE CHARGED Kate Cassels," Zoe said as she brought her car to a halt in front of Julie Woodford's bungalow.

"Sometimes, you have to take a more flexible approach to the law," Ryan said, unbuckling his seat belt. "The person she blackmailed is in a coma, and until we know whether Johnny Wilson is prepared to confirm Kate Cassels' story, we have nothing. He could say he gifted her the money."

"But she admitted it."

"And she could retract that confession claiming we made her say things under duress," Ryan said.

"Oh yeah, that's going to work," the constable said.

Zoe had the same tunnel vision as Ryan when he first entered the police force. It took him time to accept that everything wasn't black and white. There was a lot of gray—and Kate Cassels was part of that gray. "We've got bigger fish to fry. We'll need her to give evidence in court," Ryan said.

"If you say so." There was no point in arguing. There were things about Ryan's approach to criminals and the law that she would never accept.

Ryan reached for the door handle.

Zoe put her hand on his arm. "Before we go into the house, won't you tell me why we're here?"

"We're here because of you," Ryan replied.

"Me?" Zoe said, astonished.

"Yes. You reminded me of the reasons for murder—Love, lust, loathing, or loot."

"But I said that none of them applied."

"You're wrong. I think one of them does." Ryan said.

"Which one ?"

"You want to be a detective; you work it out."

Ryan looked out the car window as the bungalow door opened. Julie Woodford stepped out.

"We should go," he said.

Zoe released her hand from the detective's arm as he opened the door. The man was so annoying.

SEVENTY-SEVEN

"**Y**OU MENTIONED THAT YOUR SON HAD talked about a girl he liked and who he thought liked him," Ryan said as they entered Nathan Woodford's room.

"Yes," Julie said.

"He didn't by any chance have a photo of that girl?" the detective asked.

Julie thought about this. "Maybe." She walked across to the desk and opened the drawer under the tabletop.

Ryan and Zoe followed, moving to stand behind Julie.

The woman turned. "I feel awful about this. This is Nathan's private stuff. I'm not one of those mothers who want to know everything about their children."

"So you've never looked in here?" Zoe asked, surprised.

"No. Well, just glanced."

Even after such a long time, it was clear that Julie hadn't entirely accepted that her son would never return. And she obviously still saw him as an eighteen-year-old boy who would get angry if he found his mom had gone through his possessions.

"What about the police? Did they look?" Ryan asked.

"No. Never."

Ryan wasn't surprised. It was clear that Sergeant Robinson had decided early on that Nathan Woodford was dead and that he knew who'd done it. It was sloppy police work, but it was what happened when the cop in charge had made up his mind about a case.

"I'm sure Nathan would be okay with it," Ryan said.

"Yes, and it could really help us, Julie," Zoe added, though she had no real idea what the detective was expecting to find from the search.

Julie sighed heavily. "Okay." She started to rifle through the old papers and pens. Spotting a yellow, dog-eared sleeve, she opened it. There was a small pile of black and white photos inside.

"Could I?" Ryan said, holding out his hand.

Julie reluctantly handed the package over. "Nathan did buy himself a disposal camera once. I think it was an experiment to see if he liked taking photos."

"And did he?" Zoe asked, looking over Ryan's shoulder as he examined the pictures. The black and white shots were poorly framed shots of the sea, the beach, and trees.

"He was good, don't you think?" Julie asked the constable.

"Yes, he had talent," she said, lying.

Ryan held up one of the photos and pointed at it. "Is this the girl?"

Julie peered at the picture the detective was holding.

"Yes. That's her."

SEVENTY-EIGHT

Ellie waved as Ryan approached. She was sitting in the small out-door area of the hospital's cafe toying with a cup of coffee, a pack of cigarettes next to it.

"Hi," the detective said, taking a seat. "You look stunning today," And she did. She wore a long-sleeved white and blue striped blouse, knotted at the stomach, with tight-fitting black pants. "And you've had your hair cut too. It looks spectacular."

Ellie smiled. It was always good to be complimented, and she had had her hair trimmed and highlighted with blonde streaks this morning. The detective was charming, and observant too.

Ryan pointed to the cigarettes. "I didn't know you smoked."

"I've just started again after six years without one. I took two puffs last night, and it's as if I'd never stopped." She looked around. "But I'd forgotten that you can't smoke at a hospital, even outside."

"Why did you begin again?" Ryan asked.

"Because of Johnny. When I heard about what had happened to him, it hit me like a ton of bricks."

"You know that you won't be able to speak to him yet? He's still in a coma," Ryan said.

"Yeah. That's what the hospital told me. I just want to see Johnny, that's all." She paused. "Why would anyone want to shoot him? He's an irritating bastard, but that's carrying things a bit far," Ellie said.

"All I can say is he has a lot to talk about," Ryan said.

Ellie took a sip of coffee. "So he's in trouble." She searched the detective's face. "Big trouble? People don't get shot for nothing." Ellie leaned forward, brushing the detective's arm with her blouse. "Could he be sent to prison? Go on, tell me."

Ryan shook his head. "Sorry."

"I doubt if you'll get much out of him, though. Johnny can be as tight as a clam if he wants to be," Ellie said.

Silence. Ryan said nothing.

She stared at him. "What? You think he'll talk?"

"When someone is facing years in jail, and you offer them a deal that could shorten their sentence, they'll talk, they always do," Ryan said.

"Really?" Ellie asked.

"Yes. We rely on deals far more than people realize. So he'll tell us everything; I'm confident of that."

Silence—then Ellie glanced at her watch. "Sorry, time to go." She stood up. "And Ryan, don't forget about our dinner."

"How could I?"

She smiled. "See you later then." She turned and walked back inside the hospital.

MOST TIMES, IT WAS LIKE STATIC on a TV. And then, for a moment, the picture came clear. Out of focus blues, and browns, replaced with a figure . . . a nurse? Then bang. It all disappeared again. He was back in his world—where nothing made sense.

"Johnny. Johnny?" a voice said.

"Johnny? What? Who is Johnny?" he wanted to say. But nothing came out. "I'm sorry. I'm sorry." The voice repeated, over and over.

"Sorry? What did it mean?" He was falling, his head moving back. The light darkened. And the pressure built. He tried to move. Trapped, he was being pushed down, more and more forceful. He gasped for breath.

SHE WAS STOOPED OVER JOHNNY WILSON's hospital bed, a pillow pushed down over the unconscious man's face when Ryan and Zoe pulled her away.

"Let him go," Ryan shouted, his one arm wrapped tight around Ellie Sastra's waist. With his other hand, the detective pushed the woman's arm high up her back.

"You're hurting me, you asshole," Ellie screamed, struggling to free herself.

"What's going on?" The voice came from the doorway. Ryan twisted around. A nurse stood in the doorway.

"Police," Zoe said as she tried to cuff the struggling woman. "This woman just tried to kill the patient."

"They're lying. I did nothing of the sort. He's my ex-husband, for god sake," Ellie shouted.

"Please nurse make sure he's okay," Ryan said.

The nurse hesitated and then, decision made, moved over to the bed, flung the pillow on the floor, and leaned over.

"He's still breathing," she said, reaching up to press the emergency button above the bed.

THE DETECTIVE KNEW HE HAD TO act fast. A prisoner was usually most cooperative immediately after arrest. So arriving at the station, he straight away hustled Ellie through to the interview room, ordering her to sit down at the table. After cautioning her, he set up the recorder.

"Interview with Ellie Sastra with Detective Ramesh Ryan and Constable Zoe Yang present," the detective said into the recorder microphone before giving the time, date, and location.

"Shall we start at the beginning? Why did you try to kill Johnny Wilson?" Detective Ryan asked. Ellie stared at him. Since leaving the hospital, she had said nothing. She still said nothing.

"Perhaps there were accentuating circumstances? Things that we could use to help you lessen your sentence?" Ellie remained silent.

"You understand just how serious the charge of attempted murder is? That gets you up to twenty-five years in prison." Ellie continued staring ahead.

There was a knock, the door swung open, and the Sarge walked in. He stepped across to Ryan and whispered in his ear.

"Interview ended at 17:15," the detective said, standing up and accompanying the Sarge out.

"So, what's so urgent?" Ryan asked.

"Word from the hospital. They've brought Johnny out of the coma, and they're willing to let you talk to him now."

"Good."

"How are you getting on with her?"

"We're not. She hasn't said a word."

"Oh."

"Can you take her to the lock-up, Sarge? Zoe and I will go see Johnny Wilson."

SEVENTY-NINE

"DOCTOR GRANT. I'M MR. WILSON'S DOCTOR," the young man said to Ryan and Zoe. "I take it you've been made aware of his condition?"

"I understand he's available to talk," the detective said.

"That information didn't come from me. Those above my pay grade made that decision. They overruled my recommendation," the Doctor said.

"You don't want us to speak to him?"

"I think he should be left alone for at least another day."

That was out of the question. Like most of the police, Ryan believed the law was unduly protective of criminals. The longer he left it, the less likely he would be to find out the truth.

"Are you saying he isn't strong enough to be interviewed?" Ryan asked.

"The patient's recovery has been remarkable."

"So?"

"But still, ideally, you should wait."

"This is not an ideal world doctor. The man in there has been involved in several killings," Ryan said, pointing to the ward door. "I can't afford to wait until he's skipping around the room."

"Well, if needs must. But please, no more than twenty minutes," the Doctor said.

"Thank you." Ryan pushed open the door. Zoe followed.

Inside, Johnny was propped up against the pillow. His face was white, and he looked tired, but his eyes were alert. "Evening officers," he said.

"How are you feeling?" Ryan asked, picking up a chair and carrying it close to the bed.

"Never better," Johnny said, his voice strained. "What's up?"

Ryan waited for Zoe to put her chair down on the other side of the bed and place her iPhone on the bedside table. "We're here to interview you," the detective said.

"About the shooting?" Johnny Wilson asked.

"You remember being shot?"

"Of course. The doctor said I was lucky to be alive," Johnny said.

"No one's told you anything else."

Johnny shook his head. "Is there more? I think cheating death once is quite an achievement."

"Cheating it twice even more so, wouldn't you say?" Ryan replied.

"What?"

"Ellie Sastra tried to kill you earlier," Ryan said.

Johnny looked from Ryan to Zoe. "Is that true?"

"Yes," the constable said. "Ellie tried to suffocate you, here, in this room earlier. If we hadn't pulled her off, you would be dead."

Johnny went quiet as he thought about this. He was thinking of the dream he'd had—the one where he couldn't breathe.

"Are you agreeable to us recording our conversation?" Ryan asked.

"Are you arresting me?" Johnny asked, still thinking about Ellie.

"Why would we do that? You're a victim, right?"

Johnny nodded. "I certainly am."

"So?" The detective waited. Ryan knew that Johnny shouldn't agree to a recorded interview without a lawyer being present. But the pub owner had a huge ego and had gone through life believing he was more intelligent than everyone else. That was his Achilles Heel.

Ryan stood up. "Of course, if you don't feel up to being interviewed now, I'm quite willing to put this off to a later date." It was a lie, but one that offered a direct challenge to Johnny: So you're scared of being questioned by two half-wit cops? Really?

Johnny took the bait. "Go ahead, detective," he said smiling.

Ryan retook his seat and nodded at Zoe to start the recording on her iPhone. Then: "Interview with Johnny Wilson with Detective Ramesh Ryan and Constable Zoe Yang present," the detective said and gave the time, date, and location.

"Let's start at the beginning."

"Okay, well, a man and a woman who I'd never seen before came into the pub. They were both armed. When I tried to run, they shot me."

"No, not that beginning," Ryan said.

"What? But that's what happened."

"No. Let's start with Nathan Woodford."

"Nathan Woodford?"

"The man who disappeared fifteen years ago."

"I've just been shot, and you say my ex-wife tried to kill me, but you're asking me about something that happened eons ago?" Johnny said.

"So you remember it?"

Johnny thought about this. "Oh yes. Wasn't it his father who did that?"

"Kate Cassels says you murdered Nathan Woodford," Ryan said.

"Kate? What's Kate got to do with anything?"

"She was blackmailing you. Scott Dean confessed to her that you and he murdered Nathan Woodford," Ryan said.

Johnny said nothing, but things were clicking into place. So Kate was the blackmailer! *Bitch.*

"Kate Cassels threatened to tell the police everything unless you paid up. She gave specific instructions on where to deposit the money. You did that and put the package in the chosen store. I imagine you were feeling confident. What could go wrong? You would wait and follow whoever picked the case up. Even if they weren't the blackmailer, they would lead you to them." Ryan paused. "How am I doing so far?"

"You should write fiction, detective. You'd be good at it" Johnny said.

Ryan ignored him and continued. "Kate tricked you, though. She dressed up as a man, sent a patsy out as a distraction and took the money." The detective waited.

"Me tricked?" Johnny Wilson said after a long moment of silence. "Or was it the other way around?" He smirked.

"Okay then, maybe you fooled Kate Cassels. She didn't check the case with the money in properly. She didn't realize you had hidden a tracker inside."

"Well, that's an interesting story, but nothing to do with me," Johnny said.

Ryan shrugged. "If that's the way you want to play it." He paused. "I should tell you we have a sworn statement and a recorded interview with Kate Cassels confirming everything I've just told you."

"She's a liar."

"She isn't, but let's not dwell on that now. Let's discuss Scott Dean's death."

'What about it? Johnny asked.

"You killed him."

Johnny coughed, his face reddening.

"You all right," Zoe said anxiously.

"Sure," Johnny said, recovering. "Detective, I've changed my mind. You shouldn't write fiction. You should do stand-up comedy. First, I kill Nathan Woodford, and then I murder Scott Dean. What next? You'll tell me I'm an alien from Mars?" He paused. "We should be talking about who shot me and my ex-wife who you claim tried to murder me, not some fantastic inventions."

"Indulge me. Fifteen years after Nathan Woodford's death, Scott Dean finally decided to clear his conscience. He planned to confess to the police. You couldn't have that, so you murdered him, using the coke we found in your cellar. It was from the same batch that killed Liam Plummer," Ryan said. Johnny said nothing, his face blank.

"You don't want to say anything about all of that?"

"Nothing in the fairytale you've just spun has anything to do with me. This is police harassment, so please turn the recorder off now."

Ryan shrugged. "Interview ended 18:27." He glanced across at Zoe. "Constable." Zoe picked up the iPhone and stood up. Ryan stood up.

"You're going?" Johnny asked.

"We gave you your chance. We'll do the deal with Ellie Sastra instead."

"What deal?"

"The one we offered her. Let's go, Zoe."

Being a detective sometimes felt like being a professional poker player, Ryan thought. But like poker, if Johnny called his bluff, the game would be over. He counted slowly to himself as Zoe, and he walked to the door. Reaching five, the detective grabbed the handle. He had blown it.

"Wait," Johnny said.

Ryan, his back to Johnny, smiled. He slowly turned. "Yes."

"What are you offering?"

"We don't need you. We've done the deal with Ellie Sastra. She blames you for everything." Ryan took a step towards the bed. "We have Kate Cassels as a witness. We have the coke we found in the pub cellar—the reason you were shot by those two villains, one of whom incidentally is now dead and the other is in custody. They came looking for the cocaine—the coke that killed Liam Plummer and Scott Dean. But if you won't talk, so be it. We need nothing more from you."

"You don't? What exactly has Ellie been saying about me?" Johnny asked.

Ryan peered at Johnny. He had sold almost pure coke to Liam Plummer, killing him. He had helped murder Nathan Woodford, murdered Scott Dean, and, although the detective would maybe never be able to prove it in court, Johnny had tried to gas him—but his recorded testimony was still essential. They had caught Ellie red-handed trying to kill her ex-husband. Without Johnny's confession the detective could not confirm Ellie's role in the murder of both Nathan Woodford and Scott Dean.

"What do you think Ellie's been saying about you?" Ryan asked.

Johnny Wilson thought for a moment. Then: "Have you signed off on that deal with her?"

"Not yet," Ryan replied

"So, I could still have an agreement like that with you."

"Perhaps. It depends on what you have to offer."

"Oh, I have lots to say. But you don't get anything just like that. You have to promise that in exchange for the information I supply, you'll guarantee me clemency," Johnny said.

"No can do. I can't guarantee anything. All I can do is tell the prosecutor how you have helped out, and he can inform the judge."

Johnny thought about this. "And if I don't do it, you're going to let her take that deal?"

"Exactly" the detective said.

"That's a question for the constable, not you detective. Is that right, Zoe?"

"Yes it is," Zoe replied.

"Sit down then," Johnny Wilson said.

The officers took their seats. The detective waited for Zoe to set up the recorder on her iPhone again. Then: "Interview recommenced." He paused. "Ready, Johnny?"

"On the condition, you confirm now that I am doing this of my own free will to aid the police."

"Agreed."

"Right well, whatever she's said, she was the one responsible for Nathan Woodford's death."

"By she, you are referring to Ellie Sastra."

"Correct. She came to us—Scott Dean and me."

"When?"

"When we were all at school."

"Fifteen years ago?"

"Yes. She was in tears. She said Nathan Woodford had attacked her and tried to rape her. So she wanted to teach him a lesson."

"Those were her exact words? 'Teach him a lesson?' You remember that after all these years?" Ryan asked.

"Yes. I have a very clear memory of what was said back then."

"And what did those words mean to you?" Ryan asked.

"That we were to hurt him."

"Kill him?"

"No, of course not. We were just going to frighten him. To be honest, I wasn't convinced that Nathan had done anything to her."

"Why not?"

"For one, he was a complete geek, but more importantly, Bean loved to encourage the boys."

"Bean?" Ryan asked.

"Her nickname. Jelly Bean, Ellie."

"Okay, go on."

"Jelly Bean was the prettiest girl in the school, and everyone wanted to get into her knickers. Nathan Woodford was mesmerized by her and used to follow her around like a love-sick puppy."

Ryan reached into his pocket and produced the photo of the girl Julie Woodford had given him. He showed it to Johnny. "This is Ellie Sastra back then?"

Johnny peered at the picture of a very pretty teenage girl with long blonde hair and an angelic smile.

"Yeah, that's her," Johnny said. "Where did you get this?"

"From Nathan Woodford's mother. Nathan took her photo. He thought she liked him too."

"Classic Bean. I'm sure she enjoyed the geek's attention at first. It was flattering. A power thing. But then she got sick of it, and it started to creep her out. But he wouldn't stop," Johnny explained.

"So she made up the attack story?" Ryan asked.

"I believe so."

"And you agreed to help her."

"I was head-over-heels in love. That's why I went along with her scheme and persuaded my best friend Scotty to come with me," Johnny said.

"Scott Dean?"

"Yes."

"What scheme?"

"Bean knew Scott's parents were away that weekend, and he had the house to himself, so she passed a message to Nathan Woodford. She asked him to meet her at Scotty's place on Friday night but not to tell anyone. Bean, Scotty, and I were waiting when he arrived."

"And then what happened?" Ryan asked.

"Scotty and I began punching him. He was screaming and crying out for Bean to help him."

"What was she doing?"

"Watching," Johnny said.

"So, did she get you to stop?"

"No, she was enjoying it. And when we got bored and stopped, she went crazy. She told us Nathan Woodford still hadn't been taught a proper lesson. She slapped him really hard and then pushed him over. He tripped and fell backward, knocking his head hard. That's what killed him. Then we bundled the body into Scotty's car and drove down to his boat. We dumped him out at sea."

"But it was an accident?"

"Yes," Johnny confessed.

"So why didn't you go to the police?" Ryan asked.

"We were eighteen-year-old kids. We panicked, simple as that."

"If all that is true, why didn't Kate Cassels mention Ellie Sastra's involvement to us."

"Because Scott never told her that. He would have just said that he and I killed Nathan."

"Why?"

"Because he believed what Bean said—that Nathan had tried to rape her."

"I don't understand," Ryan said.

"Well, in Scotty's mind, we both had a choice. We didn't need to hurt the geek. But she did."

"So her hitting Nathan was somehow justified, but you and he doing it wasn't?" Ryan asked.

"Crazy, huh. But that's the thing about Scotty. He was never all there. He mixed everything up in his drug-addled mind, and I honestly think he eventually forgot Bean had even been in the house. But she didn't forget. She remembered exactly what had happened. So when Scott blurted out to me about going to the cops, it was Bean who decided he had to die. I just thought it was Scotty mouthing off again. But she has always been paranoid. She said we had to do something. She came up with a plan to use GHB and the coke."

"It was her plan?" Ryan asked.

"Yes."

"And she knew you had the coke?"

"She gave it to me. She found the packages on the beach on one of her early morning walks and brought them around. And the GHB was easy to find. I just swapped a couple of tabs for some coke." Johnny paused. "By the way, I stopped selling the coke after I read the newspaper story about Liam Plummer's death."

"But you didn't mind using the drug to kill Scott Dean?"

"Aren't you listening? I wouldn't have done it if she hadn't told me to. It was all her. And you don't think she would have let Kate Cassels off the hook either once she'd found out she was the blackmailer?"

"Would you have agreed to murder Kate Cassels then as well?" Ryan asked.

"You want me to admit that? Honestly? Of course, I wouldn't."

Yes, you would, Ryan thought. "And what about trying to kill me?"

"What?"

"You loosened the pipe on the old fire, so the gas leaked, and blocked the chimney, so it stayed in the room. And just to put the cherry on the cake, you locked my door."

Johnny shook his head. "That had nothing to do with me. It was just an accident," he said, smiling.

The door swung open, and Doctor Grant came in. He tapped his watch.

"Interview over," Ryan said.

EIGHTY

"**S**O IT WAS LOVE," ZOE SAID as the officers left Johnny's room and joined the throng of people heading out of the hospital at the end of visiting time.

Ryan smiled. "Yes. Johnny Wilson loved Ellie Sastra and was willing to do anything for her until she broke the spell."

"Trying to kill someone will do that. But how did you connect Ellie Sastra to Nathan Woodford's death?"

"Because three of the reasons for Nathan Woodford being killed didn't apply. But one did."

"Love again?" Zoe asked.

"When you're a teenager, love is the most important emotion you feel. Julie Woodford had told me that her son had a crush on a girl at school. I should have made a more determined effort to follow up. But I didn't," the detective said.

"Not until we returned to Julie Woodford's house and saw the photo of young Ellie Sastra? Zoe asked

"Yes, and then, with your help, set up the trap for Ellie."

"Feeding her the line about Johnny wanting to talk, knowing that she would try and do something about that? Zoe said.

"Exactly. And it worked," Ryan replied.

"Yes. Ellie did try to kill Johnny," Zoe said, and stopped. "When you told me what you thought would happen I wasn't convinced. I was still skeptical that Ellie would do what you said she would do."

"But you went along with the plan," the detective said.

"You're the senior officer. I do what I'm asked to do." Zoe shook her head. "It was an impressive deduction though."

"How so?" Ryan asked.

"Going from a photo of a teenage Ellie Sastra to conclude she was involved with the murders of Nathan Woodford and Scott Dean," Zoe said.

"It wasn't just the photo. I had my suspicions."

"About Ellie?" Zoe asked.

"Yes. She was a little too keen to see me all the time," Ryan said.

Zoe smiled. "Maybe that was just your animal magnetism?"

Ryan shook his head. "You're too kind."

"And you're too modest," Zoe replied.

"Whatever. We can agree to disagree on that. But the point was Ellie kept on turning up wherever I was, asking me sly questions about how things were going on the investigation. I suspected Ellie had ulterior motives, and on seeing the photo everything clicked into place."

They started to walk again.

"And what about you being gassed? You still think Johnny did that?"

"I'm almost certain of it, not that I will ever be able to prove it. They were running scared that I was getting too close."

"They?"

"Ellie Sastra and Johnny Wilson. He did the grunt work, but I'm pretty sure it was her idea," Ryan stated.

"Like it was her idea to do everything else?" The detective nodded.

"You think that they honestly believed that killing you would have put an end to the investigation."

"I don't know what they believed exactly. But just like when they were teenagers all those years ago, I think they panicked."

Zoe thought about this as the glass entrance doors slid open, and they stepped out of the hospital. Stopping outside, Ryan raised his hand to high-five his young companion. "Anyway we did it," he said. "Me and you."

Zoe's face broke into a grin as she slapped her hand hard against his.

Ryan wasn't just blowing smoke up the constable's butt. He knew the constable's presence in the hospital ward had been essential. She'd brought something to the table he couldn't. She had lived all her life in Barton's tight-knit community, and because of that, Johnny Wilson had trusted her to tell the truth. The detective doubted that the pub owner would have talked if the constable hadn't been willing to confirm Ellie Sastra's supposed deal. So now they didn't just have Ellie's attempt to kill Johnny as evidence, they also had the recording of his testimony to use against her. It was a one two knock-out punch.

"DETECTIVE?"

Ryan looked around. A middle-aged man in a purple shirt and expensive black suit was advancing towards them.

"Detective, can we talk?" Charles Plummer asked, reaching the officers.

"What about Mr. Plummer?"

"I'll tell you privately, detective," Plummer said. A black Mercedes S pulled out from a parking spot opposite and drew up alongside the trio as he spoke. A gray-suited muscular black man stepped out of the vehicle. In his early-thirties with a shaved head and a thick neck, sporting the tattoo of a knife which poked out from his open-necked white shirt.

Plummer looked across at Zoe. "If you could give us a few moments."

Ryan was torn. He didn't like someone dictating terms to him. But he was curious to find out what Plummer had to say.

"Zoe? Do you mind?"

"I'll wait for you in the car," the constable said and walked away.

"Smith," Plummer said. The driver opened the vehicle's back door.

"You first, detective."

Ryan slid into the backseat. Plummer followed. Smith closed the door behind them.

"I think we got off on the wrong foot when we met. I now agree with you that it was a drug overdose that killed my son," Plummer said.

"I don't know why Liam took drugs. Maybe I overindulged him? Maybe I didn't spend enough time with him? Does anyone truly know why children sometimes take the wrong turn?"

"What is this about Mr. Plummer?" the detective asked.

"I came to get an update on your progress in discovering the source of the drugs."

"It's an ongoing investigation. I'm afraid I can't divulge exactly what stage we're at," Ryan said.

"But from my inquiries . . ."

"You've been making inquiries?"

"Yes," Plummer said, his voice hardening. "Of course. You don't expect me to just sit around waiting, do you? I prefer to do things like this on my own. Police investigations usually leave a lot to be desired, though I understand you've been very thorough."

He waited for Ryan to say something. When he didn't, he continued. "I now believe that the coke that killed Liam came originally from Sydney. Is that correct?"

"I can't talk about that," the detective said.

"You work in Sydney; you know the city well. I've heard a name, a name that you may be familiar with."

"Please open the door," Ryan said.

Plummer stared at him before finally nodding his head. "Smith," he said. After a moment the door swung open.

"I'm sorry you won't help, detective. I thought that on this particular matter, our interests coincide." Plummer stepped out of the vehicle. Ryan followed.

"Oscar Bruno is the name I have," Plummer said quietly.

Ryan locked eyes with him. "Oscar Bruno?"

"Yes."

The detective waited a moment. "That's an interesting name."

Plummer nodded. "Thank you for your time, detective. Much appreciated."

He climbed back into the Mercedes, the chauffeur closing the door behind him.

Ryan watched as the driver got into the front of the car, and the vehicle took off.

EIGHTY-ONE

The following day Ryan drove into the only remaining space in the station car park. He released his seat belt and climbed out of the car. As he did, the front entrance door opened, and the Sarge stepped out.

"Ryan, hi," the Sarge said, seeing him. "Did you pass a police van on your way over, by any chance?"

The detective shook his head. "No." The Sarge had rung him last night to confirm he had arranged for Ellie Sastra to be moved to Kariong Correctional Centre today.

"Oh," the Sarge paused. "It's a pity you couldn't make it for a farewell drink last night."

"Sorry. I was exhausted. And it's not a farewell—more a temporary goodbye."

The tiredness was sort of true. Ryan had spent half an hour on the phone with his mother, who was always exhausting. But he wouldn't have gone anyway. He hated those kinds of events.

"Ah, here they are," the Sarge suddenly said.

Ryan followed the Sarge's gaze. A white Holden Colorado van was driving towards them. The word Police was printed in blue lettering across its hood.

"Can you wait out here with them while I get the prisoner?" the Sarge asked.

"No problem," Ryan replied.

The Sarge hurried back inside as the police van pulled up. A uniformed cop wound down the window and signaled to Ryan to come over.

"Pick up?" she asked.

"Yes. They're just bringing Ellie Sastra out."

The cop climbed out, stretching her legs and yawning. "I'm Constable Wright, by the way."

"Detective Ryan."

The uniformed officer walked along the side of the vehicle. She produced a set of keys and inserted them into the truck's side door.

Behind, the station door opened. The detective twisted around and saw Zoe and a cuffed Ellie Sastra come out. He headed back up the path to them.

"Just watch her moment, will you. I need to get some paperwork signed," the constable said, indicating the clipboard she held.

"So still not talking?" Ryan said to Ellie as he watched Zoe introduce herself to Constable Wright.

"Oh, I will be. But not now. And when I do, it will be only through my lawyer," she said, giving the detective a tight smile.

"Fair enough." He knew Ellie wouldn't go down without a fight, but go down, she would. "I have one question," Ryan said.

"I told you . . ."

"Yes, I know. Not without your lawyer. But this is personal. It's nothing to do with the case." Ryan paused. "I felt a connection between us. Did you feel that too?"

Ellie shook her head. "Wow, men and their fragile egos. I thought low self-esteem was a female problem."

"That's what we like you to think," Ryan said. "So you were always working me? Finding out how much I knew, and that was all it was?"

Ellie smiled. "That's for you to decide."

"Let's go," the constable said, arriving and hooking her arm into Ellie's arm. They headed to the police van. Zoe uncuffed Ellie, and Constable Wright guided the woman through into the back of the vehicle. Satisfied that she was comfortable, Wright banged the door shut, locking it before returning the clipboard to Zoe. The constable walked back to Ryan.

"A real tough nut that one," Zoe said as the police van took off.

RYAN LIKED TO THINK OF HIMSELF as an analytical kind of guy—not the touchy-feely type, but the warmth he had felt from Zoe, the Sarge, Jackie, and Jimmy as they said their goodbyes touched him. He guessed it was the difference between big city people and small-town folks. You could always meet new acquaintances in a place like Sydney, but that wasn't the case in a town like Barton. Most inhabitants were lifers, which should have meant that new arrivals were treated with kid gloves and watched suspiciously before making any overtures of friendship, but from Ryan's experience in Barton, it was precisely the opposite. He was going to miss being here.

EIGHTY-TWO

"I WOULDN'T BOTHER SETTLING DOWN," Detective Rob Headley said as Ryan dropped into his desk chair.

"Something up?"

"Isn't there always? Dudley wants to see you as soon as you arrive."

Ryan had already been phoned that news on his way back from Barton. It was why he had driven directly to the Sydney office rather than dropping off his case at his apartment . . . but he didn't want to tell that to Detective Headley.

Chief Inspector Dan Dudley appeared at his office door. "Ryan," he shouted.

Rob grimaced. "Told you. And he doesn't look happy."

"I best go then," Ryan said and headed over to the Chief Inspector's office.

RYAN CLOSED THE DOOR BEHIND HIM and Chief Inspector Dudley pointed to the other man in the room. In his early-fifties, he had a face that had seen life and then some. He wore a cheap thin blue windcheater over a V-necked black sweater, beige cargo pants, and black Adidas sneakers. "Paul. This is Detective Ryan," Dudley explained.

The man stood up immediately and pumped Ryan's hand vigorously. "Thank you. Thank you."

"You've heard me mention my cousin," the Chief Inspector said, levering himself into his desk chair.

"Second cousin," Paul said, finally releasing the detective from his grip.

"Second cousin? Yes, I suppose technically that's correct. Anyway, please sit down, both of you," the Chief Inspector said.

Paul headed back to his chair while Ryan took a seat opposite.

"I've bought Paul up to date on the developments."

"Developments, he calls them. Stop speaking in code. This man," he pointed to Ryan. "He's a miracle worker, and these aren't developments; they're seismic, catastrophic wonderments. He found who killed my son Nathan."

"Allegedly," Ryan said.

"Jeez, you're doing it now. There's no alleged about it," Paul Woodford paused. "To be honest, when Dan said he was sending someone up to Barton, I thought that it was a complete waste of time. It had been fifteen years since Nathan went missing. The case wasn't just cold; it was frigid. But you've been brilliant, detective."

Ryan was even more uncomfortable with praise than he was with saying goodbyes. He knew he had done an excellent job, but in his opinion, luck had played a sizeable part. And when Chief Inspector Dudley had asked him to go to Barton to try and find out something new about the Nathan Woodford case, he had been dubious too.

"Okay, well, now you've met, I need to catch up with the detective," the Chief Inspector said.

Paul Woodford stood up. "Of course." He walked to the door. "Thank you again."

"Before you leave, can I ask you a question?" the detective asked, standing.

"Go for it," Paul Woodford said.

"Well, the Chief Inspector told me that you had just returned from Britain, but he didn't tell me why you left Barton so soon after your son Nathan disappeared. The Sergeant who investigated the case believed you had killed him, though he couldn't prove it. Running off to England didn't help," Ryan said.

"That Sergeant couldn't prove it because it wasn't true. And I left because I couldn't cope. At the time, I was drinking heavily. Then Nathan disappeared. I knew that everyone thought I'd done it. No one was prepared to look any further. I was scared that if I had stayed, someone might have 'found' evidence that I murdered my son. I just had to go. But let me tell you, there hasn't been a single day since that I haven't thought about Nathan. And when I got back here and met up with Dan, he suggested putting you on the case," Paul Woodford explained.

"Maybe you should have come back earlier and pushed them to reopen the inquiry," the detective said.

"I didn't think they would be interested, not when that request came from the prime suspect. Besides, they're not you."

"And what about your wife, is there . . ." Ryan paused, letting his words hang in the air.

"No, that ended long ago. I did speak to Julie this morning, though, and she's as thrilled as I am now there's been some closure," Paul Woodford said. He pulled the door open. "You've made me so happy, detective. Thank you."

As Paul Woodford left, the Chief Inspector told Ryan to sit down again. "Since my cousin . . ." The Chief Inspector stopped. "My second cousin . . . Well since he has got all of that off his chest, it's my turn. I think, in hindsight, I may have come on a bit too heavy. But I hope you understand that the scene we played out in this office was for the benefit of the others," Dudley said, indicating outside. "I couldn't just send you up to Barton for no reason. Detectives don't get released to go off to investigate a cold case for a member of their boss's family."

Ryan was glad to hear the Chief Inspector's apology. Dudley had played his role well as a racist pig. If anything, it was a little too pitch-perfect.

Dudley leaned across the desk. "Now, to the other matter. You have the evidence?"

Ryan reached into his pocket, and produced his iPhone. He placed it on the desk. "All on here. Do you think it's enough?" Ryan asked.

"Internal Affairs have been investigating him for months. What you got and what they've found out will be more than enough to convict him." The Chief Inspector reached for his desk phone, dialed, and waited. "Phil, Dan here. You can send them up now."

"All done," the Chief Inspector said, putting down the phone, standing, and walking to the door. Opening it, he bawled. "Headley. Here. Now. And bring your cell phone with you."

Moments later, Detective Headley hurried in. "Sir?"

"Take a seat," the Chief Inspector ordered.

Rob Headley looked across at Ryan.

"He's staying. I called you in to thank you for helping Detective Ryan."

"No problem Chief. We're all in this together," Detective Headley said.

"Ryan?" Dudley said, indicating Ryan's iPhone.

The detective picked up his cell, opened it, and scrolled through the messages. Finding one, he quickly typed, "Thank you," And sent it.

Detective Headley's phone buzzed in his pocket. He took it out and looked at the text.

"It's attached to the information you sent to me about the boat. I wanted to make sure I have the right contact for you," Ryan said.

"Well, as you can see, I've just got that message, so yes you do have the correct number," Headley said.

Ryan went back into his cell. Opening the mail symbol on the front screen, he scrolled through his emails, opened one, and held his phone up, showing it to Chief Inspector Dudley. As he did, there was a knock on the door.

"Come," Dudley said.

Two suited men in their late-thirties entered. Detective Headley turned to stare at them.

"They are from Internal Affairs, in case you're wondering Headley," Dudley said.

"If you can just wait for a moment, officers." The two men remained at the door.

"Detective Headley, you've just confirmed your phone number. Now show him, Ryan," the Chief Inspector said.

Ryan twisted the screen around and pointed to the email. Headley leaned forward to view it.

"It's a photo of Detective Ryan, along with the address of the Singing Pelican pub, where the detective was staying, and a description of his car—a blue Ford Focus."

"So?" Headley asked.

"So, this is a copy of the original message sent to Leo Moretti aka The Lion—one of the criminals who kidnapped Ryan. It was on his phone—a phone we now have in our possession. The question is, why does the person who sent this message to Leo Moretti have the same phone number as you?" Chief Inspector Dudley didn't wait for the answer. "Hand over your gun and your badge, Headley . . . now."

After a show of astonishment and an insistence that he was perfectly innocent of what was alleged, Detective Rob Headley reluctantly obeyed.

"I'M NEVER HAPPY WHEN I DISCOVER A BENT COP," Dudley said as he watched the Internal Affairs officers march Detective Headley out. "But that should end all the leaks to Oscar Bruno that have been coming from this department."

"You couldn't have done that before I got back?" Ryan said.

"Maybe, but I wanted to see Headley's face when you confronted him with the evidence. Now forget him. He's dead to me. I've got another important job for you. I want you over at Long Bay Hospital. I've arranged for you to have a preliminary chat with Micky Docker," The Chief Inspector said.

"Me?" Ryan said, confused.

"You're thinking that because you shot Micky Docker, you're perhaps not the best person to interview him?" Dudley said.

"Something like that."

"That's precisely why I need you there. You saved Docker's life, and he knows it. So, if he's going to talk to someone, that someone should be you," the Chief Inspector said. "So, on your way, Ryan," Dudley said and then peered down at his desk and shuffled through papers.

Ryan didn't move. He wasn't sure he agreed with the Chief Inspector's logic.

Dudley looked up. "That wasn't a request, Ryan. It was an order . . . Go!"

EIGHTY-THREE

It took Ryan twenty-five minutes to drive from the police head-quarters to the Long Bay Correctional Centre in Randwick. Constructed over a hundred years ago, Long Bay is Sydney's central prison and has more than one thousand inmates—and it's where Micky Docker would reside until his trial. But Micky wasn't in the central jail yet. Because of his leg wound, he was resting in the complex's hospital.

The hospital building is a new addition to Long Bay. It sits on the western corner of the site and houses over one hundred prison patients. But just because it's classified as a hospital doesn't mean it's easy to get into. It's still considered a "Maximum Security Institution" and has its own secure entrance, surrounded by an impressively high metal fence.

Ryan parked his car outside the perimeter and walked to the gatehouse. The detective understood the Chief Inspector's enthusiasm for getting someone over to speak to Micky quickly. It was an excellent time to interview him—he was alone and undoubtedly feeling sorry for himself. Unlike the late Big Jay and The Lion, the detective knew little about Micky Docker or his dead companion Stack, except that they worked for Oscar Bruno—and Ryan was still dubious about Micky's willingness to speak to him.

The detective showed his ID at the first barred gate, and after passing through the metal detector, was ushered in. Ahead he could see the three-level hospital building—its glass and gray walls, a sharp contrast to the gothic stone of the rest of the prison. Ryan followed the short-covered walkway to a second security gate. Here he flashed his police ID to a fat walrus-mustached prison guard.

"Hands up," the guard said. "I have to pat you down."

"But I'm a cop?"

"That's the rules. I do it, or you don't get in," the guard said.

There were always more-than-my-jobs-worth in any profession, and Ryan knew picking a fight with any of them was a waste of time. The detective raised his hands.

Search complete, the guard waved Ryan down the short metal-walled corridor that led into a well-lit lobby. Once there, the detective showed his ID to the woman staffing the entrance desk. She told him he was to take the elevator to the third floor. Here someone would direct him to Micky Docker.

ON REACHING HIS DESTINATION, RYAN EXITED the elevator and walked across to the nurse's station opposite. A young, slim nurse in dark blue scrubs smiled at the detective. "How can I help?"

He offered her his ID. "Detective Ryan. I've come to see Micky Docker."

"Mr. Docker is in ward five, detective." She pointed to her right. "Fourth door down."

Ryan set off down the hallway, but he had only taken a few steps when a shout came from behind. "Detective?"

Ryan stopped and waited for the nurse to reach him. She waved a piece of paper in the air.

"I almost forgot. You need to wear this." It was a paper name tag, his name written on it in blue ink. The nurse slapped the tag on his suit lapel.

"Must I?" he said, grimacing. Sticky labels always left ugly marks on clothes.

"Sorry, it's the rules. And how else would we be able to tell who's who?" the nurse said.

"I don't think there's much of a problem there. You won't get another officer coming to see Micky Docker today," Ryan said.

"That's where you're wrong. There was a policeman here a short time ago. He's only just left."

Ryan's frowned. "You sure?"

"Yes," the nurse said.

Abruptly abandoning her, Ryan sprinted down the hallway. Reaching ward five, he pushed the door open. A brown sheet was pulled over the single hospital bed. The detective yanked the cloth back. A man lay in the bed. Blood gushed from a broad, jagged gash running from one side of his throat to the other. It was a very dead Micky Docker.

EIGHTY-FOUR

THE SUN WAS JUST BEGINNING TO fade as the afternoon drifted into dusk, but Smith still had more than enough light for what he needed to do.

He knew how important it was to dress comfortably for the job and had dressed accordingly. Smith had forsaken his usual day wear—a gray tight-fitted suit and white shirt—replacing those clothes with a loose-fitting black sweatshirt and a pair of dark gray sweats. For head cover he had chosen a black baseball cap, its peak facing back to protect him from the sun.

Earlier, Smith had steered the powerful sixty-two-foot boat, the Fandango, into position across from the luxury Point Piper mansions. He had been concerned that his vessel would stand out, but on arrival Smith realized that he had been worrying unduly. Bigger, more expensive craft were moored all around.

Smith had never been a big fan of show-pony vessels. Brought up on the coast, he had spent his youth on his father's boat—a no-frills craft that had been built for just one purpose, fishing. All the brown calf leather, Roman marble, and teak from Thailand furnishing the Fandango did little for him. However, the boat's perfectly flat deck made for an ideal shooting platform.

Smith adjusted the butt of the bolt-action Arctic Warfare sniper rifle to fit more comfortably into the hollow of his shoulder and peered through the Schmidt and Bender telescopic sight. He had already been lying on the deck for five hours, never once letting his attention wander. The wait didn't bother him. And he was confident something would happen soon.

OSCAR BRUNO WALKED OUT OF THE mansion and made his way to the cliff edge. Stopping, he took a drag on his cigarette, blowing the smoke into the air. He was thinking about buying a boat, maybe one like the little sixty-footer moored directly across the bay. It looked like it would be fun to mess around on. But the drug dealer knew doing fun things wasn't possible at the moment. He was far too busy for that.

Bruno flicked the ash off the end of the cigarette. He was already regretting the act he had put on in court. Now he would have to repeat his performance whenever he left Villa Bruno. It wasn't something he relished.

Bruno sighed. Nothing seemed to be going right for him recently. Losing Big Jay and The Lion had been a body blow. He had liked . . . Bruno stopped . . . liked was the wrong word . . . He had got used to . . . yeah, that was better . . . he had got used to having them around. Of course, they had messed up the kidnapping and let that bastard cop go, but there would be other chances. Now that did cheer him up.

"Boss?"

He turned and saw The Owl running towards him.

"Well?" Bruno asked.

"It's done." The Owl said.

"He's dead?"

"As a doornail."

"Thanks," Bruno said, gesturing for The Owl to leave.

Bruno swiveled back around, to stare out once more across the harbor. The news was good . . . but then again, maybe not that good. He would have preferred to have killed Micky Docker himself, slowly.

And that was the last thought Oscar Bruno ever had. Smith's shot smashed into his skull, tearing off bits of bone and burrowing into his brain. The drug boss fell back, the blood spurting out onto the immaculately manicured grass. By the time he hit the ground, he, like Micky Docker, was quite dead.

EIGHTY-FIVE

GRASPING HIS SUITCASE, AN EXHAUSTED DETECTIVE Ryan slowly climbed the stairs to his Potts Point apartment. He had spent the rest of the day at the Long Bay Hospital dealing with Micky Docker's death and trying to discover how a fake policeman slash assassin had somehow managed to evade so many security checks. He'd obviously had inside help, but proving that wasn't going to be easy.

Entering the apartment, Ryan picked up the letter pushed under the door. He glanced at it uninterested. It was probably a missive from the Body Corporate. Dropping the unopened envelope onto the living room table, he went through to the bedroom to unpack.

After that chore, and now hungry, Ryan leafed through restaurant take-away menus. Deciding on Thai, he pulled out his cell, dialed, and waited while absently picking up the envelope. It was addressed to Detective Ramesh Ryan. That was strange. The Body Corporate usually sent their letters to Mr. Ryan. He put the phone on speaker and ripped the missive open to reveal a plain sheet of postcard-sized white cardboard. Intrigued, Ryan pulled it out.

"Hello?" a voice from the phone said as the detective flicked the card over.

"The Thai Connection Restaurant . . . Can I help you?" the voice asked.

"Sorry. Changed my mind," the detective replied and clicked off his cell. He stared at the words printed in bold black capital letters: **"IT'S DONE."** What did that mean?

There was a knock on the door. Ryan put down the card and walked across to open up.

"About time," Mumta said, hugging him. "It's been so long."

"I've only been away a couple of weeks, mom," Ryan said as he peered over his mother's shoulder at the smiling young woman standing behind.

Disentangling herself, Mumta signaled for the woman to step forward. "Anya, this is my handsome son Ramesh."

The detective offered the woman his hand and took a good look at her. Her straight, shoulder-length black hair framed an engaging face. She wore a black V-neck mesh maxi dress and black knee-length boots.

"Nice to meet you, Ramesh," the woman said in a lilting voice.

"Likewise, Anya." He grinned. She really was beautiful.

"Are you going to invite us in, or are we going to stand out here all night?" Mumta asked.

"Sorry, come in."

Ryan stood by the open door as the two women entered.

"Take a seat, please," Ryan said, indicating the sofa.

As the women sat down, the detective's phone rang.

Ryan picked up the cell, glancing at the screen. It was Chief Inspector Dudley's private number, the one he'd used to update the him on progress on the Nathan Woodford investigation while he was in Barton.

"Sorry, I have to take this . . . Chief Inspector," he said, walking away and making for the privacy of the kitchen.

"Sorry to disturb you, detective, but I have important news. Oscar Bruno is dead."

"What?"

"You heard me. Bruno was shot at his home this evening. Good news, huh, though I suppose I shouldn't really say that, but what the heck? The man was a shit," Dudley said.

Bruno was indeed a shit—someone with no redeeming qualities. His death was more than good news. It was fantastic news. Suddenly the words **It's Done** on the card made sense . . . and Ryan knew precisely who had done it.

A hand suddenly reached across from behind and snatched the phone. The detective spun around. It was his mother. She spoke into the cell:

"Hello, I'm sorry, but I'm Ramesh's mother, and whoever you are, I can assure you your news can wait. I haven't seen my son for several weeks."

Ryan grabbed the phone back. "Sorry, Sir. My mother . . ." He stopped as he stared at his mom, who was glaring back at him. "My mother just wants to talk to me."

"Quite right too. Don't worry about it, Ryan. Oh, but before you go, there is one other piece of news. I've just been informed that a cop's gone missing in Gosford. He goes by the name of Kavia Gupta and apparently is an IT wizard." He paused, "The place seems to have suddenly become a criminal hot spot. Anyway, I'll leave you to your mother. Goodnight." The phone clicked off.

Mumta took a step closer to Ryan. She whispered: "What do you think of Anya?"

"What?" the detective said distractedly as he mulled over what the Chief Inspector had just said.

"Pay attention, Ramesh. Anya's ravishing, isn't she?"

"Yes, she looks nice. But why is she here?" he asked.

"For a detective, you are slow on the uptake sometimes. To meet you, of course."

Ryan shook his head. "Mom. This is the twenty-first century. Mothers don't arrange for their adult children to meet people they think they should date."

"Oh no. I leave that to you, do I? My thirty-eight-year-old unmarried son whose apparently just been trying to date a serial killer? At least Anya's not one of those." She pointed into the living room. "Come along, Ramesh, best not to keep her waiting."

CLIVE FLEURY IS AN AWARD-WINNING WRITER of novels and screen-plays, including most recently the science fiction book "Kill Code: A Dystopian Science Fiction Novel." He is also a TV/Film writer, director, and producer who has worked for major broadcasters and studios on a wide variety of successful drama and documentary projects, in the US, the UK, Europe, Australia and the Middle East. He has written and directed four feature films, one of which, "Big City Blues," starred Giancarlo Esposito, the late Burt Reynolds, and Balthazar Getty. His most recent film, "Sons of Summer," is a surfing movie set on the Gold Coast of Australia and stars Temuera Morrison and Isabel Lucas. Clive currently spends his time between Florida and Sydney, Australia.